THE SECRET OF US

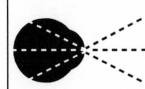

This Large Print Book carries the
Seal of Approval of N.A.V.H.

THE SECRET OF US

ROXANNE HENKE

THORNDIKE PRESS

A part of Gale, Cengage Learning

Detroit • New York • San Francisco • New Haven, Conn • Waterville, Maine • London

GALE
CENGAGE Learning

Copyright © 2007 by Roxanne Sayler Henke.
Scripture taken from the HOLY BIBLE, NEW INTERNATIONAL VERSION®.
NIV ® Copyright © 1973, 1978, 1984 by International Bible Society.
Used by permission of Zondervan Publishing House. All rights reserved.
Thorndike Press, a part of Gale, Cengage Learning.

Thorndike Press® Large Print Christian Fiction.
The text of this Large Print edition is unabridged.
Other aspects of the book may vary from the original edition.
Set in 16 pt. Plantin.
Printed on permanent paper.

LIBRARY OF CONGRESS CATALOGING-IN-PUBLICATION DATA

Henke, Roxanne, 1953–
    The secret of us / by Roxanne Henke.
        p. cm. — (Thorndike Press large print Christian fiction)
    ISBN-13: 978-1-4104-1208-9 (hardcover : alk. paper)
    ISBN-10: 1-4104-1208-3 (hardcover : alk. paper)
    1. Married women—Fiction. 2. Married people—Fiction. 3.
Self-actualization (Psychology)—Fiction. 4. Large type books. I.
Title.
PS3608.E55S43 2009
813'.6—dc22   2008038784

Published in 2009 by arrangement with Harvest House Publishers.
Roxanne Sayler Henke: Published in association with the Books & Such Literary Agency, 52 Mission Circle, Suite 122, PMB 170, Santa Rose, CA 95409-5370, www.booksandsuch.biz.

Printed in the United States of America
1 2 3 4 5 6 7 12 11 10 09 08

Love is patient, love is kind . . .
it is not rude, it is
not self-seeking, it is not easily angered,
it keeps no record of wrongs . . .
(Love) always protects,
always trusts, always hopes, always
perseveres. Love never fails.
1 CORINTHIANS 13:4–8

Many waters cannot quench love;
rivers cannot wash it away.
If one were to give all the wealth
of his house for love,
it would be utterly scorned.
SONG OF SOLOMON 8:7

Talking about love . . .
this book is dedicated to Lorren.
Of course.

PROLOGUE:
LAURA

Life can turn on a dime . . . or the tap of a brake pedal.

One minute you're a 20-year-old college student, sitting at a stoplight, impatiently drumming the steering wheel, because if the light doesn't turn green soon you're going to be late for your art history midterm. The next minute you're sitting in an emergency room, and the guy who smashed his BMW into the rear bumper of your car is sitting beside you, still apologizing.

"Honest, all I did was glance at my watch to see what time it was. The light was red, and I was already late for a meeting and then . . ." One side of his mouth turned up. "I guess you know what happened next."

"Yeah." I touched the goose egg I could feel rising between my eyebrows where my head had hit the steering wheel. I looked at the guy who had already promised he'd take care of everything. If I could trust my blurry vision, he looked really cute. *I should have plucked my eyebrows last night.* I held the two pieces that used to be my glasses in my hands.

He nodded at the broken plastic in my lap. "Sorry about those, too."

I fingered one tortoise-shell earpiece. "I usually wear contacts. I was only wearing these because I was running late."

"You too, huh?" He grinned as though we had much more in common. "Don't worry. I'll take care of everything."

"You already said that."

He held up his right hand as if he was already in court. "Well, this is my promise." He lowered his hand then held it out to me. "Donnie Dunn," he said as we shook hands. Maybe he had told me his name out on the street, out by the police car, before the ambulance hauled us away. If so, I'd forgotten. I put my hand in his. "Dunn," he repeated, as if everything that came after was already a done deal.

Fast forward an hour, and you're limping out of the hospital with crutches and a date for the next night.

Within a year you have a husband. And there you have it. A whole new life.

And then 23 years later, late one night you turn over in bed, look across the king-sized expanse and wonder, *Do I know this man? Have I ever really loved him?*

I slipped out of bed and tiptoed into the bathroom, closing the door quietly behind me. The soft glow of the nightlight was all I needed. I stared at my empty eyes in the dark mirror.

There was a cough from the bed just outside the door. *Oh, please, Donnie, stay asleep.*

I stood in front of the sink and laid my forehead against the cool marble of the countertop. I needed to clear my head. I needed to put some semblance of order to these thoughts that had kept me awake, more often than just tonight.

After 23 years, did he care anymore?

More importantly . . . did I?

LAURA

And two shall become one . . .

"So, what do you think, Mom? Lemon chiffon or the red velvet? Or do you think one of the others tastes better?"

From across the table, my daughter's words slid through the netting of my faraway thoughts. I glanced at my watch. Who knew picking a wedding cake would take this long? If we didn't wrap it up soon I was going to be late for the art guild meeting. And to think I thought I'd have time to go grocery shopping between this appointment and my meeting. With Stasha living at home until the wedding, it was taking some readjustment for all of us, including the fact that there was one more person I needed to remember to feed.

Speaking of feeding, 200 guests would be eating this wedding cake at the end of August. Just over two months from today. I

13

knew Stasha was as anxious to check this *one-more-thing* off her long list as I was to get to my meeting.

I blinked my eyes and stared at the four cakes sitting between us on the table. The sugary frosting from the tastes I'd had of all four slices coated the inside of my mouth. I moved my tongue around, trying to distinguish the flavors. At this point, they all tasted the same to me. I sighed to buy myself time. Make my answer something that would appease Stasha, not make her dissolve into a puddle of impatient tears. "What do you think Josh would like?"

Anastasia brushed an imaginary stray hair from her eyes. "The only kind of cake he likes is chocolate. But that's too predictable."

The lady from the bakery picked up a long knife and pointed it at one of the cakes. "The red velvet cake has cocoa in it, so technically it is a chocolate cake." She paused, giving me time to remember the price sheet she'd sent ahead of our meeting. Of course it was the more expensive cake. Not that Donnie would care. "It's very elegant," she added. "And good."

"Let's go with the red velvet," Anastasia said, her eyes flickering to mine for confirmation. "Josh will like it."

14

I forced a smile onto my face. "Sounds like a good choice." I reached for my purse. If I hurried I might be able to get to the meeting a bit early. Maybe make a few phone calls from my cell phone in the parking lot. I had promised Karen I'd try and track down a couple of the artists she was hoping to display in her new gallery.

The gallery you *should be opening.* Another thing not to think about now.

"Great choice." The bakery lady put aside her knife and slid the cakes out of the way. From a nearby shelf she pulled a thick binder and placed it on the table. "Now, we'll want to decide on a *look* for the cake."

Oh, good grief. A *look.* What next? I felt like giving her a *look.* One that would have nothing to do with wedding cakes and everything to do with the ridiculous amount of time these minute details consumed. I took my hand off my purse and forced it to lie still in my lap. I wanted nothing more than to rub my temples. The headache that seemed to accompany each of these wedding-planning events throbbed as if an amped-up punk band was tuning up inside my head. Instead I turned up the corners of my mouth and let my eyes crinkle into the appearance of a smile. I wasn't about to let my only child suspect anything was wrong.

I closed my eyes momentarily against a sudden emptiness. Even I couldn't put into words the vague unease I'd been feeling. The sense that after 23 years of marriage to her father I didn't know if — no, I wouldn't, *couldn't,* think about that now. Stasha had been planning her wedding day since she was five.

Sixteen years and a college degree hadn't damped her enthusiasm one bit. She had been collecting ideas for years. Now it seemed Stasha planned to use them all in one elaborate day. A day I had vowed to get through smiling. She would never know the questions I'd been grappling with these past months. *Is this all there is? Do all marriages eventually turn into . . . companionship? Friendship? If you could even call it that.*

Empty. That was the word that best described the arrangement we had unknowingly ended up with. I pressed a hand against the side of my face. Maybe this would pass. It wasn't as if Donnie and I hadn't had rough patches in the past.

But this is different.

Hormones? I prayed whatever I was feeling was simply hormones. The alternative was just too scary.

As the cake lady pattered on, explaining the intricate details that made each style of cake unique, I couldn't help but compare Stasha's plans with the wedding I'd planned so many starry-eyed years ago.

"Are you sure you don't want something different?" My mom made her point by going several blocks out of her way to drive past the large Lutheran church I had attended as a child.

I gazed out the car window as we drove past. She had managed to arrange our route so that the church was on my side of the car. "I'm sure." I turned her way. "I haven't lived here the past few years. All our friends are in Carlton."

When I had shown up on my parents' doorstep all those years ago with a huge grin and a bigger diamond, it wasn't hard to see the surprise on their faces. "Isn't it a little soon?" Mom asked right after she sort of hugged me.

I swung my arms wide. "Not when you're in love." I tried to assure her a justice-of-the-peace wedding was exactly what we — I — wanted. "Besides, this will be so much easier for you. All you have to do is show up and be happy for us."

Mom cast a last glance through my car window at the church. "Well, that's all I've ever wanted for you, Laura. For you to be happy."

I shifted my chair to get a better look at the photo of a lavish cake Stasha was holding my way. *Happiness,* I reminded myself as I nodded my approval. Like mother, like daughter. Like grandmother. We'd come full circle. Too bad my mother was no longer alive. Her granddaughter was planning the wedding she'd wanted me to have.

Like my mother, all I wanted for Stasha was happiness. Which was why I planned to let Stasha have her perfect day. I would wait until the ink on her marriage license dried and the photos of the beautiful bride and her loving family were in an album.

Then . . . then I might consider . . .

No. I could never do that.

Are you sure?

Yes. Leaving Donnie wasn't an option. When I said "I do," I had meant it.

You've changed. Donnie's different. You've grown apart.

Oh, how well I knew that. Stasha tilted another elaborate wedding cake picture my way. One part of me pointed to the picture and shook my head, another part of me kept up the silent debate.

You don't have to do anything now. Stasha's wedding isn't until August. You've lived with Donnie for 23 years; another two months isn't going to matter one iota. Just

18

think about what you'll say.

To tell the truth, it was getting harder not to think about it. Donnie was wrapped up in yet another big ad campaign. Never home, as usual. The story of his life, and mine. There would be time for us later. Always later.

When will your time come?

I thought my time would have been here by now. As it was, I'd put off my painting, my dreams of travel, of having my own gallery, of having a life, waiting for my husband to —

To what?

Exactly. In the past 23 years I'd learned that Donnie's work was what counted. What mattered within the four walls that made up our house. The expanse of space that encompassed the agency. In the tangled web that was our marriage.

Which was why I needed to have a serious talk with Donnie. Not an "Oh, by the way" kind of talk. We'd had those. This time I needed my husband to sit down and listen, really listen to how unhappy I was in this union of ours.

No, not now. Not when Stasha is planning her wedding. Not while Stasha was living with us for the summer. We already had all the emotions we needed under one roof.

There would be plenty of time later, after the wedding, for what I needed to say to Donnie.

I knew Donnie. I knew the way he'd react if I told him how I was feeling. First he'd deny that he worked so much. Then he would tell me about the good life he was providing for me. For us. That would be my cue to start back-pedaling, to make excuses. *We do have a beautiful house. Yes, I love my sports car. Of course I'm happy Stasha is getting the wedding of her dreams. No, I'm the one who's sorry.* I'd start to cry. Donnie would put his arms around me until my tears dried. I'd go back to same old, same old. He'd go back to work. After this many years, even our arguments were scripted.

No, this time when I talked to him, things would be different. This time I wouldn't let him comfort me into thinking I was the one who had been wrong all along. I didn't plan to let his familiar platitudes distract me. This time I would press on, press him, until something changed. Or else.

Or else what?

I vaguely took in the picture of the cake Stasha was pointing to. I nodded. Whatever she wanted would be okay with me. My daughter wouldn't know how far my thoughts had strayed from wedding cakes, flowers, and linen colors. I had a much larger problem on my plate. What would be an "or else" for Donnie? Donnie knew I'd never leave. I knew I'd never leave. The vow I made didn't allow for that option.

But there was another thing I knew. I knew I didn't want to continue living the way we were. Roommates. Glorified room-mates. Sharing a house and a last name. Not much else. Oh, we slept in the same bed, but that's all we did there. If this was what 23 years of marriage amounted to, I wasn't so sure I wanted it anymore.

What are your alternatives?

There was the rub. The only alternative was to upset the comfortable applecart that was our marriage.

Comfortable?

I coughed at the sudden tightening in my throat. Even in my unhappiness I had to admit there was a certain comfort in the familiar. I didn't know exactly how I wanted my marriage to change, just that I did.

As Stasha and the cake lady discussed the endless shades of white that frosting could be, I let my mind drift again. I wasn't quite sure how Donnie and I had gotten to this point, and I didn't have a clue how we'd get out of it. All I knew was that what we had was no longer enough. At least not for me. I planned to let my husband know exactly how I felt. And I wouldn't back off until we had an answer to what ailed us.

What if there isn't one?

I gritted my teeth against the thought. There just had to be. No one should be expected to live in a shell of a marriage. A relationship that looked strong and pretty from the outside with nothing but vapor inside.

"Mom. *Mo-om?*" Stasha was waving her hand in front of my face. "Where are you?" She was laughing, obviously in the dark about my conflicted emotions. Which was exactly where I wanted her to be. Clueless. She deserved her measure of happiness. Soon enough she'd find out what marriage was all about.

"Right here," I said, forcing a smile, giving my head a little shake, bringing my thoughts back to seemingly simple wedding woes. There would be plenty of time to think about my marriage later. If I dared think about it at all.

I'd learned, even in my thoughts, that it was lonely to live without feeling loved.

DONNIE

"Okay, so I'm thinking we talk to the dealership. Let's see if they won't let us use their biggest tractor. I'm talking big." I lifted both of my arms into the air to underscore my point. Actually, I had no clue what size tractors came in, but that wasn't my department, and that's why we were having this meeting. So my staff could grab my vision and run with it. "We take this tractor out to the airport and have it waiting at the Exec-Jet landing strip. When Martin and his people get off the plane, that's the first thing they see. Their tractor. At the airport." I sat back then quickly forward as a new idea popped into my head. "We could have the tractor escort the limo back here to the agency where we've got ice-cold drinks and snacks waiting." Now I sat back. "Someone find out what they like to eat. And drink." I could see my assistant, Arlene, make a note.

I was used to silent pauses during these

brainstorming sessions. Sometimes it took a few long seconds for a good idea to settle.

"Uh, Don. Mr. Dunn?"

It was the new guy. What was his name? I wracked my brain. We'd added staff like pinball points lately. It was hard to keep up. Jeff. Yeah, Jeff. "What're you thinking?" I wiggled the fingers of both hands, encouraging him to get things rolling. If there was one thing I hated it was brain-dead brainstorming. I had to give the new guy credit for being the first to speak up.

He tapped the end of his pen on the table, in rapid-fire motion. He'd better have something good to say, because the noise was getting on my nerves. "Uh, I grew up on a farm and, well, tractors don't go all that fast. Especially in city traffic. That escort back here might be long and slow. I doubt that's the impression we want them to get of the agency."

I liked this kid and pointed at him. "Those are the kinds of things I'm looking for. You're right." I cast my eyes around the table waiting for more feedback.

A voice from the far end of the table. "We could set up a mini farm scene. Hay bales? Maybe a cow?" It wasn't hard to tell that even Justine wasn't sold on her idea.

Across the table there was a snicker from

24

Ben. I cut him off with a glance. They all knew the rules for these sessions. No idea was too "out there." It wasn't that laughing wasn't allowed; sometimes we came up with our best ideas in the middle of snort-out-loud laughter, but his scoff had a different tone. But then, Ben and Justine always seemed to be on opposite sides of the table.

I bit back a remark and waited for more ideas. Personnel issues were the bane of my existence at the Dunn Agency. If the only thing I had to worry about was brainstorming, this business would be a piece of — no, I refused to say "cake." Clichés were another thing not allowed around here.

"Come on people; give me something." I lifted my hands. Begging.

"I think your idea of having a tractor, a big tractor, waiting at the airport is genius." My business partner Matt would tell it to me straight. "It's the last place you'd think of seeing a tractor, so it'll let Martin know right off the bat that we do things differently around here. It will also let them see how accessible the community of Carlton is to their product. Jeff's right about a tractor being too slow for an escort. So let's think what else we can do to wow this client into moving their business from Minneapolis to the Dunn Agency. North Dakota may not

25

be high on their list, but they did ask us to pitch the account, which means the door is open. They're listening. We've got to convince them we're the perfect agency to handle their product." Not for the first time, my old college pal put my thoughts into words.

"Exactly," I chimed in. "Now, let's start thinking out of the box." I sat back, my cue to my staff to start throwing ideas on the table.

I picked up my can of Mountain Dew, my fourth of the day, and took a long swallow. If we won this account, it would be a peacock feather in our cap. A sign that the Dunn Agency was ready to do business with the big boys. Not that we weren't already the largest agency in Carlton, maybe in all of North Dakota. But I had my eyes on a bigger prize. I wanted to expand the agency to Minneapolis. In my mind, and Matt's, even Chicago wasn't out of our league. At least not eventually. But it was going to take a few big accounts like Martin's to create the momentum we'd need to move into the bigger markets.

Arlene leaned near my ear. "Would you like me to get you another Mountain Dew?"

I nodded. I had to give her credit, she knew me well. Sometimes I thought she knew me better than Laura.

You spend more time with Arlene. She should know you well.

Funny, Laura herself had pointed that out to me a couple years ago.

No. Not so funny.

Yeah, Laura would have pointed that out, too.

I sneaked a look at my watch. It was already after four, and this meeting was just starting to roll. In a couple of hours someone would pull out a take-out menu and begin taking orders, and the next thing I knew, I'd be eating another supper here instead of at home.

"Here you go." Arlene whispered as she set the icy can at my elbow. "Do you want me to give Laura a call and tell her you might be late?"

Once again I glanced at my wrist. I shook my head. If everyone was hitting on all cylinders this afternoon, maybe we'd be done by seven. Seven-thirty at the latest. I'd make it home for a late supper.

"What do you think, Donnie?" Leave it to Ben to brownnose.

"What do I think?" I needed to cover for the fact that I'd zoned out for a minute. Time for a pep talk. "I think we're gonna get this account. The Martin Corporation is the largest farm implement manufacturing company in the Upper Midwest, next to Deere. If we land this account, it will be a gold star on all of our résumés. Let's put it this way, if we sign Martin, you won't be finding coal at the bottom of your Christmas stockings this year."

Cheesy, but money always talked. I popped the top on my Dew as a new round of brainstorming began. I could have added that I had a wedding to pay for. A lavish wedding with a sit-down dinner at the country club. Live band. Open bar. The works. But since most of the people at this brainstorming session weren't invited — we'd limited the agency invites to the few staffers who had been here long enough to know who Stasha was — it was probably best to leave out that part of my incentive plan.

Besides, I did my best to keep my personal life separate from business.

What personal life?

I hooked a finger around the collar of my shirt and tugged at it. I might as well have had Laura sitting on my shoulder. Then again, why bother bringing her in? I was channeling her comments clearly enough without her.

Another gulp of Dew, and I pushed my

chair back from the table, forming my hands into a T — time out for a bathroom break. One of the advantages of owning the company. Besides, I needed to clear my head. It wasn't doing any of us any good to have my mind unfocused.

As my staff continued tossing ideas around, I walked into my office. A private bathroom was only one of the perks I enjoyed. I stood for a moment and gazed out my corner office windows. Fourth floor. Top floor. A North Dakota skyscraper. If I had my way, one of these days I'd be looking over the rooftops of downtown Minneapolis. I headed to the bathroom. But Minneapolis wouldn't happen until this meeting today took off.

I washed my hands. Splashed some cold water on my face. Hoped it would give me a second wind. Borrowed energy that my usual intake of caffeine wasn't quite providing today. I should probably give Laura a quick call, let her know I might be late. Phone calls to keep her informed were among the promises I'd made to her after our last . . . discussion.

But then again, if I told her I was going to be late, that I might not be there for supper at all . . . I glanced at the phone, seeing a can of worms instead of a receiver. I didn't

29

have the time or the energy to get into our familiar argument. If I made it home in time, fine. If not, well, been there, done that too. Her frustration would blow over. Eventually.

For a brief second I let my mind imagine what a free night at home might feel like. When was the last time I'd stretched out on the couch, my head nestled in Laura's lap while her hands gently fingered my hair, drifting and dozing as if I didn't have a care in the world?

I gave my head a small shake. No time for rhetorical questions. I didn't dare ask Laura when I had last been really relaxed. She'd tell me. That was one thing about Laura. She always let me know where I stood, but she was quick to forgive. Only one of the many reasons I love her.

But I didn't have time to count those reasons now. I had a brainstorming session to wrap up.

From the looks of the kitchen when I walked in from the garage, I hadn't missed much in the way of supper. The counters were bare. No lingering aromas. Maybe Laura had met a friend for dinner. That would take me off the hook.

I set my bulging briefcase on the kitchen

table. The wall clock read 8:45. If Laura had cooked dinner, the food would have been put away a long time ago. I took a last, warm swallow from the soda can in my hand and headed to the closet where we kept the garbage can and recycling bin. The garbage can was filled to the max.

Could you please take out the garbage on your way out?

Two small fingers of guilt walked their way up my back. Laura's words from much earlier this morning. If there was such a thing as a doghouse, I was in it. Best to cut my losses. I pushed at the refuse at the top of the rubber can. An empty yogurt container and an empty jar of Fisher's salted peanuts pressed back against my hand. More guilt. I recognized the rubbish as Laura's stand-by meal. Yogurt and dry-roasted peanuts. Something she always had on hand. Something that didn't need heating. Food that wouldn't dry out waiting for me to show up. Food I wouldn't have called a meal.

Laura might not, either.

Okay, so I messed up. Again. What was I supposed to do? An ad agency doesn't run on air. We wouldn't have this humongous house if it weren't for my hard work. Stasha wouldn't be planning the wedding of her dreams if it weren't for all the long hours I put in. I worked up my side of a good argument as I yanked the garbage bag from the bin.

There was a small shriek from the kitchen hallway. "Oh — !" Laura stood in the doorway with one hand over her heart. "You scared me. I didn't know you were home."

Then luck was on my side. Maybe she'd think I'd been home for ages. I could see Laura's eyes flick to my briefcase on the tabletop. Fat chance of that "been home for ages" excuse working tonight. She knew that if I'd been home that long, my briefcase would be by my chair in the family room, open at my feet.

I braced myself for the coming argument. *You didn't call me about dinner. I thought we — you — promised you'd call if you couldn't make it. How long do you think I waited to eat before it finally sank in that you weren't coming home? Again.*

I twisted the top of the heavy bag into a knot and pulled it tight, waiting for a noose of similar constriction to tighten around my own neck. I straightened, waiting for her to start in. Maybe she was loading her figurative rifle, waiting until I got back inside from taking the garbage out to the garage so she could unload both barrels at once.

"Where's Stasha?" I asked, hefting the bag off the floor. Diversionary tactics were sometimes best.

"Out with friends." Laura walked to the sink and filled a glass of water, no doubt preparing to shore up her argument with the silent treatment.

Okay, if that was the way she wanted it, I could also load up during my short jaunt. I turned and hauled the bulky bag into the garage, setting it in the far corner, right next to a second bag of garbage I'd apparently forgotten to take out earlier in the week.

I stood with my hand on the doorknob and took a deep breath. Yeah, maybe I deserved what was coming, but what was the alternative? That I quit work? Sell the agency? Laura had to know my work kept her in fine form. Nice clothes. Great jewelry. Vacations to some of the finest places in the country.

Those are business trips.

Well, sure they were. But we still went to some pretty nice places.

How entertaining do you think it is for Laura to sit alone in a fancy hotel room while you're in meetings all day? Four walls are four walls.

Well, it wasn't tough duty. I couldn't feel too sorry for her. If she brought it up, that's what I'd say. Words at the ready, I opened

33

the door to face the battleground. The kitchen was empty. I surveyed the imaginary battlefield. It was hard to fight when the enemy was nowhere in sight. I took my time unzipping my briefcase, riffling through the papers inside as if I was searching for something important. In truth, I'd expected Laura to be standing in the kitchen with her hands on her hips, ready to fire words of accusation at me. I was finding it hard to switch battle plans when I didn't know what tactic the enemy was using this time.

Laura isn't the enemy.

I rubbed my face with my hands. It had to be late if my whiskers were scratching. I was well aware that Laura had all the right in the world to be upset. I had promised her I'd call if I'd be late, and I hadn't done that. Not any of the times I'd missed supper this week.

Okay, so I would go on the offensive and apologize. I picked up my briefcase and carried it with me into the family room, with "I'm sorry" on the tip of my tongue. Laura wasn't there either.

I sat in my familiar recliner. I wasn't going to be foolish about this. No need to start an argument if I didn't have to. If Laura wanted to sleep it off, I'd let her.

I bent down to my briefcase and pulled

out the creative brief I'd brought home to read. Another hour, give or take some dozing in my chair, and I'd tiptoe into the bedroom and slip into bed. Fight averted.

Just as I was congratulating myself on a brilliant battle plan, Laura walked into the family room tightening the tie on her bathrobe, a book tucked under her arm. She'd had plenty of time to prepare an argument. I bent my head to the brief, hoping it looked as though I hadn't noticed her coming into the room.

Laura walked to the couch, switched on the light, then settled down into the leather and opened her book.

Wasn't she going to say anything?

I couldn't help it; I accidentally looked up. Laura was bent over her book. Couldn't she sense the elephant in the room?

Involuntarily, I cleared my throat. Laura glanced up from her book, her eyebrows raised as if to ask, "What?"

I gave her a half smile, shook my head, and lowered my eyes to my work. It was hard to concentrate when her silence was so loud. Couldn't she hear it? How could she read? I wasn't getting anything accomplished.

I might as well take my lumps and get it over with. This time I purposely cleared my throat to get her attention. When she looked up, I said, "Everything okay?"

She nodded as if she didn't have a care in the world. "Fine," she said as she turned a page of her book. "Everything's fine."

She went on reading while I tried to work. *Everything's fine,* she said. But I knew better. Something wasn't fine.

STASHA

I stood in the doorway between the kitchen and the family room trying to pick up the vibe. It wasn't hard to figure out that I'd walked in on the middle of something. It didn't seem as if my mom and dad were fighting, but I couldn't quite figure out what it was they *were* doing — or not doing. Something invisible, but very real, hung in the air. I was tempted to tiptoe backwards, back into the kitchen and right out the side door. Let Mom and Dad settle whatever it was they weren't talking about right now. Trouble was, I had nowhere to go once I got to the garage.

That was the problem with moving back home between college graduation and my wedding. I was trapped in limbo land. I'd tried explaining it to Jen over dinner earlier tonight.

"It's just so weird being back in my old room." I waved a fork with a clump of Cajun chicken salad on the end. "I mean, my mom still has my cheerleading letter on my bulletin board. And my old doll is sitting on a chair in the corner." I leaned forward. "And behind my door there's still a poster of that group we were so nuts about in like eighth grade. I can't even remember why we thought they were cute. It's like I moved into a time warp." I pushed the bite of salad into my mouth and chewed.

Jen looked at me as she took a long drink of her Diet Pepsi. "So, take down the poster. Move the stuff."

I rolled my eyes. She didn't get it. "That's the problem. It doesn't really seem like my stuff anymore. It's like it's my mom's. But it's still mine. Or not . . ." My words trailed off. It was hard to explain how moving back home made me feel. I put down my fork and sighed. "I miss Josh."

Jen stirred her catsup with a french fry and didn't say anything. I shouldn't have said that about missing Josh. Jen didn't have a boyfriend, and she was 21, just like me. She liked to pretend that being single was everything *Cosmo* cracked it up to be, but I knew better.

"Hey." I reached a hand across the table. "Maybe you'll meet someone at the wedding. You know how the bridesmaids always

38

have the most fun."

"Yeah." Jen smiled and leaned her head toward the Elizabeth's shopping bag in the booth beside her. "The dress I got for the rehearsal is a killer."

Now it was my turn to stir my salad. Jen and I had met to go shopping, which was hard to do when I didn't have a job or money. As it was, I was eating supper on the 20 bucks my dad had slipped me the other night. It was different for Jen. She'd gone to college right here in Carlton, interned at a computer graphics company, and was hired before she even graduated. She had her own apartment, a cool used car, and a job. But no boyfriend.

And I had Josh. I comforted myself with the fact that my situation was temporary. As soon as Josh finished summer session, we'd be married and start living what I called "real life."

"Did you find a job yet?" Jen pushed a french fry into her mouth.

I'd wondered when she'd ask that. It seemed like the question of the day these past weeks. My mom seemed to think she wasn't doing her duty if she didn't dance around the question at least once a day.

I could feel my jaw tighten as I searched for the easiest explanation. Once again I found myself waving salad through the air. "When I got back to town I turned in applications at a few places here in the mall."

"The mall? Like retail? I thought your degree was in mass communications."

"It is, but —" I stuffed the salad into my mouth and gave it three vicious chomps before I swallowed and tried to explain. "By the time I got back, most of the part-time summer jobs were already filled with high school and college kids who got here before I did. I had an ad sales interview at one of the TV stations, but it seemed pointless to take it. I mean, I'd barely get started, and I'd have to quit for my wedding." I pointed my fork at myself. "Who'd want to hire me right now?"

She shrugged as if I finally had a point.

"Besides," I added, "we'll be moving after we get back from our honeymoon."

"Moving?" Jen dropped her jaw. "I thought Josh wanted to stay here. In Carlton."

How did she know that? I stared back at her until I remembered. I had told her. Me and my big mouth and two Amaretto sours two weeks ago. I'd spilled my guts like a Samurai warrior.

"He does," I admitted. "But there's no way I'm staying in Carlton, and he knows it. I want a career. I want to live in a big city. Not in this pretend town that likes to think it's big-time."

Oh, great. I could tell by Jen's face that I'd just stuck my foot in my mouth — and possibly stomped on her dreams.

"I mean . . ." How could I explain this? With both hands I pushed my hair behind my ears and leaned toward her. "I've watched my dad. He runs this small agency, and it consumes his life. All he does is live, eat, and breathe work. If I work in a large company, I won't have to have that kind of responsibility all the time. I want a life too."

Jen chewed her sandwich and didn't say anything. I couldn't tell if she understood what I was trying to say. For that matter, I wasn't sure of everything I was saying either.

Sometimes explaining something to Jen helped me figure it out myself, so I took a breath and went on. "And then I look at my mom, and she doesn't even have a life. I mean, she majored in art history in college, and what has she ever done with that? She makes her club meetings sound like a job, but they're not; they're just clubs she joins to fill her time and make it seem like she's busy." I sat back and sighed. "I guess I'm afraid if I stay here I'll end up like my dad

41

or my mom. And I just want to find out who I am."

Now, an hour later, I realized I'd probably said more to Jen than I should have. My instant analysis had left me unsettled. Here I was, standing in my parents' family room, feeling like an intruder. Dad was in his recliner reading some papers he must have pulled from his briefcase on the floor. Mom was on the couch, a book in her lap, reading. It was a scene I'd witnessed a thousand times while I was growing up in this house, but tonight, something was different. If they'd been arguing I would have heard their raised voices long before they knew I was home. At least if that had been the case, I would have known what was going on. But, as it was, my mom and dad almost never argued. At least not that I ever heard. So that hardly seemed the problem now.

I hoped Josh and I would have a relationship as good as theirs. And it couldn't start soon enough. All I had to do was bide my time for another six weeks.

I cleared my throat to let them know I was back in my luxurious holding zone. "Hey, what's up?"

Mom glanced up from her book. "Hi! I didn't hear you come in." She threw a quick glance at my dad and then patted a spot on the couch next to her. "Want to join us?"

It didn't seem there was much "us" to join, but I sat near her anyway. I grabbed an *Oprah* magazine off the coffee table and put my feet up as if I belonged. Even though I'd lived away from home for four years, it didn't seem I'd been gone long enough for this not to feel like home anymore. But that's exactly how it felt. As if I was a visitor. I couldn't wait for Josh to finish the extra summer session he was taking to get his coaching certification. Then his assignment was to get here and get married. And then life would begin.

When we'd planned our wedding for late summer, we had forgotten about the fact that I would be done with college in May and he wouldn't finish up until early August. It hardly paid for me to find a temporary apartment in the town where we had both gone to college; who knew where we'd be moving once we were married and found jobs? I moved out of my sorority house right after graduation and came back to Carlton. Josh would live in his apartment with his roommates until second summer session was over. I hadn't realized how hard it would be to spend the summer away from Josh until I'd spent almost four weeks doing it.

"Did you have fun tonight?" My mom's finger held her spot in her book.

"Yeah," I answered, "but Jen didn't want to go to a movie after supper." I tried to bite back the rest of my sentence, but it fell out anyway. "She has to work in the morning." I waited for what I knew was coming.

Mom pressed her lips together as if she also was biting back a response. I had to give her credit; she did a better job of not bringing up a sore subject than I did. The thing was, she didn't have to say a word; I already knew what she was thinking. I'd complained to her often enough how bored I was. She had told me more than once to get out and find any job I could, just to fill the time and save some money for our marriage. I tried. I really did. Well, sort of. I couldn't see the point of trying to find a decent job that I was going to quit in a couple of months anyway.

"I'm going to talk to the manager of Brews-n-News tomorrow." There, that would keep her off my case for 24 hours. As if I had gone to college so I could end up making expensive coffee drinks. I quickly pretended to be engrossed in my magazine.

I had to admit I'd spent more time reading than job-hunting. I'd forgotten how much fun it could be to read just because you wanted to. Which was probably exactly why my mom was so engrossed in the book on her lap. But then, what else did my mom have to do?

I turned a page of my magazine and studied her out of the corner of my eye. Didn't she ever want to do more with her life? More than just sit here and read? More than waiting for my dad to come home from work?

I licked my finger and turned a page. My life was going to be different. As soon as our wedding was over, I had no doubt I would be working at an important and interesting job. Somewhere besides Carlton, North Dakota. For the time being, I was going to be a bride. I was justified living in la-la land for just a little while longer.

I glanced up from my magazine and caught my dad staring at my mom as if he was waiting for her to say something. Suddenly it dawned on me. Maybe they'd been talking about the honeymoon. My honeymoon. The honeymoon my dad had promised me since I was a little girl. I bit back a smile. No wonder they had been so quiet when I walked in the room. They probably thought I'd forgotten and wanted it to be a surprise. Fat chance I'd forget something that cool.

I laid the magazine in my lap and faked a tired stretch. "I think I'll go to my room. I want to e-mail Josh. Then maybe I'll work on my résumé and check out some jobs on-line before I go to bed." There, that should give them the hint that I'd be out of the room the rest of the night. If they wanted to plan a surprise, I wasn't about to get in their way.

About the only thing that had changed in my old bedroom was that there was a computer in it. Sometime in the past four years my parents had tried to move into the computer age. They had traded the clunky computer I used during high school for high-tech central. Flat screen, no less. Hooked up to high speed DSL. Top shelf. There was even a fax machine on my old desk. Even though they rarely used the computer — my dad said he had enough e-mail to wade through at work; my mom said, "Why e-mail when I see my friends all the time?" — I was glad they had it. It helped me keep in touch with my far-flung college friends. And Josh.

If I was lucky I'd have a dozen or more e-mails waiting that would take the rest of the night to read and answer. At least it would look like I was busy.

I clicked on Outlook Express and waited for the familiar screen to appear. I hoped there would be at least one e-mail from Josh. He tried to send one at least once a day, in addition to calling if he found the time. Unlike me, he didn't have time to sit around and be bored. In addition to his classes, he was coaching Little League with a city parks program and umping organized amateur softball games any night he could pick up a game, which meant extra money.

A small twinge of lazy, "you need a job" guilt stabbed at my conscience as I impatiently clicked at the e-mail icon again. *Come onnn.* How could a nanosecond feel so long?

THIS PAGE CANNOT BE FOUND BY
YOUR SERVER.

What? Argh! Technology glitches. I hate them. I closed the page and tried again.

THIS PAGE CANNOT BE FOUND BY
YOUR SERVER.

I hit the heel of my hand against the edge of the desk. What was I going to do with a whole night if the computer was down?

You told your parents you were going to work on your résumé. You don't need the In-

ternet for that.

I swallowed hard as I clicked on the e-mail icon for a third time. The truth was, my résumé was as done as it was going to get. *Nothing will change until you actually start sending it out.*

I tilted my head back as far as it would go and tensed the muscles in my neck as tightly as I could. Maybe the numbing pain that spread through my neck and shoulders would make these thoughts go away.

No. Not tonight.

As I tapped at the mouse again and again, I heard my thoughts echo. *You're not qualified for a real job. No one will hire you. You're a fake and a phony. Even after four years of college you don't know anything.*

"Hear from Josh?" My mom was standing in the doorway. If they'd discussed my honeymoon, it sure hadn't taken them long.

I glanced away from the screen. "I haven't checked my e-mail yet."

"Did you find out anything about those jobs online?"

Sometimes it would be nice if my mom didn't remember absolutely everything I said. Maybe these computer problems tonight were a gift after all. I pointed impatiently to the screen. "There's something wrong. I can't get connected."

Mom held up a palm as if she was taking an oath. "Don't ask me. I know nothing about that machine." She came into the room and smoothed my hair off my neck, bending to give a spot under my ear a soft kiss. "I'm not going to be able to do this much longer," she said quietly. "Pretty soon you're going to be married, with a husband and a home of your own. An exciting job. Maybe some kids someday." She chuckled softly as she walked back into the hall. "My little girl is all grown up."

I knew she meant her words to be encouraging; everything she'd said was stuff I was anticipating, but for reasons I couldn't pinpoint, a lump filled my throat.

I turned the computer off; I didn't have much to tell Josh anyway. There was a whole lot I needed to figure out as I brushed my teeth, pulled on the oversized T-shirt I slept in, and crawled into bed.

I lay on my back and stared at the ceiling. I wanted my real life with Josh to start. But not the other real life, the one where I needed to prove myself. Prove that I was brilliant and talented. Prove that I was everything my dad was and everything my mother wasn't. It was time to live up to all my dreaming. All my big talk.

And I was scared to death.

LAURA

I pulled the phone receiver away from my ear, staring at the mouthpiece as if looking at it would help decipher what I'd just heard. "Can you say that again?"

"I phhinnk der's somephing wrrronnng."

If I didn't know better, I'd swear my mother-in-law had been drinking more than orange juice to start her day. "What's the matter?" I asked, and at the same time thought, *Whatever it is, I don't have time for this today.* My eyes drifted to the calendar hanging on the wall near my phone. I had promised to help Karen paint the walls of the gallery this afternoon. Before that I had Bible study and a lunch date with Carla, my old college roommate.

"I haave a terrrrible headaaache." Eleanor's voice whispered. "I'mm diizzzy."

Something had to be dreadfully wrong for Eleanor to be calling me for help. My mother-in-law was as feisty as they came.

Some of my friends complained to no end about their mothers-in-law, but the only complaint I had was that she'd brought up her only son to have an even stronger work ethic than she had. Eleanor was never sick.

"Do you want me to come over?" She lived less than 15 minutes from us, in an older section of Carlton. In my mind's eye I could see the neighboring houses on either side of her small bungalow. Large. Imposing. Too far for Eleanor to walk if she truly needed help.

"Yesss. Pleeease commme." Her voice seemed to fade.

"Eleanor." I spoke loudly, not sure if she could comprehend my words. "I want you to go to your couch. Lie down until I get there. Okay?" There was no response. "Eleanor? Did you hear me?" Silence. Then a familiar buzz. She must have hung up the phone. At least she could still do that. *Maybe I should call an ambulance.*

Instead, I grabbed my purse and car keys and headed for the door. There was no time to leave a note for Stasha. Besides, she knew I planned to be gone for most of the day. At the last minute I turned around and grabbed my Bible and study book. Possibly something as simple as an inner-ear infection was making Eleanor dizzy. With any

51

luck I'd be able to tend to her and still make it to Bible study.

As I headed through the side streets that would take me to Eleanor's, I held down the speed-dial button for Donnie's extension at the agency. I seldom called him at work, and I knew all the warnings about talking on a cell phone while driving, but this seemed important enough to take the risk.

"Dunn Agency. Arlene speaking." Donnie's assistant's familiar voice was unexpectedly comforting now that my day had suddenly been turned upside down.

"Arlene, it's Laura. Is Donnie available?"

"Oh, Laura. I haven't seen you in so long. How are you?"

Under any other circumstances, I would have loved to chat with Arlene. After working for Donnie since he'd started the agency 20-some years ago, Arlene was like a member of the family. But today, the niceties would have to take a backseat. "Arlene, I'm afraid I might have a bit of an emergency on my hands. I think I'd better talk to Donnie. I'm on my way to his mother's house right now."

"Oh. Okay. Let me buzz him."

I drove with one hand as static-filled "hold" music tried to entertain me. I hoped

I wouldn't lose the call; Donnie would have no patience with dead air.

"Laura?" It wasn't Donnie; it was Arlene back on the line. "I'm afraid he's not picking up. I paged him, but I think he may have already left for a meeting he had scheduled this morning. Do you want to try him on his cell phone?"

If Donnie was in a meeting, he wouldn't appreciate the interruption, especially if his mother turned out to have something as simple as an ear problem. I was almost at Eleanor's house. I'd check things out, then call back. "Just tell him I called, and have him call me when he has time."

"Will do," Arlene said as I pulled into my mother-in-law's driveway.

As usual for this early in the morning, Eleanor had her single-car garage door closed, which provided the only access to the inside door that she normally used. I hurried out of the car to the front door. Sultry mid-July heat, rare for a North Dakota morning, pressed heavily against my skin as I rang the bell. I waited only a second and then turned the knob. Locked. Of course. If Eleanor had planned to go anywhere this morning, she would have used the door to the garage. I rapped loudly. "Eleanor!" I knocked again. "Can you open the door?"

I peeked through the sidelight, the long, narrow window framing one side of the doorway, hoping to see her making her way down the short hallway. Nothing but polished hardwood and an ornate runner. It occurred to me that Donnie kept a spare key to check on the house when his mother took one of her frequent trips. A lot of good that did me now.

I might feel foolish about this in a minute, but I'd feel more foolish if I didn't do it. I opened my cell phone and dialed 911. While I gave directions to the dispatcher, my eyes landed on an out-of-place rock at the base of a shrub near the door. It might as well have had a sign on it reading "Here's the key." I picked it up and dug inside the small opening. Sure enough, there it was. Quickly I inserted the key into the lock and let myself inside. "Eleanor? It's Laura. Are you —"

I saw her feet first. "Oh!" I couldn't keep the alarm out of my voice. She was lying on the living room floor near the end table where she kept her phone. I knelt at her side and tried to feel her neck for a pulse. Watching *ER* every Thursday night had taught me only the basics. "Eleanor, can you hear me?"

Her eyelids fluttered, but only one opened. One side of her mouth sagged open. The other struggled to form a word. Whatever it was, it came out as air, but I welcomed her effort all the same. At least she was alive.

I took her limp hand in mine. "An ambulance is on the way."

She closed her eye.

I prayed.

An hour later, I stood beside Eleanor's gurney as the emergency room doctor announced the diagnosis.

"I'm guessing your mother-in-law has suffered a transient ischemic attack. TIA we call them. Or mini stroke." The doctor's assessment didn't seem as grim now that Eleanor was sitting up in her bed, looking as if nothing had happened.

"I'm ready to go home now." My mother-in-law sat up and started sliding her legs to the edge of the bed.

As if we'd practiced together, both the doctor and I reached out an arm and said in unison, "No."

"No way," I added. My frantic drive behind the ambulance was fresh in my mind. I wasn't about to take this patient home an hour after we'd arrived.

The doctor backed me up by putting a

firm hand on Eleanor's leg. "You may be feeling better now, but you're at high risk for a subsequent stroke. Your sudden recovery from the symptoms of a TIA may not appear life-threatening, but that can be deceiving. The next couple of days will determine the outcome of this attack."

"I feel fine." She waved both her hands in front of her body, then held out her open palms to the doctor. "Honestly, I don't see any reason to stay here. I was supposed to be at my golf league this morning, and I've already missed that. I know they're wondering where I am. I don't want to miss the luncheon too."

The doctor and I exchanged a pointed look before he spoke. "We're going to put you on an aspirin regimen and observe you for the next 24 to 48 hours."

"Well, could you make it 24? I'd hate to miss birthday club on Thursday."

The doctor looked intently at Eleanor. "I can see I'm going to have my hands full with you." I hoped she was getting the message that she wasn't going anywhere anytime soon.

Eleanor's eyes met mine. "What should we tell Donnie?"

"What should we tell him?" Oh, good grief. "We're going to tell him exactly what happened. That you had a mini stroke and you have to stay in the hospital for two days."

Eleanor rubbed at a spot just under her ear. "I don't want him to worry about me."

I didn't have the heart to tell her it might do her son some good to have something to worry about besides his work.

It took a few more minutes for the doctor to explain in detail what had happened. The bottom line was that Eleanor wasn't leaving the hospital for a while. When he left, Eleanor crossed her arms over her chest and actually "Harrumphed!" Outside of a cartoon, I'd never seen anyone actually do that before.

"You're lucky, you know," I said, repeating the doctor's observation. "This was a minor stroke. It could have been much worse." I pulled a chair next to the gurney. "You rest. I'll be right here."

Eleanor laid her head back into the pillow and closed her eyes briefly. "No, Laura, you should go. I'll be fine."

"I'll go in a while," I said.

"Really, you can go." Eleanor fluffed the stiff pillow behind her head and sank back into it. "It's certainly not relaxing for me to try and rest, knowing you're sitting there watching me try to do it."

I mentally put myself in Eleanor's hospital gown and realized she was right. "You're sure?"

"Absolutely positive," she said waving me toward the corridor.

"I'll be back tonight. Promise."

"Bring Donnie with you."

Knowing Donnie's schedule, that was one promise I wasn't ready to make. I raised my hand in a noncommittal wave as I walked out the door.

"I could wring his neck," I said to Karen as I slashed my paintbrush across the wall of her soon-to-open gallery. What I was ready to do to my husband would put him in the hospital right beside his mother. The deep maroon of the paint reminded me of blood. Donnie's to be exact. "He still hasn't called. He doesn't even know his mother had a stroke and is in the hospital."

Karen knew I needed to let off steam. My remarks didn't need much in the way of a response, only an occasional acknowledgment that she was listening and that she agreed with me.

"I've left two messages on his cell phone and two messages with Arlene. If he doesn't care about his mother any more than that!" I jabbed the paintbrush into the can as if it was a knife. It was as hot in here as the July heat outside. Karen was trying to save every dime she could to finance this gallery, which meant no air conditioning. Today I didn't mind; I needed to let off steam in more ways than one.

"Maybe his phone battery went dead."

I certainly didn't need Karen making excuses for my husband. "Dead. Now there's a word that might apply to Donnie if he doesn't call soon."

"Give the guy a break, Laura." Karen smoothed paint on the wall as if she was meditating. "If he knew about his mother, you know he'd call. Obviously, he hasn't gotten any of the messages yet."

She was a fine friend to take his side. Almost every time we got together all she did was complain about her husband, Todd. I certainly had good reason to complain about mine this afternoon. Tears of frustration stung my eyes. I slapped more of the blood-red paint on the wall in uneven strokes. "I spent the whole morning tending to this emergency with his mother. I missed Bible study. I had to call Carla and cancel lunch. I haven't seen her in months, and I was really looking forward to catching up. Know what I had for lunch? A Whopper at Burger King. If I die of high cholesterol, it will serve Donnie right." Short, crisscrossing brushstrokes punctuated my angry words. "And what did Donnie do all day? The same thing he always does. Went about his business as if there wasn't anything in the world more important than his agency. I could strangle him."

Karen held her brush still, a half-smile on her face. "Come on." She wiggled the fingers of one hand toward her chin. "Tell me how you really feel."

I couldn't help it. A burst of frustrated laughter filled the space between us as my pent-up anger finally let go. Just as quickly, it was replaced with tired tears. "I was just so scared," I said. I bent to dip my brush in the paint, rising to cover my livid brush strokes with a gentle, even coat. I blinked away the tears. "I really did think Eleanor was going to die on her living room floor while I sat there and watched."

"I don't blame you for being scared." Karen's affirmation of my fear helped dispel more of it. "I don't know if I would have even thought to call the ambulance. I might have just froze. Or freezed. Or however you say it." She laughed. It wasn't the first time she'd invented a word.

"Freezed." I repeated, laughing. "A technical medical term for acting stupid without moving."

"Like this." Karen held her paintbrush over her head at a crazy angle and struck a pose.

I could always count on Karen to get me out of a bad mood. I knew my frustration wasn't all because of Eleanor. There was only one month left until Stasha's wedding, and I somehow felt as if we were forgetting something important. Many a night I'd stayed awake ticking off all the things we had planned as if they were sheep jumping a fence. But with a professional wedding planner and a banquet manager, we couldn't possibly have overlooked anything, except maybe signing a check. And they would have reminded us about that.

"Look out!" Karen was still holding her goofy pose. I reached out helplessly as a large drip of red paint headed for Karen's blonde hair, highlights I knew she'd paid good money for. At the same instant, Karen looked up and saw the glob heading her way. Instinctively, she jerked the brush away from her head, flinging the large blob onto my royal blue shirt, an old one of Donnie's that I'd put over my sleeveless white blouse to protect myself from exactly what had just happened.

"Sorry." Karen smiled an apology as she

stepped toward me to wipe off the paint.

I held up a hand. "Wait. I think I'd be better off doing this in the bathroom. I don't want the color to bleed through the fabric onto my blouse."

"You're right." Karen reached for my paintbrush. "I'm going to wrap these in a plastic bag so they don't dry out, and then I'll run down the street and get us a couple of Diet Cokes. We deserve them."

"Sounds good." I headed to the bathroom in the back as Karen went out the front door. I stepped to the sink, holding the front of my shirt away from the fabric beneath. What would be the best way to tackle this paint-removal project?

With one hand I unbuttoned the big overshirt, carefully slipping out of it. I laid the fabric across the basin of the sink, stretching it tight, using my right hand and the front of my legs as a stretcher bar. This was latex paint; plain water would do the trick.

With my left hand I reached for the faucet, but like a little kid faced with a mud puddle, I couldn't resist sticking my forefinger into the messy glob of color. There wasn't much paint, but there was enough for me to make a couple of swift swipes. *Hills in the distance.* Instant images of the vivid landscapes I used to paint tugged from somewhere deep. The maroon paint against the blue fabric was an unlikely color combination that sent my mind whirling. *A brilliant sunset turning the hills red against a stormy sky.*

I scribbled at the paint, filling in the small hill with my tiny palette. Oh, if only I had a touch of white. Or just a dab of cadmium orange or Naples yellow.

You haven't forgotten the colors.

No, I hadn't. Even after all these years. *Cerulean blue. Burnt umber. Cobalt. Violet.* The possibilities of what I could do with those colors were endless.

You should paint again.

With a sudden fierceness, I missed painting. The tightly stretched blank canvas waiting for me to fill the space with color. To fill in my imagined vision of the world around me. It was as if I was back in the studio; I could smell the mix of oil paint and turpentine — my perfume during my college years when I'd studied the masters, when I'd made my first feeble attempts at creating my own masterpieces.

Ha! I couldn't help but smile. My freshman effort on a large canvas didn't look a whole lot better than the makeshift canvas I now held over the sink. And yet I'd learned from that effort, receiving the smallest bit of encouragement from my instructor. "You've got a good eye for color, Laura," he'd said as he passed by my easel.

Even now I could remember the swell of pride that filled my chest and fueled my desire to learn more. By the end of the semester, my instructor was using my canvas as an example of the innovative use of color.

I had never told my college story to Karen. None of my friends knew I used to paint. They never guessed that many of the pictures they had admired in my home had been done by me. Even so, it had been me that Karen had asked for advice on what color to paint the walls of her gallery. We both knew she'd need some walls covered with the creamiest of white. Certain paintings popped on white. But she wanted more in her gallery than the starkness of a single color that many of the larger city galleries featured. That's why I'd suggested we do one wall in maroon with a gold glaze over the top. We'd painted a couple of the free-standing room panels in the gallery a cobalt blue. But we had to remember that this was North Dakota and not New York. Folks around here had an eye for hunting prints in editions that were issued by the thousands. We knew we had a job ahead of us, educating many of the locals about the value of owning an original piece of art.

We? What's up with that?

With a heavy finger I pushed my simple painting into the basin and turned on the water. Along with the paint, I would wash away the evidence that I still toyed with my old dream. The dream that someday I would be the one opening a gallery. That my paintings would hang under spotlights in featured spaces.

When had I given up the dream? As hard as I tried, I couldn't remember. I'd been in college studying art. I'd met Donnie. There had hardly been time to paint during our whirlwind courtship. We got married and started the agency. I helped with the office work those first years. We'd had Stasha. And somehow in the course of it all, I had started a life, one without painting.

Avoiding my face in the mirror, I swished the fabric under the running water, watching as the water turned crimson, then pink, and finally clear, the way my dream had somehow dissolved. Maybe someday I'd start again. I could set up my — what was that? From the other room I heard a faint sound and turned my head to listen. Was Karen back already? I turned off the water. "Karen?" I called. If someone had walked in, it wouldn't be the first time a curious passerby — "potential customer," Karen and I called them — had wandered in. "Anyone there?"

Quickly I squeezed the fabric, not quite sure if I should take the time to flatten it or simply leave it in a lump in the bottom of the sink while I went to check on the noise. Oh! How could I be so dense? It was my cell phone. I dropped the wet shirt into the sink and raced for my purse in the middle of the room. I had been listening for it all day, and now when it finally rang I'd almost missed it. I didn't take time to see who was calling. "Hello?"

"Where have you been?" It was Donnie, sounding as exasperated with me as I was with him.

"Me?" I didn't know whether to get mad or laugh. He certainly wasn't in any position to be criticizing me.

"I've tried calling you twice. Well, three times including now."

If he wanted to play that game I could tell him I'd called him four times, counting the messages I'd left with Arlene. Had he really tried to call, or was he just covering up for all the messages I'd left? I knew I had no reason to doubt him. As absentminded as he sometimes was, he was fairly transparent. If he said he'd tried to call, he probably had. But how could I have missed his calls when I had done nothing but listen for them?

I pulled the phone away from my ear and glanced at the screen. Sure enough, I had messages I hadn't noticed. I had a sudden vision of my purse on the floor of Burger King and the loud birthday party of three-year-olds in the two booths beside me. The stop at the gas station where I'd quickly swiped my card and filled the car with gas, my purse resting on the passenger seat and my phone out of hearing range. My earlier rant to Karen suddenly made me feel small and petty. *Forgive me, Lord.* The messages I'd left for Donnie had been purposely vague. *Something about your mother.* By the time I'd called, there had been no reason to rush. I'd just wanted to share the news and my worry. I took a breath. "It's your mom."

"What about her?" I could hear the impatience in his voice. I wasn't sure if he was still angry with me, worried about his mother, or afraid that whatever it was would interfere with his work.

"She's had a . . ." How should I say this so he wouldn't get overly concerned? Eleanor would more than likely be perfectly fine. The doctor himself had said so. *Consider it an early warning sign. We'll watch her closely from here on.*

I'd start over. "Your mom is fine. Really." I found myself holding up a palm as if to hold off any questions he might ask before I could explain it all. "She had a small stroke. A TIA, the doctor called it."

"A stroke? How is she? Where is she?"

So much for my upheld hand. I lowered it as I gave him the story, all of it — her slurred phone call, my call for the ambulance, her seemingly miraculous recovery once we were at the hospital. All par for the course for a mini stroke, for those who were lucky. I paced around the empty gallery as I talked, wanting Donnie to know how scared I had been, wanting him to say I'd done exactly what he would have done. That he'd come pick me up, and we'd go to the hospital together.

"So . . . she's fine." Bottom-line Donnie. After 23 years I should have known better than to expect much from him.

"Well, ye-es. They do want to keep her for observation. The next 48 hours are critical." I paced to the door. Karen was out on the sidewalk talking to someone, a Diet Coke in each hand.

"Where are you now?" Donnie's voice grew muffled, as if he was talking to someone nearby.

Ahhh . . . Maybe he was planning to come

get me after all. "I'm at Karen's gallery, helping her paint."

He spoke back into the phone. "Well, Mom can't be that bad if you're off painting."

As if the whole morning I'd spent at the hospital was a coffee party. Karen stepped inside and handed me a cold Coke. I propped the phone between my shoulder and chin and twisted the cap off the bottle as if it were Donnie's neck. Instead of making a snide comment, I took a long swallow.

"Laura? You still there?"

Let him worry for a second while I swallowed. It would serve Donnie right if I hung up on him. "I'm here." My words were as icy as the liquid I'd just gulped.

"Good. I thought for a second we'd gotten cut off." He was so oblivious. "So then, Mom's going to be fine?" He paused for the smallest of moments, as if he knew he should stop while he was ahead. As usual, he didn't. "I've got the Martin people flying in this afternoon. I spent the morning at the airport coordinating our presentation. They're due in any minute. If you could just tell Mom . . ."

Whatever else he had to say, I didn't want to hear. I talked to him in my head. *And I spent the morning at the hospital with* your *mother.* Of course, he didn't hear a word of my unspoken hostility. He hadn't really heard me in . . . what? Weeks? Months? Years? I was wallpaper to him, nothing but a background to his busy, more important life.

What had possessed me to think I might take up painting again? It must have been the heat — or the paint fumes. For a moment I'd forgotten that the whole world revolved around Donnie Dunn.

I murmured "goodbye" and ended the call, a new resolve settling somewhere deep. The world could continue to turn around Donnie for a while. For Stasha's sake, I'd let that happen. But after the wedding . . .

DONNIE

Talk about lousy timing. I snapped my cell phone closed and rubbed the back of my neck. My mother was lying in the hospital on what could be one of the most important days of my career. What was I supposed to do?

You're just like your dad, Donnie. I could hear Mom say it. It was a good thing to be like my dad in her eyes. He'd worked hard, given us a good life. I knew that if he were still alive, he'd be amazed to see how my company had grown; it was now worth several million dollars. His dreams of getting ahead had been fine for his time. He had wanted a nice house for his family, a new car every few years, my college tuition, and enough left over so my mom would be set in case he died before she did. With some wise investing from his insurance sales job, he had done all that. He'd had big dreams, but mine were bigger.

There was a faint hum in the distance. My eyes scanned the sky. The Martin plane was due to land any minute.

Matt stood at my side, his hand shielding his eyes from the late afternoon sun. "Think that's them?"

Even though I had no idea what the Martin plane looked like, I used my hand as a visor too. "Hope so." I looked around. Everything was in place. The local dealership had lent us the biggest piece of machinery the company made. It was spit-polished and parked not far from where Andrew Martin and his cronies would get off their plane. Four of my staff people were lined up in matching T-shirts printed with the Martin logo and the new tagline we were hoping they would pick for the company. We weren't quite sure how many people the Martin folks were bringing for this meeting. I'd rather be safe than . . . nope, couldn't use *sorry* . . . too cliché. I'd rather have too many people here to welcome them than not enough. That's why I had some of my staff here as a welcoming committee. We could comfortably fit eight in the limo. Andrew, Matt, and me, for sure. We'd see who else got off the plane, assess their apparent rank in the company, then do a quick shuffle to see how we'd get them all back to the agency. We had two shiny black Town Cars at our disposal as well.

The plane appeared to grow larger as it approached for landing. If this was the Martin plane, they did things first-class. A twin-engine jet. Impressive.

I fingered my cell phone. If it wasn't them, I might have a second to call my mother at the hospital and see how she was doing.

"It's them." Matt was straightening his tie, looking down at his shoes as if he was checking to see if they needed a second polishing.

Too late to think about polish now or about calling my mother. The large "M" on the side of the plane came to a stop right where we'd hoped. I pushed back my shoulders. I'd never been in the service, but I felt as if I was waiting for some kind of inspection. Well, in a way I was. They were here to inspect our agency, to see if we passed muster compared to the big boys.

I ran a finger around my collar and jutted my chin into the air to give myself some breathing room. I was ready. If we won this account the sky was the . . . no, couldn't say *limit*. Let's just say this account would be a solid stepping-stone to Minneapolis.

Matt loosened his tie, unbuttoned the top

button of his collar, and then pulled his tie off. He tossed it on my desk and sank into the chair across from mine. "So, how do you think it went?"

My tie joined his on the desktop. I stretched my arms over my head, linked my fingers, and rested my head against my palms. "I think it went good. Really good."

Matt smiled. "Yeah. I did, too. They sure liked the chicken wings."

"Let's hope they like the agency as much." I sat back up and put my forearms on the desk. There was still work to do to get ready for our full presentation in the morning. "Everyone knows the Martin people are going to be back here at nine tomorrow, right?"

"Everyone knows. They're going to wear the caps we had printed with the logo tomorrow."

"Good." I picked up a pen and tapped it against the desk. "I hope Andy has a chance to look over our book before he comes in tomorrow." The book was an agency's bible when it came to featuring their work. Ours included highlights from our best accounts, showcasing the creative talent of our agency. "They did get a couple of copies, didn't they?"

Matt closed his eyes for a second, thinking. He opened them wide. "Shoot, I can't remember — I'm trying to think if anyone was carrying a copy when they left."

I pressed my lips into a thin line and gave my pen a hard thump. "I really wanted them to have a chance to go through it before we meet tomorrow. Some of the material I plan to present at the meeting references our previous work."

Matt tilted his head from side to side, stretching his neck. "Man, the night went so fast, and it seemed like there was so much I was trying to remember to tell them, without making it seem like I was dropping info." He scratched at his head. "I have no idea if they got the book or not."

"Donnie? Matt?" Arlene stood in the doorway.

My head jerked up. I'd thought Matt and I were the only two people left in the office. "What are you still doing here?"

Arlene shrugged her shoulders. "Cleaning up. Trying to figure out where to put chicken bones so we won't smell them in the morning."

Leave it to Arlene to think of that. The cleaning crew only came in two nights a week, and tonight wasn't one of them. "Put them in a garbage bag," I volunteered. "I'll carry them out to the Dumpster on my way out." Even though Carlton didn't have a crime problem, carrying garbage into a dark alley wasn't part of Arlene's duties.

Arlene held up a finger. "What I wanted to say was that I couldn't help overhear you two wondering if the Martin people got a copy of the book. I just wanted you to know I had gift baskets delivered to their hotel rooms. They each had one of the T-shirts in them, the baseball cap, and a copy of the book. And some other stuff . . ." Her sentence trailed off as if what she'd done wasn't all that much.

"Arlene." I didn't even try to hold back the stupid grin I could feel forming. "You are marvelous. I don't know what we'd do without you."

A weird twinge twitched her mouth. Maybe she was trying to hold back a grin herself.

"And with that" — Matt pushed himself out of his chair — "I'm going to call it a night. Tomorrow is going to come early enough. Don't worry about the chicken bones. I'll take them out."

"Thanks." I looked over the papers and notes on my desk. Something Matt had said before he left was niggling at my brain: "I'm going to call it a night." Call! That was it. I needed to call my mother at the hospital. I reached for the phone, but one glance at the small clock on my desk told me it was much too late to call anyone, especially someone in the hospital. I ran a hand over my face. Could life get any more complicated?

"Uh, Donnie? Don." Arlene stepped into my office. The woman had been my right arm almost since the day I'd open the Dunn Agency. She'd been here when everyone called me Donnie and had been part of the transition when I'd somehow turned into "Don" to the new hires that had come on board the past few years. She knew this business as well as she knew me. Arlene never asked for my time unless it was urgent — or she wanted a raise. "Can I talk to you for a minute?"

I nodded. It was late. Whatever she wanted wouldn't take too long. As well as Arlene knew me, I knew her. It didn't take me but a blink to read her. She was standing in the doorway fidgeting with a letter-sized piece of white paper between her hands. It might as well have been a poster reading "I want a raise."

I was whipped from the high-stress entertaining we'd done tonight, but I wasn't surprised at her timing. What better time to ask for an increase in salary when she'd already put in a 40-hour week, and it wasn't even Friday? Even though Matt and I were equal partners, somehow over the years I'd become the go-to person when Arlene wanted a pay increase.

"Come in." I motioned her in.

Arlene was as sharp as they came. I paid her well, but she knew she was worth more. We played this game every year. So be it. I clicked my pen. If she wanted a raise, she'd get one. But first, we'd have to play a little hardball. Eventually I'd let Arlene think she'd batted it out of the park.

"Were you happy with the way things went tonight?" Arlene sat in her familiar spot across from me.

"Fantastic. And that's a quote." I couldn't help but smile. So much for my poker face in this discussion.

"That's good." Arlene looked down at the paper in her hands. No doubt a list of all the reasons I should raise her salary. She looked back at me. "Pretty soon you'll have an office in Minneapolis. Maybe Chicago."

"Well." Her comment caught me off guard; I rubbed at the side of my jaw. "I suppose that's part of the plan. Eventually." As tired as I was, it was hard to imagine being any busier.

"And with Stasha getting married next

month," Arlene looked down at the paper in her hand, and then looked up at me and smiled, "who knows? You might be a grandpa sometime soon."

Me? A grandpa? Every now and then Laura said she'd like grandchildren someday. But soon? I was too busy to sit in a rocker and shake a rattle in a baby's face.

"So, what's up?" *Let's get this conversation going so I can get home, get some sleep, and get back here in the morning.*

Arlene cleared her throat, then turned the paper in her hands my way, and slid it across the desk. I didn't glance at it. I'd let Arlene make her case. Whatever she said, I already knew the answer was yes.

"Donnie, you know I've been with you almost since the day you unlocked the door of the Dunn Agency." She took a deep breath. "You saw potential in me when I brought nothing to this job but a résumé that said 'stay-at-home mom.' "

I nodded, and she smiled almost as nervously as she had the day I had interviewed her.

"I want to thank you for that," she added as she looked me square in the eye.

"Sure." I waved off her words. It had been Arlene who had done me the favor of coming to work for my small agency.

Arlene had been the first person to answer the help-wanted ad I had placed in the *Carlton Register.* I had moved the agency — if that's what you could call the two clients I had back then — out of our spare bedroom and into rented office space. Arlene had answered my ad in person. More than ten years older than me, her kids in school, she was looking for a job to fill her time. I remembered thinking that her age — not quite 40 — would give my office a look of maturity, an air of confidence I wasn't feeling at not quite 30. In the 20 years since, I'd attended her children's three graduation receptions and three weddings, and stood on the sidelines as her husband survived a triple valve replacement last year. Arlene and I went way back.

I didn't need her list. Plus, I had some work to get done to prepare for tomorrow. Without looking at her letter, I slid the paper back her way. "Arlene, the answer is yes. Let me do some figuring and get back to you."

A nervous smile twitched one corner of her lips.

"No, Donnie." Once again she pushed the paper toward me. "You didn't let me finish. I don't want a raise." She smoothed an invisible wrinkle in her skirt. "Donnie," she began slowly, "Marlon has been talking about retiring ever since his surgery. We've got another grandchild on the way around Christmas. Jill just told us." Jill was their daughter in Texas.

She paused as she ran a finger along the edge of my desk. "I'd like to go down and spend some time once the baby is born."

"Sure." I lifted my hand in a generous gesture. "No problem. We'll work something out."

She pulled in a slow breath and then released it. "I'm sorry. I've been trying to think of a better way to —" Arlene closed her eyes for a long second, then looked back at me. She spoke quickly. "I know this isn't the best time to tell you this, but the thing is, Donnie, in this business there will never be a good time to resign."

Resign? I felt an odd thrumming near my ear, as if something was coming at me. I could hear it approach, but it was coming much too fast to see. I braced myself.

Once more she pointed to the piece of paper in front of me. "I'm resigning, Donnie. I'd like to be done by the end of the month. I'll be glad to train a replacement."

My head bobbed as if I understood, as if I was agreeing. Slowly my nod turned into a no. There was no way I could run this place

81

without Arlene. Especially not now, with this new business almost on our plate. All I could think to say was, "What can I do to make you stay?"

She shook her head. "Nothing." She folded her hands and rested them on the edge of my desk. "I've thought about this long and hard. I've prayed about it. Life is short, and the fact is, I want to spend what's left of it with Marlon. We want to do some traveling, visit the kids. After helping plan Stasha's honeymoon trip, it's made me want to go to Europe. Italy would be nice."

The words slipped out. "Laura's always wanted to go there too."

Arlene smiled. "Then you should take her."

My response was instant. "I can't. I'm too busy. And now with you —"

Arlene held up a finger. "Maybe you didn't hear me, Donnie. Life is short. You don't have forever. None of us do. I don't want to keep working at this pace anymore."

Easy for Arlene to say. She wasn't sitting in my chair. I might have been able to make time for a trip before, but now, with her leaving, there was no way.

Arlene stood. "I wish I could have timed this better, but to tell you the truth, I've already postponed telling you twice." She smiled apologetically and said, "I'd better finish up."

"Yeah, me, too." I pulled a file folder in front of me and flipped it open, but instead of getting to work, all I could think about was the time crunch I was about to experience, trying to hire and train someone to fill Arlene's practical shoes, all the while juggling the new business coming our way.

I sat back in my chair and ran a hand through my hair. I didn't have time for this.

"You don't have forever. None of us do. I don't want to work at this pace anymore."

As if I wanted this rat race. Ha. Who wouldn't love a trip to Europe? Sure I'd go. *We'd* go. Someday when I have more time.

The thrumming in my head continued until I was forced to sit back and rub my temples. There went everything except work for the next six months . . . or more. The story of my life. Arlene hadn't hit the ball out of the park; she had hit a line drive, right into my solar plexus.

STASHA

It wasn't supposed to be like this.

I was a bride. I was getting married in two weeks. I was supposed to be shopping and laughing and having lunch with my friends. Instead, I sat at the computer in my old bedroom with tears streaming down my cheeks. Jen was at work. So were my other friends. I had taken a part-time job at a coffee shop. And I felt like the loser of the century.

"I hate this." I clicked through the pages of Monster.com. The résumés I'd sent out over the past month might as well have gone to Pluto for all the response I'd gotten. There was no way to follow up, no one I could call. I was at the mercy of a faceless, alien potential boss-person. "Stupid cyberspace," I said as I clicked over to Jobs.com.

This afternoon Josh and I had an appointment to look at an apartment to rent — in Carlton. At that thought, another stream of hot tears fell over the rim of my eyes and rolled onto my hands on the keyboard. We weren't supposed to live in Carlton. We were supposed to be moving into some funky uptown apartment — or maybe even a loft — in Minneapolis, or St. Louis, or anywhere but Carlton, North Dakota. But until I landed a job in one of those places, Josh said we couldn't afford to move anywhere. "Money," he said. I hated that too right now. Well, what I hated was not having any.

Josh was home from summer school and was camping out at his parents' house until the wedding. He was graduated and certified to teach junior high math and coach whatever sport needed him. The only glitch in the plan was that I was supposed to have a job offer by now. How lame was it that I already had a nodding acquaintance with some of my regular coffee customers? Once I got a real job, Josh could substitute teach wherever, until a permanent position opened up. For now, we were forced to find somewhere, anywhere, to stay until we had something more permanent than the construction job Josh had picked up when he moved back to town. And my stupid coffee shop gig.

My mom said we could stay here while we looked for jobs, but Josh refused to move into my old house. "I'm not living off your dad," is what he said. "This is our life. We're going to make it happen on our own. Besides, they've done enough. A wedding and a trip to Italy — if we can't take it from there . . ." He didn't have to finish the sentence. I knew how stubborn he could be when it came to asking for help.

As least I had Italy to look forward to. My dad had remembered his long-ago promise. When he'd started the conversation last night, I was sure he was going to give me the "you-need-a-job" talk.

"Stasha?" Dad had put down his fork and cleared his throat. It was one of the rare nights he was home for dinner. I was so used to him being gone lately that it almost seemed weird to have him home.

Mom had made meat loaf, one of Dad's favorites — not mine. But I wasn't about to complain. It was free. And other than doing my own laundry and running now-and-then errands for my mom, I hadn't done much to contribute to the family over the summer. When my dad said my name like that, a zing of panic shot through me. With Dad it was usually casual conversation: "How you doing? Josh done with school yet? Sure you don't want to come work at the agency?"

I shot a glance at Josh. If my dad had his way, we'd be staying in Carlton. I was going to have to step lightly around Dad's questions.

If Dad was going to start in on that again, I was prepared with my little speech about how I needed to make my own life. If I worked for him, I wouldn't feel as if I'd gotten a job on my own merits. I would leave out the part that I wouldn't live in Carlton if my life depended on it.

"I was wondering what you had planned for after the wedding," he said.

I knew it. I put my fork down. Before I opened my mouth I tried my best to remind myself that Dad had financed my summer of leisure. And the wedding he'd be hosting in short order hadn't come cheap. Nice would be a good thing to be right now.

"I'm looking for a real job," I started. "I really am. I sent out at least 20 résumés over the Internet, and I'm looking for more places, and Josh is going to —" Out of the corner of my eye I could see Josh pause with a huge forkful of mashed potatoes suspended between his plate and his mouth. He knew this conversation could get ugly.

Dad held up a couple of fingers, stopping my flow of words. "I meant, for a honeymoon."

"Oh." I could have saved myself the run-on sentence. I wasn't about to mention that I'd hoped for a trip to Italy, not after a summer of mooching. Being the only child of a workaholic who made up for it by throwing nice things my way might have left me a little spoiled, but I knew better than to expect something that big. I shrugged and looked down at my meat loaf. "Josh thought maybe we could drive to Minneapolis and see the Twins play." I couldn't help it; I rolled my eyes, which was exactly what I'd done when Josh had said it in the first place. Josh was nodding like a bobblehead baseball figure.

I could see a smile tugging at the corner of my dad's mouth. My mom picked up her glass of milk and took a long swallow. I knew what they were thinking. Going to a baseball game was a lame idea for a honeymoon, but with no money and no idea where we were going to live, what choice did we have?

"Do you have your tickets already?" Dad said and put a bite of meat loaf and mashed potatoes into his mouth.

"I doubt it," I said. Since Josh had started his construction job, he was dead tired every night. He barely had the energy to come over and hang out, much less make honeymoon plans. The other night he'd fallen asleep on the family room couch in the middle of telling me what project he'd worked on that day. For all I knew we might end up spending our honeymoon in Carlton on my parents' couch. That would be an exciting story to tell our kids.

My dad pushed his chair away from the table, walked over to where he had set his briefcase, and reached inside. He pulled out a manila envelope and held it out to me. "Here are some tickets for you two."

Knowing my dad, some client had given him box-seat tickets at the Metrodome. Josh would be happy. I forced a smile. At least we'd be going somewhere besides Carlton. "Thanks." I reached inside the envelope and pulled out a brochure. ROME, it read.

Rome?

"Rome!" I jumped up so fast my chair fell over. "Italy? You remembered!" A high-pitched squeal and a bouncing hug hardly began to tell him how excited I was. Josh and I were going to *Rome!* I held the brochure in both hands. "Are you *serious?*"

Dad was grinning from ear to ear. He glanced at my mom. "I told you she'd remember."

"You were right." Mom dished herself up another spoonful of peas.

89

"Thank you!"

I held the tickets in the air so Josh could see them.

"You're welcome." Dad reached for the peas too. "You'll have to thank Arlene. She made all the arrangements through the company travel agent." He paused with the bowl of peas in the air. "Your mom said you and Josh both have passports, right? If not, we're in big trouble."

"We do." I was nodding as if my head might fall off. We both had taken a semester abroad in college. It hadn't been the same semester, and I had missed Josh so much I thought I might have to swim across the ocean to see him. Now I was glad, because it meant we both had passports.

Whoa! The ring of my cell phone abruptly brought me back from my memory to my bedroom. As I jumped from my chair to grab the phone from my bed, I looked over at my wedding dress hanging from the door frame of my closet. In one week this boring, miserable summer would be over. Once we were in Rome, I would have a ten-day reprieve from checking my e-mail 20 times a day. There would be a job offer waiting for me when we got back. There just had to be.

"Hello?"

"Stasha, hi. You ready?"

Oh my gosh. Josh. What time was it? "Yeah," I said half-jogging to the bathroom with the phone pressed to my ear. "Where are you?"

"I'm in my truck about four blocks from your place. Wanna meet me outside?"

"Sure." I reached for my makeup. Four blocks! I'd never be ready in time.

You had all day to fix up. All I'd done was sit in front of my computer, acting like I was doing something. How would I ever hold a job when I couldn't even be ready to go apartment-hunting at four in the afternoon?

I looked down at my clothes. Sweatpants and a T-shirt. *Sheesh.* Josh would hardly buy the excuse that I hadn't had time to get ready. He'd taken off from his job early so we could go see this apartment together. He had spotted the "For Rent" sign across the street from where he was working and went over to ask if we could see the apartment. The rent was cheap. All it needed was my approval.

Heck with the makeup. I wasn't scary without it, just pale. I dashed back to my bedroom and climbed out of my sweatpants and into a pair of cutoffs. Through my open window I could hear Josh's truck idling

91

outside. My light blue T-shirt would work. I slid my feet into a pair of flip-flops. Josh tapped the horn. I could already imagine his face. He hated it when I was late. It wouldn't be the first time we'd fought over my idea of time. Or lack of it.

As I grabbed my purse and ran down the stairs, I remembered how mad I used to get at my dad when I was little. He'd promise we'd go to the Dairy Queen, or for a bike ride, or shoot baskets when he got home from work. How many times had I sat on the front steps, my chin in my hands, waiting and watching for him to come down the street in his black car, feeling less and less excited the longer I waited? Feeling less and less important.

"Sorry." I hopped into Josh's truck, leaned over and gave him a kiss on the cheek before I fastened my seat belt. "I was checking for jobs online and lost track of time." That part was true. I didn't have to tell him about the time I spent crying or the hours I'd spent fantasizing about Italy.

He was biting the inside of his cheek, a sure sign he was losing patience with me. He'd get over it soon enough.

"I'm really looking forward to seeing this place." I looked out the side window as we pulled away from the curb. My parents' house was the biggest one in our cul-de-sac. "It looks like it could be in a magazine," Jen had told me the first time she came over. I was seven when we moved into the house, which had been custom-built. Even I felt as if I was walking through the glossy pages of a magazine the first few weeks we lived there. Then it simply turned into my house.

I angled toward Josh. "Just think, this apartment could be our first home." I left out the part that it wouldn't be for long. I reached across the seat and touched his arm. "Are you excited?"

At least he'd quit biting his cheek. He threw a glance my way and finally smiled. "Yeah, I am."

"Good." I sighed and crossed my arms over my chest, listening to the country station on the radio while I let my mind imagine what our first place might look like.

"Here it is." Josh pulled to the curb and scrunched down, looking past me out the window to the old house standing at the end of a very cracked sidewalk.

I looked from the house to Josh. How could he possibly be smiling?

I followed his stare and found myself gazing at two stories of chipped grey paint and an upper balcony that was so warped it could be a featured attraction at a county fair fun house, except this didn't look one bit fun.

"This is it?" I sounded breathless. This just couldn't be — oh, I got it, it was a joke. I was just about to start laughing when I saw the "For Rent" sign in the dirty window near the front door. I closed my eyes and swallowed hard.

Josh opened the door and climbed out of the truck. "It's the upper level that's for rent. The owner lives on the main floor."

By the time Josh walked around the pickup, I had managed to get my door open, but that was about it. This just simply couldn't be the place Josh had said was perfect for us.

I trailed behind Josh as he walked up to the front door and knocked. While we waited, he turned and put his arm around the small of my back, pulling me close. "I think you'll like this," he said.

I looked at the side of Josh's head. Was he nuts? What had ever given him the idea that I would like peeling paint and a house that smelled musty from the front step? I was going to go through the motions, but I could already tell there was no way this was going to be our first home. "What's taking so long?" I shifted to my other leg. "Are you sure someone is home?" If I had any luck at all, maybe the owner wasn't home. Maybe they'd left town and weren't ever coming back.

The door opened an inch as an old eye looked out. The door closed, and I could hear a sort of shuffling behind the door, then it opened all the way. "Come in." A man who was bent over a walker stood in the entry.

I felt a twinge of guilt for my impatience. No wonder it had taken so long.

"Mr. Miller, this is my fiancée, Anastasia Dunn."

The old man stuck out a twisted hand. "Call me Leon," he said. He looked at Josh. "You got a pretty one."

"You can call me Stasha," I said as I put my hand in his. His skin was rough, his grip as firm as a hand curved with arthritis could be. How come I suddenly felt like crying?

Not everyone has had a life as good as yours. I blinked against the sting in my eyes.

Mr. Miller waved his hand over his shoulder. "You'll have to go up by yourselves. I haven't climbed those steps in years, so the way it looks is the way the last renters left it. I can't help it." He turned his walker so we could get by. "I'll wait for you down here. Take your time."

I gave Josh a wide-eyed stare as we walked

down the hallway to a set of stairs near the back of the house. I wasn't sure what my look meant. All I knew was that I felt sorry for this old man, but I didn't know if I wanted to live in his house.

Josh led the way. "There's a back door," he explained as we passed it. "That's how we would get in. We wouldn't have to walk through the whole house every time, and then there's another door at the top of the stairs."

I could see that. In fact, I could hear it. The door squeaked loudly as we walked through it.

"I can fix that with some WD-40," Josh said.

I stood in the threshold of what Josh thought would be our first apartment. To my left was a kitchen. From where I stood I could see rust stains in the old porcelain sink. There was an eating nook tucked in a back alcove, which was painted icky blue. To the right was a living room with all four walls painted a dull brown. I wondered if Leon knew what his renters had done over the years. The only saving grace was the two large double-hung windows that faced the street and let in a lot of light. I could see through the dirty glass that the sagging balcony was only for show. The only way out to it was through a window.

"The bedroom is back here." Josh took three steps, and there we were.

I put a hand to my mouth. I wasn't sure whether I should laugh or cry. The sloped ceiling, in fact the whole room, was covered in a rose-patterned wallpaper — and the pink roses were huge. The only time I'd seen anything similar was in a movie that took place during the Depression.

"Do you like it?" Josh looked at me as if there was no doubt. "Your favorite color is pink, isn't it?"

Not anymore.

The only thing I could think to say was, "Is there a closet?"

"Over here." Josh ducked his head as he maneuvered past the angled ceiling toward the back of the room, where there was another tiny alcove with a window that faced the backyard. On the right he opened a dark varnished door to reveal a space not any wider than the door itself.

"Josh." He had to know that my shirts wouldn't even fit in there. Not to mention my skirts and pants and dresses and shoes.

"I won't need to use it," he said. "I'll keep my stuff in a dresser."

What did he expect me to say? That I loved it? He had to know me better than that. If he didn't, we were in big trouble. I bit my lips together just in case I accidentally started to say what I was thinking.

While I stood looking into the coffin-sized closet, I could hear Josh walking through the kitchen and back into the living room. From the doorway of the bedroom I could see him stand near the front windows and run both hands through his hair. He stuck his hands in the back pockets of his jeans and headed back toward me.

I turned and faced the backyard window. I didn't want him to see whatever expression was on my face. I knew it couldn't be pretty.

"Say something."

I shook my head.

Josh came up behind me and put his arms around me, nuzzled his mouth against my neck. "It'll only be for a little while."

I could feel a sob pushing at the back of my throat as he rested his head next to mine. This wasn't at all how I imagined our first home. Not old. Or musty. Or small.

"It'll be different when we clean it up and get our stuff in here."

I wobbled my head against his. The china we'd registered for wouldn't fit in the tiny kitchen cupboards. I didn't want to live here. I didn't want to clean it. Even soap and water wouldn't make brown walls a different color. I didn't care about the old man downstairs and how bent over and poor he looked. Someone else could rent his place. I'd tell Josh we'd have to find something else. I opened my mouth.

"Stash, I've looked around. Every place wants us to sign a long-term lease." He paused, taking in a deep breath, pushing it out. "Besides, it's all we can afford."

I closed my mouth. There wasn't anything I could say to that. Not part-time coffee shop me. I closed my mouth. For better or worse — it was starting even before we said our vows.

"I'm going to tell Mr. Miller we'll take it."

All I could do was nod my head and let hot tears run down my face.

LAURA

Italy! As I pulled a yellow bowl from the kitchen cupboard I slammed the door, opened it, and slammed it shut again. I'd been doing a lot of slamming the past three weeks. Not that it made me feel any better.

I glanced at my wall calendar, then at my watch. I had 45 minutes before I needed to be at the art guild's potluck luncheon. A half hour to make a salad and 15 minutes of driving time to try, one more time, to stuff away the simmering anger I felt toward Donnie over the trip he'd given Stasha and Josh.

I opened the fridge and yanked out a head of romaine lettuce, a cucumber, and two carrots. I plucked the peeler out of the utensil drawer, and with short, violent strokes I started ripping off the rough peel of the carrots. Of all the places Donnie could send Stasha on her honeymoon. He could have sent them to Paris, or London, or Timbuktu for that matter. Sending them to Rome? Donnie might as well have slapped me in the face.

I set the carrots down and picked up the cucumber. In short order I peeled it, sliced it, and tossed it into a bowl. The romaine leaves crunched between my fingers as I yanked them apart, rinsed them, and then ripped them into pieces.

Grabbing the grater from the drawer, I took a deep breath. I had to let this resentment go. Three weeks ago Donnie had made his announcement at the dinner table — "Here are some tickets for you" — and I was still seething. It wasn't as if the gift had come as a complete surprise. One night in our bedroom, months before, Donnie had tossed out his idea.

"What would you think of us sending Stasha and Josh on a honeymoon?" Donnie had walked out of the bathroom pulling a stretched-out, faded T-shirt over his head. He tugged at the old gym shorts he wore as pajamas. "That could be our wedding gift to them."

I laid down the *American Artist* magazine I'd been reading in bed and looked his way. "I was thinking we could get them a painting. An original. Maybe a watercolor. Something they'd always have." If it hadn't been so long since I'd picked up a paintbrush, I would have loved to paint the picture myself.

Donnie tossed back the covers on his side of the bed, jostling my magazine as he crawled into bed. "They'll always have memories of their trip."

"Well, yes, but I was thinking of something more tangible, I guess."

Donnie turned on his side, facing me, propping his head on his bent elbow. "Think about it. They're still kids. They're probably going to move ten times before they settle down. And by the time they have a house, their tastes might be totally different."

I wasn't letting go that easily. "A landscape never goes out of style."

"Neither does a good trip."

How would you know? When was the last time Donnie and I had taken a trip that wasn't connected with business? I knew the answer to that — never. I refused to count the times early in our marriage when vacation meant a long weekend at my parents' house in Flanders. It was all we could afford back then. Now we had the money, but no time. At least Donnie didn't have the time.

I picked up my magazine and stared at a painting of an ancient cityscape done in vibrant pastels. Who wouldn't want to walk those narrow, intriguing streets? Donnie had done next to nothing to help plan this wedding other than writing checks. I should be glad he was getting involved. "What did you have in mind?"

Donnie punched at his pillow and then turned onto his back. "Oh, I don't know. Maybe a cruise somewhere. I thought I'd have Arlene check with a travel agent and come up with some ideas. Do you need a passport to take a cruise?"

I bit back the "how-would-I-know" remark on the tip of my tongue. "Stasha and Josh both have them."

I could see Donnie close his eyes as if that settled it. "Good."

And that had been the last I'd heard of it until he had surprised both Stasha — and me — with his over-the-top gift. More than once since that dinner I'd opened my mouth to tell Donnie how I felt. But every time I tried to say the words, they got stuck in my throat. Was it selfish to want this trip for me and not for Stasha? The words I tried to say turned into a lump of unshed tears and then hardened into a rigid coal of bitterness.

I had lived with that lump for too long now. Face it; I wouldn't be going to Europe any time soon. My yearning for adventure would have to be satisfied by a drive through Carlton with a salad as my travel companion. I rolled my eyes as I slid the carrot against the sharp metal of the grater. The carrot turned into a jagged pile of shreds on the cutting board, just like my dream of someday exploring the museums of Italy.

Oh, Lord, I'm tired of carrying this anger around. Help me give it to You.

Once again, I breathed deeply and blew the air out in a huff that lifted my long bangs. Stasha was getting married in three days. It would do no good to ruin her wedding by pouting. Today's luncheon was the last thing on my calendar that was not wedding-related. Guests would start arriving in Carlton tomorrow afternoon. Rehearsal was the following evening, the wedding on Friday. By next week at this time, Stasha would be a married woman in Italy, and I'd be left with a stack of wedding gifts to deliver to her and Josh's apartment. I'd have Donnie's tux returned and my dress at the dry cleaners. I'd have another month of meetings to attend. Same old, same old.

No, not same old — because then I would have my talk with Donnie.

My heart skipped a beat at the thought. As often as I'd tumbled the conversation around in my brain, the idea of actually turning my thoughts into spoken words scared me. What if Donnie called my bluff?

I stopped grating the carrot for a second, then resumed. There was the fatal flaw in my long-laid plan; there was no bluff. I had nothing to hold over his head. I wasn't about to walk out. I only wanted more of his time and his attention — the two things he didn't have to give, or didn't want to.

There was that bitter coal again. I set the grater aside. With both hands I reached into the deep bowl, turning and twisting the cool cucumber chunks and lettuce into a mix that looked the way my thoughts felt — impossibly jumbled. What if, after my talk, Donnie did decide to work less? What if the things that I thought would make my marriage better actually didn't? What then?

There was a pit-like feeling deep in my stomach, and it had nothing to do with the fact it was almost lunchtime. *Maybe you should just accept that this is what a long-term marriage looks like. Wine and roses are for people like Stasha and Josh, not for 40-somethings who have nursed each other through the flu and juggled vehicles for oil changes and argued about carrying out the garbage.*

I flicked stray pieces of lettuce off my fingertips. What if I wanted wine and roses?

Was that so wrong?

Nothing is stopping you *from bringing a little romance to the table — or the bedroom.*

But I was tired of everything in our relationship always being up to me.

Then tell Donnie what you need.

Oh, I planned to, all right. With a twist of my wrist I grabbed a towel from the handle of the fridge and wiped my damp hands. What really made me mad was that I shouldn't have to tell him. If he couldn't notice that something huge was missing in our relationship, he had to have a . . . a . . . I glanced around. Right in front of my eyes was a metaphor I could use. Donnie had to have a cutting board in place of his eyeballs.

And why quibble about the speck in someone else's eye, when a board is in your own?

I blinked twice. The words from last week's Bible study filtered through my anger. I wasn't the one with a board in my eye; Donnie was. He'd spent our whole marriage oblivious to the fact that I had needs too. I glared at the salad in front of me as if it was my husband. It was surprising the whole bowl didn't up and wilt under my laser gaze. A tiny thought crept through my tunnel vision: *Something's missing.*

Of course something was amiss. That's what I had been talking to myself about all morning. My marriage was as insubstantial as iceberg lettuce.

You're using romaine.

Picky. Picky. Did it really matter? Lettuce was lettuce.

So then, marriage is marriage? Every marriage is alike?

No, that couldn't be possible. Just about every couple I knew seemed to be more in tune than Donnie and I were. Take Karen and Todd, for instance. Even though she complained about him often enough, it was obvious she adored the daylights out of him.

They went through counseling, remember? Marriage takes work.

I closed my eyes against the thought. I was tired of working at it. After this many years, I'd thought marriage would be easy. It wasn't. I turned to the fridge to find the salad dressing I'd made, and then paused as a new thought filtered in: *Many waters cannot quench love.*

The snippet of a Bible verse Stasha wanted read at her wedding now mocked me. Maybe many waters couldn't quench love, but years worth of neglect could drown it.

Are you going to believe your fears, or My truth? Many waters cannot quench love.

My only option was too bleak. For now, all I could do was to grab on to the only life preserver in sight and hope it would hold me. As I turned to the fridge to get the dressing, a jolt of color caught my eye. Good grief, there were the shreds of carrots lying right beside the bowl. For someone who claimed to love color, I'd just about brought a monochrome salad to the luncheon. I tossed them into the mix. There. Already the salad looked better.

Everything's a bit better when there's some color to it. Even a marriage.

I stared at the bowl. If I didn't get off this train of thought I'd never make it to the luncheon. I wasn't going to solve my marriage crisis standing alone in my kitchen.

You'll never solve any problem in a marriage alone. *A marriage is a partnership. It takes effort. Planning. It doesn't just happen; you need to add a variety of things, mix it up. A little oil and vinegar enhances the flavor.*

I'd certainly been generous with the vinegar part of our marriage these past months. But right now, the way I felt about Donnie, I'd have a hard time mustering the gumption to add oil, spices, or anything else of interest to our plain old side-salad of a marriage.

Speaking of oil and vinegar . . . I opened the fridge and grabbed the bottle of home-made vinaigrette from the shelf. I needed to get a move on. Today was busy enough; there were wedding festivities over the next several days, and I'd promised to help Karen with her gallery whenever I could.

And you'll be president of the art guild starting in September. You've got Bible study and — I slapped at the bottom of the dressing bottle. The honey-mustard vinaigrette I'd mixed up last night was as stubborn as my conscience when it came to reminding me of all the responsibilities I had. *And when will you ever have time to paint?*

One more thing my conscience wouldn't let me forget. But yes, I'd rather think about painting instead of my marriage. Distraction had been my deliverance all summer. More than once I'd imagined Stasha's old bedroom as an art studio. I could tear out the carpet and put in hardwood floors. The corner windows faced east and south, a perfect view if I wanted to paint a sunrise — or anything else, for that matter.

Make that nothing else. No use dreaming about something that wasn't going to happen. There already weren't enough hours in a day. I drizzled the dressing over the salad and tossed it harder than necessary. Somewhere in all my musing, my anger had dissipated, and I was left with a familiar melancholy. This was the way it was. Donnie would send our daughter on the trip of a lifetime. I would stay home and look at the pictures when she returned. I'd stay busy with the art guild, Karen's gallery, and a million other details that consumed my days. Dreams were for the young, not a middle-aged, would-be painter. Best to get on with the things I could do. In a hurry I crumbled feta cheese over the salad and dotted the top with Greek olives — another reminder of a country I'd never see.

The ring of the telephone startled me. Quickly I rinsed my hands and reached for the phone. "Hello?" Whoever it was, I didn't have time to chat.

"Laura?" Eleanor. Donnie's mom. "I was wondering what time you were coming."

My stomach did a stutter step. The second I heard her voice I remembered the doctor appointment I said I'd drive her to, the one I'd forgotten to write on the calendar. I closed my eyes as if the date and time were on the inside of my lids. Two o'clock today. I'd have to leave the luncheon early in order to pick her up and get her to the doctor on time. It would be touch and go, but I could do it.

Ever since her TIA episode, Eleanor had developed a kind of fear I found hard to understand. Although her doctor had cautioned her to take things slow for a time, Eleanor had grown extra cautious. The mother-in-law I used to know had been feisty and independent, but over the past weeks she'd started phoning more often, asking if I could pick up some groceries for her; she wasn't sure she should be driving yet. Or she wondered if I thought it would be okay for her to carry her small bag of garbage to the curb for pickup.

"Here," she'd said to me one day when I stopped by to drop off a prescription. She pointed to a large cardboard box on the floor of her entry, then nudged it an inch toward me with her foot.

"What's that?" I could see the neatly folded clothes in the box; I just didn't know what she expected me to do with them.

"Oh." She waved a hand through the air as if they were nothing. "They're some of Donnie's old clothes I saved from when he was little. Silly." I could see a slight flush of color in her cheeks. "I don't know what I thought I needed them for."

I knew. I had saved many of Stasha's things, too. "For memories." I picked up the blue plaid Western shirt folded on top. I could only imagine Donnie as a miniature cowboy.

"You can take them." Eleanor cleared her

111

throat. "I won't be here forever."

Compared to the woman who was ready to bolt from her hospital bed the day of her episode, this new mother-in-law was a person I didn't know.

I sighed silently, turning my mouth away from the phone. I would fit her appointment in somehow. "I'll be there by 1:15. Can you watch for me?"

"Of course I can." Now there was the Eleanor I knew.

I hung up the phone and jotted a quick note to Stasha. Who knew what time I'd get home? After her morning shift at Brews-n-News, Stasha was going to spend the day trying to spruce up her new apartment. I had seen it and could understand why Stasha wasn't as enthusiastic as Josh, but I knew better than to side with Stasha on this. They were starting a new life; they needed to make a decision together about where they would live. If there was one thing I'd learned from Eleanor, it was to stay out of their business.

There had been times when I wished Eleanor had interfered a bit more. Donnie could have used someone besides me to nag him about how much time he spent at work. I knew Eleanor had struggled over the same issues with Donnie's dad. She had to know how I felt. Apparently the workaholic gene had been passed on, as well as the gene called "longsuffering wife."

As if you can call your life "suffering."

I cringed. Just about any woman I knew would trade lives with me in an instant. I covered the salad with plastic wrap and picked up the heavy ceramic bowl. I would go to my meeting, hurry to pick up Eleanor, sit at the doctor's office, and make a list of all that needed to be done over the next few days. *For better or worse.* I could hardly classify not getting to go to Europe as worse, not when I listened to the news every night. But still, it was hard to let go of my dream.

Balancing the salad bowl on my hip, with my free hand I grabbed my car keys and my purse, and turned the doorknob with the tips of my fingers.

Oh, good grief, the phone was ringing again. What was this . . . Grand Central Station? Whoever it was would have to leave a message. I had to get going. I took one step into the garage.

What if it was Eleanor? What if, in the couple of minutes since I'd talked to her, she had another episode? What if she needed me now?

With guilt as my guide, I stepped back

into the kitchen, threw my purse and keys on the counter, and picked up the phone. "Hello." Maybe not the nicest I'd ever sounded.

"Finally. You're home." The clear voice of my college roommate, Carla, greeted me. I'd canceled our lunch date weeks ago, made a mental note to call her, and forgot. I'd also erased the two phone messages she'd left in the meantime, always intending to call her back.

Now I really felt guilty. "Oh, Carla." I shifted the heavy bowl on my hip. "Would you believe I've got a lettuce salad in my hand and am on my way out the door? I'm running late for a lunch meeting, and then I have to take my mother-in-law to the doctor this afternoon. Can I call you back?" I would keep my promise this time.

"You're too busy." Her light laugh came through the line. "I know you've got the wedding this weekend. Let me ask you a quick question, and we'll talk later. Would you like to take an adult ed class this fall?" She didn't give me time to turn her down. "I thought it would be a good way for us to spend some time together. We could meet for dinner before class and have time to catch up. The reason I'm calling is that the sign up deadline is Friday. Judy's going to come too. It'll be fun. What do you think?"

Carla had always been the organizer in our group of friends. Now she not only had enthusiasm but also my guilt on her side. I didn't have time to take a class, but how could I say no to one of my dearest friends — a friend I'd put off too many times lately?

"When does it start?" I scrunched the phone between my shoulder and my ear, and lifted the page of my wall calendar. The squares of September were already half-filled.

"It begins the second Tuesday and runs for eight weeks, 7:30 to 9."

An evening class would be better than something during the day. I already had art guild, Bible study, book club, and my promise to help Karen at the gallery to fill my days.

I looked at the clock on the wall. If I didn't leave this second I'd be late for the luncheon. "Sure." If I changed my mind, I'd explain why to Carla later.

"It'll be fun," she said. "I'll sign us up. See you at the wedding."

I hung up the phone, picked up my purse and keys a second time, and hurried out to my car. It was only as I was speeding to the meeting that it occurred to me I had no clue what sort of class I'd just agreed to take.

Trust Me.

I signaled, tapped at the brake, and turned the corner. Almost there. I knew God had a sense of humor. And I did trust Him. I just wasn't so sure I trusted Carla. Knowing her, she would sign me up for a trapeze class.

I smiled at the image as I pulled to the curb and reached for the door handle. Oh well, I didn't have to worry about the class now. By the time the wedding and Stasha's elaborate honeymoon were over, I might feel like throwing myself into thin air from a trapeze bar.

Before I got out of the car I took a quick glance in the rearview mirror. My smile had been replaced with a crease between my brows. I lifted a finger as if I could smooth away the silent thoughts that had put it there. Only I knew I was walking a tight-rope. On one side, a net to catch me — Donnie. Safe. Predictable. Emotionally void. On the other side, something new. Scary. Somehow enticing. The unsettling thoughts made my stomach plunge. Was it fear? Or simply the unknown?

No! Don't even think about —

There was a time when I wouldn't have dared toy with the thought of life without Donnie. But lately, it felt as if I was living alone even when he was home. *Stop it!*

116

But that was the trouble. I couldn't stop thinking about what my life could be like, what I might be missing. Watching Stasha and Josh together was a reminder of all that love could be. Should be. Had been.

And that was the trouble. My love for Donnie was in the past tense.

I pulled the heavy salad bowl onto my lap, got out of the car, and walked to my meeting carrying my burdens. There was nothing I could do with these troubled thoughts today. The next three days would hold celebration. I'd put on a mask for the sake of my daughter.

DONNIE

I glanced at my watch. With a little luck I'd be able to work in a quick phone call between the pictures and the wedding. I could make another call between the ceremony and the reception if I had to. The Martin account wasn't the largest account the Dunn Agency had ever pitched, but it was the second largest. After two months of wooing, they told us they would have a decision by sometime Friday. Well, it was Friday, the one day out of the whole year my daughter had picked for her wedding day. For now, I had no choice but to smile and say *formaggio.*

"Cheese." For the hundredth time I smiled as the flash blinded me, then I automatically looked once more at my watch. Stasha and Josh were going to Italy for their honeymoon, thanks to the Dunn Agency. My daughter couldn't begrudge me one important phone call to see if I had a new client.

I held up a finger to get the photographer's attention.

"Two more quick group shots, then you can have a break." The kid who claimed to be a professional photographer cut me off as he adjusted his camera. "Patience, Dad." He flashed a too-wide smile my way. He'd been calling Laura and me Mom and Dad since he walked in the door of the church. I wondered if he'd change his tune if I signed his check with a scrawling *Dad.*

He positioned his head behind the lens. "Okay, here we go. On three. One . . . Two . . . Thr—"

I felt the sudden thrum of my cell phone in the pocket of my tuxedo slacks. I forced myself not to reach for it until the flash went off. There. I shot my hand into my pocket and flipped open the phone. Arlene, who had agreed to stay on until we heard yea or nay on the Martin project, had orders to call the minute there was word about our bid for the contract. With the wedding scheduled for 6:00, I was counting on the fact that Arlene would be able to take the call and make it to the ceremony. "Donnie here."

Laura nudged me with her elbow; I glanced her way. I had promised her I would turn off my phone during the wedding. Well, this wasn't the wedding. Not yet. Not until guests started showing up. The look of irritation on her face pushed me to the far side of the church. Laura had told me a thousand times I talked too loudly on my cell phone. I lowered my voice. "Any word?"

A low chuckle came from the phone. "You're supposed to have that thing turned off." It was Matt.

"Yeah, and you're not supposed to be calling. Now we're both in trouble."

He laughed again. "I suppose Laura's glaring daggers."

"And the photographer, who looks old enough to be in junior high, by the way."

"Feeling old?"

Leave it to Matt to cut to the bottom line and bring feelings into the conversation. Ever since his breakup with Kathy, he had developed a sensitive side I wasn't used to. I couldn't help but take a quick glance at my daughter, posing in the center of the church aisle, her gown arranged around her as perfectly as those Barbie dolls she used to play with. When had she grown into a young woman old enough to get married? It seemed like just last week Laura had told me we would be having a baby. Where had 21 years gone?

I swallowed against the unexpected lump

in my throat. Now was not the time to think about things I'd missed. "Look ahead, not back" was my motto. I turned my head away from the bridal party. "What's up?"

"Still waiting. Andrew Martin called and wanted some more info on the estimates we gave them. He said they still hoped to have their decision made by the close of the day. They're anxious to move ahead with the campaign for the new product line."

Through the receiver I could hear Matt clicking his tongue against the top of his mouth, a nervous habit he'd had since college. Waiting was not his forte. Or mine.

He cleared his throat. "I don't know about this one, Donnie. I usually have a sense about these things. This one has me worried. It's strung out so long."

So that's why he'd called. I didn't have a pulse on this client either, and I didn't like the feeling. But it wasn't my job to spread panic among the troops. My job was to assure them no matter what the client decided, the Dunn Agency was still top-drawer. No matter what Martin decided, it still would be.

"Relax, Matt," I said into the phone. "This client isn't going to make or break us. You know that."

I could hear his sigh. "Remember those

one-on-one games we used to play back in college? We were intense. Neither one of us wanted to lose. I still don't."

Oh, I remembered all right. That was one of the reasons I'd asked Matt to work with me when I started the firm. His competitive edge was as sharp as mine. I wanted him on the same team.

"We won't. No matter what happens."

"Dad?" This time it was Stasha crooking her finger at me. "We need you for some more pictures."

"Gotta go, buddy. Let Arlene handle the phone and get your butt over here. You're one of the host coup—" I cut myself off. Matt's divorce was still a touchy subject. "You're supposed to be greeting people, so get here and greet. Whatever Martin decides, this wedding is happening."

I felt a hand on my arm as I closed the phone. Laura.

"Donnie, your daughter is getting married today." Her voice was resigned. "You might want to be here for it."

I deserved that. I made a point of reopening my phone and pressing the button so she could see I had turned my phone off. "I'm yours for the rest of the day." I pocketed my phone and wrapped an arm around the soft cloud of material covering her shoulders. She looked as pretty as her perfume smelled. Oh sure, there were some crinkles around her eyes that weren't there 23 years ago. Her middle was softer now too. So was mine. But we were both fit and trim. We made a good-looking couple, if I had to say so myself.

As we walked, I squeezed Laura closer to me. Her light-brown hair glinted with the highlights I paid for every few months, in contrast to the gray hair at my temples. But I had to admit, I liked the look the silver hair gave me. It softened that trying-too-hard, studied-casual appearance of so many of the younger guys in the ad business. And I'd cut off my right ear before I'd get a pair of standard-issue, black-framed glasses, the "uniform" in my creative line of work, it seemed. No thanks. When I needed to study a contract, my wire-rimmed reading glasses did the job just fine. I didn't need glasses to see how beautiful Laura was this afternoon.

"Okaaaay." The photographer rubbed his hands together as if he was a Boy Scout trying to start a fire. "We want a picture of just Mom and Dad." He flashed his cheesy grin. "The couple responsible for the lovely bride."

Tired clichés. I couldn't stand them. Apparently Laura couldn't either. I felt her back stiffen as I guided her to the spot the young photographer indicated. I clenched my teeth and stood where he told me. I watched as he adjusted the hem of Laura's dress. She had been distant lately. But what mother of the bride wouldn't be?

Hasn't this "distance" been going on longer than —

No. I cut the thought off. Both Stasha and Laura had been in their own world for months. Planning a big wedding took time and a toll. There was nothing wrong that a walk down this aisle wouldn't fix.

I pulled in a long breath and tilted my head against my shoulders, stretching against the tension held there. In our own ways we had both been under a lot of stress these past weeks. Laura planning this wedding, me with my never-ending days at the agency. With a sudden fierceness I longed for a moment when someone — Laura — would assure me it was all worth it.

Out of the corner of my eye I appraised Laura. The copper-colored fabric of her dress made her skin appear pearl-like, unusual this late in the summer. Most of the women around here were sporting desperate-brown, short-North-Dakota-summer tans. Laura had never been one to go along with the masses. Maybe that was one of the reasons she had married me. "Conventional" wasn't in my vocabulary, which was why advertising was the perfect fit for me.

The photographer looked through the camera lens, stepped back, and surveyed the picture of the two of us he planned to snap, if he ever got around to it.

I fingered my cell phone. Of all the days for a wedding.

I had tried explaining what might happen today to Laura as I climbed out of bed before sunup. "I just want to run by the office before all this wedding business starts and check on a few things."

Laura rolled over in bed and lifted her head from the pillow. "You're going to the office? Today?"

"Just for a few minutes." I slipped one leg into a pair of pants, then the other. I pushed a belt through the loops. "I'll be back before anyone even gets out of bed."

Anastasia was sleeping in her old bedroom. The rehearsal dinner had gone late last night. I didn't expect either of them up before mid morning.

Laura raised herself on one elbow. "I was hoping you'd be around to take your mother to the hairdresser. We all have appointments this morning, but I didn't want her to have to wait there for the rest of us to get done. She hasn't been feeling well, you know."

I concentrated on buttoning my shirt. So what else was new? As far back as I could remember, my mother had had something to complain about.

That's not true.

Yes, it was. I slipped my feet into a pair of loafers. She had nagged my dad all the time about things that needed doing around the house.

There were things that did need doing. Remember how long you waited for him to put up a basketball hoop for you?

Yeah. Well. Now I had a better idea of what his life had been like. Work could consume a guy. Laura had it figured out. My mom should have too.

She's lonely. She just wants your attention.

A stab of guilt knifed through me. I looked at my watch as I slipped it on my wrist. "I'll be home by nine."

"Uh-huh." Laura laid her head back against the pillow and stared at the ceiling.

I put my left hand on the doorknob and held up my right hand. "Promise."

Across the room I could see Laura close her eyes as if she was already falling back to sleep.

Good. I could make my getaway. It was

only as I stood in the hall and began quietly closing the door behind me that I heard her faint words.

"He'll never change."

Laura's sleep-cloaked words from early this morning haunted me now. I had run into the house at 10:30 ready to explain the problems that had cropped up as I prepared to leave work the first time, and then the second. It was hard to explain when there was no one home to talk to.

I ran my hand up and down Laura's back as we waited for the photographer to adjust his lens. Laura was right; I would never change when it came to providing a good life for my family. It wasn't money I was working for; it was for Laura. And Stasha. For moments like this.

Another thing that would never change was my love for Laura. She put up with my quirks. She had been through it all with me over the years. She had been nothing less than a cheerleader when I was laid off from Carr & Company. When was that — almost 22 years ago? I had just about stepped away from my dream of working in the ad business after that, but Laura wouldn't let me take the easy route.

"You are not giving up." She stood over me with both hands on her hips. The torn corner of the ratty couch I'd had since college was proof positive that I needed some sort of job, and soon.

Laura bent down, pulled the classified ads off my lap, and glanced at the ink circles I had made. "These are nothing but entry-level jobs. You've worked in the ad business for over five years. You're not going to go out and start selling ads at some" — she rubbed her barely pregnant belly — "radio station." She sat down beside me and threaded her arm through mine. "You've got too many great ideas."

"And a baby on the way. I need a job, Laura. Now."

"Start your own agency."

I laughed. "Oh, and did I mention I have a wife to feed?"

"We won't starve."

I looked at her as if she was nuts, because just then she was.

"We won't." I saw the stubborn set of her chin. "I've got my job at the clinic. The baby isn't due for five months. I have paid maternity leave. We've got health insurance and a BMW we can sell if we get desperate."

She knew my car was my pride and joy. "There's motivation."

"Donnie." She wove the fingers of one hand between mine. "Your mind is your best asset. You've got a little money in your retirement plan. We could cash that in and use it for startup money. It's not as if we don't have a few years to replenish it." At age 26, I could hardly argue with her.

I always told Laura she should have majored in business instead of art history. Her urging turned out to be the best thing that ever happened to me — to us, although it didn't seem like it at first.

The Dunn Agency started out in the second bedroom, nursery-turned-office of our rental apartment. It had taken all of those five baby-waiting months to land my first client. Five months of phone calls and cold calls trying to convince the small business community of Carlton that Donnie Dunn could do wonders for their business if they just gave me a chance. I dangled just about any lure I could find, short of offering my services for free.

At first no one took the bait. Then, at last, I got a nibble from the owner of a new strip mall on the north end of town. He was taking a chance opening a row of shops in a previously noncommercial area of town on the first of December that year. Who knew my lame ad-campaign — "Go north! That's where Santa shops!" — would be the start of a business relationship that continued to this day?

Stan and his wife would be at the wedding tonight. We had both come a long way since those days. Stan now owned ten strip malls across the state. For the past several years I had been quietly laying the groundwork to open a branch of the Dunn Agency in Minneapolis. I already had the corner on the ad market in this part of North Dakota. I was looking for a new challenge before I turned 50 in two years. Maybe then I would start thinking about scaling back.

"Okay, parents, that's it for now." The photographer released us with a wave of his hand. Just as I took a step off my mark he reminded us, "But I'm going to need all of you right after the reception line for the photos with the groom."

Apparently the "keep the bride out of sight" tradition was old enough for Stasha to consider it retro. The older I got, the more I realized that "everything old really was new again" if you waited long enough.

Speaking of waiting . . . as I walked to the rear of the church, I fingered the cell phone in my pocket. With any luck I would now get put in solitary with the rest of the men. If so, I could sneak in a last-minute phone call.

"Donnie?" My mother was sitting in the

rear pew, no doubt making a list of things that should still be done before the wedding got underway in less than an hour, and she would expect me to get right on it.

Don't knock her. Where do you think you got your attention to detail from? Your business wouldn't be what it is today without that fine-tuned gift.

But my gift was much better spent doing tasks in my office, not piddly woman stuff at a wedding.

Maybe distraction would be my friend this afternoon. "Mom, isn't this great?" I looked around at the decorations hanging from the ends of the pews, the flowers, candles, and ribbons filling the front of the church. "Laura and Stasha did a super job planning all this, didn't they?" I didn't mention the wedding planner, who charged almost as much as an expensive ad campaign to turn their brilliant ideas into reality. My mother didn't need to know about that. She would only add it to her list of things to fret about.

"It's all beautiful. I've never seen —" My mom held a tissue near her mouth and coughed.

I shifted from one foot to the other, waiting for her to catch her breath.

"Oh, my." She pulled in a breath and started coughing again.

"Are you okay?" I bent close.

The spasm passed. "Goodness." She patted at her mouth with the tissue. "I hope that doesn't happen during the wedding."

"Me too." I glanced into the foyer of the church and saw the first guests beginning to arrive. If I hurried downstairs I could slip into the men's bathroom and give Arlene a quick call to see if Martin had made a decision. A "yes" would make this day perfect. I put a hand on my mother's shoulder. "You just sit here. I'll run downstairs and make sure the ushers get up here and get you to a seat up front."

She cleared her throat in a way that made it sound as if she was going to start all over again. "I'm really not feeling all that well."

"It's been a busy day. Once you get seated, all you have to do is relax." I patted her shoulder. "I'll save a dance for you at the reception, right after I dance with the bride — and her mother." I winked. "Put it on your dance card."

With an amused smile and a shake of her head she waved me off. I hurried downstairs and into the bathroom, relishing the seductive chime of a cell phone finding new life.

"Don." The pastor was washing his hands. "Big day." He reached for a paper towel. "Are you ready to give your daughter away?"

After I make a phone call. "Is a father ever completely ready to do that?" I slipped into a stall, hoping he'd get the hint.

I could hear him chuckle outside of the stall. "Oh, you'd be surprised at how ready some dads are." He launched into what sounded as if it was going to be a long-winded story.

It was.

"Thanks, Dad." Stasha looked up at me with the same deep-brown eyes her mother had, her white veil forming a cloud around her perfect face. Now I remembered why I stayed in this crazy business — to make my little girl smile just like that. She turned her head and faced the white-carpeted aisle. "Ready?"

I couldn't find my voice. Instead I nodded.

A tune that sounded vaguely familiar seemed to grow loud enough to fill the church, giving us our cue. At the opposite end of the aisle the pastor waited along with Josh and four attendants on each side of the aisle. Laura stood and turned our way, signaling the congregation to rise.

It was only Stasha and me there in the foyer. My last time alone with Stasha Dunn. Within minutes she would belong to another man. There was a hushed rustle as 200 faces turned to watch our walk.

Just as I lifted a foot to begin the short journey, I heard the outside door of the church whip open. I turned my head to see Matt hurrying inside. He caught my eye. Flashed me a grin I couldn't miss reading. He lifted both thumbs up. *We got it!*

I turned and beamed at Stasha. "Time to go."

As we began our walk, I nodded at the friends and strangers on either side of the aisle. Everyone was smiling back at me. Their look said it all. This day was perfect. *Perfecto,* as someone who didn't know Italian might say.

Perfect.

Except —

I rubbed my damp palm against the side of my tuxedo slacks. As soon as I turned Stasha over to Josh, I was going to have to figure out a way to quietly turn off my cell phone.

STASHA

"Happy?"

I looked up at my new husband. At that instant I knew I'd never forget the soul-piercing look of love in his eyes. If my thoughts sounded like a cheesy romance novel, well, all those clichés were coming true right now. I smiled back at Josh as we swayed together to the first dance at our wedding reception. I hadn't stopped smiling since the minister had said, "I now present to you Mr. and Mrs. Joshua MacKay." The muscles in the sides of my cheeks were starting to ache. Could a person be too happy? If so, then I was. I held Josh's glance and nodded. "Very happy."

He laid his cheek against the side of my head and pulled me close. "Me too."

This day had been everything I dreamt it would be. My mom, Grandma Dunn, and I had some quality girl time in the morning as we got pampered at the hair salon. After lunch, Mom did her best not to cry off her makeup as she and my bridesmaids helped me get into my wedding gown at home before heading to the church for pictures. So what if my dad had spent half the time checking his cell phone? He always juggled ten balls at a time. I wasn't all that different.

That's one of the reasons I knew Josh and I were meant for each other. He was low-key, like my mom. I was Type A, like my dad. If it worked for them, I knew it would be a good match for Josh and me too.

I took a slow breath, taking in the faint fragrance of the white rosebud pinned to Josh's lapel, then nestled my cheek against the tightly woven cloth of his tux. He looked so handsome tonight.

Josh's arms squeezed me close, reminding me to enjoy this moment. I squeezed him back, but it was hard not to think about all the things that would be happening in the next few months. After our honeymoon in Italy, our first mission would be to find jobs. Career kinds of jobs. In the meantime, we would be living in our cheap upstairs rental above Mr. Miller. I knew that in a few months we would be laughing at the ugly apartment where our married life started. No place to go from there but up.

I let my eyes drift shut as I swayed in Josh's arms. Tonight, even the thought of our musty apartment seemed romantic. It would be our first home.

"Love you." Josh broke through my thoughts as our first song ended.

"Me more." It was my shortcut way of saying I loved him more. He shook his head, pointed at his chest, then at me. Part of the ritual. *No, I love* you *more.*

We held hands. "Same," we said in union. Then we laughed.

As the next song started I felt a tap on my shoulder. "Got time for a dance with an old guy?" It was my dad, holding his arms wide.

I looked over at Josh and raised my eyebrows. "Sorry, I loved this guy before I even knew you."

Josh clapped my dad on the back. "I can take a hint. Guess that's my cue to go dance with my mom."

My dad put one hand on the small of my back, took my hand in his, and stepped us into a slow, waltz-like rhythm. How many times had he danced me around the living room in just this way?

Not many. He was too busy working, which was why this dance was so special. It wasn't often I got to spend one-on-one time with my dad. "You're a good dancer," I said.

137

"It's like riding a bike." He twirled me in a wide circle. "I used to do a lot of dancing with your mom years ago." He nodded over my shoulder at someone I couldn't see. He slowed us to a gentle sway. "Are you as happy as you look?"

"I am." I couldn't stop grinning.

"I'm glad."

We danced in silence, my wide smile finally releasing into a comfortable, closed-lip curve. My dad and I were so much alike. He would understand if I told him I was already thinking past tonight, to a new city and a new job. My new life with Josh. *Our* new life.

Before I could say anything, he spoke. "We got the Martin account today."

I leaned back. "You did?" Last night during the rehearsal dinner Dad had brought me up to date about the newest client the agency had pitched. A few days earlier he had first mentioned it and what it might mean for his business. "Great! Looks like you got a wedding present."

He shook his head as if he couldn't believe his good luck. "A son-in-law and a new client, all in the same day. Life doesn't get much better than that."

I was back to grinning again. "Sounds like a line from an ad campaign."

"An overused ad campaign. I'd say that company needs a new creative team leader." My dad winked. We both knew who he was thinking about. "Come work for me."

I had worked at my dad's ad agency enough during the summers in high school. It was like having a couple of years of entry-level work experience already. Because of that experience, I was sure I would be qualified for lots of jobs in a city like Chicago.

Like all the other times my dad suggested I come work for him, not one fiber in my being was tempted to say yes. I didn't want to follow in my dad's footsteps. I wanted to create my own path. I pressed my lips into a "you know the answer to that question" smile and gently shook my head. "That'd be too easy, Dad."

As we slow-stepped to the music, he shrugged one shoulder. "Hey, you can't fault a guy for trying. Just promise me one thing."

"What's that?"

"You won't go to work for my competition."

I lifted my hand from his shoulder and swatted at his back. "You don't have to worry about that."

The last strains of music faded. We stopped dancing and stood facing each other. The corners of my dad's eyes crinkled as he held my hands and smiled down at me. "You look so much like your mother."

I suddenly felt self-conscious, and my eyes flicked away from his. People told me that all the time. I had learned to consider it a compliment. I could see Mom standing at the side of the dance floor visiting with one of her cousins. She was beautiful tonight. I squeezed my dad's hands. "You should go ask her to dance."

He squeezed back. "You're right. I should."

I'd only taken two steps toward the edge of the dance floor when Jen stopped me. She wrapped me in a hug. "Stasha! I can't believe you're married!"

My dad wiggled his fingers over his shoulder at me as he kept walking. I hugged Jen back. "I can't believe it either!"

Jen started jabbering away as if we hadn't talked through half of the rehearsal dinner last night or at the house getting dressed just a few hours earlier. "The wedding was beautiful. I think I have a crush on the best man. Do you think I should go ask Byron to dance? Or just hope I catch the bouquet and be content in knowing I'm next?" She laughed as she tilted her head and fluffed her hair. Her eyes were fixed on a spot behind me. I had no doubt that "spot" was wearing a tux and was oblivious to Jen's stare-down. Jen's idea of flirting was so subtle most guys didn't know they were involved. Mostly, she would blabber on and on to me for weeks about her new obsession until the guy started dating someone else.

The first notes of a slow song drifted through the room. "Go ask him to dance." There. I couldn't get much more direct.

"Think I should?" Jen was running a finger over her lower lip.

"It's a wedding, Jen. People meet at these things all the time." I was starting to feel like Cupid. Speaking of which, where was Josh? I wanted to dance with my boyfri— *husband.* I smiled as I thought the word. I was married now.

I glanced down at my wedding ring. Married. I loved the sound of that word. I loved all the meaning behind it. Josh and I had the rest of our lives to spend together.

"Go." With a lift of my chin I urged Jen to follow her heart for once. She took a deep breath as she closed her eyes and nodded, more to herself than to me. When she opened them she headed toward Byron, approaching him from a direction he couldn't see. But then, I already knew that love was like that, coming at you when you least expected.

The way it had come with Josh and me a year ago. My on-again, off-again college boyfriend had broken up with me again. But this time, instead of hanging my hopes on the idea that we might get back together, I had sworn off men completely. So, I didn't pay much attention to the conversation Josh started with me one afternoon when I was sitting on the grass outside the student union trying to soak up some sun and study at the same time.

"Mind if I sit here?" He tossed out the words as he searched for a place for himself on the grass near me.

I looked up from my psychology book. There was a wide lawn of green, spring grass surrounding us. He could have sat anywhere. I might have given up on men, but I wasn't blind. He was cute. I opened the palm of my hand and motioned to the grass. "You've probably paid as much for this seat as I have."

He smiled as he sat down and pulled a book from his backpack. "You must have gotten the e-mail about student fees going up next fall."

"They are?" I really didn't pay much attention to those sorts of things. I just let my folks know what I owed the registrar, and Dad would write a check.

"Along with tuition." He opened the book in his lap. "It's a good thing next year is my last year. I'm not sure I could afford another one."

I pushed a strand of hair behind my ear. So he was finishing up his junior year. "Me too."

He turned a few pages of the book in his lap until he got to the place he was looking for. "Are you on work-study? I haven't seen you around."

"Oh, I didn't mean 'me too' about affording another year, I meant about it being my last year." Why was I explaining myself to this cute stranger? I could feel a warm flush rising in my cheeks, one that wasn't caused by the afternoon sun. "I'll be graduating a year from now."

Little had I known that chance conversation would last long enough to give me the worst sunburn of my life — and a date with Josh MacKay. Love happened when I wasn't looking.

Now I was looking. Where was my husband? My eyes scanned the room for his familiar silhouette. Sure enough, he was behind me, shoulder-to-shoulder with Byron as Jen headed their way. Jen might have been walking toward them, but Josh's eyes were on me. Goosebumps ran down my arms as he crooked his finger for me to come near.

I started walking his way, noticing off to my left that my dad was lifting his arm to let my mom know he was right behind her, ready to take her in his arms for a dance. I knew how hard my mom had worked to make everything perfect today. All that was left was to celebrate. Did she still get goosebumps at his touch? Did she feel warm and happy every time she looked at him, the way I knew I always would with Josh? I paused. Her smile would be worth waiting to see.

Just as my dad was about to touch her arm, Matt, Dad's friend and business partner, stepped to his side and grabbed his hand, shaking it as if they'd just landed the catch of the century. Well, according to what my dad had told me about this new client, maybe they had.

As my mom turned to see who was behind her, her eyes glanced off Dad, and she smiled politely at Matt. She accepted a hug, said something to Dad, and then headed in the direction of the women's bathroom. It looked like my mom was going to miss out on that dance. I could hardly fault my mom for taking refuge for a minute. All this wedding-planning stuff had been stressful on both of us.

I'd had a *Bride's* magazine-like idea of what planning a wedding would be like. The reality turned out to be an article I had never read on any printed page. It was the between-the-lines stuff that had caused headaches, arguments, and more than a few tears. But all that was over now. Mom had to be as happy as I was with the way this night had turned out.

As I watched, Dad crossed his arms over his chest. Matt mirrored his stance. Knowing Dad and Matt, they might talk shop for an hour. Knowing Mom, she'd understand.

I smiled to myself. If only I could freeze the moments of this day. The tender kiss Mom gave me as she clasped onto my wrist the thin silver bracelet Dad had given her on their wedding day. The way my dad's eyebrows lifted in surprised delight at his first glimpse of me in my wedding gown. The look in Josh's eyes as he stepped forward to meet me as I walked down the aisle. The look that passed between my mom and dad when the pastor asked, "Who gives this woman . . . ?" My memories were the scenes a photographer would never catch. Snapshots of memory, only for me.

I made a slow circle, taking in the sounds

and faces of this perfect night. Tonight was just the start of the memory album that would become my life as Anastasia MacKay. No doubt all brides had the same sort of memories tucked away in their hearts. Someday I was going to have to ask my mom what her special memories were. After 23 years of marriage, I could hardly imagine what she'd say.

I lifted the hem of my dress and turned to walk toward my husband. I only hoped my marriage to Josh was half as good as my mom's and dad's marriage was.

LAURA

With the edge of a kitchen knife I pushed week-old red velvet wedding cake off a plate and into the garbage. Stiff crumbs and sugary frosting clung to the platter as if they didn't want to let go of the dreamy night they had been created for. I knew the feeling. As long as I'd had wedding plans to hang on to, there had been a chiffon-like buffer between life as I'd always known it and what lay ahead.

Now, while Stasha and Josh were on their honeymoon, it was as though someone had pushed a "pause" button on my life. The wedding was over, the photos not yet processed, and my life was steeping in some sort of darkroom, waiting to see what would develop. I scraped at the pebble-like crumbs, the knife screeching against the plate as if crying, "Enough!" Okay. A short soak in hot water would take care of what was left. It was an idea that sounded all too appealing. I could use a long soak in a hot tub myself.

You don't have time for that.

I almost laughed out loud. I didn't have time? That was all I had these days. With more force than necessary, I squirted dish soap into the sink and filled it with hot water, pushing the sugar-crusted plate beneath the soapy surface. The ripples of water slowed their concentric ebb and settled into flat-surfaced monotony. *My life in a sink.*

I sighed at the sad irony. Now that the hectic weeks leading up to the wedding were over, my life had come to a standstill. The rented tuxedos had been returned. My worn-once dress was in the back of the guest room closet. The flowers that hadn't been left at church, or dropped off at a nearby retirement home, had spent a week wilting in three vases around the house. I had thrown them out yesterday before I picked up Stasha's gown from the cleaners. The fancy dress, in its expensive box, was under the bed in what used to be her bedroom. I hoped that in the not-too-far-off future Stasha would have room to store it at her new home. But for now, their rental apartment wasn't big enough for more than necessities.

Well, maybe a bath wasn't a necessity; most days it would be nothing but pure luxury. But today I needed the comfort of that warm water like a long hug — something that had been in short supply around here.

And whose fault is that?

I clenched my teeth and headed for the bathroom. It was hard to hug someone who wasn't around.

And when he is here?

As I snapped the bathtub drain tight and turned on the hot water tap as far as it would go, I could feel the hard kernel of resentment pulsing inside me. Who wouldn't feel resentful after 20-some years of being a mistress to an advertising agency?

Tears pushed at my throat as I poured a capful of bubble bath into the rushing stream of water. Maybe now that I had stuffed the last of the wedding cake in the trash, I would be able to drown the hurt feelings I had carried since the wedding reception. Donnie knew how much I loved to dance, and yet he had chosen to spend his time — all but the wedding-party dance — glad-handing guests. No one would have accused him of being unsociable if he had twirled me around the dance floor a couple of times.

It must be nice to have no one to worry about except himself. I slipped out of my clothes and into the tub. How long would I nurse my grudge this time? I sank into the enveloping warmth of the water, toying with a thought. What would life be like if I had no one to worry about but myself?

Empty.

I splashed at the water. That wasn't true. I'd be carefree. My days would be full.

With what? Why don't you fill them now?

In frustration I closed my eyes and dipped my head back into the water, letting the liquid warmth seep into my hair and cover my ears, as if warm water could drown my thoughts. I didn't want my conscience playing devil's advocate. My marriage was over. It had started smothering me years ago and died completely these past months. There wasn't one big thing, just a thousand little ones that turned into a sandstorm that stung my heart until there was nothing left. I would have to come to grips with the fact that I had two options. I could accept my marriage as is. Or . . .

I swallowed my discomfort as I felt another swell of tears push into my throat. There was one thing I said I'd never do. I'd never abandon my marriage. Oh, I had made allowances in the back of my mind for things like physical abuse or a horribly addictive drug problem that affected my child. I knew the Bible gave permission to leave an adulterous union. It had been easy to rationalize what I might do when all the options were things I couldn't imagine Donnie doing. Even now, just the thought of the many empty hours I had spent in my marriage sent an arrow of ache into the center of my heart. An unexpected sob caught in my throat. What I hadn't imagined was this loneliness.

I tilted my chin into the bubbles until the water was level with the crease in my lips. Blowing my sorrow across the surface of the water, I imagined a tiny sailboat fluttering ahead of the storm I was creating. I was the person in that boat, tossed around, unsure of what lay ahead. *Show me what's next, Lord.* The prayer was a breath, a plea, the first I had uttered in weeks. My faith hadn't exactly been at the forefront as I juggled my options.

I wonder why?

I felt a quick shiver of chagrin as I pushed my head out of the water and leaned my back against the hard surface of the tub. I knew why. What was there to pray about? I didn't have any options. When I had said "Till death do us part," I had meant it. I just hadn't imagined that what died would be my love.

Once again I lifted my knees and pushed my shoulders beneath the water, creating small waves to rock me, to give tepid, pitiful comfort. I hadn't ever wanted my marriage to turn out this way.

This too shall pass. The mantra I'd repeated so many times when Stasha was a colicky baby tried to soothe me now. *This too shall pass.* I hoped it would. But what if I had my talk with Donnie, and he insisted there was nothing wrong? What then?

You can always leave. As hard as I tried not to think about leaving as an option, little snippets of what lay outside my wedding vows crept in. It was hard not to dream about a different life. Anything was better than my empty reality.

No! You can't leave. This too shall pass.

I already knew the coming days wouldn't be easy. Donnie wouldn't be happy when I demanded he work less, be home — be with me — more. I knew when the going got rough, I would need to look past the immediate and focus on the bigger picture.

What is the bigger picture?

Starting a new life.

With Donnie.

Or without — I couldn't say it, even in

my thoughts. For a second it was as if the bath bubbles I was staring at were a mirror image of my mind — an indistinct blur, little bits of sparkle bursting into nothingness, a reflection of my marriage.

What about commitment?

A quick ember of anger burned in my chest. Ask Donnie about that. He was committed to his business.

What about your *commitment?*

Ha. I should be committed. I had stuck this marriage out for 23 years, practically raising Stasha by myself while Donnie built up his agency.

Isn't it your *agency? Both of yours?*

It didn't feel like mine. Donnie had his business. I was left with this empty, beautiful, silent house.

I turned on the tap and lay back as a new stream of hot water fell into the tub. My heart might be empty, but my tub could be full. *Sheesh.* I was turning into a caricature of a bitter woman soaking in her sorrows. The next thing, I'd be writing bad poetry in a cold attic with an empty Jack Daniels bottle tipped at my elbow. In spite of it all, my lips curved into a wry smile. I wasn't quite that bad. Not yet. I still had time to make my plans. I did own part of the agency. If all else failed, Donnie could buy my shares and, if I was careful, I wouldn't have the money woes many women did when their marriages broke up midstream.

Stop it. What you think, you become. Fix your thoughts on what is true and good and right. Think about those things.

I swished my shoulders in the warm water. Why was it so much easier to think about leaving my marriage than staying in it?

It's always easier to run from a problem than to stick it out and solve it.

Donnie and I had spent years wrestling the same old conflict. As if questioning God, I turned my eyes to the ceiling. *Isn't that enough?*

Seventy times seven. That's how many times you need to forgive.

I had never been good at math, but in this case I knew multiplication wasn't the point. The numbers might bear me out, but the logic wouldn't. I sighed into the humid air of the bathroom. There was no winning this argument with myself. Either way, the solution would involve change.

There had been a brief time when I'd thought of trying to force Donnie to sell the whole business. If I was forced to give up my dreams, he should, too. The past few months had made me more practical. With all the bustle of the wedding it had been easy to pack away my acerbic thoughts for Stasha's sake.

What about for My sake?

I pushed the thought aside. I had come to the conclusion that just because something wasn't right, it didn't necessarily mean it was wrong. Twenty-three years was enough trying.

I turned off the hot water. Was that the phone ringing? I turned my head toward the door. Maybe not. Besides, whose call would be worth hopping out of a hot bath for? Certainly not Donnie.

Somehow all my thoughts these days seemed to circle back to him.

I pressed my warm, wet hands against my face. I had hoped this bath would provide a respite; instead my thoughts were as jumbled as ever. I picked up the soap and lathered my legs for a shave. The triple-bladed razor with a built-in aloe moisturizing strip was advertising overkill — a product pitch someone had no doubt dreamt up while taking time away from a loving family. I made one swipe over my shin, then another. I couldn't tell one iota of difference in this razor. My time-jaded eyes examined the molded plastic. Life was so much simpler years ago. What seemed like necessities to Stasha and Josh had been luxuries — or had not even been invented — when Donnie and I got married.

Take that new mattress, for example. When I had taken Stasha shopping for a new mattress, she acted as if she bought new beds as a hobby. "Our apartment might be kind of tight, but I think in the long run we'll be happier with the king-sized bed." Who wouldn't be? But then, why would I expect a different choice from a daughter who only remembered her parents sleeping on a king-sized mattress?

I remembered pulling my credit card from my clutch purse and handing it to the salesman. This bed was only part of the gift Donnie insisted on giving Stasha to start her new life. I had a hunch that if we had given Josh a traditional dowry of two cows and a camel, it might have been cheaper.

As the salesman wrote up the purchase, I took a deep breath and pressed my fingers against the bridge of my nose. I couldn't help but remember the sagging double mattress Donnie and I started our marriage with. We hadn't had a clue that two people weren't supposed to roll together into the valley that formed in the middle of the well-used mattress. The bed had been Donnie's mom and dad's. I imagine they had been relieved to pass the old thing on to us and graduate to something new. We had been thrilled with the donation, too young and too broke to care that it was old and used.

I could still recall the way we had pushed and pulled, sweated and laughed that heavy mattress down the steep stairs that led to our half-basement first apartment. We angled the box spring with its torn cover through three doorframes and into the bedroom, then went up for more. Donnie had turned at the sound of my "Watch it!" and practically knocked me out with the iron rails that made up the sturdy frame. By the time we got all the parts in place, we were too tired to do anything but flop on the bare, faded mattress and take a nap — an occasion we dubbed our "First Sleep" to mark the day we moved in. We didn't have much, but that bed was ours — our make-shift retreat, a place where the world was bound by the edges of a mattress and held us close. It was a place to make love, hold each other, and dream. What would our lives look like?

Had we had the nerve to look ahead 20 years? It seemed to me we had. But we couldn't get very far in our imagining. A house, children, and careers were nothing but dreams, impossible to imagine when love was so new. What happened to those two, "we've got the world on a string" young people we had been back then?

I poured a quarter-sized drop of shampoo into my hand, rubbing the liquid into a lather in my hair. It had been complicated to watch new love bloom between Stasha and Josh. There were so many reminders of the way things used to be between Donnie and me. My only consolation now was that Stasha would have Josh to cling to if I decided to —

Say it. Say it out loud.

My mouth worked in silent practice. No. I couldn't. Not quite yet. I would wait until Stasha got her wedding photos back. I wanted the memories of her wedding to hold nothing but happiness, so when she looked back years later she would remember only good things about that time. I knew it was a stupid, arbitrary deadline. Photos. So what? But I needed some kind of line in the sand, or I'd never get up the nerve. I'd wait until she was started in her new life. Then I'd start mine.

I leaned back into the tub and dunked the suds out of my hair. I knew the coming weeks wouldn't be easy, but it wasn't as though my ultimatum would blindside Donnie. He had to know things were as good as done between us.

Done. Dunn. "Hi, I'm Donnie Dunn."

The way it had all started, and the way it might end.

Done.

DONNIE

"When it rains, it pours."

With the flat edge of my hand I made a slashing gesture across my neck. Matt knew I hated clichés. We wouldn't be anything in this business if we relied on the old and familiar to make an impression.

Matt chuckled. "Well, in this case it's true."

I leaned back in my office chair and held up one finger. "Okay, I'll concede this once." I couldn't help but grin. Not only had we won the Martin account last week, we had also been approached to present a bid to Carlton Industries, only the largest manufacturer of industrial equipment in a ten-state area. There were people on this floor working on a creative brief as we spoke. "Any problems so far?"

Matt linked his hands behind his head and pressed his neck into them. "Only that we have more business than people to do it."

"Nice problem, but not good." I pushed myself forward and picked up a pen. Somehow I could always think better with something in my hands. I twisted the pen between my fingers. "The thing is, if we hire more people and don't get the CI account, we're overstaffed."

"Yeah, but if we don't hire anyone we might not get the presentation done in time. We're not the only agency invited in on this."

"Overtime?" Even as I said it, I knew it wasn't the answer.

"Everyone is at their limit now."

I knew that. The constant pressure was the main reason Arlene insisted that she really was leaving. I was still trying to get her to change her mind, but I wasn't having much luck. It was standard operating procedure to work as late as it took to get a project done. Deadlines were constant and constantly being pushed. The word "burnout" had no doubt been invented in an ad agency, which is why it tended to be a young person's game. Besides Arlene, Matt, and me, I could count on one hand the number of people on staff who had been here more than ten years. At 48 I was pushing the parameters of the business. There were never enough hours in a day to get a job done the way we wanted to. You learned to think quickly and creatively, or you didn't last.

I clicked the end of the pen, a nervous gesture that drove Laura nuts if I did it around her. "The thing is, if we hire someone new, the learning curve might take longer than the time we have to get this project up to speed."

"Do we have a choice?"

The buzz of the phone intercom broke into our conversation. Arlene knew that if Matt and I were talking, she was allowed to interrupt. Matt and I spent too much time discussing the details of running the agency to have our phones blocked half the day.

I leaned forward and picked up the receiver. "Yes?"

"The bride on line one." Arlene's voice held a smile.

Ah, Stasha. As I reached to connect the call I motioned to Matt that I wouldn't be long. He pushed his thumb over his shoulder, indicating he'd come back later. Knowing it was Stasha on the other end of the line pushed my immediate business problems aside. "How's Mrs. MacKay?"

"Oh!" Stasha sounded surprised. "We haven't called her yet."

I couldn't help but chuckle. "Honey, I

meant you, not your mother-in-law."

Her laughter could have been coming from next door instead of from across the ocean. "Dad, I called because I just had to tell you" — her voice softened — "thanks. This place is . . ." I could hear her whisper something to someone. I assumed it was Josh. She returned with *"Fantastico."*

The excitement in her voice was palpable. A warm feeling filled my chest. "I'm glad," I said. "You deserve it. You and Josh."

"Dad, you should bring Mom here sometime. You know how much she loves art and architecture and fashion and, well —" She took a breath. "It's all right here. She'd love it. So would you."

I had no doubt I would.

"We'll travel the world someday." I had said those words to Laura years ago, holding up three fingers as if I was a too-old Boy Scout, as if Laura needed proof that I would keep my word. "Promise."

At the time, Laura's eyes had focused on something I couldn't see. Probably pictures of the insides of museums she had read about, statues she had studied in her many art classes. "The only place I'm really dying to see is Rome," she had said.

I had promised her I would take her there someday. I would — as soon as we could afford it, when the agency was up and making a profit. "Rome it is," I had said as I kissed her on the lips. "And Paris." Another kiss. "And London." Another. "The Isle of Capri. And —" My vocabulary of exotic locales had been exhausted.

I had meant it back then. I really had. Why hadn't we ever gone to any of those places? It certainly wasn't the money. Laura had never begged, only softly suggested, "Do you think we could take that trip to Rome next year?"

"Maybe," I'd answer. "Let's see how things go."

Go, they had. Each year busier than the one before. One more project that needed completing before I could keep my promise. How had it happened that our daughter was on the trip Laura and I had always planned to take?

"Have you called your mother?" I could only imagine how Laura might feel hearing about our trip from Stasha.

"I tried calling Mom. I didn't want to bug you at work. But no one answered at home. I left a message."

Oh, great. I could imagine Laura standing in our kitchen, listening to Stasha's exuberant message on the answering machine.

"Dad, you've really gotta come here

sometime. Soon. The Trevi Fountain is so cool. Mom would love it. It's huge, but it's tucked away in the middle of a bunch of buildings and little side streets. When you come around the corner, there it is. And it's like . . . wow!"

Oh, man. I hoped Stasha had kept her message to Laura less detailed than this. "So, you'll be home in, what?" I glanced at the calendar on my desk. "Five days?"

"Actually," she sighed. "Four and a half. We're half a day ahead of you." There was a short burst of static on the line. "I'd better go. I don't have much time left on this phone card. Things okay in Carlton? With you and Mom?"

"Your mom's fine." At least I hoped she was. I'd been at the office most of this week getting the concepting started on the Martin account, brainstorming talking points for the Carlton Industries pitch, not to mention the other fires that needed tending. Now that I thought about it, I had hardly been home while Laura had been awake. Maybe when I hung up I'd give her a call and suggest we go out for dinner. Laura loved eating out. "We're going out to dinner tonight."

Another promise you won't keep?

No, really, I was going to call her as soon

as I hung up.

"Daddy." Stasha hadn't called me that since, when? Age three? I felt a sudden urge to blink my eyes. "Really. Thank you for this trip. It's more than I — we — ever imagined."

"I'm glad you're enjoying it, honey." I couldn't resist adding one more thing. "And I've got a job waiting for you when you get back." Hint. Hint.

"Dad." I could hear the "no way" without her saying it.

"Hey, it doesn't hurt to keep your options open. You eat better when you have a paycheck." In my mind's eye, I could see Stasha rolling her eyes.

"We're not going to starve, Dad. Josh and I both have college degrees. And you know we are not going to live in Carlton. I've got to go."

Why had I opened that can of worms? I didn't want the conversation to end like this. "Say hi to Josh. You guys have fun. Does your mom know what time we're supposed to pick you up from the airport?"

"Mom's got all the info. Give her a kiss from me."

A kiss. When was the last time . . . ?

"Love you." Stasha's words let me off the hook from that thought. *"Ciao."*

"Chow," I echoed as I hung up. I looked at my watch. I had a late lunch meeting in an hour, time enough to call Laura and run the dinner idea past her.

My hand hovered over the phone. *Are you sure you have time? What about the CI presentation? What about the media plan for the Martin account?*

What about the fact that Laura would be listening to Stasha's phone message from Italy any minute, if she hadn't already? I reached for the receiver.

"Uh, Donnie?" Arlene stepped into my office. With the light system on our office phones, she had the advantage of knowing when I wasn't on mine. "Do you have a minute?"

I didn't, but that was nothing new. "Sure." I pulled my hand back from the phone and picked up a paper clip. "What do you need?"

Arlene sat across from me and turned two sheets of paper my way. "I need you to make a decision on my replacement." Very deliberately she touched the top of each of the papers. "I've narrowed the applicants down to these two for you."

I turned the paper clip in my hand, sticking the fingernail of my thumb between the bent metal and holding it there. Arlene hadn't wasted any time. She said she would stay until the Martin people had come to a decision. It had been barely a week, and she was planning her escape.

Is that what you think leaving this job would be? An escape?

For a split second it was as if a weight lifted from my chest. Thriving on pressure was the nature of my game, but obviously it wasn't called *pressure* for no reason. Sometimes the responsibility of managing this business weighed on my shoulders like bricks. This morning the thought of slipping out from under that heavy load was surprisingly enticing. Was this the way Arlene felt when she thought about leaving this job? As if she was suddenly freed from a cage? I couldn't let on that I knew the feeling all too well. Instead I said, "I was hoping you'd change your mind."

"You should know me better than that by now."

"A guy can hope." I pulled the résumés toward me, put on my wire-rimmed reading glasses, and skimmed the two pages. "They look almost identical to me."

A sly smile turned up one corner of Arlene's lips. "Believe me, they are not identical."

"You've interviewed them?"

She nodded. Noncommittal.

I looked back down at the résumés. Emma and Elle. Even their names were alike. Work histories almost matched up. Educational background . . . ditto, except for their graduation years. Emma had graduated almost fifteen years before Elle. I lifted one hand in the air. "I don't know. You decide."

"I can't. That's why I'm sitting here."

I didn't have time for indecision. I sat back. "Give me the *Cliff Notes* version."

"Here's the problem." Arlene pulled the papers back and held one up. "Emma reminds me of me 20 years ago. She has kids in school and wants a job to fill her time. She hasn't worked in a number of years, but she's enthusiastic, just like I was. She wants to prove she can do the job."

"She told you that?" I hoped Arlene hadn't invited a lawsuit with her questions.

"No, she didn't have to. I just know it." Arlene picked up the other paper. "Elle is young. Well, younger. She worked for a few years to pay for business college. She just graduated. She wants to work in the ad business and is willing to do what it takes to learn the ropes. She couldn't afford four years of college, so she got a two-year degree and wants to go back to school part-time to finish the rest when she has time. She wants to work, and she needs someone to give her a break." Arlene laid the paper down and sat back. "See why I couldn't decide?"

I flipped the paper clip between my fingers. Age discrimination crossed my mind as I thought briefly about not hiring Emma. But all I had to do was look at Arlene sitting across from me to know that age didn't matter when it came to being a good employee. A few years of life experience were sometimes worth more than the freshness of being right out of school. Then again, I couldn't help but remember Stasha's phone call minutes ago. Just like my daughter, this Elle needed a break. If another employer was trying to decide between someone who wanted a job just to get out of the house and my daughter . . . well, I knew who I'd tell him to pick.

"Let's go with Elle." There. Done.

Arlene gathered the papers. "This should be interesting." There was a crafty gleam in her eye.

"What?"

"You'll see" was all she said.

A cliché. Arlene was standing across from my desk introducing me to my new personal assistant, Elle Arneson, and all I could think was, *She's a cliché.*

I stood, swallowed, and stuck out my hand. "Nice to meet you." I tried to keep my eyes above her neck, but it was hard. Long legs, short skirt, high heels. She was wearing a blouse that could use one more button, topped by a jacket that was . . . what was the word? *Fitted.* Long, blonde hair framed her blue eyes. I tried to concentrate on those. "So, has Arlene showed you around?"

"Yes, she has, Mr. Dunn." Her voice had a seductive, Janis Joplin-like rasp to it. "I've heard so many good things about your agency. I'm really looking forward to working with you."

I cleared my throat and tried to avoid looking at Arlene. After all these years, she had to know what I was thinking. "Call me Don," I said, clearing my throat. Sheesh. Why hadn't I picked Emma instead? This gal was trouble on heels, at least for any member of the male species who had blood pumping in his veins.

She's too young for you.

Not that I was thinking about it . . . her. I might be too old, but I wasn't blind. Not yet. But if I didn't quit staring I might be soon. *Wonder if she has a left hook?* I glanced at her hand. No fist and no ring. I fingered the back of mine.

171

"Mr. Dunn. Don. I'm looking forward to working for you."

I rubbed my damp palm against my slacks. "Well, uh . . . glad to have you on board." *Talk about a cliché.* "I'll let Arlene teach you the ropes." *Sheesh.*

I held up one palm. "Bye now. Thanks. See you."

Bye now? Thanks? See you? I could feel a flush rising around my neck as the two women left my office. It had been a long time since I had been tongued-tied around a woman.

Arlene stepped to the side to let Elle exit first. Elle didn't look back. Arlene did. She gave me a one-sided grin and raised one eyebrow as if to say "I told you so." Then her expression turned serious. "Don't turn conventional on me."

I knew exactly what she meant. Without looking back, I reached for the arms of my chair and pulled it under me. I looked down at the file on my desk, but it was hard to concentrate. Elle was a knockout, no question about it. The question was, could she handle the work?

I shuffled the papers in front of me. The physical reaction I'd had when I looked at Elle unnerved me. Even the first time I saw Laura I hadn't had a feeling like that. Of course, I met Laura during a fender-bender on her way to a midterm. She hadn't exactly been dressed to impress the boss.

Wonder what Laura will say when she meets Elle?

Just the fact that I was wondering made me feel guilty. Knowing Laura, she would engage Elle in conversation and find out about her hardscrabble life — a father who abandoned her mother when she was pregnant, a mother who battled a debilitating disease most of her life, leaving Elle to care for her when she wasn't in school. A sibling who died in —

Oh, stop it! Even my imagination was making excuses to justify hiring a woman so beautiful.

You didn't hire her. Arlene did.

There. That was my excuse.

You don't need an excuse. You need to go home to your wife.

I would. Tonight I would make a point of being home in time for dinner. I'd spend the evening talking to Laura. I'd ask about her day, tell her about the young woman Arlene had hired to take her place. I'd tell Laura that Elle was young enough to be my daughter. That I planned to take her under my wing. Give her a leg up in the world.

I leaned back in my chair and closed my

eyes, trying with all my might to stop the clichés running rampant through my addled brain. If nothing else, I had learned one thing today. Clichés had a purpose. They filled in for originality when a person was too dumbstruck to think for himself.

STASHA

A burst of quick Italian was followed by, "KLM flight 5056, departing Rome for Amsterdam will begin boarding, starting with rows . . ."

No one waited to hear the rest of the announcement. As if we'd been trained along with Pavlov's dogs, there was a rustle of activity as most of the waiting passengers, Josh and I included, reached for our boarding passes and carry-ons and shuffled to form a straggly line.

As we waited our turn to board the plane, I looked over the people who would be our travel companions for the coming hours. Most of them looked bored. Or maybe they were tired. As zonked as I was. My eyes met Josh's. He didn't need to say a word; we were both exhausted. We'd certainly made the most of our ten days in Italy, not to mention our nights. There was a hint in Josh's eyes of all we had experienced. I pressed my lips together and tried to hide my smile. Josh seemed to be thinking about the same things I was. What the heck; I smiled at him full-force. Isn't that what honeymoons were all about? We were newly-weds, and I didn't care if everyone on this flight knew it.

Somehow, right now, boarding the plane in Italy to head back to Carlton, it felt official: Josh and I were a married couple. We had said our vows, our honeymoon would be over in — I looked at my watch; even after ten days in Italy I still had a hard time figuring out the time difference between Italy time and Central time. I'd be generous. In a little under 20 hours, taking into account plane changes in Amsterdam and Minneapolis, Josh and I would be walking into our first home — if you could call our cruddy, temporary apartment in Carlton a home. Anyway, it held all our earthly possessions, except for all the stuff I still had in my old room back at Mom and Dad's.

We were headed back to the real world. Priority number one was sleep. As tired as I was, even if I slept all the way back to the United States, I knew that with all the interruptions on the plane, I'd never catch up on all the sleep I missed. Just thinking about it made me yawn. I'd need all the sleep I

could get to face priority number two —
checking to see if my résumé had drawn any
interest.

I picked up my backpack and shuffled
forward three steps. To be honest, job hunting had been at the back of my mind for
the past month. Now that our honeymoon
was almost over, it didn't take my tired
brain long to remember the question I had
been asked at least a thousand times at the
wedding reception. "So, what will you do
after your honeymoon?"

I had spent enough time leading up to the
wedding worrying about that very question.
Didn't people know enough to let me enjoy
one night without thinking about the rest of
my life? There wasn't much to say. And now
I had to face the fact that other than job
hunting, I had absolutely nothing waiting
for me back in Carlton except my lame job
at the coffee shop.

And thank-you notes. Even though my
mom wasn't in Rome to remind me, she
somehow managed. I rolled my eyes as I
hoisted my backpack higher on my shoulder
and shuffled forward a few more steps. Just
another day, or three, to catch up on sleep,
and then I'd be ready to face the real world.

"Signorina?" The airline attendant scan-
ning the boarding passes held out her hand

toward me. "Miss? Your boarding pass?"

The line in front of me had disappeared. I shook my head and stepped forward. I must have zoned out for a second. I couldn't wait to get on the plane and crash. Okay, bad word to use in an airport. Sleep. All I wanted was to sleep.

The flight attendant scanned my boarding pass. *"Grazie."* Then Josh's. *"Grazie. Buono viaggiare."*

Whatever. I was too tired to care what she had said. Good something. "You too," I muttered just to leave a good American impression.

Josh stepped to my side as we walked down the sloping corridor onto the airplane. "It seems hard to believe at this time tomorrow we'll be back in Carlton."

Great. As if I needed reminding the honeymoon was over. Real life was about to begin. Even though I didn't need to, I automatically ducked my head as I stepped into the plane.

"Buona sera. Good evening." The male flight attendant motioned for me to head to my right.

I turned as Josh stepped on the back of my shoe. I shot him a look. Enough with the closeness. We'd been glued together for ten days. I was ready for a little breathing space on the trip home.

"Sorry." He was breathing down my neck as he pointed over my shoulder. "I think our seats are up a little on the left. I can take the window." As if he was making a sacrifice.

I had planned on sitting by the window. That way I wouldn't be bugged by all the people traipsing up and down the aisle during the long flight home, and I could sleep undisturbed.

It's not all about you anymore. Josh might want the same thing.

I took in a slow breath as I stood back for him to climb across the aisle seat to the window. My window.

Let it go. The mantra my Aunt Jane had suggested during a silly "Give Your Best Advice to the Bride" bridal shower game echoed now. So this was what she had meant. I exhaled. It would be ridiculous to start a fight over something so petty, especially after the fantastic time Josh and I had just had together.

I plopped my backpack on the seat and scrunched myself into our two-seat row so others could continue down the aisle. Thank goodness we hadn't been stuck in one of those claustrophobic five-seat middle rows. Maybe my aisle seat wasn't so bad. I unzipped my carry-on. All I needed was to grab a paperback out of my pack, something to read until I fell asleep. Mission accomplished. I shoved my pack into the overhead bin, then turned and settled into the seat. Minnie Mouse must have sat in this seat on the previous trip. *Or you've gained weight from all the gelato you ate the past ten days.* Either way, the seat belt needed adjusting. There. I leaned my head back against the seat, sighed deeply, and closed my eyes.

"Could you put this up for me?" Josh was passing his backpack to me.

A flash of irritation hit me. Couldn't he see how tired I was? Why couldn't he have put it up there before he sat down? Before I got settled? I blew out a puff of angry air and unbuckled my seat belt.

If there had been a stranger sitting next to you and he had asked the same thing, you would have said, "Sure. No problem."

Well, yeah. But Josh had to know how tired I was. A stranger wouldn't.

Josh would gladly do it for you.

The steely air inside my lungs began to soften. He would. *Let it go.* From between my raised arms I glanced down at Josh. He was leaning over, arranging my seat belt so when I sat back down it would be ready for me to buckle up. *You've married the nicest guy in the world.* I sat down and kissed Josh on the cheek. "Love you," I said, hoping he could hear what I had left unsaid: *I'm sorry I was irritated with you.*

"Me more."

I couldn't help but smile.

"Same," we said in unison, as if we'd been made just for each other.

Once again I leaned my head back against the seat. As soon as the plane took off I planned to recline my seat the entire one and a half inches, stuff my sweatshirt in the crook of my neck, and sleep. Until then I would practice dozing.

"I wonder if our great-grandparents ever imagined being on one side of the world one day and back home later the same day?"

Did Josh really expect me to answer that?

"Doesn't it twist your brain to think that we're here in Italy, and back in North Dakota our families are having a normal day?"

Couldn't he see that my eyes were closed? For a reason?

"Look. There's our luggage. There's that green luggage tag you put on my duffel bag. At least our clothes will make it to the United States. That's good to know, isn't it?"

Where was the duct tape?

"We're going to be flying all night. Think they'll serve us supper and breakfast?"

Apparently Josh was going to narrate the entire trip.

I bit down, clenching my teeth together to keep me from saying something I shouldn't. These two small seats were too confining to start a fight. The duration of a transatlantic flight was a long time to be mad at someone whose shoulder was pressed against yours the whole way. Certainly he could tell he was irritating me. Josh and I had dated steadily for a year. We'd gone through long days of midterms and finals. We had been married for ten days. He had to know I got cranky when I didn't get enough sleep.

Tell him.

He should know.

He can't read your mind.

He can see. How about my body language? My eyes are closed.

Do you know what he's thinking?

Well, duh. Sure. He's thinking about being home tomorrow, about our luggage being loaded onto the plane, about what he's going to get to eat on the way.

And why do you know all that?

Because he said it.

*My point exactly. He told *you.**

182

I pressed my eyelids together and thought about this one corny country song that Josh loved. Go ahead, hand me my "Stupid" sign. Of course Josh didn't know how I was feeling.

So . . . tell him. Tell him how tired you are.

A ball of stubbornness stuck in my throat. It wasn't one bit romantic for me to have to tell Josh how I was feeling. If he really loved me, he'd know.

I opened one eye just a slit and looked at him from the corner. He was leaning forward, looking out the window. Then he turned and looked over the people in the seats behind us. He reached forward and pulled the safety instructions from the seat pocket and read through them as if we might need to use them.

A faint thrum of fear made my fingers tingle. What if we did crash? What would we do? In my imagination I could hear the exiting instructions shouted in a language I didn't understand. Even if we survived the crash, maybe we'd never get out. But we had to. We had so much life ahead of us.

I could see Josh scan the rows in front of us, then the rows behind. I knew he was counting how many rows there were between us and the nearest exit. He'd done the same thing on every leg of our trip. I sighed deeply and reached out to squeeze Josh's arm. I didn't have to worry about anything. Josh would take care of me. Crabby or not, he loved me. "Love you," I said for the second time in as many minutes.

"Just a minute, I'm counting." Josh settled back in his seat. "Five. We're five rows from the nearest exit. It's behind us."

I smiled as I leaned my head against his shoulder and closed my eyes. His words were the most romantic thing I'd heard all day.

I looked out the oval of the airplane window as the plane descended into the small Carlton airport. After being in airports in Rome, Amsterdam, and Minneapolis all within the past 20 hours, the Carlton airport looked positively miniature. Josh insisted I have the window seat on the last leg home. Now that I had been stuck next to the body of the plane this past hour, I realized I should have appreciated the airy freedom the aisle seat provided. Josh had done me a favor by sitting next to the window while we crossed the ocean. I'd have to remember that next time.

Next time. As if there would be a next time anytime soon. This trip was going to have to serve as a fantastic memory for years to come. From here on out Josh and I would have to become contributing members to the national economy. In other words, employees and taxpayers. Reality shimmered right below our airplane.

I could see the runway blur under the wheels of the plane. I pressed my head back against the seat and tensed, waiting for the rubbery bounce that would mean we were on solid ground. Home.

There. As the plane shuddered its way to a near stop, I opened my eyes and reached for the backpack I'd stowed under the seat in front of me for this leg of our journey. I was more than ready to climb into our new bed and sleep lying down, to make up for the half-sleep I'd gotten on three planes. I was suddenly grateful for the time Josh and I had spent getting our first apartment at least somewhat set up.

The delivery guys had just left after setting up the king-size frame and mattresses. Josh and I had jockeyed the big bed away from the wall enough for me to sidestep my way between the wall and the bed. With my teeth, I ripped the plastic off the sheets that had come with the mattresses. I was ready to finish the job.

"Let's make the bed."

Josh rolled his eyes. "Let's just leave it for

now. We won't be sleeping in it for another week. "Unless . . ." He wiggled his eyebrows at me.

I drew out the flimsy piece of cardboard from between the tightly folded sheets and lobbed it at him. "You're such a guy." I couldn't help but laugh. Truth was, I was looking forward to using this bed as much as Josh was.

"Here, grab the other side." I unfurled the fitted sheet across the bed. "Oh, wait a sec. I forgot the mattress pad." I unzipped the bulky bed covering, a shower gift I hadn't appreciated until now. It didn't take long to slide the four corners over the sides of the thick mattress, then the fitted sheet. In tandem we tucked in the bottom of the soft blue top sheet as if we'd been doing this together for years. Obviously Josh's mom had taught him to make a bed. I would have to thank her.

"I'm going to open up that blanket your aunt gave us for a shower gift." I slithered out from my side of the bed and started toward the living room where our shower and early wedding gifts were stacked.

Josh trailed behind, veering off when he saw the TV sitting in a corner. "I'm going to hook this up so I can get my PlayStation running."

It was my turn to roll my eyes.

"Don't worry," he added. "I'll hook up the computer too. That way we can check on our job offers." His tongue worried the inside of his cheek. "Or not."

"Don't even say that." I was tempted to toss the plastic-wrapped blanket at him. "Think positive."

"And pray." Josh squatted in front of the computer on the floor. "We can use all the help we can get."

"Yeah, that too." I'd been trying to remember to pray about finding a job. But between studying for finals, planning the wedding, my job at the Brews-n-News, and getting this apartment set up, I hadn't been doing too great in the talking-to-God department. Oh well, I'd have more time soon. I held up the blanket and raised an eyebrow, reminding Josh we hadn't finished making the bed.

"Do you really need me to spread a blanket on top of the sheets? I'd really like to get the computer running."

Men. I knew his ulterior motive was to play Minesweeper.

I left Josh in our small living room while I spread our only blanket over the sheets. As I tucked the blanket between the mattress and box spring, it dawned on me that

187

maybe I should have washed the sheets first. But with the laundry room down two flights of stairs in Mr. Miller's basement, and no detergent in our cupboard, well, how dirty could new sheets be? Taking care of my own place might take some getting used to.

"Welcome to Carlton." The flight attendant's announcement reminded me that I wasn't quite in that ready-and-waiting bed.

I turned and smiled at Josh. At the time I had made up the bed, I imagined a romantic first night at home, with candles lit all around the bed, that sort of thing. After ten days of being together 24/7, and almost a whole day spent in a succession of airplanes just trying to get home, my only fantasies were of sleep.

It would be after midnight by the time we got our luggage and left the terminal. Right now I was wishing we had left our car in the parking lot instead of having my mom pick us up. Paying for ten days of parking had seemed like a waste of money, but right now, I'd give most anything not to have to dredge up the enthusiasm I knew my mom would expect. She would want details about our trip that I couldn't begin to remember with my jet-lagged brain. I'd have to promise her a detailed account ASAP.

I followed Josh off the plane, through the

small terminal to the baggage area. "Mom!" There she was, smiling and waving.

She held her arms out to welcome me home. "Oh, it's good to have you back."

I wrapped my arms around her too. I hadn't realized it, but I had missed being in the place I called home. *You won't be calling it home for much longer.*

As the too-loud buzzer announced the arrival of our luggage, I let my mind finger the thought. In short order Josh and I would be moving. Somewhere else would soon be that place I called home. I could hardly wait.

"Man, it's good to be here." Josh dropped his huge duffel bag at the foot of the stairs, dug a hand into the pocket of his jeans, and pulled out the key to our apartment.

I followed him up the steep steps. I didn't dare let go of my suitcase. I'd never have the energy to pick it up again. Thankfully, Mom understood why I couldn't even start telling her about our trip. I promised I'd call her the next day.

As Josh turned the key in the lock and pushed open the door, it occurred to me that this was our first time walking into our apartment as husband and wife. We'd come and gone a hundred times over the past two weeks, combining our crummy, college-accumulated furniture, finding places for old lamps and end tables dragged from our parents' basements, stacking in one corner of the living room all those boxes we hoped to unpack in another apartment. But tonight, for the first time, this was our home.

"Ready?" Josh turned and grinned at me. So, he also realized this was a first too.

"Yup." I tugged at my souvenir-loaded suitcase.

Josh touched my hand. "Let go."

It was sweet of him to offer. "It's okay, I can get it."

"No. Let go. There's something I want to do."

I could feel my eyebrows puzzle together. "Okay. Thanks." I released my hand from the luggage and stepped aside. It wouldn't hurt my pride to let Josh do some of these things for me. "What — ? Whoa-aaa . . ."

Before I had a chance to figure out what was happening, I was swept off my feet into Josh's arms, carried over the doorstep into our apartment, and placed back on my feet with a kiss to make it official.

"Silly." I could feel myself blush. Who knew this guy of mine even knew about that old-fashioned tradition? Much less that he'd do it.

"Welcome home." He slid his arms around

my waist and kissed me again.

"You too." I kissed him back.

"Think we should close the door?"

"Umm-mm-m-mm." It was hard to talk with his lips on mine.

Now that I should be sleeping, I couldn't. My head lifted and lowered with Josh's heavy breathing. As overtired as I was, I couldn't help but smile. It turned out Josh was glad I insisted we have our bed ready.

I eased myself out from under Josh's arm and slid to what was now officially my side of the bed. How could he be so dead to the world and I be so awake?

The cool wall of our bedroom was next to my shoulder. In order to climb out of bed I had to thread myself out of the blankets and slip off the end of the bed. Maybe a king-sized bed hadn't been the best idea. I glanced over Josh's body to his side of the bed. There was barely room for my chipped nightstand on the other side. When I got my job and Josh and I went house hunting, we would need to remember that our bedroom had to be big enough so we could get out on both sides of the bed. It was a small luxury I never thought about when I didn't have to share a bed.

I wandered into our living room — if you

could call one couch, one chair, and a mess of half-unpacked boxes and wedding gifts a living room. I switched on the floor lamp Josh had brought from his stash of stuff, squinting against the sudden brightness and the mess. We had a long way to go to turn this place into a home — even if only for a brief time.

I stood in front of the stack of shower gifts. It was easy to remember how much fun it had been to open them. I ran my hand over the nubby surface of a thick navy towel. There were four of them somewhere in this pile. We had received just about everything we'd registered for at Herberger's and Target, and lots of things we hadn't. A glint of light bounced off a crystal bowl in an opened box. My great-aunt Barbara had given it to us. "For when you entertain," she had said at the shower. Ha. As if we'd be able to do any entertaining *here.*

A sudden anxiety thrummed in my chest. There was so much to do. There were all these boxes to unpack, gifts to sort, people to thank. There was no way we'd be able to use all this stuff in our small apartment. I had a feeling we'd be hauling much of it back to my parents' basement. They'd have to store it until we had a house big enough to fit it all in.

I had taken a lot for granted over the years — the spacious house where I'd grown up, for one thing. Somehow it never occurred to me that I wouldn't always live in a big house. Things were a lot different from when my parents started out in their tiny apartment. Salaries were smaller then — expectations too. My dad took every chance he had to tell me about his humble beginnings, starting his business in what would be my nursery.

"It doesn't hurt to start at the bottom. It makes you appreciate things more."

I certainly wasn't opposed to hard work. I just planned to manage my job better than my dad managed his. I was going to have a great career *and* a great life with Josh, once I slogged through all these gifts and our combined boxes of stuff. Just the thought made me exhausted . . . as if I could get any *more* worn-out. I plopped into the vinyl recliner Josh had brought along from his apartment, trying to block the pile of presents from my vision with my heavy eyelids. If I couldn't see it, maybe I wouldn't be so overwhelmed by all there was to do . . . starting tomorrow.

I rubbed my eyes as I stared at Josh, already hunched over the computer screen barely five feet from where I had been sleeping in the recliner. I pushed at the footrest with my heels and sat upright. I hoped he didn't remember the argument we'd already had over that chair; Josh knew its days were limited to our first paycheck. Mousy-brown, torn vinyl, armrest cup holders that only a guy could love. Yuck. I didn't dare tell Josh I'd slept like Sleeping Beauty in that thing.

"Morning. I think." I waited for a response. Tried again. "Good morning." Had he left his ears in Italy? Some first morning together. I'd try again. *"Buon giorno."*

"Huh? Oh! You're up." He turned a bit in the kitchen chair he was using at the computer and gave me a sleepy smile. "I was trying to be quiet so you could sleep."

"What time is it?"

"In Carlton or in Italy?" Josh looked at his empty wrist. "I think I'm still on Italy time." He glanced at the corner of the computer screen. "It's almost noon — here."

I rubbed sleep crust from the corners of my eyes. "No wonder I'm starving."

"Me too. What are you making for lunch?"

Me? Lunch? As if we had food in the apartment. As if I was suddenly in charge of meals. I'd never dreamt of being a Stepford Wife, and I didn't plan on becoming one now. We needed to get something straight. "I suppose we're going to have to go grocery shopping this morning. Uh . . . afternoon." I hoped he noticed the emphasis I put on *we.*

"Yeah, I suppose we will. Don't we have some leftover wedding cake or something?"

If this was Josh's idea of meal planning, things didn't look good. I might end up with kitchen duties by default. Right now I needed a shower, then food. As if in protest at being second in line, my stomach growled. Josh had already turned back to the computer. He probably wouldn't hear me, but I said it anyway. "I'm going to hit the shower."

"Hey — I think . . ." His eyes were glued to the screen.

Even if he wasn't listening to me, I'd heard him. "Think what?"

"Wow. Get this." He sat back in the chair and pointed at the computer. "I have three schools interested in talking to me about a job. One of them is right here in Carlton."

Right. Josh knew how I felt about staying here. We were too young to spend the rest of our lives stuck in nowhere North Dakota, just like my parents.

Stuck? You can hardly call the lives they've lived "stuck."

Well sure, Dad traveled with his business. Sometimes Mom went along. They had a great house. Cool cars. But look at them. All my dad talked about was work.

He loves what he does.

Still, there was more to life than that. And look at my mom. She'd never done anything with her art degree. She stayed home, raised me, helped Dad start his business, and did some volunteer work. I wanted more than that for my life. If Josh took a job here, it would be all too easy to walk right into those same deep ruts my mom had slogged through. No way. I shuffled into the kitchen. I didn't need to hear about a possible job in Carlton. What I needed was a Diet Coke.

I swung open the fridge door. If it hadn't been for the yellow stain on the bottom shelf, our fridge could be a display model in an appliance store. Empty. I thought for sure there had been a couple of cans of soda left from when we were getting the apartment set up.

As if in answer to my thoughts I heard the pop-fizz of a can opening in the living room. I leaned back and looked around the doorway. Sure enough, there sat Josh with one empty Diet Coke can on its side on the floor, and a new can, the last can, tilted to his lips.

Had it occurred to him I might like something to drink, too?

Obviously not. But then, I wasn't so sure I would have thought past my own thirst either. So this is what it was like to have a home of your own and a husband. No one stocked the fridge when you weren't looking. There were now two people under the same roof who drank Diet Coke.

I shuffled back to where Josh was sitting. "Can I have a sip?"

He looked at the can as if he hadn't realized he was holding it. "Uh, sure."

It was practically empty. How could he drink half a can of Coke in the time it took me to walk from the fridge to his chair?

He tilted his head toward the computer screen. "Look at this job. They want to interview me ASAP."

All I could see were the words at the top of the screen: Carlton Central Junior High School. No way was Josh going to that interview. He wasn't going to take the first teaching job that came along. He might not be picky, but I was. I also wasn't worried. I knew there was a perfect job waiting for me. As soon as I logged into my e-mail I'd have a better idea of what our future held. I wasn't going to assume he could read my mind about something this important. "You know how I feel about staying in Carlton. Josh, there's a reason you have a job offer in Carlton. And the reason is that no one else wants that job. Besides, hasn't school started already?" I knew that North Dakota schools had started while we were in Italy. "Those offers have to be old."

"These are positions they weren't able to fill."

"Jo-osh." I had nothing more to say.

Josh shrugged and moved the Carlton job offer into his "Jobs" folder. "It's nice to know they're interested."

Well, at least I could be encouraging about that. I reached out and rubbed the back of his neck. "You're going to make a great teacher," I said, and then shifted the conversation to a more hopeful note. "You said there were a couple of other leads?"

Josh clicked the mouse, changing the screen. "One's somewhere in Minnesota. The other was in some town in North Dakota I've never even heard of."

For some reason my heart seemed to fall into my empty stomach. It had never occurred to me that Josh might be offered a job in a town even smaller than Carlton.

Suddenly I was wishing we were back in Italy. There were more museums to tour, ancient churches to wander through, fountains where we could throw in a few *centesimos* and wish life could always be as carefree as our honeymoon.

That's not real life.

I nudged Josh's shoulder with the soda can. "Let me check my e-mail."

He slid off the chair, and I slipped into the warm spot.

"Don't we have some Pop Tarts or something?" Leave it to Josh to go from job hunting to food in a nanosecond.

"You can check." I knew the mish-mash of boxes in the kitchen would keep him busy rummaging. "If you find some, see if you can unearth one of the toasters we got for a shower present. Make one for me too."

There, that would keep him from looking over my shoulder. Knowing Josh, he would want me to jump on the first job I was offered. I had a plan for our life, and this was where it would start. Quickly I maneuvered the mouse, typed in my password, and waited for the screen to change.

I have a plan for your life, too.

The quiet reminder filtered through my anxious thoughts as my inbox filled the screen. My whole life my mom had told me that God had a bigger plan than I did. I was more than ready to find out what it was.

I scanned through my e-mail inbox. Spam.

Spam. Spam. Tons of e-mails from my college friends. I'd get to those later. Right now I had other priorities.

Man, how many people were there who sent spam? I deleted as I went. Gone. Gone. Gone. Here was a screen name I didn't recognize. Maybe it was the recruiter for the advertising firm in New York where I'd sent my résumé. There was an excited buzz in my ears as I clicked on the unfamiliar e-mail and waited to see what my future held. BUY SOFTWARE AT A DISCOUNT. Maybe not. Delete.

I clicked through the list. By the time I was finished, I had gone through at least 25 "How does it feel to be married?" e-mails and deleted some 50 pieces of spam, and I was left staring at what was, for all intents and purposes, a blank screen. It didn't hold one piece of e-mail that really mattered.

"So?" I could tell Josh had something in his mouth.

A minute ago I would have insisted that he share, but right now I didn't have an appetite for anything. I stared at the screen, my hopes falling as fast as a kite with no wind. There must be some mistake. I clicked the "check mail" icon again. Same screen. Maybe my mailbox had filled up while I was gone and the offers that were surely coming my way had bounced back into cyberspace.

I could feel Josh breathing down my neck. A hot surge pushed from somewhere in my chest and rose into my face. I checked for new mail again. Nothing.

Josh cleared his throat behind me, leaned forward, and asked, "So, where are we going to be moving?" His question wasn't a slam, but still it hurt. Josh had exactly three job possibilities. I had exactly none.

LAURA

The only word I could put to this feeling was jealousy.

I watched Stasha run her fingers over Josh's knee as they sat beside each other on our couch recounting their honeymoon. "And then we walked, well, climbed all the way to the top of St. Peter's Basilica. That's in Vatican City, where the pope lives. It's something like 600 steps to the top."

"Um, 323." Josh put his hand over Stasha's and squeezed. No wonder he was a math teacher.

"Well, it felt like 600." Stasha sighed as if she'd just finished the hike.

Josh raised his eyebrows at me and bit his lips together, trying to hide a smile, acknowledging the fact that he and I now shared inside knowledge of my sometimes-diva daughter. His wife.

There it was again, another pang knocking at my heart. I wasn't sure if it was reluctance over having to share my daughter with this young man, envy over the fabulous trip they'd just taken, or simply bafflement over the love they both wore like an emblem for all to see. Had I ever really felt that way about Donnie? Had it shown like this?

I glanced at Donnie, sitting in his recliner at a right angle to the couch. I had to give him credit — he had kept his promise to be here tonight. He was even leaning forward, forearms on his knees as if he wanted to catch every word. See every photo.

He's a good man.

Of course he was good, just never around. When he was, his mind wasn't anywhere in sync with what was going on around here.

It is tonight.

Once in a blue moon didn't count. Enough waffling. I had made up my mind. I had told myself that when Stasha's wedding pictures arrived, it would be "D" day. Well, "C" day, at any rate. Big *conversation* day. My eyes flicked to the end table where the thick album of proofs was waiting. I'd picked it up Saturday and saved it until tonight, when I knew Stasha and Josh were coming over for dinner to show us their honeymoon photos. I planned to surprise them with their wedding photos as soon as they were finished replaying their trip.

I planned to surprise Donnie with something completely different tomorrow night.

"And you should have seen the goofy uniforms the Vatican guards have to wear." Stasha paused to laugh as she passed a photo to her dad.

Donnie smiled and handed me the picture of a guard in an oddly striped uniform.

Josh picked up where she left off. "They were designed by Michelangelo."

Stasha again. "I thought the guy was supposed to have an eye for design."

It was as though they were two people sharing one thought process out loud. Were there pairs of twins who were any more in tune? Certainly there were psychologists who studied people who were so alike and yet not related. Had Donnie and I ever been on the same wavelength the way these two lovebirds were?

I doubted it. I looked at him again. He asked Josh a question and laughed at something Stasha said. When had he last laughed that way at something I said?

"I'm going to get our dessert ready," I said abruptly and headed for the kitchen.

I grabbed four plates and forks and cut the apple pie into six slices. I'd picked up the pie from the bakery on my way home from helping Karen at the gallery most of the day. Today we had uncrated several paintings by an artist from Wyoming. That was after I had stopped by Eleanor's to pick up a sweater she wanted dropped off at the dry cleaners. Did Donnie have any idea what I had done today? No. But it didn't matter. After tomorrow night, Donnie would have no choice but to pay attention. I had my exact words all planned out.

"It's very simple, Donnie. You need to choose: the agency or our marriage."

DONNIE

Another day, another dol— Nope. Couldn't say it. I rearranged papers on my desk. It was hard getting my head in the game this morning. I had so much to do that it was difficult figuring out where to start. I reached for another procrastinating sip of Mountain Dew. *Empty.* Not even 9:00 a.m., and I'd downed one Dew already. More caffeine might do the trick. I pushed myself away from my desk and walked out of my office toward the break room.

"Good morning, Mr. Dunn." Elle looked up from the keyboard at her computer station just outside my office.

"Morning." I lifted my fingers and tried to act casual, as if Elle and Arlene were interchangeable. Casual. Right. I paused by Elle's desk. How could I ignore the electric blue shirt she was wearing? It made her ice-blue eyes pop. Of course, her eye makeup could have something to do with it. Funny, in all the years I worked with Arlene I had never noticed if she wore eye makeup. Speaking of which — "Where's Arlene?"

"Oh," Elle stopped typing and looked up. "Arlene's taking the morning off. She thought I could handle things until she gets here after lunch." Elle held up crossed fingers. "So far, so good."

Under normal circumstances I might have cringed at the cliché, but somehow, coming from Elle's glossed lips, it sounded cute. Except I was missing a cold Dew on my desk. Arlene had taken on the task of bringing me a soda every morning, without my ever really noticing. Now that she wasn't here, I noticed.

"Did you need anything?" Elle started rising from her chair.

I held up a palm. "No, that's okay. I'm just going to get something to drink."

"Do you want me to get it for you? Is that something I'm supposed to be doing?"

Now was the time to let her know. But the thought of telling Elle to make sure I had a fresh beverage at my elbow suddenly seemed outdated and chauvinistic. A cliché of its own. "No, no," I said as if it was out of the question. "The exercise is good for me."

Elle's eyes flicked to the break room ten feet away. "Exercise. That's funny."

Yeah, just call me Jay Leno. Enough loitering. I made a beeline for the break room, then the fridge, popped a can of Dew, and started drinking. *Need to cool off?*

If I did, I wouldn't admit it. I walked back to my office, not letting my eyes so much as flick in Elle's direction. If she thought I was aloof, great. It might be best for both of us.

And Laura?

I set the can on the desk and turned to the window. I had nothing to feel guilty about. I could hardly help talking to — or looking at — my personal assistant while I was at work, could I?

I stared at downtown Carlton from my fourth-floor vantage point. The trees in planters along the boulevard were showing signs of fall. Mid-September in North Dakota might still be summer in most of the country, but here in the Upper Midwest you never knew what the month might bring.

Change.

Change. Weird. That was a word I'd kept thinking last night, too, as Stasha and Josh shared photos from their honeymoon and details of their trip. She had graduated from college only a few months ago and now she was a wife. Soon she would have a career. Thing were changing so fast I could hardly keep up.

Laura would, though. I could tell by the way she kept eyeing Stasha — stealing glances at the way she'd lean into Josh or touch his arm, the way Josh would turn and smile at Stasha, then share his grin with us. I remembered what those heady days of getting-started-in-life were like. It was as if Laura was cataloging it all, filing memories of our daughter in a mental album to take out and page through later. I knew if I ever forgot the details, Laura would be there to fill in the blanks.

Are you so sure?

An uneasy weight tugged at a muscle at the base of my neck; I massaged it with my fingers. Last night I had done my best to concentrate while they talked about their trip to Italy — and to pretend I had never promised Laura any such thing. If I had any luck at all, maybe Laura had forgotten those long-ago promises.

She hadn't said anything about our taking a trip in, what? A year?

Just because she hasn't said anything doesn't mean she doesn't remember. You need to apologize.

For what? How could I apologize for something I hadn't done?

That's the very reason you need to.

Why open Pandora's box when I didn't have to?

Before it's too late.

Late? How could it be too late? Laura and I had years ahead of us. One of these days I'd start to think about retirement. We weren't even 50 yet. There would be lots of time ahead of us to go to Italy or any place Laura wanted.

Before it's too late.

I kneaded the tight spot in my left shoulder again. Maybe tonight I could tell Laura that I hadn't forgotten my promise. I couldn't take off across the globe just yet, not with Arlene leaving and the full plate of business. But soon. Someday, I would give her the trip of her dreams.

Movement on the street outside caught my eye. I watched as a woman who looked a lot like Laura got out of her car and walked into the coffee shop just a few doors down the sidewalk — Brews-n-News, where Stasha worked part-time. I craned my neck. Maybe it was Laura stopping in to say hi. Maybe she would drop by my office next.

A deep *thud* of a heartbeat turned me away from the window. I wasn't so sure I wanted her here. She hadn't yet seen Arlene's replacement. And I wasn't so sure I wanted her to, at least not until I got my ogling eyes back where they belonged.

I also wasn't so sure I wanted to see her any earlier than I had to. Whatever she had up her sweater sleeve last night, well, she'd promised to share it with me tonight.

I sat at my desk, pushed the soda can aside, and pulled the Martin media plan front and center. I tried to concentrate on the words and numbers, but instead I found myself rehashing the puzzle of last night.

Laura and Stasha had oohed and ahhed over every picture in the wedding album while Josh and I acted appropriately enthused. After dessert, the kids left, and Laura and I sat in the living room and read. Soon enough, Laura cleared her throat and said, "Donnie?"

I looked over the top of my reading glasses and over the top of the newspaper I hadn't had time to read until the day was practically over.

Laura met my gaze. She licked her lips and played with the diamond necklace that rested against her collarbone. "Umm . . ."

I raised my eyebrows. *What?*

"We need to talk." Laura closed the magazine she was reading.

If this was going to be a drawn-out, post-wedding, post-honeymoon conversation about how wonderful everything went, I wasn't up for it. My eyes fell on the briefcase at my feet. As soon as I scanned the headlines, I had the Carlton Industries creative brief to look over, then the competitive review for the Brody Corporation. CI wasn't the only client we were pitching; Brody had asked us to present to them as well. Their business would be as much of a coup as the Martin account had been. I wanted them both.

The newspaper rustled as I lowered it a couple of inches. "Laura." I closed my eyes for a long second. "I'm sort of tapped out tonight. You and Stasha did a great job on the wedding. If there are bills left to pay, I'll leave my checkbook on the table, or just put them on the credit card. We can pay it off at the end of the month."

Laura looked as if she was biting back words. Maybe she was, but I didn't have the mental energy to listen to them tonight. "Okay?" It really wasn't a question.

"Sure." Short, but not so sweet.

I lifted the paper.

She cleared her throat. "Could we talk tomorrow night then? There's something I need to discuss."

Discuss. I never did like that word. Maybe it would be best to simply get it over with. I turned my wrist and looked at the time.

Almost 10 and I had a good hour or more of reading ahead of me, if I didn't fall asleep in the recliner. "Sure, tomorrow will work."

"Will you be home?"

"I'll try." It was the best I could do.

The buzz of the intercom startled me back to the open file on my desk, back to the day of work I needed to clear off my desk. It would be hours before I would find out what Laura thought we needed to discuss. "Mr. Dunn, call on line one."

I reached for the phone just as Matt stepped through the doorway of my office. I held my thumb and index finger a quarter-inch apart. *This long.* I motioned for him to sit down, then made quick work of the phone call.

"What's up?" It was the way we started almost every morning around here — Matt and me and 20 minutes, a meeting of the minds before we got too busy to think straight.

Usually Matt started right in on whatever fire needed tending; today he tilted his head a fraction of an inch toward the door and spoke low. "Hubba."

"Quit drooling." My voice was low too. I wasn't interested in finding out the particulars of a sexual harassment case. "Besides, she's too young for you."

"Says who?"

"Says a man who is old enough to be her dad. A guy who's the same age as you."

Matt wiggled his eyebrows. "Tell that to the tabloids. No one cares about age anymore. Haven't you heard? Fifty is the new 30."

"Since when did you start watching *Oprah*?"

Matt shot me a smart-mouthed grin.

"Besides," I reminded him, "she's not 30 yet."

"Is she single?"

I rolled my eyes. Ever since his divorce, Matt had been on the prowl. I had no idea if Elle was or wasn't. "She's not to you." I drew a notepad near me and picked up a pen; it was time for business. "I'm hoping to expand this agency, not close it. So, stay away."

Matt drew his chin back. "Whoa. Methinks thou dost protest too much."

Matt could dish it out. So could I. "Better to warn you now, than bail you out later. Bail the business out."

A flash of irritation narrowed Matt's eyes. He never did like being told he couldn't do something, a trait that was an asset in advertising but possibly lethal when it came to my assistant. He cast a last-jab glance over his shoulder, as if he could see through the wall to where Elle sat. As long as all he did was look, I wouldn't say any more.

"What fire do we need to put out first today?" There was a stack of little embers simmering on each corner of my desk. Put them all together, and we'd have a blaze of major proportions. Matt had always been good at knowing in which order we needed to concentrate our efforts.

Matt leaned forward, his forearms on his knees. "We've got concepting to do on the Martin account. Plus they're talking about doing some media, TV and magazine, next spring. We need to start on that now. They'd like the deliverables ASAP. We should do some focus groups before the CI pitch. And other than Justine, we have no one working on the Brody business." He sat back and clicked his tongue against the roof of his mouth. "Our biggest problem is that we don't have enough manpower to do it all."

I scribbled a hard circle on the paper in front of me. "What do you suggest we do?"

Matt cut to the chase. "We need bodies."

I could feel the muscle in the base of my neck throb. The problem wasn't so much finding people to work, it was finding qualified people. There was a steep learning curve in this business, tempered by the fact that if these prospective clients selected a different agency to do their work, Matt and I would be left with a group of trained people with no work to do. Laying off people was not my favorite part of this job.

"Freelancers?"

Matt crossed his arms over his chest. "We're gonna have to."

Freelance contractors were more expensive. Hiring someone for a short-term job with no benefits came at a price.

"I'll have Arlene make some calls. Uh . . ." Old habits died hard. "I guess I'll have Elle start. Arlene won't be in until after lunch."

"Oh, great." Matt knew what Arlene did around here, the relationships she had formed with many of our contract folks. Elle wouldn't know who would be best to contact for the work we needed done.

A chunk of cement weighed in my stomach. All of a sudden, my new assistant didn't seem nearly as attractive as good-old Arlene. And she'd be gone for good in two weeks. "Maybe we can wait until after lunch."

"Yeah, maybe." Or maybe not.

It took an hour for the idea to percolate from the back of my brain to the forefront.

"I'm going to step out for a minute." I

216

threw the words at Elle as I walked past her desk.

She jumped as if I'd caught her online shopping. "Oh! Did I miss an appointment on your calendar?" I could see her scrambling to look at the daily planner near her keyboard.

"No. I'm going to step out for a second. Get some coffee."

Elle stood. "I can get you some."

"It's okay." I paused with a hand on the back of her computer screen. "I'm going to have a quick meeting while I'm out too."

"You are?" She sat back down and clicked a few keys. "You aren't scheduled for any meetings this morning."

Ah, the prison-like joy of a shared calendar, my life for all to see. "Something came up." There were a few privileges that came with ownership. I patted the top of Elle's computer screen. "I'm going to get that coffee now. Be back soon."

Her words followed me out of the office. "Arlene told me you didn't drink coffee."

I didn't — except in an emergency. And considering all the work facing the agency right now, and the fact that I was going to have to cancel Laura's discussion tonight, today I felt compelled to have a cup. Maybe two.

I pushed my way out the door onto the sidewalk and took a breath of bracing, mid-September air. I needed all the help I could get for what faced me a few feet down the sidewalk. Today I hoped a cup of caffeine, and a little finagling, held the cure to what ailed me.

STASHA

"Enjoy." I handed a double-espresso skim latte to Cathy, one of my regulars, and then looked over her shoulder to see how many more people I'd have to wait on before I could have a cup of something myself. There were six people in line. *Wait.* Make that seven. My dad, of all the non-coffee-drinking people to be in a place like this, stepped in behind Steve, a soy cappuccino regular.

I began filling the next order. *What is Dad doing here?* Ouch. A burst of steam hit the back of my hand. I pulled it back and pressed it against my apron, trying to soothe the sting. *Focus.* If my dad was standing in a line for coffee, he had more on his mind than I thought. In the 21 years I'd been alive, I had never seen him so much as take one sip of the stuff. Maybe he'd finally lost it. Oh well, coffee was a better alternative than something stronger to drink. I would find out what he planned to order in a few minutes. "Here you go," I said to the stranger next in line, handing over his coffee.

It was hard to concentrate on filling orders when the corners of my eyes kept tabs on my dad. I had worked here part-time since the middle of summer, and not once had Dad stopped in. I was kinda glad. Four years of college made me way overqualified for this job. Maybe my dad had an urge to see where my tuition dollars had landed me. I could feel a flush spread over my cheeks, a redness not caused by the steam machine.

Now that Josh had taken an extended job as a substitute at Carlton Junior High, I would be stuck behind this counter until Christmas.

"Over my dead body," I said to Josh when he told me he was taking the teaching job in Carlton. I had my hands on my hips as if I was his mother or something.

"It's only three months." Josh crossed his arms over his chest. "Besides, we're both going to be dead bodies if neither one of us has a job that pays enough to buy groceries."

The truth of his words stung each morning when I tied the maroon coffee shop apron around my waist and stepped behind the counter. It might look as if I was filling coffee cups, but in reality I was biding my time. I held out hope that my résumé would attract someone's attention — besides the "Get Rich Quick Stuffing Envelopes from Home" kind of offers that had filled my in-box. If I had to, I'd move somewhere and start my career. Josh could join me when the teacher who had taken maternity leave put her baby in day care and came back to work. I glanced down the short coffee line. I hoped my dad could tell that this wasn't where I planned to spend the rest of my life.

Steve was next. Good — Greg, the manager, could have the grand privilege of serving my dad his first cup of coffee and save me the embarrassment.

"The usual?" I asked Steve.

"Already got it." Greg held out Steve's order.

Great. I felt as if I was playing store, calling my dad as a customer. "Next." For the first time since I'd worked here I hoped I wouldn't get a tip; knowing my dad, he'd slip me a twenty. If any of my coworkers noticed, I'd feel so bogus.

"I'll have a cup of coffee. The closest thing you have to Mountain Dew."

"Da-ad." I stood across the counter and

leveled a stare at him. "You don't drink coffee." It was weird enough to see him standing in line. Weirder to be waiting on him.

He angled his chin to the blackboard offerings hanging behind my head. "You're the second person who's told me that today. I'm stepping out of my box. Give me a cup of something."

I threw a thumb over my shoulder. "We sell Coke if you're desperate."

He stared at the chalkboard as if he was studying for a test, looking for an answer to an important question. He lifted his eyebrows. "No, I think I'll have a coffee drink. Surprise me." Before I turned, he added, "Do you ever get a coffee break?"

I opened my mouth to say "not usually," but before I could speak Greg chimed in. "As soon as the line is down, go ahead."

"Thanks." Dad nodded at Greg. "Must be one of the perks."

I couldn't believe my dad said something so lame, as if Greg hadn't heard every coffee pun in the world. I rolled my eyes as I turned to prepare his surprise.

Dad found a corner table and was waiting there for me. I put our two drinks on the table, untied my apron, and then sat across from him, cupping my hands around my plain-old Colombian coffee.

He took a sip, then licked his lips. "This isn't half bad. For coffee."

I smiled. "You can hardly call that coffee." I nodded my head toward his cup. "That's a half-caf, espresso shot, with steamed milk and a shot of mocha."

"Yeah," Dad deadpanned, "I thought so."

I lifted the plastic lid from my cup, took a sip, then put the lid back on. One thing I'd learned working here was that I didn't like cold coffee. That was about the only discovery I had made at my mind-numbing job.

My dad took another swallow and then nodded toward my coworkers trying to look busy behind the counter. "I was watching them while I was standing in line. You guys must do everything humanly possible to a coffee bean." One side of his mouth turned up. "Who knew? My creative team could have a field day with an account like this."

Leave it to my dad to turn a coffee break into more work. I took another sip of my coffee, wondering if I should ask why he was here. If he was going to ask if Josh and I needed any help, any money, I wasn't sure what I'd say. Until Josh got his first paycheck, things were tight. I had a feeling even after he got his check we wouldn't be on easy street. I had discovered that a part-time coffee shop job was fine when a person lived with her parents, but not so fine when you were trying to pay rent, car insurance, health insurance —

What health insurance?

I twisted the cup in my hands. Josh and I didn't have health insurance right now. Neither one of our temporary jobs offered the benefit. I didn't dare tell my parents; they'd go ballistic, and I didn't need more stress than I already had. But if Dad did offer to help and I said yes, Josh would be the one throwing a fit.

Dad continued to watch my coworkers as he picked up the black stir-stick and twisted it between his fingers. "As if we need another account right now."

The words were mumbled, but I heard them just fine. Suddenly I had a feeling I knew why he was here. I could feel a slight whooshing in my brain. An over-caffeinated buzz. As it was, this cup was my first of the morning. If my hunch was right, there was another reason for the hum in my head. I held the cup midway between the table and my mouth, a smoke screen for what might come next. I took another sip buying time while I shaped my question. "What gives?"

Before the words were completely out of my mouth, he leaned forward. "Stasha, don't say no. For once, please listen to what

224

I have to say first."

I knew it. I took the lid off my cup, set it aside, and stared into the murky brown liquid. Finally, I looked up. "Dad, if this is about coming to work for you —"

He held up his palm. "Please, just listen."

I already knew the answer to his question, but after the wedding he had given Josh and me, and after the honeymoon of a lifetime, if he wanted to talk I figured I owed him the courtesy of listening.

"Okay, here goes." He set his cup at the edge of the table, then folded the stir-stick between his fingers. "We're shorthanded. I may only need you for a few weeks — a month or two if you can spare it. You already have some experience at the agency. You know how we do things. All I need is another pair of hands for a while. I know you'll make more at the agency than you do here. If you find another job and have to move — fine. Any time you can give me, I'll take."

I didn't want to work at the agency. Not my dad's agency. Not in Carlton. It would be like being back in high school again. All those summers I was the gopher — the go-for-this and go-for-that person. I wanted a real job. A career. And I was willing to wait.

"Dad —"

He cut me off. "Stasha, please, think about my offer before you say no."

A thousand thoughts ran through my head at once — the next-to-negative balance in our checkbook, how I concocted new coffee drinks as a way to help me fall asleep, Josh leaving for work in dress pants, shirt, and a tie, me in blue jeans and a T-shirt. After four years of college, I hadn't come much further than when I was working at the agency all those summers ago. But I wasn't about to give up my dream.

I looked up from my coffee, into his eyes. "Dad, I don't have to think about it."

He was already shaking his head, anticipating the answer we both knew was coming.

I looked over at the coffee counter at my coworkers mixing shots of syrup in a cup and daring each other to drink them. I looked at the old man who sat at a table in the window. Same man, same table, every morning. Reading the newspaper word for word, nursing his plain coffee and one free refill for two hours.

The words that came next surprised both of us. "Okay, I'll do it."

LAURA

"And then there are the cutting instruments to consider. For some quilts you'll need to cut out the same shape up to 200 times."

There was a mild gasp, probably from me. The fact I was sitting in a quilting class instead of asking Donnie to choose between the agency or our marriage had me in a dumbfounded stupor. I still wasn't quite sure how Carla's late afternoon phone reminder convinced me I needed to be here instead of doing what I had planned for months.

I looked to either side of me. The group wasn't large. The instructor held up a finger and looked straight at me. "Now I don't mean to scare anyone; I hope you look at this as a challenge. Quilting can be as basic as sewing large random square patches together with a machine" — she paused as if she were being transported to someplace far away from the high school classroom where we were being held captive — "or it can become a highly intricate art form, combining a variety of materials, colors, threads, and imagination."

Imagination. The first word she had said all night that captivated me. All evening my mind bounced between what I had thought my evening would hold — the beginning of the end of my marriage as I knew it — and the surreal reality of a beginners quilting class.

Out of the corner of my eye I sneaked a look at Carla. Quilting? Was she serious? I was beginning to think I'd prefer the trapeze class. At least then I'd be doing something, not just sitting here trying to figure out where in the heck I was going to find a template and a rotary cutter. Already I was wondering how much they would bring in when I sold them at the church rummage sale next spring — when this class would just be a memory.

Oh, good grief. I crossed my arms over my chest. I had made up my mind. If Carla bought the stuff, I'd borrow it from her, but I wasn't going to invest an arm and a leg in her passing fancy. I still had two boxes somewhere down in the basement filled with half-finished cross-stitch projects and practically the whole line of DMC six-strand embroidery floss. I had scoffed at that hobby, too, when Carla conned me into trying it. Then I got hooked and couldn't stop, until one day I realized I was spending all those hours stitching someone else's vision, filling tiny squares with colored thread as if it was some sort of fine art. Well, maybe it was, but not for me. If I was going to spend all that time at something, I wanted it to be my vision, my art.

And so . . . ? You did . . . what?

I looked at my lap. I had quit cross-stitching and joined the Carlton Art Guild. Got my art fix secondhand instead of doing what I really wanted, which was painting.

The instructor gathered her demonstration materials into a plastic bin. "For our next session, you'll need to bring the basic supplies on the list I handed out. Select one of the three pattern choices and be prepared to start cutting your fabric."

It was as if we were at the Indy 500: "Ladies, start your scissors."

"Oh." She looked at the ten of us. "Don't forget to pick up your fats."

I turned and looked at Carla. "Fats?"

"I'll tell you later," she whispered.

I glanced across Carla at Judy. She shrugged her shoulders. She didn't know either.

"Caaa-rrr-la!" I rolled my chin through the air like a whiny three-year-old. "I don't want to learn how to quilt." We were sitting at Applebee's sharing a Thai chicken pizza. It was hardly enough for the three of us — Carla, Judy, and reluctant me. Apparently just the idea of quilting made me hungry. "Let's order another one. And I still don't get it; why do they call them fats?"

"See? You really are interested." Carla waved our waitress over and pointed at the crumbs on our plate. "Can we have another one of these?" She picked up her water glass and took a sip from the straw. "I don't know why they call them fats. Maybe because it's chunks of fabric tied together, and they look fat. I haven't been in the class any longer than you have."

"But you want to be there. I don't," I countered.

Judy sipped her decaf, strangely quiet. Not at all the raucous wild woman I had known when the three of us were roommates. It had taken me half a semester to warm up to Judy. Everything she did was loud. When she talked on the phone, we heard every word. When she laughed, we covered our ears. If Judy wanted to say something, you might as well stop and listen, because you'd be forced to anyway. Eventually I learned that her boisterous personality was a cover. Judy didn't like being alone. Being the life of every party — even when there wasn't one — was her way of ensuring she'd have people around her. She had settled down a lot in the years since we had roomed together, but she still enjoyed being the center of attention. Good thing she had married Bill, a quiet guy who didn't crave the spotlight. Judy was more the "Let's try belly dancing" type; quilting had to feel like sitting in quicksand to her. I had a feeling we were both getting sucked into some kind of muck. I looked to Judy for backup. "I can't believe you want to take this class."

I expected her to bellow, "Thank you. Thank you. I thought for sure all three of us had lost our sanity. Quilting! Just call me Betsy Ross. Now let's find something fun to do." Instead she twirled her teaspoon in her fingers and said, "It's something to do."

I lowered my chin and looked at her through the slits that had become my eyes. "What have you done with Judy?" Our old joke when someone acted out of character.

Carla widened her eyes at me as a warning.

"What?"

Just then a loud cheer broke out from a table near the bar. Our heads turned automatically. A group of college guys were cheering for something on TV.

"At least someone is having fun." Judy took another sip of coffee and looked at me over the raised rim. "Bill left me."

"No." My eyes flicked to Carla. She blinked slowly. Confirmation. She already knew. Another thing she was going to tell me later.

Judy nodded as she set her cup on the table. "Three weeks ago."

Right after Stasha's wedding. I wasn't quite sure why, but my heart started thudding inside my chest. Her words hit a mark she hadn't been aiming at.

If I'd had my way tonight, I would have been discussing this very thing right about now. I doubted I would have chosen Applebee's for my confession, though. But I couldn't think about my problems now. It was Judy who needed my attention. "But why? I thought you two were —"

"The perfect couple?"

People think the same thing about Donnie and you.

I pushed the thought aside. "Well," I gazed into my coffee cup. On more than one occasion I had wondered how mild-mannered Bill could put up with boisterous Judy day in, day out for all those years. I knew how often she got on my nerves even now, but I would never say that to her. "No one's perfect." Let her think I meant Bill.

"True." Judy wrapped her hands around her coffee mug, her support of some sort. She lowered her eyes. "He was verbally abusive. It got bad."

"Bill?" My tone might as well have said, "I don't believe you."

Her eyes met mine. "I didn't believe it either at first."

"What would he say?"

Carla nudged my leg under the table and gave me a look that said we could talk about this later, alone. But it was too late.

"Oh-hh," Judy tilted her chin in the air and blinked rapidly. "It started with things like telling me not to talk so loud. Hey, I grew up in a home with six kids; we had to talk loud. Old habits are hard to break, but I tried talking softer. Then he started telling me how what I said was stupid, that no one cared about what I had to say." She paused and licked her lips as if tasting the bitter words. "It was worse when he was drinking."

We had been together with Bill and Judy

as couples dozens of times, and we all had a drink or two, but I had never seen him out of control. "Bill drinks?"

Judy looked down at her cup. "Oh yeah. He drinks."

What else didn't I know? I leaned forward to hear more just as the server brought our second Thai pizza. "Here you go." She picked up the empty dish and replaced it with a steaming platter. Carla and I stared at the chicken and cheese as if we had never seen a pizza before. Judy pointed at the plate. "You want any of this?"

Not anymore. We both shook our heads. She slid out of the booth, picked up the pizza, and carried it to the table of college guys. Her voice carried across the restaurant. "Here you go, boys. Enjoy." Her return trip was followed by shouts of "Thanks!" and "You rock!"

Judy waved to the guys as if she didn't have a care in the world, slid back in the booth, and picked up her coffee cup. "Where were we? Oh yeah, Bill. As if I could forget." She lifted a shoulder. "What can I say? He's gone. I gave him an ultimatum — me or the booze. Guess which he picked?" Her eyes filled with tears. "Doesn't do much for a gal's self-esteem."

My mouth felt like a gaping hole, a clown's

mouth waiting for a bean bag to be thrown in. "What are you going to do?"

What will you *do?* That was the real question, the one I didn't dare ask myself. I waited for Judy's answer, wondering if whatever she said would give me some direction.

She took a deep breath, looked at Carla and then at me. "Right now I'm going to take a quilting class."

Well then, so was I.

Why did I feel as if the rug had been pulled out from under me? Instead of turning left, the route that would take me home from the restaurant, I turned right, as if I could drive away from Judy's announcement.

Her words rang in my ears. *He's verbally abusive. It's worse when he drinks. He chose booze over me.* Suddenly, my brooding these past weeks seemed incredibly petty, as if sitting alone in a quiet, beautiful home, waiting for my faithful husband to get home from running his lucrative business, was hard duty. So what if I spent a lot of time alone? Compared to what Judy had been going through, my life was nirvana.

A sarcastic breath of air puffed from my lips. What did I think I would say to Donnie tonight? That I wanted to end our perfectly fine marriage? I should have my head examined. I should have thanked Carla for insisting I attend the quilting class. I should be thanking my lucky stars —

Or Me . . .

A peculiar chill ran down my arms. Had Carla's idea of taking a quilting class been entirely her idea? Had her insistent call this afternoon been instigated only by her?

Oh, Lord. I closed my eyes for the briefest of seconds as I drove down the nearly empty four-lane road. I opened them; I needed to see exactly where I was going, or rather, where I had been headed. If I'd had my way tonight, my marriage could very well be over. Instead, as unlikely as it seemed, I had spent the evening at a quilting class, of all things — an intervention by fabric, needle, and thread.

I am the Weaver . . .

I hadn't sought God about any of this. My guide had been my hard heart — my self-serving righteousness, my wounded pride and hurt feelings. I could change all that now. I pressed the blinker and turned toward home.

Forgive me for what I've been thinking, secretly planning. Help me see all the good things in my life. In Donnie. Give me a new attitude about my marriage. Help me be grate-

ful for what I have. Help me to quit picking at what I don't.

As I drove toward home, I imagined the small, Tiffany-style lamp I knew was lit in my front window. Carla, Judy, and I had sat at Applebee's much longer than I had anticipated. Donnie would be home by now. He must have found the note I had left.

Sorry, something came up with Carla. Let's talk tomorrow night.

I wondered if he had been even the tiniest bit peeved that I was the one to be a no-show for a change. It would do him good to find out what it felt like to get stood up.

So, you're retracting your prayer already?

The heat of conviction seared under my coat. How was it that within seconds of praying for my marriage, I could climb right back onto my high horse and start galloping?

I'd try again. *Lord, let me see Donnie through new eyes. The eyes that once saw only his love for me, and mine for him.*

There. That was better. In a couple of miles I would be home. Donnie would be there. It wasn't often he was the one waiting for me. Tonight would be different — a chance for a new start. Who knew? Maybe he would be waiting up. We could sit together, snuggle on the couch. We hadn't done that in —

Snuggling . . . that's not all we hadn't done lately. We hadn't made love in — Anger burned in my chest. Was it terrible to want to be hugged now and then? Touched? Loved? When was the last time . . . ?

To tell the truth, I couldn't even remember. All I knew was that it was sometime before that *other* night. The night, the date — I remembered it all too well. I might as well have written it on the calendar. But no need; it was seared in my brain. Such a stupid ritual, when I stopped to think about it. "Birthday in the Bedroom," we called it. I cringed thinking about it now. While some of my friends had no qualms talking about their sex lives, I had never been one to talk about that sort of thing. Good thing. I'd die of embarrassment if one of my girlfriends ever asked if we celebrated Donnie's birthday last January the way we always did.

We had invented our private celebration on Donnie's birthday the first year we were married. We didn't always "celebrate" in the bedroom, though. I couldn't help but smile as I remembered how inventive we thought we were, as if we had discovered something no one else had ever tried. We had been so young and naïve in our own way. But that was okay. It worked for us, for a long time.

Until this past birthday, nine long months ago.

"That was nice." I pulled my coat around me and tightened my scarf as we left the restaurant. A biting January wind whipped around my legs. I should have worn slacks on such a freezing night, but it was Donnie's birthday, and I wanted to look special.

"Yeah." Donnie turned his back to the wind and buttoned his leather coat. "Nice." His tone held the same distraction it had all night.

"Where's the car?" I stood on tiptoes and faced into the wind. Donnie had dropped me off at the door on our way to his birthday dinner. I had been secretly hoping he would offer to let me wait in the restaurant while he went and brought the car around.

"It's this way." He bent his head into the wind and started walking.

I scrunched my neck down into the collar of my coat and followed. Irritation bit at me as sharply as the crystallized snow pitting against my nylon-covered legs. How many times over the past years had I told Donnie how cold and treacherous it was to walk outside in a North Dakota winter in heels? It wouldn't pay to remind him now. He would say what he always did: "Dress warmer."

I didn't want to start an argument, not on his birthday. I stood on my side of the car as Donnie fumbled through four pockets trying to locate the car keys. How could he not know where they were? Couldn't he feel the bulge of his overloaded key ring weighing down one of his pockets? Every time we went out, he — we — went through this same song and dance.

I tried to keep my chattering teeth together and bite back the words on my tongue. They slipped out. "Hurry up!"

As he pulled the keys from one of his pockets and opened the door, Donnie threw a look at me over the roof of the car. If only I had been able to hold the words in for a few more seconds. If only he had thought to use our automatic starter and have the car warmed.

"Isn't the auto-start working?" It was a not-so-subtle dig. I leaned over and turned the fan on high.

Donnie snapped it down to low. "All you're going to get is cold air. Let the car warm up first."

"We'll be home by the time the car is warm."

How many winters had we had this exact same conversation? Each of us trying to prove we knew the most about thermodynamics, or whatever it was that caused men and women to live at completely opposite ends of the body-temperature spectrum. I burrowed down into my coat, determined not to move until the air around me warmed up or we arrived home. Already I could imagine the warmth of my electric blanket.

After the stilted conversation Donnie manufactured this evening, I certainly didn't feel the least bit romantic. I cast a sidelong glance at my husband. It certainly didn't look like he had sex on his mind either.

But we had always celebrated Birthday in the Bedroom. A transparent cloud of warm air followed my sigh into the cold car. If Donnie didn't remember, would it be so bad if I didn't remind him?

"Tradition" — the tune of the old song from *Fiddler on the Roof* echoed in my head. Just because we had always ended his birthday with the same tradition, would it be so terrible if this one year we skipped it? I didn't feel like making love, not one bit, not after the aloof way Donnie acted all through dinner. Whatever he had on his mind seemed more important than talking to me.

Feelings follow action.

I knew. I had learned the truth of those

three words when Stasha was an infant. How often did I feel like changing her diaper? Feel like walking her across the floor as she wailed? Feel like giving her a bath during those few weeks when she was deathly afraid of water? And yet, even in those times when I hadn't felt like caring for her, somehow simply going through the motions had kindled a deeper sort of love.

In all our years of marriage I certainly hadn't felt like having sex every time Donnie did, but I had learned that feelings really did follow actions. The times I had turned him down — and there had been plenty of those times when Stasha was a toddler — I was left carrying a load of guilt on a cold shoulder as heavy as a block of ice. The times I greeted Donnie's sometimes-stumbling overtures with a soft kiss and a hug almost always helped bridge an emotional gap that often hung between us in those early years.

It was easy to remember the days when I was a stressed-out young woman, trying to figure out how to be a wife, hold down a job, and encourage Donnie in the business he was trying to build. Then Stasha came along, adding more stress. I had learned that both marriage and making love were often about compromise.

If it was Donnie's birthday, it was tradition. It wouldn't kill me to set aside my frustration with his preoccupation over dinner, to overlook the 30 feet of icy parking lot I'd had to tiptoe across, to ignore the cold car that was slowly warming. Feelings follow action. When we got home, I would take action. Hopefully, the feelings would follow.

We didn't talk as we drove the short distance home. I doubted Donnie had a clue about the thoughts tumbling around in my brain. I often wondered how men could be so oblivious to women's emotions.

I sat silent as Donnie pulled the car into the garage and then turned off the engine. He had refused to let me tell the waiter it was his birthday. I had been hoping for at least a cupcake to share after dinner. Now my mind scrambled through my kitchen shelves trying to come up with a makeshift birthday cake. I had quit baking him one the year Stasha went off to college. A two-layer cake lasted much too long when there were only two people to whittle away at it. Would a piece of banana bread count?

"Well," I said as I stepped from the garage into the kitchen, determined to salvage what was left of the night. "Would you like some ice cream? I think I have some hot fudge topping in the cupboard. I'll heat it up." I left out the part about the small candle I was planning as a centerpiece on his sundae.

"No thanks," he said. "I'm full." He slipped off his coat and carried it to the hall closet, holding out his hand to take mine.

"Are you sure?" I forced a smile. "It's your birthday. It's not official until you blow out a candle and make a wish."

He hung up the coats. "I have to review the Westwood Mall media plan tonight."

"Tonight?" I could feel my eyebrows rise. "It's —" I looked at my wristwatch — "after nine." It felt much later. Nine o'clock wasn't later than many of his late-night work sessions.

"Yeah, I know. That's why I need to get at it. We've got a meeting with the Westwood folks in the morning."

"Oh." Why did I feel like a balloon with a slow leak? As if my good intentions were slowly evaporating into thin air?

"Thanks for tonight. Dinner was nice." Donnie leaned over and kissed my cheek.

My cheek. Did he really not remember his birthday tradition?

He closed the closet door and began walking toward the den. Suddenly an image of an imp — make that a sultry vixen — flowed through me. Well. If he really didn't remember, I'd make him recall our annual celebration.

"Donnie?" I stood in the entry and crooked my finger as he turned. "Come here."

"What?" He looked puzzled as he slowly turned and stepped my way.

I took a measured step to meet him and waited as he drew near. I put my arms over his shoulders, pulled him close, and whispered in his ear. "I have a present for you." I molded my body close to his so there would be no doubt what kind of gift I had in mind.

His arms wrapped around me. He held me in a long, tight hug and then released me as if I had been dropped into a snowbank. "Can I take a rain check?" he asked. "I've just got so much to do tonight."

A hot flush filled me, a different sort of heat than I had been feeling a second earlier. I was embarrassed at the way I had thrown myself at my husband and humiliated by the way he had so abruptly turned me away. His rejection stung as if he had slapped me.

That had been nine months ago. Months when the bitter hurt of dismissal hung between us like a thick wall. Had Donnie even noticed that we hadn't made love in all those months? I hadn't meant to count, but my subconscious did. The first few months mortification and anger kept me from turning to Donnie for solace. Somewhere along the line, those feelings turned into a stalemate. If Donnie didn't need me, I didn't need him. Eventually my hurt feelings turned into a lazy complacency. It was easy to put on my nightgown, read my book, turn out the light, and go to sleep. Was a sexless marriage so bad? At least we didn't fight.

You're not being loved, either.

I tried to ignore that part. Some days, some nights, were easier than others.

You're lonely.

As I pulled into the driveway, tears filled my eyes. Was being lonely reason enough for divorce? After listening to Judy's story tonight, my reasoning seemed fuzzy at best.

With any luck, Donnie would be in bed, asleep. I'd have another long night to examine my feelings and decide what I should do.

Feelings follow action.

Okay. I got it. Tonight I wouldn't do anything. Tomorrow I would do my best to change my attitude toward my husband. Deep down, I knew he was a good man. He wasn't verbally abusive like Judy's husband.

He didn't drink to excess. He wasn't unfaithful as my friend Sheila's husband had been.

When I thought about my marriage in those terms, about all the things Donnie could be besides a workaholic, I felt remorse for all the little failings I'd held against him. I could change things, starting tonight. I'd go into the house, hang up my coat, get undressed, crawl into bed, and scoot all the way over to Donnie's side.

As I drove into the garage and watched the garage door slide down behind me, it didn't escape my notice that in my schedule for the night I had left out "put on my nightgown." I got out of the car and tried to hold back a mischievous grin. I could already imagine Donnie's sleepy surprise, feel his arms surround my bare skin. My plan was long overdue.

Earlier tonight I had been prepared to throw our marriage away. After talking to Judy and God, I was ready to do what it would take to salvage what was left and try to build something new.

I let myself into the house and looked for the note I had left on the table for Donnie. Gone. Good — that meant Donnie was home. At this hour he'd be in bed. I set my purse on the counter and slipped my coat onto the back of a chair. I tiptoed up the stairs and down the hall, although as soundly as Donnie usually slept I could have been wearing cement shoes and kicking a bowling ball ahead of me and he wouldn't have woken up. Even so, I wanted this reconciliation of sorts to be a surprise.

The bedroom was dark, and with just the light from the hall, it was hard to see all the way over to the far end of our large bedroom to the bed where Donnie would be slumbering away without an inkling of what was about to happen to him. I slipped out of my shoes and tiptoed into the room. "Whaa-aat in the —" I clamped my hand over my mouth as I tripped over what felt like a leather-bound rock on the floor just inside the door. "Ouch!" I couldn't help it. My toes hurt! I lay there for a second, rubbing my big toe, waiting for Donnie to wake up and turn on the light.

Nothing. No sound from the bed. No light. As my eyes became accustomed to the darkness I could make out the bulky form of Donnie's briefcase by our bedroom door. No wonder my foot hurt. He carried what he called the "brains" of the agency home in that bag every night — a bag containing a never-ending pile of paperwork that felt like an iron brick against my foot. I got on my hands and knees to get up. Certainly Donnie hadn't slept through all my commotion.

"Donnie?" I whispered. No sound of rustling from the bed. If my big toe quit throbbing, maybe I could carry on with my plan of a love attack. Gently I stood, testing my foot. It was aching, but whole. Light from a nearly full moon filtered through the bedroom curtains. Now that my eyes had adjusted, the room seemed almost illuminated. The bed was neatly made.

How could that be? My hand groped for the light switch on the bedside lamp. My eyes needed proof. The room was empty. No Donnie. Instant anger surged through me. *What?* Had he come home, checked the kitchen, the family room, the bedroom, my usual haunts, and then thought he was home free?

In my renewed anger I had no trouble imagining his thoughts. *Ah . . . we don't have to "talk" tonight. Laura's gone, and I have the house to myself. Whatever was so important will probably be forgotten by tomorrow. It's my lucky day . . . make that night.*

I scanned the room. Somehow my brain couldn't register the fact that he really wasn't here. Had Donnie's car not been in the garage when I pulled in and I simply hadn't noticed? His parking space was usually empty when I drove in. It would be more likely for me to notice if his car *had* been there than not. As hard as I tried to recall I couldn't. As if I expected him to be hiding somewhere, I opened the door to the walk-in closet and peered in. Then it dawned on me; at loose ends without me home, he had more than likely wandered downstairs and was asleep in front of the television set.

I didn't recall hearing the TV, but I went back down the stairs. No, the television wasn't on, nor was Donnie asleep in the recliner. I had already been through the kitchen. Other than a glance into the living room and the den, there was nowhere else to look. I doubted he would be down in our messy basement this time of night. Even so, I opened the door and called down. "Donnie?" It was dark and silent.

Where was he? He wouldn't be at the office without his briefcase.

A devil of suspicion danced on my shoulder. After all his years of long hours at the office, this wasn't the first time it crossed my mind he might be seeing someone. Even so, I'd never had reason to think he might be. No notes in a pocket, no lipstick on a collar. Not that I looked closely, but I wasn't stupid. I watched *Oprah.* I knew the signs.

I poked my head out the kitchen door and into the garage. Sure enough, his car was gone. How did I not notice that?

My anger turned to puzzlement as I climbed the stairs to our bedroom. My husband wasn't home, and it was almost midnight. All the evidence, the little bit I had, was against him.

Two could play this game, if you could call the unraveling of a marriage a game. I would change into my nightgown and robe and wait up for him. I would get the explanation from the horse's mouth . . . although that wasn't exactly the body part that came to mind right now. I walked into the closet, stepped out of my clothes, and slipped my nightgown over my head. A few minutes ago I had been thinking of making love to Donnie; now my strongest urge was to wring his neck.

My robe was in the bathroom. Before I went downstairs to slow-cook my annoyance, I needed to wash off my makeup. I pushed my feet into my slippers and then shuffled to the bathroom. As I reached for my robe, I noticed a slip of paper on the counter. It took only a glance to recognize Donnie's scrawl. My heart started an erratic thump. What if Donnie had also been contemplating ending our marriage and beat me to it? What if I was the one being left? Panic filled me. As often as I had thought that leaving Donnie would solve my problems, now I could clearly see it wouldn't.

Lord. Lord. A silent, desperate prayer . . . for what, I wasn't quite sure. Tentatively I reached for the note.

MOM TAKEN TO HOSPITAL BY AMBU-LANCE. LEAVING NOW. MEDFIRST. CALL ME. D.

Oh, Lord. A different prayer this time, but just as desperate. I scrambled back to the closet and pulled on the same clothes I had taken off moments ago. *Please let her be okay.* How much time had I wasted being angry at Donnie tonight? *Be with Donnie.* My mother-in-law might be dying. *Be with the doctors.* I had suspected my husband of having an affair. *Forgive me.* Why in the world had Donnie left me a note? In the bathroom, of all places?

It's the one place he knew you'd see it.

Why hadn't he called?

You had your cell phone turned off all night.

As usual. I didn't live and breathe being connected the way Donnie did. I reached

252

for the bedside phone and speed-dialed Donnie's cell number. I tapped my foot as it rang. *Pick up.* I should have run downstairs and called from my cell phone on the way to the hospital.

"Laura?" One word, tense and relieved all at the same time.

"It's me. What's wrong?"

He sighed before he spoke. "They think she had another stroke." For a second his voice was muffled. I could hear another voice in the background. Donnie spoke again. "I'm not supposed to use my cell phone here. Can you believe it? Wait a sec."

It wasn't often someone told Donnie Dunn he couldn't do something. In the midst of all this, I found that thought comforting. If sheer willpower could see to it that Eleanor got the best of the best, Donnie would do just that.

"You still there?" He was back.

"Yes."

"I'm still not sure how Mom ended up here. She must have called 911 herself. I got a call from the hospital around ten."

"You've been there two hours?" I could imagine Donnie looking at his wrist.

"It seems longer."

I remembered the day I had found Eleanor lying on her living room floor. I knew how long a minute could feel when you were waiting for help, for answers.

"How is she?"

There was a shaky breath from Donnie's end of the line. "Not good."

"What?" I hadn't expected that. In this day and age, at 70 Eleanor was still considered young. She was also healthy, for someone who had had a mild stroke, anyway.

"Laura, the doctor isn't sure she's going to make it through the night."

"What?" And to think that while this had been unfolding I had been sitting at Applebee's, thinking of leaving my husband. "Are you still there?" I wasn't sure if he was still on the phone. There was a huff of air into the phone. *Was he crying?*

"Donnie?" I wanted to hug him. Hold him.

Another puff. A gasp for air. He had never been good about expressing his feelings. "I'll be there, Donnie. I'm coming as fast as I can." I hurried down the stairs, grabbed my coat, snatched my purse, and ran to the car. As I backed the car out of the driveway and turned toward the hospital, Donnie's last words echoed in my brain: "I need you, Laura."

How could I have ever thought I didn't care about this man? That we weren't somehow connected at the heart?

"I need you, Laura."

"I'm coming," I said into the night.

DONNIE

"I need you, Laura"? What had I been thinking? I shut off my cell phone, snapped it shut, and slipped it into my pocket. I blinked my eyes a few times. Hard. There was no need to get emotional. As far as I knew, Barbara Walters wasn't doing an interview with me tonight. I straightened my shoulders. A deep breath, two, would go a long way toward getting much-needed oxygen to my addled brain. I needed to be at the top of my game when I went back to talk to the doctor. The prognosis he had laid out was not acceptable. I was going to make sure he knew that.

I took a couple of steps, paused while the emergency room doors slid open, then stepped outside. Crisp early October. The brisk night air was exactly what I needed.

I rubbed the back of my neck, trying to relieve the tightness there. Maybe my refusal to take "Sorry, there's not much we can do but wait" for an answer was due to some latent gene left over from my Depression-era grandparents. As far as I could remember, no one had ever said, "Donnie, you have to be tough." It was just something I knew. It was who I was. Tough, do-it-yourself Donnie.

And how's that working for you?

Fine. I walked out from under the canopy that hung over the emergency entrance, out to where I could see the almost full moon. It was a mystery how the sky could look so calm when just behind me my mother's life lay in the balance.

It's not the sky that's calm, Donnie, it's the heavens. It's all in My control.

A huff of air puffed from my lips. If only it was that easy, turning everything over to God. I had no doubt that if the inside of my mother's brain was still functioning, she was praying. More than likely not for herself . . . probably for me. I blinked up at the stars. *Oh, God . . .* It had been a long time since I had prayed. *God . . . My mom . . .*

I stopped. What was the use? Who knew if He even heard someone like me?

I do . . .

I was overtired. My mind was taxed to the limit. I rubbed my hands against my face, the faint stubble of my midnight beard scratching them. I'd have to remember to shave, or Mom would be sure to remind me. If she ever spoke again.

No. I refused to think the grim thought. She would speak again. She'd sit up and walk. I was sure of it. If the Carlton doctors didn't have answers, I'd find doctors who did.

I turned. It was time I got back to my mother's side and start her on the path to recovery, if I had to see to it myself. That stubborn philosophy had served me well when I was getting the agency up and running. It kept me hanging on when more than one client had left for another firm. It was all part of the game. Setbacks didn't defeat me, they made me want to work all the harder to prove . . . to prove . . .

What, Donnie?

I paused at the emergency room doors. What *was* I trying to prove? That I was the best at what I did. Period.

I'd love you anyway.

The strange thought stopped me in my tracks. It was something my mom might have said.

Or Me. Listen to Me . . . I'd love you anyway.

A sudden lump pushed its way into my throat. Unconditional love. The love of a mother for a child. My mother.

Or a Father . . .

If I didn't get a grip, they'd be putting me in a double room along with my mom. I straightened and pushed the baggy middle of my shirt into the waistband of my slacks. The doctor's white coat proclaimed his authority. It would be best if I'd look as pulled together as possible when I began the confrontation. *Negotiation,* I reminded myself as I stepped through the doors and walked down the too-bright corridor to the room where my mother lay. The good doctor didn't know he was dealing with Donnie Dunn. Believe me, he would.

"It's going to take time to assess the damage done by this latest stroke, Mr. Dunn." The doctor tugged at the ends of his stethoscope. As young as he looked, his action reminded me of a kid pulling on the strings of a sweatshirt hood. I wondered if it had ever occurred to him that it might be *his* mother lying here someday.

"I understand assessment. What I don't understand is why you can't run those tests right now."

He cleared his throat. Nerves. I could tell. "Right now, we're hoping the medication we've given her will alleviate further damage, like another stroke or a heart attack.

We've got her on a thrombolytic agent and an anticoagulant. Providing she responds . . ."

His eyes darted to my mother, lying inert on the bed. I could read the doubt behind his glance. Tubes protruded from her arms and her nose. A monitor beeped rhythmically near her head. It was a picture out of a movie. Except it was *my* mother.

"I don't think you understand. I want the very best for my mother. Money is no —"

He put a hand on the light blanket covering my mother's foot. "I know you do, Mr. Dunn. We all do. We're doing all we can at this point in time."

"If it means transferring my mother to a larger hospital to get the best care . . ." I left the rest of the sentence to his interpretation. I didn't want to come right out and tell him he looked too inexperienced to know what he was talking about.

"Oh . . . no . . ." Laura stood in the doorway, one hand covering her mouth, her eyes on my mother. She turned her tear-filled gaze to me.

I pressed my lips into a hard line. Falling apart would do my mother no good.

Laura stepped to my side, leaned her head near my shoulder, and rubbed my arm. "How are you doing?"

There was a thickness in my throat. I cleared it away. I nodded my head toward the doctor. "We were just discussing the best treatment options."

The doctor held out his hand. "I'm Dr. Banning. You are . . . ?"

"His wife," Laura said. "Eleanor's daughter-in-law. Laura Dunn. How is she?" As upset as Laura had seemed when she walked in the door, she got down to business surprisingly fast.

The doctor flicked his eyes to me, then away. As if he knew he should look me in the eye but couldn't do it. His voice held apology as he directed his comments to Laura. "She's not well. I had hoped for better brain activity by now. Her low level of consciousness leads me to suspect Mrs. Dunn may have suffered a cerebral hemorrhage."

"A what — ?" My words were louder than intended, but they seemed to get his attention. It was the first time he had mentioned a hemorrhage in my presence. "You suspect?" Was he grasping at straws? "I want definitive answers, not some — some —" I waved a hand in the air — "speculation. This isn't the commodities market we're talking about. It's my mother."

"Mr. Dunn." Now he did look into my

eyes, which suddenly worried me more than when he had avoided my gaze. "Every patient we treat is someone's loved one. I understand that. We all do. While medicine can produce great results in many cases, it's an inexact science when it comes to the brain." His eyes rested on my mother for a moment. He motioned his hand toward the door. "Would you step outside with me for a minute?" Laura and I moved just outside the doorway. Dr. Banning stood with his back to the room. His voice was low. "I do understand your concern for your mother. I'm concerned, too. I need to tell you there is an extremely high rate of death associated with cerebral hemorrhage. My immediate task is to keep her alive through the next few hours. If she survives the night, then we can think about what the future might hold."

From somewhere deep inside, it felt as if my heart was being thwacked by one of those thick, padded mallets used in ancient-Chinese-gong-rituals. Dr. Banning's voice reverberated. *Death. Death. High rate of death.*

It was Laura who spoke. "What can we do to help?"

Dr. Banning sighed deeply. It suddenly occurred to me that this night had not been any shorter for him, than it had for me . . . or my mother. Giving him a hard time wasn't going to serve my mother any better. I chimed in. "Tell us, what can we do?"

He hesitated. "If you're praying people, I'd advise you to start."

I had already tried praying and I hadn't gotten very far. But Laura nodded. "I already am. What else?"

A surge of warm love flooded through me. Laura and I hadn't had much to test our relationship in recent years, unless a couple bad colds and a nasty case of the flu counted. Sure, we'd had an aunt or uncle pass away. A couple of our friends. But none particularly close. My dad had died before I met Laura, and both her parents passed away within a couple of years after our marriage. Anastasia hadn't ever broken a bone, or even needed stitches. If the phrase, *We'd led a charmed life,* wasn't a cliché, I'd apply it to our life. I put an arm around Laura's shoulder.

A nurse paused near the three of us and Dr. Banning looked her way. "Doctor, you're wanted in ICU."

He nodded, then turned back to us. "We'll get some scans of your mother's brain as soon as she stabilizes. We'll move her to ICU and monitor her through the night.

The next several hours are critical. I'd advise you to stay in touch with the hospital."

"We'll be staying." Laura's tone left no doubt.

If I ever won the lottery, I'd refurbish the ICU waiting room. La-Z-boy recliners. Blankets. A plasma TV with a remote just for guys like me. I stifled a groan. As short and restless as the night had been, it was good to know my sense of humor was intact. From my uncomfortable vantage point on a vinyl couch, I opened my eyes and scanned the small waiting area. The low drone of the TV was the only thing that reminded me of home. I peeled my damp hand and the side of my face off the imitation leather and pushed myself into a semi-sitting position. Laura was curled up in a chair that looked more suited to a visit to the principal's office than it did for sleeping. Someone I vaguely remembered wandering in sometime after 3:00 a.m. was now dozing on the other couch. The smell of burnt coffee served to remind me I needed a Mountain Dew.

I swung my legs off the couch and stood, stretching to loosen what felt like a permanent kink in my back. Even though Laura and I had been up and down a half-dozen times during the night to check on my mother, the mild exercise wasn't enough to counteract the effects of a bad couch.

I wandered into the wide corridor and looked for a pop machine. Finding none, I headed toward the elevator. The cafeteria would be sure to have what I craved, if it was open. As the elevator doors opened I looked at my watch. A little after 5:30 am. I rubbed my face. If I were 30 years younger, I might be able to pass my stubble off as hip and urban. As it was, I needed a shave and a shower before I went into the office in two hours. *You can't go to work. Nothing's changed overnight. Your mother is hanging between life and death.*

I *had* to go into work today. I knew that my mother, if she were cognizant, would understand. Whatever was going to happen over the next few hours would happen whether I was by her side or in the office. I'd stop back at lunchtime. If anything changed, Laura would call. Besides, today was the day Stasha was starting at the agency. I needed to be there to make sure she was assigned to the right project.

Matt can handle that.

No. I needed to be there. Stasha's presence at the agency had come with a caveat . . .

"I'll only work for you if you promise me one thing." Stasha wrapped the strings of her apron around her hand. I wasn't sure who she was imagining she was strangling.

Maybe me. "Anything." I held up my right palm as a promise. "What is it?"

Stasha untangled her hand from the strings. She leaned forward across the small coffee shop table. "I don't want people thinking the only reason I got this job is because I'm related to you." Under her breath she added, "Even though it is."

"It is not," I shot back. "What do you think I wrote all those tuition checks for? My health? If I remember right, you have a degree in communications. You are *exactly* who we're looking to hire."

She rolled her eyes.

"Would I lie to my own daughter?"

"See." She sat back in her chair. "That's what I'm getting at." She tied the strings of her apron into a bow and then pulled it apart as she looked into my eyes. "You have to *promise* not to treat me like your daughter. The other people can't either."

I chuckled. "What am I supposed to do, give them lobotomies?"

"Very funny." Another eye roll. "You have to tell them the deal."

I tilted my chair onto the back two legs, pushed back, and balanced there as my mind clicked off the key people in the office. Now that Arlene had gone, there were only a few people left who had been at the agency during Stasha's high school summers, when she'd been our errand-runner. In the four years she'd been away at college she had spent her summers away from Carlton. Her time at the agency was limited to a Christmas break drop-by to say hi. I thought of her high school graduation photo on the credenza in my office. It didn't even look like the young woman sitting across from me. I lowered the chair legs to the floor. "I don't think that will be a problem, Mrs. MacKay."

Ah-ha. Score one point for Dad. Stasha couldn't help but smile. She struggled to pull in the corners of her mouth. "I'm serious, Dad."

I pointed a finger at her. "Don't call me Dad. I'm Mr. Dunn to you."

Once again she smiled.

I pushed away from the table and stood. "Usually I give my new employees a firm handshake. Would you allow me one exception?" I held out my arms.

Stasha smiled as she slowly nodded her head and stepped into my embrace, hugging me in return. As her head pressed against my chest, I heard her murmur, "I'm serious about this, Dad."

"Me too, Mrs. MacKay. Me too."

That was why I wanted to be at the office this morning for Stasha's first day. There would be no favoritism. I would run interference if I had to. *Now there's a catch-22.* Having Stasha at the agency might be harder than I thought it would be.

I stepped off the hospital elevator and followed the signs to the cafeteria. I'd grab a Dew and a cup of fresh coffee for Laura, make a brief stop to check on Mom, then head home for a shower. Laura had called Stasha late last night to tell her about her grandmother but had convinced her it was unnecessary for her to come . . . yet. Laura would call Stasha if anything changed. So far, it hadn't.

The clink of dishes let me know I was almost at the cafeteria and that it was open. I should have guessed almost everything in a hospital ran 24/7. An ice-cold Dew was just what I needed to jump-start what I knew would be another long day.

A quick survey of the cafeteria told me things were self-serve. I grabbed the largest cup available, filled it with ice, then pressed the Mountain Dew button. A small spurt of yellowed liquid trickled out, then stopped. I pressed the button again. Nothing. This couldn't be. I looked around. A sleepy-eyed cashier caught my eye. I pointed to the dispenser and raised my eyebrows.

"Uh, yah," she said as if she had no idea what a caffeine-addiction felt like. "Must be out. Someone will change it. Hang on."

Hang on. That's all I'd been doing since ten o'clock last night.

Longer than that.

A thick line of tension stretched tight inside my head and pulled into the base of my neck, into that tight muscle in my shoulder. A bass fiddle string waiting to be plucked.

Or snapped.

It didn't take much thought to imagine what the reverberation would feel like. As if the string had already been twanged, I drummed my fingers against the side of my icy cup. Images of the stack of work waiting for me on my desk crowded between the pictures of my mother during the night. The ER, the ICU, the flicker of fluorescent lights, the soft beep of monitors. Dr. Banning's words, "High death rate." Stasha starting work today only served to remind me how short-staffed we were. The Martin account, Carlton Industries, Brody — they all needed attention. Not to mention our regular clients. And in all the commotion I'd never once thought to ask Laura what she wanted to discuss.

Without thinking I pressed the side of the chilly cup against the back of my neck. Cold comfort.

"Long night?"

I looked to my left. "Stan?" Quickly I wiped the condensation from the cup against my slacks and reached out my hand to shake his. The last time I'd seen Stan had been at Stasha's wedding. He was a client and business friend. "What are you doing here?"

"I suppose I should ask you the same thing." By the relaxed look on his face, I had a hunch that his purpose here wasn't quite as traumatic as mine.

"My mother," I explained. "They think she had a stroke last night."

"How's she doing?"

It was harder to say the words than I thought. "Not good."

Stan lowered his gaze for a moment. "I'm sorry to hear that."

Somehow sympathy only made me feel worse. "What about you? Are you as desperate for a Dew as I am?"

"Coffee's my vice." He held up a half-full

cup. "Actually, I was hoping to find some cigars. The bubble-gum variety." He grinned. "First grandchild an hour ago."

"You're kidding!" My mind scrambled. Did he have two daughters or three? Or was it two girls and a boy? What were their names? I had a vague recollection of being at a wedding. Or had he introduced me to his kids when we bumped into each other at Westwood Mall? Laura would remember. I covered my ignorance by shaking his hand, again. "Congratulations, Grandpa."

"That sounds so weird," he said, still smiling.

"Get used to it." I took a sip of the melted ice at the bottom of my cup. "So, boy or girl?"

Another grin. "Boy. Joshua."

If he did have three girls, now would be a good time to tease him about finally adding a guy to the family. One of these days I planned to start paying more attention to these sorts of things. For now, all I could say was, "That's my son-in-law's name."

"I remember. Guess it's still a popular name."

"Guess so." Idle chit-chat was better than thinking about the day ahead or the night I'd just spent. As Stan filled me in on the details of his evening, my knowledge of his business acumen somehow didn't compute when I tried to imagine him as a grandfather. All my life I'd prided myself on avoiding clichés, but I had to admit my idea of a grandfather consisted of white hair and a rocking chair. And not much to do.

If that was the case, Stan didn't have time to be a grandfather. The last time we talked, he was thinking about expanding into Minneapolis, the same place I had my eye on. That kind of business commitment wouldn't leave much time for rattle-shaking.

"I'm thinking of selling off a couple of my properties." From somewhere far off Stan's quiet announcement filtered through the clutter of thoughts in my mind. "You interested?"

"What?" I hoped Stan interpreted my question as surprise and didn't recognize that I'd been standing here, phoning in my side of the conversation. "Repeat that?"

Stan chuckled. "Yeah, you heard me right." As he took a sip of his coffee, he grew serious. "My daughter had a lot of trouble with this pregnancy. She was on complete bed rest the last month. A couple of times we were afraid she was going to lose the baby. I don't know," Stan sighed heavily. "Made me wonder what I'm working so hard for."

There were a bunch of things I could think of. His Lexus. His wife's little red sports car. The box he'd bought at the sports arena. His condo in Florida.

He didn't wait for me to remind him. "Do I need more stuff? Or more time?"

Time. I needed it, too. If only money could buy more of it.

"I want to show my grandson how to pitch a curveball." Stan lifted his cup and took the last swallow. "What could be more important than that?"

"Not much," the little-boy, Roger Maris wannabe deep inside said. Another part of me was already calculating which of Stan's properties might interest me. I hadn't thought much beyond the advertising business, but who knew? Maybe there were new fish to fry. *Isn't that a cliché?*

Maybe it was. But it applied perfectly. Someday, when I had a grandchild, I'd have time to be complacent. Until then I planned to capitalize on Stan's urge to downsize. I reached out and clapped Stan on the shoulder. "Enjoy that grandson of yours."

He lifted his empty cup as if toasting me. "I plan to."

"Uh, mister?" The cashier lifted her chin towards the beverage kiosk. "Pop machine's fixed now."

"Thanks." I stepped to the machine, dumped my melting ice, and refilled my cup with my favorite liquid. I really didn't need the jolt I'd been craving from the soda anymore. Stan's offer had sent my adrenaline surging. There was nothing I liked better than a challenge. Who would have guessed my mother's calamity would present an opportunity to me? Right here in a hospital cafeteria, no less.

I dug in my pocket, pulled out two bucks, told the cashier to keep the change. What was a little loose change when I might have so much more in just a matter of months? If I hadn't been holding a cold cup in my hands, I might have rubbed them together. Suddenly I couldn't wait to get to work.

What about your mother?

She'd understand.

So would Laura.

STASHA

Elle leaned her shoulder close to me and motioned with the slightest lift of her chin. My gaze followed hers as my dad breezed by the doorway of the agency coffee room. She lowered her voice. "Mr. Dunn is *so* hot."

It was a good thing I wasn't drinking anything at the moment. If I had been, it would have been spewed across the table where we sat. As it was, I almost choked on the bite of chocolate chip cookie I had in my mouth.

Elle reached toward the plate of cookies on the break table and broke off a piece. "Don't you think?"

I swallowed. Hard. Obviously the few staffers who knew me hadn't spread the word that I was Mr. Dunn's daughter. I didn't know what would be worse — agreeing with Elle or admitting I was his child. In my mind, the word "hot" did not belong

275

in any sentence that included my dad.

I took a deep breath and shot her an annoyed look. "He's married." I had to make this convincing. I silently gulped. "Isn't he?"

She smiled. "I'm not."

Now I was really annoyed. "Besides," I said, trying to sound casual-like, "he's like, what? Almost 50? And you're?" I didn't know how old she was, but I took a general stab at it. "A lot younger."

Elle rolled her eyes and flipped a page of the *InStyle* magazine in front of her. She pointed to a picture of Harrison Ford and the much-younger actress on his arm. "It doesn't matter to them."

I pretended to laugh. "Well, that's Hollywood. In case you don't remember, this is Carlton. *North Dakota.*"

"So what?" She flipped another page. "That's supposed to make me blind? You've got to admit, Mr. Dunn is *choice.*"

Oh, brother. I washed my cookie crumbs down with Diet Coke. "He's not my type, I guess." *You think??* A faint line of perspiration dotted the edges of my hairline, underneath my side-swept bangs. Thank goodness. I wouldn't want Elle to get the impression my father was causing me to break out in a sweat.

So far, Dad had managed to keep our

relationship quiet. Not that it would be the end of the world if someone found out. But if I was going to get a fair chance at making my mark in this business, I wanted to do it without the baggage, or favoritism, that came along with the bloodline. I felt sort of bad keeping the whole truth from Elle. She was turning out to be my first friend here. But then, we had a connection we hadn't known until I walked in that first day.

"Hi!" The tall blonde stopped mid stride as she headed into the ladies room, the same place I was headed. She pointed at me. "You're the girl from the coffee shop. Do you deliver now?"

I recognized her, too, but I didn't remember her being quite so tall. When I worked at Brews-n-News I only saw the top half of people from across the counter. I looked down now. Sure enough, three inch heels lifted her to eye level with me. I certainly remembered Elle, although I didn't know her name then. The guys behind the counter always elbowed each other out of the way to wait on her.

"Actually," I stuck out my hand. "I work here now."

I could feel a question in her handshake. "You make coffee?"

I couldn't help but laugh; I was almost as

surprised to be here myself. I stepped through the swinging door into the bathroom. She followed, as I explained, "That coffee job was only temporary." I left out the part that this job was in the same category. "I majored in mass communications, graduated last May, got married in August, and worked at the coffee shop." I stepped into the bathroom stall next to her. "Living on love and minimum wage wasn't all it was cracked up to be."

I could hear her laugh in the echo of the bathroom. "Have you worked in an ad agency before?"

I was thankful for the divider between us so she couldn't see my mouth working, trying out an answer to her question. Did my summer job here count? My semester-long internship at college?

Thankfully, she didn't wait for my reply. "I haven't. I love it. There's always something new. And the people here are so great. By the way . . ."

From under the metal divider there was a flutter of fingers near my ankles. "My name's Elle."

"Stasha," I replied, fluttering my fingers over hers.

That unlikely introduction led Elle to think we were best buddies, as if we went way back — all the way to the coffee shop. I didn't mind. I could use a new friend, as long as she didn't keep bringing up my dad. If I had anything to say about it, she'd never find out until it didn't matter anymore. Like when Josh was finished with his teaching stint and I found an out-of-state job. Luckily, our coffee breaks were almost always on the run, with not much time to chat past the basics. Today I had a lull between projects, so I'd sat here longer than usual.

Elle was still staring at me, waiting for more of an answer about our hot boss — or watching me squirm. A change of subject was in order. Quick. "I hope my grandma gets better soon." I twisted the cap off a soda bottle and took a drink.

Elle looked surprised. "Is she sick?"

Oh, crud. As soon as the words were out of her mouth I remembered. My grandma was Donnie's mother. Mr. Dunn to Elle, Dad to me. Grandma. Mother. Another connection I didn't want to advertise. After two weeks on the job, I was learning that deception was harder than I thought. Well, maybe not actual deception, more like omitting a few key details.

It was no secret that Mr. Dunn's mother was seriously ill. My dad had had Elle send out an interoffice memo letting everyone know he might be in and out of the office the next few weeks. From what I could tell, he'd been mostly in.

It was my mom who spent hours by my grandma's bedside. First at the hospital, now at the nursing home where they'd transferred her after the insurance company said her hospital coverage had reached its limit.

I'd been to see Grandma twice when she was still at the hospital. All she did was lie there, occasionally opening her eyes, looking around as if she was trying to figure out where she was, and then going back to sleep. If it was sleep. The doctors couldn't tell us whether she could hear us or understand what we said.

It made me sad to remember how alive my grandma had always been. Somehow I thought she'd always be there to bake pumpkin pie for Thanksgiving dinner and give me cool gifts for my birthday. I remembered how she'd thrown custom to the wind the night of my wedding. She didn't ask Josh to dance, she asked me. That was the grandma I missed, not the grandma who did nothing but silently lie in bed. It was harder to see her than to feel guilty about not stopping by. Maybe that was the way my dad felt too. My mom, on the other hand, acted as if sitting by my grandma was her full-time job.

There had to be a happy medium when it came to balancing work and life, but neither my dad nor my mom seemed to know what that looked like.

Neither did Josh. But I didn't want to think about him right now either. I avoided Elle's question by quickly standing. "Oh! I just remembered, I have an off-site commercial to shoot this afternoon, and I've got to call someone."

It was the truth, just maybe not as dire as I made it sound. I hurried down the hall to my cubicle, already stacked high with papers and client products. Two weeks worth of stuff that made it look as if I'd been here for an eternity. Or would be.

I reached for my Rolodex and found the number of First and First Bank. Once I confirmed the time of the shoot, we'd be all set. It was my first big project for my dad.

Mr. Dunn, I mentally corrected. I was starting to understand why he'd always been so late coming home. About the only time the phones around here stopped ringing was when the main receptionist turned on the voice-mail system after six. The early part of the day was spent putting out fires, and the real work began *after* six, when the executives and grunts like me tried to get one step ahead before tomorrow. Which reminded me — I needed to call Josh and let him know the commercial shoot didn't start until the bank lobby closed sometime after six. I'd be home late. Probably really late.

Then again, what was the use? If things went the way they had since he'd started teaching, I would more than likely beat him home. Until I married a teacher who doubled as a coach, I hadn't known that teachers had to do all kinds of things besides teach.

"What would you think if we had Mr. Swenson walk from the front door of the bank up to one of the teller windows?" I began, taking a breath to finish . . . "then he could turn to the camera and say his line."

Ben, the creative director in charge of filming the commercial, gave me a long look. I took another breath and kept talking. "It might give us a little movement, instead of having him just stand there while the camera zooms in." I hoped my voice sounded more confident than I felt. I had never done anything like this before, but I'd watched enough TV to know that talking heads were boring.

Slowly Ben nodded. "I like it." He turned to the cameraman, Ryan, and gave him instructions, then turned back to me. "Go ahead and do a walk-through of the scenario for Ryan. I want to get the lighting in place before we bring in Mr. Swenson. No sense wasting his time while we set up the shot."

Lucky Mr. Swenson, the bank president, got to sit in his plush office and get some work done. The rest of us were working like crazy trying to shoot three 30-second spots. In theory we were talking about a minute and a half. The reality was turning into infinity.

It was already after eight, and we had filmed three bank customers telling the camera what they loved most about First and First Bank. Then we moved on to the tellers and captured them as they gushed about their *awesome* customers. Of course, what else would they say, with three customers standing right there? They were gone now.

Ryan picked up one of the umbrella-style lights and moved it three inches, then moved another one not much farther. With my foot I nudged a cord lying on the floor, trying to look as if I was contributing. The job description for creative director's assistant should have included: "Good at standing for long periods of time doing nothing."

Ben thrust a piece of paper at me. "Read this for me."

I quickly scanned it. "Looks good to me."

"I meant *out loud*. It's Mr. Swenson's lines. I want to time them."

"I don't know how fast he talks."

"Pretend you do." Ben didn't hide the fact that I had fallen from my lofty position as production genius just seconds ago to newbie numbskull.

"Here at First and First, we put customers first." Now that I read it out loud, it sounded weird. I looked up. "Don't you think that's a lot of 'firsts' for one sentence?"

Ben's forehead crinkled. "Yeah, I do. We're gonna have to rewrite it. Why don't you see what you can come up with."

A second ago you were whining to yourself how boring this was. Here's a chance to show what you've got.

"Sure," I said taking the script from Ben's hand. The little buzz I often felt when faced with a challenge propelled me to the nearest desk. I sat down, grabbed a pen out of the holder, and started writing. I could do this.

When I returned with the rewrite five minutes later, Ben looked it over and said,

"Not bad. Read it for me." He pulled out a stopwatch, waited a second, then pointed at me. "Go."

My heart thumped as I read. "First and First isn't just a name; it's the way we feel about our customers. Every day you're number one with us."

For the second time tonight Ben gave me a long look. "Sure you haven't done this before?"

"No." Nervous sweat coated my palms. Was it good enough to put on film?

"Someone get Mr. Swenson. We're ready to rumble." Ben lifted his chin. "Good job, MacKay. We could use some new blood in copywriting."

A wave of relief washed over me. I'd done it. What I'd written was good. More than good. "Cool," I said, trying to act it.

As Ben waved Mr. Swenson into place, he tossed one more compliment over his shoulder. "I'll put in a good word with the boss for you."

Wow. "That'd be great." Maybe. For a second I'd forgotten who the boss was. Ben had no clue. I crossed my arms and leaned against the nearest wall while Mr. Swenson rehearsed the copy I'd written. I hoped my dad was as cool about this as I'd managed to be. Hopefully, our interest in the advertising business and our acting ability was in the gene pool we shared.

"That'll do it." Ben shook Mr. Swenson's hand. "Great job. If this banking thing doesn't work out for you . . ." He smiled and motioned toward the camera.

Mr. Swenson laughed. "I think I'll stick with what I know." He turned to shake my hand too. "Thanks for the great lines."

His warm wash of words wrapped around me. Tonight was the first time anyone had ever complimented my writing skills. And it had happened twice. I hadn't done much, but that was the essence of this industry. Short. Sweet. To the point. And pack an emotional punch if possible. Somehow I'd done just that.

"Mr. Miller?" Slowly, I let myself in the back door that Leon insisted we keep locked. It didn't matter to him that I had to take my life in my hands to pick my way across the cracked sidewalk that ran around the weedy side of the house. Not even a down-and-out burglar would consider breaking into a house as chipped and peeling as Mr. Miller's. It was hard to explain to Leon. Easier to simply tiptoe my way in the dark — heaven forbid we turn on the back porch light; that used electricity — and tiptoe in the back entry we shared. I peeked around the door frame. Just beyond was Leon's kitchen. The light over the sink was on, so he had to be up. I'd discovered that Leon often liked to hang out there while he had a piece of toast and a glass of milk. Not that he was spying on us or anything.

"Mr. Miller?" I called softly. "Leon?" If he was still up, I didn't want to give him a heart attack. I had given him fair warning. I stepped in and flicked on the light going up the stairway to our apartment.

Just then, the door to the bathroom just off the kitchen opened. There stood Leon, framed by the door, in nothing but his walker and his birthday suit.

We both froze for what seemed like five minutes. Then Leon turned and hobbled as quickly as he could down the hallway toward his bedroom. "Just got out of the tub," he mumbled over his back. "You kind of picked a bad time to come home."

No kidding. I ran up the back steps to our apartment, giggling to myself. Josh didn't know he'd missed the floor show. I couldn't wait to tell him about it.

"Josh?" I whispered loudly as I slipped into the apartment and closed the door behind me. We still hadn't figured out how much of our upstairs life Mr. Miller could hear. I decided to make sure he wouldn't overhear this. "Guess what I just saw."

Nothing. I poked my head into the living room on my right. A quick glance to the left showed me the kitchen was all clear, too. In fact, after just a few steps I realized I had the apartment to myself.

Suddenly I felt a little embarrassed. It would have been one thing if I'd been able to share my unexpected homecoming with Josh; it was something else entirely to know I was in my house with a naked man. Even if he was almost 90 and couldn't climb the steps, it was still weird. I wanted my husband.

I toed my shoes off my feet and tossed my coat over the chair near the door. I never did get a chance to eat supper. The kitchen was dark, and I didn't bother to turn on the light. One look in our nearly empty fridge, and I realized I was too tired to even spoon yogurt into my mouth. I closed the fridge, walked into the bedroom, and flopped on the bed. The second I fell there, I realized the mistake I had made. Getting back up to get undressed was going to be impossible.

As I tried to muster the energy to lift myself off the bed, vague thoughts drifted through my mind. What was Josh doing out so late? His coaching practice never went this long. Maybe he stayed late to grade papers. Or change the bulletin boards in his classroom. It seemed that there was always something that kept him at school.

Not so different from an ad agency, is it?

No. I was finding out almost any career took a good chunk of time from a day.

Snatches of my first commercial shoot played in my brain. *Every day you're number one with us. Good job, MacKay. I'll put in a good word with the boss for you. Thanks for the great lines.*

All of a sudden I was kinda glad Josh wasn't home. If he asked how my day went, I'd have to say, "Great." And I wasn't quite ready to admit to him — or myself — that maybe, just maybe I liked — make that loved — my new job.

LAURA

As if I was giving my mother-in-law a one-armed hug, I lifted her off the bed just enough to stick another pillow behind her back. "Ugh." I hadn't meant to grunt, but dead weight was heavy.

"Daaay?" Eleanor's eyes sought mine.

These days it was fill-in-the-blank with her. For all I knew she could be asking if it was a nice day, a cold day, or simply day.

"Yes," I said, taking a stab in the dark, "it's a chilly day out there." Who knew? Maybe my skin still held the cold from the November air outside, and Eleanor felt it.

"Ummmm," Eleanor answered, if she was actually replying. It was hard to know if her random sounds were an attempt to communicate or mindless verbalizing.

Mindless? Even though I hadn't said anything, I clamped my hand over my mouth. I hadn't meant it like that. I busied myself by fluffing her pillow and then held

290

a cup of water and a straw near her mouth. Maybe this time she'd be able to sip on her own.

Her mouth worked around the straw as if some part of her knew what to do, but somewhere along the synapses in her brain there was a misfire.

"Auugg." She leaned back against the pillows. If it was frustrating for me, I could only imagine how she felt, if she even understood what I'd been trying to do.

The CNAs and RNs cheered her one-word conversations as if Eleanor had scored a touchdown at the Super Bowl. I had a hard time mustering the same enthusiasm. I wasn't sure I wanted to readjust my memory of the Eleanor I knew and replace it with this shell of a person laying in a bed. Not if it meant this.

I pulled the blanket up, lifting her arms to rest outside the cover. Her eyelids fluttered closed. Sleep was a blessing. I prayed Eleanor was dreaming of better times — games she played as a child, trips she took with her husband, times she scolded Donnie for some silly prank he'd pulled. Anything was better than her present reality.

I took my familiar seat in the padded chair I'd positioned near her bed. From here I could keep watch over Eleanor. A glance to my right let me see if one of the constantly rotating staffers was making their rounds, and when all was quiet, I could lift my eyes and look out the large picture window. It wasn't called River's Edge Nursing Home for nothing. I only wished Eleanor could appreciate the beautiful view she had. The trees lining the riverbank were bare now, a layer of snow covering the land on either side of the slow-moving stream. The water hadn't frozen yet, if it ever did. I glanced at Eleanor, inert on the bed. Sad to imagine, but it looked as if I'd be here for the long haul. I'd get to see if the river did freeze, then thaw, and flow swiftly again. Watch as green leaves sprouted on tree branches. Life's cycle framed in a glass-paned rectangle.

Eleanor stirred on the bed, her hand struggling to rise as if reaching for an object, her fingers not cooperating. This was certainly Eleanor's frozen winter.

What about you?

If a lifetime had a winter, this was surely mine, too. My life was as colorless as the scene outside Eleanor's window. Drab. Gray. The portrait of a dead marriage painted in monochrome and a vinyl chair pulled close to a nursing-home bed. I gave my head a small shake and reached for the sewing in the basket I'd brought along to help pass the time. Carla did not accept Eleanor's illness as an excuse to miss quilting class. "The first rule of caretaking is to take care of yourself," she had said, as if she was an expert.

From the top of the basket I lifted my current project. My third block, more undone than finished. With both hands I smoothed the fabric over one of my legs, feeling the warmth of my fingers through the squares of cloth. The others in the class were treating our weekly lesson as if it was a speed competition. Eight weeks was long enough, the instructor said, to give us a good start on the basics of piecing together a quilt. And yet, several in the class were almost finished with their entire project.

They needed a life. I couldn't help but roll my eyes. My life now meant keeping my debilitated mother-in-law company. I'd rather have a completed quilt any day.

You don't have to sit here every day.

I don't sit here all the time.

Close enough. Two hours every afternoon. An hour or so most evenings.

The truth was, if I didn't sit here, who would? A now-familiar ember burned in my chest. Donnie had been here to see his mother a few times, of course, but not as often as he should have been. I flipped the quilt piece over and ran my finger over the seams and stitching on the back. Even the underside had a symmetry about it. If only my life were as neatly sewn together. Instead my relationship with Donnie was frayed, raveling in a way no simple stitch could stop.

I can stop it.

It was too late for prayers and platitudes. I knew the old advice; the way a man treated his mother was the way he'd treat his wife. I should have paid more attention to that wisdom 23 years ago. It was too late now. But I planned to change that as soon as Eleanor recovered or at least stabilized. Donnie and I had a history together. Part of me would always love him, but I wasn't willing to spend what was left of my life as one lonely woman in a two-person marriage. If there was a good time to ask a husband to leave, it certainly wouldn't be when his mother was incapacitated. I owed Eleanor more than that for her only son.

I inserted the needle just once into the fabric, cinching it there, then fingered through the scraps of fabric in my basket. Unlike Carla and Judy, I decided after the first class that quilting was never going to be a lifelong pastime. For Judy's sake, I stayed in the class: "material moral support," I secretly called my decision. I also decided I wasn't going to spend a fortune investing in a hobby I didn't plan to continue.

At our second class the other women got busy laying claim to the classroom sewing machines, marking their territory with baskets of colored fabric.

"Let me see what colors you picked." Carla was poking her fingers into my basket.

I swatted at Carla's hand. "You're going to mess it up." In reality I was hoping she wouldn't notice my half-hearted attempt at fabric selection. "What did you pick?"

As if she'd been waiting to be asked, Carla pulled several neatly cut layers of crisp fabric from her basket. "Fall colors," she said, fanning the scraps with her hand.

Burnt sienna. Evergreen. Yellow ocher. There was a tug in my chest as I easily recalled the names of the colors. "Pretty." I nodded my head toward the machines. "You'd better find a place."

I was hoping she didn't insist on me sitting next to her. I'd done the math; there weren't enough machines for all of us. My guess was that the instructor was going to have us play musical machines, taking turns while some cut fabric, some sewed, and some ironed small seams flat. With any luck

I could avoid having Carla or Judy see my pitiful attempt at quilting. I wouldn't need a machine tonight. As it was, I hadn't even opened my new pair of scissors, my only purchase. I'd passed up investing in the "fats" the instructor was selling. In fact, an hour earlier, I had sifted through the bag of old clothes Eleanor had given me, trying to imagine old shirts and skirts into a quilt. A crazy quilt of castoffs.

I wasn't anxious to hear what Carla, or "never had an opinion she didn't express" Judy, would have to say about my fabric selection.

A rustle in the bed where Eleanor lay brought me back to the here and now. I wished I could share with Eleanor what Judy had said. Or, more accurately, what she had yodeled. I smiled now as I lifted the brown plaid rectangles and blue chambray squares onto my lap. "Hey, pardner, you fixin' to quilt yourself a saddle blanket?"

While others in the class outpaced me, I was a throwback, hand-piecing my fabric. It was slow and tedious, just like the hours I spent at Eleanor's bedside each day. I had no finished project in mind. No goal. The other women in the class teased me, calling me Ma Ingalls, their *Little House on the Prairie* quilter. It was okay. I looked at this new hobby as a temporary fix, a way to stand by Judy during her divorce, time to spend with my old friends, help in taking my mind off my fix for a few hours once a week. As soon as Eleanor got to a stage where I felt comfortable leaving her care for Donnie to supervise, I would pack up my scraps and not look back.

Then what?

My mouth suddenly dry, I ran my tongue over my teeth. I'd figure out something. The shock of Judy and Bill's breakup had worn off. Donnie didn't have a drinking problem, but emotional neglect had to count for something.

Emotional neglect? Since when have you turned into a drama queen?

Maybe there wasn't an official name for what had happened to Donnie and me, but whatever it was, it was making me miserable.

And it's all about you . . . *right?*

I didn't want it to be. I wanted it to be about Donnie *and* me. The last I looked, it took two people to make a marriage, and if one of them wasn't cooperating, well, the simple truth was I was tired of doing this marriage business all by myself. I pulled the needle from the fabric and caught some of the brown plaid fabric with the sharp tip of the needle and began sewing it to the blue chambray. "Ouch!"

Dang. Everyone else used a thimble. My finger automatically went to my mouth. I didn't think I nicked it enough to draw blood, but it still stung.

"Owww." Eleanor was looking at me, wide-eyed. Her eyes traveled to the fabric that hung from my other hand. She took a slow breath. "Cowwww." Another breath. "Boyyyyy."

In spite of my shock at her one-word sentence, I couldn't help but laugh. It was as if she and Judy were in cahoots. "Not you too."

She closed her eyes, opened them once more. "Donnnieeee." Her eyes again went to the quilt square in my hand.

Now I felt like the dense one. I lifted the fabric. "Donnie was a cowboy?"

Her head rested against the pillow as one side of her mouth attempted a smile. At least I thought it was a smile. Part of me wanted to reach for the call button. The fact that Eleanor had connected her thoughts and speech in a way that sort-of made sense seemed like an event that should be recorded. Then again, looking at Eleanor, eyes now shut, seemingly back in her cocoon of a world, the news could probably wait.

Instead, I ran my hand over the brown plaid, the blue chambray. Had Donnie really thought he was a cowboy when he wore this shirt?

I remembered the day I'd pulled the shirt out of the box of old clothes Eleanor had foisted on me several months ago. I hadn't given the small shirt a second thought in my frantic search for quilt fabric. It was hard to imagine my husband, Mr. Advertising, as a little boy who dreamed of riding broncos and lassoing cattle. But then, he'd always been a character who liked being the center of attention. I could very well see him in the middle of Eleanor's living room, whooping it up as if a black-hatted bad guy was chasing him on a wild stallion. What had happened to that little boy?

He channeled his wild imagination into a creative career. He's using his gift.

I smoothed one finger over the cotton. I could sense a softening inside me, a door opening the smallest bit. So this was what made Donnie tick.

No. The harsh word slammed the door closed. I'd seen what Donnie's creativity had done to our marriage. All his energy went to his work, while I got nothing.

What are you so afraid of?

I picked up the fabric and took a fast

stitch, then another and another. Who cared if my stitches weren't perfect? They mirrored my life. I wasn't afraid of anything. The only thing I didn't want to think about was the promise I'd break by asking Donnie to leave. I'd thought marriage was forever. Once Donnie was gone, the biggest promise I had ever made would be broken. That's what I was afraid of: breaking my promise.

Then don't.

An ache of loneliness kept time with the beat of my heart. The steady rhythm of my stitching. If only it was that simple.

A quick knock on the open door to Eleanor's room startled me. I turned my head as a man's vaguely familiar face leaned in the doorway. Had he caught me quilting or dozing? I wasn't sure. "Yes?" I said, trying to cover my fogginess, lifting my quilting as if I'd been hard at it. He'd caught me snoozing red-handed. Well, brown plaid-handed.

"Hi." The man lifted his hand in greeting as he stepped into the room. Now I remembered. Tall, dark, well-built. I'd passed him in the hallways of the nursing home on several of my visits. It was hard not to notice a young, well, younger healthy face in this place. Someone not in a nurse's uniform. We had developed a nodding acquaintance.

I imagined he was a doctor making rounds, although I knew he wasn't Eleanor's doctor. What could he be doing here, other than waking up sleeping visitors? A guilty wash flooded my cheeks. I supposed there wasn't a law against napping in a nursing home, although if I kept it up they might start charging me. Maybe he was looking for one of his patients.

"Can I help you?"

"I'm looking for Eleanor Dunn."

"This is Eleanor." I crossed my arms over my chest, nodded my head toward the bed behind me. "I'm her daughter." I left off the in-law part. Let him think he was dealing with a blood relative.

"Pleased to meet you." He stuck out his hand, and in three long strides he was across the room in front of me.

He was taller up close. His eyes were darker brown too. And his smile more engaging.

I stuck out my hand. "Laura," I said, not smiling. "Laura Dunn. Eleanor's daughter." *In-law,* I whispered to myself, honest on the inside, anyway.

"It looks like I'll be seeing a lot of you then."

"Is that so?"

"Yeah," he said, nodding to the empty bed

301

in the opposite corner of the room. "My mom's finally getting transferred from her swing bed into a permanent room. It's been a long haul for her. We were hoping she'd recover enough to go home, but her doctor doesn't think that's going to happen."

In the briefest blink, his eyes scanned me; his look wasn't suggestive, but his quick assessment left me feeling suddenly exposed.

"By the way, I'm John."

Such an ordinary name for a man who didn't look ordinary at all.

"Laura," I said. "Oh, I guess I already told you that." Someone should just whisk me back to junior high. If he thought I was an adult, I should try to act like one. "So," I said, pushing a strand of hair behind one ear, "you said your mom is going to be Eleanor's roommate? I was wondering when someone would move in here. The roommate she had when she first came here die— Uh . . ." Someone dying in a nursing home was nothing unusual, but somehow bringing it up just now didn't seem appropriate.

John looked out the window, then back at me. "Don't worry, I know what's next." His eyes scanned the small room. "After this. I'm not worried, and neither is my mother. From all reports, heaven isn't a bad place to spend the rest of your life." He drew in a long breath and puffed it out. "But we're not worrying about that right now. Mom broke her hip, and with osteoporosis she's probably not going to get out of her wheel-chair. She's given me the go-ahead to close up her apartment." He stuffed his hands into the back pockets of his slacks. "One good thing is that my mom's been really co-operative about this transition."

"That is nice. Fortunately, or maybe unfortunately, cooperation is an issue we haven't had to deal with." I thought of Elea-nor's house, sitting empty, the heat turned as low as it would go. We were going to have to decide what to do about it one of these days. I had no doubt Donnie would have something to say about selling his childhood home, if I could ever pin him down to talk about it. Any conversation I'd tried to have with him about his mother had been met with evasiveness — like the one we had when we learned she had to leave the hospi-tal.

"Well, what do you think?" I had asked him as we walked out of Eleanor's hospital room and made our way past the nurses' station.

"About what?"

How could he not know what I was asking? Donnie walked faster. I hurried to keep up with him as he strode quickly down the hospital corridor. Eleanor's doctor had just told us we needed to find a place for her to be transferred to. I couldn't imagine Donnie could be thinking about anything but that.

"I have a meeting I need to get to," he said. "Let's talk about it tonight."

"Tonight?" I stopped in my tracks. When he didn't turn around, I ran to catch up. "Your mother is lying in a hospital bed, practically comatose, and you have a meeting to go to?" A nurse gave me a sidelong glance as she walked past. Somehow I doubted this was the first tense family conversation she'd overheard.

Donnie didn't miss a stride. In my rush to keep up, my foot caught on the industrial carpet. I stumbled, quickly caught myself, and hurried on as if I was afraid of being left behind. All morning Donnie had looked at his watch, as if spending a few hours with his mother was a huge inconvenience in his all-important schedule. Enough was enough. I stood stock-still, hands on my hips. If he didn't notice, I didn't know what I'd do.

Donnie glanced over his shoulder, took a few more steps, and looked back again. Finally he stopped and turned my way.

"Listen, I'm sorry if I don't have the names of nursing homes in Carlton on the tip of my tongue. In case you don't remember, I have a business to run. I've spent as much time here as I could the past few days. We're presenting the new ad campaign to the Brody people this afternoon. I told Matt if I could possibly be there, I would. This is one of the biggest accounts we've ever pitched. They want TV, radio, print. What's it going to look like to the client if the president of the company is a no-show?"

I was seething. "What's it going to look like if you're not here for your own mother?"

"I've *been* here. For three straight days." Donnie puffed his cheeks with air, huffed it out. "What am I supposed to do? Huh? What? Tell me. Go ahead, you tell me, Laura. She doesn't even know I'm here."

"She does know," I countered.

The soft ding of a patient call button sounded somewhere behind me. Over the loudspeaker a doctor was paged as Donnie and I staged a stare-down at the Not-So-OK Corral, the hospital corridor.

He sighed. "Look, nothing is going to change in the next" — he shot his arm from his cuff and looked at his watch — "four hours. We can talk about it tonight."

"*If* you're home," I shot back.

305

As usual, Donnie had been right. Nothing had changed by that evening, and not much more had changed in the weeks that passed, except that Eleanor was in a different bed and every now and then surprised us with an unexpected word like "cowboy."

I glanced at Eleanor now. Her eyes were closed, as they were most of the time. I turned to John. "I'm afraid Eleanor isn't going to be much company for your mother."

John smiled. "You haven't met my mother. She can talk enough for both of them."

There was something about the way he talked about his mother that was oddly appealing. As if I starred in *CSI,* I began collecting clues about the man. Obviously devoted to his mother. A professional of some sort, judging by the sport coat he wore over a shirt and tie. His job must be somewhat flexible for him to be at the nursing home in the middle of the afternoon.

He pulled one hand from his pocket and gestured from the empty bed to Eleanor's. "I just hope my mother will let your mom rest if she needs to."

How long had it been since I'd done a ring check? Twenty-three years? My heart did a funny little blip, as if my radar screen for these sorts of things had suddenly been activated after years of inactivity. He wasn't wearing one. But then, that didn't necessarily mean anything. Donnie didn't wear his wedding ring either. The first week we were married he complained that the two words engraved on the inside, *Love Always,* irritated his skin. I'd tried smoothing them down with my thumb as we drove to our honeymoon hotel, but the ring ended up in my jewelry box by the time we arrived back at our apartment. The fact that Donnie didn't wear his ring never bothered me. I didn't need a piece of metal to bond him to me. Standing in Eleanor's room, watching a handsome man wave his left hand around for all the world to see, it occurred to me that while maybe I didn't need the assurance of a ring, other women might need the warning: *Hands off.*

Are you warning yourself?

Oh, good grief, no. My right hand lifted to finger my earring as he spoke.

Preening?

No. I pulled my hand away from my ear and ran it beneath the hair at the nape of my neck, fluffing things a bit. This was ridiculous. I folded my arms across my chest. There. I wasn't sure if what I'd been doing was flirting, or if it was simply an uncomfortable fidget. It had been years since I'd been aware of my movements in this way. I'd had a silly, school-girl-type crush on Donnie's business partner, Matt, ages ago. We were all a lot younger then, more social. Matt's wife, Kathy, and I were friends. She confided all kinds of husband things to me. Little things that made Donnie pale in comparison.

"Matt makes the bed every morning. I don't even think about it."

"Matt always goes out to the kitchen and gets the coffee started. Can you believe he doesn't even drink the stuff?"

One day when Kathy and I were at Westwood Mall, window shopping and chatting, she told me, "Matt's home scrubbing the kitchen floor."

That's when I decided maybe I'd gotten the short stick.

I started noticing Matt in a way I hadn't before. He was more than just a business acquaintance, he was a really, *really* nice guy. He laughed at my jokes. He noticed my new sweater. Who wouldn't fall for a guy like that? The only problem was, he was married, and so was I. His wife was my good friend, and I loved Donnie; I really did. It's just that I wanted him to be more like Matt.

I didn't dare breathe a word of my infatuation to Kathy, but I did tell Donnie, just not in so many words.

"Matt makes Kathy's coffee in the morning."

"Matt makes the bed while Kathy showers."

"Kathy told me Matt scrubs the kitchen floor. On his hands and knees."

Donnie was oblivious.

I found myself daydreaming about my dream man. I picked at all the things Donnie did that irritated me.

"Could you *please* put your dishes in the dishwasher?"

"Do I have to remind you *every week* to take out the garbage?"

"Has it ever occurred to you that there *isn't* a laundry fairy? It's *me* who folds your clothes and puts them in your drawer."

I was married to Donnie, and he wasn't perfect like Matt.

I knew my thoughts weren't helping my marriage. In fact, they could very well destroy it if I didn't get them in control. Then two things happened.

Donnie and I were in church one Sunday, sitting in our pew as we usually did, more out of habit than faith, when the pastor got up to speak on marriage.

I shifted on the padded seat. Did he know

my struggle?

Of course I do.

I pulled a hymnal from the holder and held it in my lap. I wasn't in the habit of hearing God talk. Or of listening to much of what the pastor had to say. He opened his Bible. "I want to read three verses before I share my message with you today." He turned a page, found his place. "Better to live on a corner of the roof than share a house with a quarrelsome wife." There was a low chuckle from the congregation. I wasn't laughing.

"The next verse is also from Proverbs. A quarrelsome wife is like a constant dripping."

I clutched my hymnbook with the conviction of the guilty. There was out-and-out laughter this time, with a distinctively baritone quality to it. That one apparently hit a chord with the men.

The pastor raised one finger. "Just in case you get the wrong message here, I don't feel these verses apply strictly to the women. There are lessons here for all of us."

That quieted things down in a hurry.

"Now listen up." He looked down at his Bible and then, for some odd reason, straight at me as he recited the third verse. "Love forgets mistakes; nagging about them

310

parts the best of friends."

If I wasn't careful, I might lose Donnie *and* Kathy.

Later that afternoon, Kathy and I went to a matinee. As we were sipping our Diet Cokes waiting for the movie to start, Kathy said, "It just drives me *nuts* the way Matt will stand, twist at the waist just once, and then crack his knuckles."

I swallowed the Coke in my mouth. "Matt cracks his knuckles?" I'd never noticed.

"Oh, gosh." Kathy rolled her eyes. "You have to have seen it. Or heard it. I tell him to stop it all the time."

Funny how once she mentioned Matt's bad habit, I started noticing it too. He did stand there with his hands on his back, twist to one side, and then intertwine his fingers and crack his knuckles like a construction worker. Not only did it drive Kathy nuts, it started bugging me. Donnie and his familiar quirks started to look down right normal, bearable in a way Matt's knuckle-cracking wasn't.

That's what I needed to do now, find a fault in the man standing in front of me. John was still talking. It seemed his mother's gift of gab had been inherited.

Well now, that could grow irritating. But then, a little conversation could be kind of nice. How long had it been since Donnie talked so freely with me?

John jingled the change in his pocket.

Now that could really drive a person bananas.

"Oops." He grimaced and took his hand out of his pocket. "My secretary gets on me all the time for that. Sorry."

So maybe he really was perfect.

He nodded his head toward Eleanor. "It looks like she might be waking up. Do you mind if I introduce myself to her?"

In my sudden fascination, I'd forgotten all about my mother-in-law in the bed behind me. "Oh. Here. Let me." I turned to Eleanor's side. "Eleanor," I said talking as if I was an actress saying my lines for an audience. "This is John. His mother is going to be your new roommate."

Eleanor's eyes found his. "Ahhh," she gurgled. Maybe it was hi.

"Pleased to meet you," John said, stepping next to her, holding her hand between both of his.

I wondered what his hands would feel like if he held mine like that. Liquid warmth spread across my chest, into my neck. I'd heard of women having a resurgence of sexuality in midlife. The phenomenon was happening as I stood there. Someone should just shoot me, put me out of my misery.

Okay, so what I was feeling wasn't painful. Just unsettling. There were emotions tugging at me in a way I hadn't felt about Donnie in . . . what? I turned away from the picture of John holding Eleanor's hand and stared out the window. I couldn't remember the last time I'd had these sorts of feelings for my husband.

"Here we are." The overly enthusiastic voice of a nurse's assistant rounded the corner, throwing a much-needed wet blanket on my fantasizing. She was pushing an older woman in a wheelchair. "This is your new room, Cecelia. You'll be living with Eleanor."

"Glory be and pass the mayonnaise." Cecelia flashed a smile and lifted her hand in greeting.

"I forgot to tell you," John walked toward his mother as he caught my glance. "Mom has a bit of dementia. Some days are better than others."

The nurse patted Cecelia's shoulder. "Moving to a new room can be a little upsetting. Once she's settled in, I'm sure she'll be fine."

As if on cue, an aide pushed a metal cart into the room filled with what looked like all of Cecelia's earthly possessions.

"Mom likes her stuff," John said, lifting a small television from the end of the cart. He moved it to the dresser across from the foot of Cecelia's bed.

"Who are you?" Cecelia was giving me the once-over. "You're not Shirley, are you? If you are, I don't like what you did to my son." She pointed a finger at me. "I don't like you, do I?" Her brows puzzled as she looked to John. "Is that Shirley?"

"My ex," John quickly explained as he glanced my way. "No, Mom, this is Laura. Eleanor's daughter."

"Where's Shirley? I don't like her, you know."

"I know, Mom. Shirley moved to California, remember? She's remarried now."

Cecelia's face suddenly cleared. She looked at me. "I never did like that Shirley. She was bad news from the get-go. Put that over there." She pointed to the nurse who had a framed photo of John and his mother in her hands. "You'll like this place." She seemed to be talking to Eleanor now. "I've been here for weeks. Food isn't so good, but it isn't bad either. Could use more salt. I used to love to cook. If I could only make my apple pie again. You liked my pie, didn't you, Johnny?"

John winked at me. "Don't say I didn't

314

warn you." He looked at his mother. "Yes, your apple pie was the best."

So then, he was not only good-looking, he was also a saint.

"We had an apple tree in our backyard. You like apples, don't you?" I wasn't sure who she was talking to now. But it didn't matter. Cecelia didn't wait for an answer. "I like apples. I like squash, too. They don't serve squash here. When I . . ."

Oh, boy. I looked at Eleanor. She seemed unusually interested in the commotion in the room. I pressed the button on the bed and lifted the head of her bed into more of a sitting position. Having a roommate might be a good distraction for her.

What about her roommate's son?

Distraction was the perfect word.

"Can I help?" I picked up a cardboard box filled with clothes and started arranging them on the closet shelves. Sticking my head in a laminated rectangle might suffocate the disquieting thoughts dancing through my mind. As I sorted cardigan sweaters from polyester slacks, Cecelia kept up a running dialogue — make that monologue — filling the room with chatter that required no attention. Good thing, since the only thing I *could* concentrate on was the alluring, spicy scent of the cologne that the only man in the room was wearing.

And the fact that I was in big, infatuated trouble.

DONNIE

"They don't like it." Matt slammed the edge of the file folder against my desk and slumped into a chair.

I flinched. "What? Who?" I hadn't heard him come into my office. My thoughts had been a million miles away from my office. I'd been imagining myself climbing Mount Everest. I was alone. No business to manage. No mother to worry about. No wife to please. Not even a Sherpa to guide me. I was blissfully alone.

"The Brody people. They don't like it." Matt clicked his tongue against the top of his mouth, a soft staccato that did nothing for my nerves.

"Since when?"

"Since a half hour ago."

"But they signed off on all of it, the media plan, everything, two months ago."

"Tell them that. I've been on the phone with them for the past 30 minutes." Matt stood across from my desk and stared at me. "What do you want to do?"

Go to Bali. Climb a mountain. I wanted to be anywhere but where I was. I tossed my pen on my desk and pushed into my chair. First things first. "What don't they like?"

"Everything. Nothing." Matt paused, then added, "They can't quite say. It's just not what they want."

I was at a loss. We sure hadn't started out like this. Justine's presentation had been flawless.

"And this chart shows the current attitude of your customers versus the desired attitude we're after," Justine had said, standing to the side of the screen as she paused the PowerPoint presentation so the client could study the research our agency had done.

Coming straight from the hospital, I had slipped into an empty chair at the back of the room. With any luck the Brody folks would think I'd been here since the lights went down. I lifted my chin and pushed my head straight back; my muscles were as taut as a tightrope.

The Brody Corporation had their fingers in all sorts of pies. They were looking to us for a campaign to unify their corporate identity to their shareholders. It hadn't been easy brainstorming this one. Corporate leasing. A chain of drive-through coffee kiosks. A franchise for movie rentals. And last, but certainly not least, partial ownership in a race-car sponsorship.

The report from the creative team after the first brainstorming session was a tongue-in-cheek suggestion that the Brody Corporation decide what they really wanted to do, and then come to us. Of course, we'd never tell that to the Brody people. We were hired to be innovative. We would earn our keep on this one. The second session report was no better. A tagline facetiously stating: We're Experts in Everything.

Hardly stellar work. We didn't get paid for half-baked ideas. We were up against a deadline. I called an emergency meeting, dictating a memo and telling Elle to send it to absolutely everyone who worked at the Dunn Agency. There were 42 heads in this building, and I wanted them all at this meeting.

Matt gave an overview of the account to the troops. I finished up. "Okay, people, I want you to *think.* Nothing is off limits. We're not going home until we've got this one nailed."

Elle sat at the table with paper and pen.

Her job was to write down any and all suggestions. We'd cull through them after the initial flood of ideas.

Silence.

Ben cleared his throat, opened his mouth, then lifted his coffee mug and poured coffee into the place where words should have been.

"Come *onnnn*." I pleaded.

"They like to mix it up." Stasha's familiar voice sounded tentative.

"Yeah," Elle chimed in. "It seems like they're always doing something new."

"That's it!" I snapped my fingers and pointed my index fingers at my daughter and Elle. "You got it." I pushed myself away from the table, strode to the whiteboard and picked up a black marker. *Brody Corp . . . Always Something New,* I wrote.

I followed with, *We like to mix-it-up!*

From that admittedly small beginning, the creative team took the ideas and built a solid campaign around them. The Brody folks had jumped on board with both feet. And now, it seemed, they wanted off the train.

"We can't lose this account," I said to Matt.

"I know, but what do we do? Tell creative to start over?"

"Either that or get the Brody people back

on board. It would be easier to —"

The buzz of my intercom interrupted me. I held my palm toward Matt. We were used to this. I pushed a button. "What?"

Elle was all business. "Ed from Westwood Mall management on line two."

Westwood Mall was another of our larger accounts. They needed new campaigns each season, new signage, radio spots, TV. Our whole team jumped when Westwood called. They were our bread and butter.

Matt nodded. This was a call I needed to take. I picked up the receiver. "Ed, great to hear from you. What can I do for you?"

"Get our merchant sales figures up." He didn't beat around the bush.

I'd allow myself the cliché. There were more important things at hand. I leaned toward the phone. "Mind if I put you on speakerphone? Matt's here with me. Two heads might be better than my thick one."

Ed laughed. "Sure, I can use all the help I can get."

I hit the speaker button and settled the receiver into the cradle. "What seems to be the problem?"

"We're heading into Thanksgiving, and usually by now we see a jump in pre-Christmas revenue. It's not happening, and our merchants are worried. They think foot traffic is down. Of course, it wouldn't have anything to do with the economy or their merchandise," Ed paused to take in a long breath. "It's all the mall's fault, you know."

"Of course it is." I was sure Ed could hear the sarcasm in my tone. We'd been through this before. "How can we help?"

Obviously, Ed had given this some thought. He didn't miss a beat. "We want to change the in-mall signage. Try some new colors, graphics."

Matt lowered his chin and gave me a wide-eyed stare. *Now?*

I spoke for the both of us. "You realize the lead time on a project like this could be several weeks."

"We need to get sales up now. We don't have several weeks."

Neither did we. But it wouldn't do to tell him about the crunch we were in with the Brody folks. I wide-eyed Matt right back. "So, what were you thinking, Ed?"

"Everyone has shopping to do in December, and we want them at Westwood, not Carlton Corners. I was hoping we could shoot for a big splash the second week in December. Newspaper. A 60-second TV ad. We'll roll out some 30-second radio spots. A clever jingle people can sing all the way to the mall."

And the real Santa could make an appearance, too.

"Uh, Ed." Problems with the Brody account. An already overworked staff. I didn't want to burst his snow globe, but what he was asking wasn't possible in the time frame he was suggesting.

As if anticipating my response, he said, "I know. It's a lot to ask in a short time."

Impossible. But I knew Westwood also did some contract work with another firm in town. I wasn't about to hand over the Westwood account on a Christmas platter. I looked to Matt to get a read from him. Elle tiptoed into the office and slipped a pink memo note into my hand. *Laura on line three.*

As if I had a pen in my hand, I scribbled in the air. *Take a message.* Laura knew my time at the office was jam-packed. She rarely called unless it was something major. I felt a sinking sensation in my stomach. *My mother.* Was there anything more this day could throw at me?

Matt nodded at me sideways. *I suppose we have to take it.*

"Ed, we'll do what we can. Let me get a team right on it and get back to you."

I hung up the phone and rubbed at the pulsing muscle at the base of my neck.

"What team?" Matt had pushed himself to the edge of his chair, poised to run, if I had to guess.

I massaged my neck.

"You okay?"

"Sure." I moved my hand to my left shoulder and kneaded the joint. What were the signs of a heart attack anyway? Was a stroke hereditary? I thought of the note Elle had slipped me: *Call Laura.* It had to be about my mother.

I looked over at Matt. "I think it would be in our best interest if we convince the Brody people that our original idea is in their best interest. It'll take too much time and manpower to reinvent the wheel. Send someone over there and sell them on it."

A quick flash of our Brody brainstorming session gave me a new idea. "Let's assign Stasha and Elle to the Westwood team."

Matt looked puzzled. "I can understand Stasha, but Elle?"

"Hey," I said, "those two came up with a seed idea that we turned into the whole Brody plan. We're going to need some new brainpower on the Westwood account. Tell you what." I pushed myself away from my desk and stood up. "I'll have Elle call over to the Brody building now and see who's around. Maybe she can set up a meeting.

I'll run over there and talk to whoever I can corner, convince them their shareholders will eat up our original plan."

Matt pressed his hands against the arms of the chair and slowly stood. "And I'll start putting together a team for the Westwood account." He closed his eyes for a moment. "We're going to have to work practically around the clock to get everything done."

"You're preaching to the choir, Buddy," I said, remembering how often we'd been through this routine before.

Matt turned to leave my office. "Now you know why I'm divorced."

My eye landed on the pink slip Elle had given me. *Call Laura.* I might have a lot of worries, but I didn't have to worry about Laura. She'd understand. Matt's ex, Kathy, had never learned the demands of the advertising business.

I clapped Matt on the shoulder. "Look at it this way; you won't have to feel guilty about leaving anyone sitting home alone all weekend."

Matt gave me a sidelong glance. "That's supposed to make me feel better about devoting my life to this place?"

I cuffed his shoulder with my fist. "All this hard work will be worth it."

Matt turned and looked at me full on.

"When? When will that happen?"

I opened my mouth. "Uh . . ." To tell the truth, I had thought it would have happened before now.

Before I could come up with an answer, Matt posed another question. "What is the payoff, anyway? An empty house? No one to do anything with? What? Tell me, Donnie, because I'd like to know."

And I thought I was having a bad day. I tugged at my shirt cuffs.

His chin jutted out, a challenge. Why did my incessantly ringing phone have to go silent now? I shrugged. I didn't know what the payoff was, but I was sure I'd know when it arrived. "Well," I started, "I know we both have plenty of —"

Matt held up a palm. "Don't say 'money,' because I can tell you I have plenty of it, and balancing my checking account doesn't give me one bit of pleasure."

I didn't know what set Matt off, but I knew we didn't have time to solve the world's problems — his problems — right now. A low thrum began in my head. Time was wasting. "I can tell you one thing," I pointed at him with my index finger. "You sure wouldn't like balancing your checking account if it was in the red, which it's going to be if we don't get our butts in gear and get busy. Do you think *I* like working this hard?"

A long silence hummed. Matt lips pressed into a hard line. "Yes, Donnie, I think you do."

His simple word, his short sentence, crackled in the air between us. My automatic reply would have been, "You're wrong. I don't." But in an instant I realized those words would have been a lie. The Donnie Dunn I knew and loved was motivated by work, not by wishing himself on a mountaintop.

I called Matt's bluff. "You're right; I do like working this hard. If you don't," I jutted my chin at him, "maybe it's time for you to get out of the business." Where had *those* words come from? I didn't want Matt to leave. There was no way I could run this place alone.

A hard silence hung heavy. Then the hollow sound of Matt ticking his tongue against the roof of his mouth. A time bomb waiting to explode. He wasn't really considering my false challenge, was he?

He cracked his knuckles, filled his cheeks with air, huffed it out. "Let me think about it." Just like that he turned to go.

"Come on, Matt." I grabbed at his upper arm. "You didn't mean that."

"Didn't I? Since when do you care? It's all business with you."

I squeezed his shoulder. "Listen, it's been a bad day. The Brody people are blowing smoke. I'll go talk to them. They'll come around. Go home. Get some rest."

"Go home? Are you forgetting about Westwood?"

I glanced at the clock on my desk. This rotten day was almost over anyway. A good night's sleep would do us all good. "No, I didn't forget about Westwood. But we're not going to get anything done getting at it this late in the day. Announce the team, and let's tackle it bright and early tomorrow."

Matt gave me a sullen nod. He didn't move, just turned and stared out the window. I recognized the look. The wish to be anywhere but here. There was more brewing in Matt than our sudden time crunch. We had worked together for over 20 years and had butted heads before, but this was different. Matt had never threatened to walk away from it all before.

I walked over and gently closed my office door, then crossed the room and put a hand on his shoulder. "You okay, buddy?"

Matt scuffed at the floor. "No." He gave his head a small shake and looked at me. "Yeah, I'm okay. Sorry." He breathed a heavy sigh as he moved out from under my hand. Once again he stared out the window. "Right before Brody called, Kathy came to see me. She's getting remarried. She didn't want me to be the last to know." He raised his eyebrows and pressed his mouth into a grim smile. "I guess she threw me for a loop." He shoved both hands deep into his pockets. "I thought I was over her."

Oh, man. I'd never been the go-to guy when it came to personal stuff. But if anyone was keeping score, I'd have to give Kathy a point for being up front with Matt. I supposed that wasn't what Matt wanted to hear right now.

What was the appropriate response? I didn't have a clue. "That's a bummer." I sounded like a college freshman.

How would I feel if I were in Matt's place? I couldn't imagine life without Laura. She was *there.* Always. She'd never been like Kathy, nagging Matt to leave work early, demanding that he not work evenings, throwing a fit when a special project required us to practically sleep at the office. Could Matt really miss someone like that?

Who was I to know what made Matt tick? Sure, we'd spent half our lives as friends. But we'd never done that kind of talking. "Sorry," was all I could think to say. I was sorry Matt was feeling so bad. I said it again. "I'm sorry."

"Thanks." Matt blinked at me, dry-eyed. He turned to the window. "I guess I sort of held out this hope. Maybe we'd get back together when things around here weren't so nuts."

The sound of a phone ringing outside my door underscored my point. "As if."

"Yeah." Matt twisted at the ring on his right hand.

So now what? There was work to do, but it hardly seemed like the time to bring it up. I cleared my throat. That seemed to do the trick.

Matt gave the top of my desk one hard tap with the tips of his fingers. "I'll get the Westwood team lined up."

Back to business, where I was comfortable. "Sounds good. I'll head over to Brody and talk to them. Check in with you after that."

Matt reached for the file folder he'd slammed on my desk earlier. He slapped the edge of it against his hand. "Thanks for listening, buddy."

"Yeah," I mumbled. What I'd done amounted to standing around looking uncomfortable. "No problem."

Matt put his hand on the doorknob. He

turned and spoke softly. "Call your wife."

I didn't think he'd seen the note Elle had slipped me. I raised a hand. "Will do. Thanks."

For what, I wasn't sure.

"Laura?" It had been tempting to head straight out the door to the Brody Corporation. To put out the biggest fire first. But if there really was something wrong with my mother, putting it off wouldn't help. "Laura?" There was a delay, static on her cell phone. "Laura? Can you hear me?"

"Oh, Donnie. There you are."

As if I could see through the line, I pulled the receiver away from my cheek and stared into it. I hadn't heard Laura sound so light, so playful in years.

I put the receiver back to my mouth. "Here I are."

Laura laughed. "I'd forgotten that one."

So had I until she mentioned it. In the early years of our marriage, whoever got home last went in search of the other one in our small apartment. "There you are" was a welcome. A discovery. Now we could be together after a day apart. "Here I are" was always the response. That and arms spread wide, pulling each other into a long kiss.

Lately, a long kiss had been as far away as

the lightness in Laura's tone. Kissing wasn't the only thing not on our radar these days. It was a good thing Matt and I didn't talk about personal stuff; if he ever asked about my sex life I'd have to clock him. In truth, I couldn't remember the last time Laura and I had — well, I'd be embarrassed to admit my performance in the husband department had been dismal at best.

Best? Hardly the word to describe your efforts at loving your wife. I switched the phone to my other ear. "What's" — there was a frog in my throat that needed clearing. I coughed. Tried again. "Is something wrong with Mom?"

"Oh, no, nothing's wrong." Laura sounded different.

"Elle gave me a note. Said you'd called. I assumed it was about Mom." What else did we talk about these days?

Again a light trill of laughter. Under normal circumstances her laugh would not have sent an odd chill down my spine. I shook off the feeling.

"I wanted to tell you that your mom got a new roommate today."

A roommate was nothing unexpected. Not in a double room in a nursing home. In my mother's current state, I couldn't imagine that a roommate would make a lick of difference to her. "Oh. Okay." There was a long pause, as if I was expected to say more. I wracked my brain. "And how's Mom?"

"Good," Laura said. "Really good, actually. Cecelia, that's her roommate's name, seems to have perked her up. Your mom is sitting up, taking it all in."

"Taking what in?" I couldn't imagine where this conversation was going.

"Cecelia's quite the talker. Your mom seems to be listening." Laura chuckled at something. "Cecilia's son was there helping her get settled. We put her clothes away and hung a couple photos. It's been quite the day. I thought you might want to stop by and see your mom and meet Cecelia."

I closed my eyes and breathed as deeply as I could before answering. "Laura, you can't imagine what my day has been like. Every time I turned around there was a blaze to put out. I'm heading out to a meeting right now. If it's not too late after that, maybe I can swing by the nursing home."

Even as I said the words, I knew I wouldn't fit it in. After I met with the Brody people I'd be right back at the office helping Matt organize the Westwood project. "Tell Mom I'll be there tomorrow. For sure."

"I'm at home now." Laura's voice cooled a degree. "I wasn't planning on going back tonight." There was a pause. Her warmth returned. "I was wondering, what time do you plan to be home tonight? You've been working so hard."

Ah. Her acknowledgment flooded through my chest. Warm pride. A sense that all this was worth it after all.

"Will you be home soon?" I could almost see Laura winding a strand of hair around her finger. What had gotten into her?

"Why?"

"Oh, I don't know. I was thinking we could have a glass of wine together. Some cheese and crackers. I bought that smoky white cheddar you like. We haven't —" She stopped, started again. "It's been so long since we've really talked." Another pause. "The wedding was such a rush. And then your mother. I thought . . . I don't know . . . I just —" A deep breath. "I miss you."

Sheesh. I put my elbow on the desk and leaned my head into my hand. There was a rock, there was a hard place. I was in between. What was I supposed to do?

"I'll see what I can do." Not much, but the best I could come up with on short notice without a creative-writing team to write me a script.

I put the key in the lock and let myself into

the house. "Laura?" I called softly, tiptoeing through the kitchen. The chance she'd still be waiting up this late was slim.

The light over the kitchen sink was on. A floor lamp in the adjacent family room cast a soft glow, along with a low smolder from the gas fireplace. On the coffee table near the fireplace were two wine glasses, an unopened bottle of something red beside them. A small bowl of crackers. A plate of sliced cheese covered with plastic wrap.

Maybe a pretty sight three hours ago, but now the tableau suggested nothing but hot water — for me.

My best bet was to clear away the evidence. I could understand Laura leaving the wine and cheese out as she stomped off to bed. But leaving the fireplace on was nothing short of dangerous. If she was still speaking to me in the morning, I'd remind her. But if Laura got up in the morning and found everything as she'd left it, the still life would serve as a sick souvenir. *Yes, Laura, your husband has let you down again.*

I made a beeline to the food. The slices of delivery pizza I'd wolfed down hours ago hadn't satisfied. Cheese and crackers would make a good bedtime snack. I walked around the back of the couch, my mind on nothing but my stomach.

"Oh, you're home." A sleepy voice from the couch.

I jumped, as what looked like an unfolded blanket on the couch moved.

"Laura. Hi." Why was I whispering? "I didn't see you there."

I should have been quieter. Should have bypassed the couch and the snack, let the fire burn and headed straight upstairs. I'd been caught red-handed. Excuses hung ready on my lips. *It took me almost two hours to convince the Brody folks to stay the course. Westwood Mall wants a totally new campaign as of yesterday.* Nothing Laura hadn't heard before. I only hoped she was too tired to argue.

Laura lifted an edge of the blanket and patted the cushion of the couch. "Sit beside me." Her voice held a sultry sleepiness I hadn't heard in a long time.

I sat. This wasn't the usual welcome when I was hours late.

Laura leaned forward and picked up the wine bottle and a corkscrew. She handed both to me with a sleepy smile and watched while I pulled the cork from the opening. With a brush of her fingers against mine, she took the bottle and poured some in both glasses. She handed one to me, lifted hers, and gently clinked it against mine.

"To us," she said, taking a sip.

"To us," I echoed. Now what? I sipped the wine, not really tasting it, and stared at the crackers on the table. My mind was still back at the agency. Tomorrow we were going to assign Ben, Justine, Stasha, and Elle to do a quick concept for the Westwood campaign. Matt and I were going to sit in as much as possible to head off any rabbit trails from the beginning. There wasn't going to be time for any missteps on this project. I was giving up my personal assistant for the next couple weeks — a small price to pay to keep a major client satisfied.

"I think your mom likes her new roommate."

"Um." I took another sip of wine. My glass was almost empty. How'd that happen? I poured a little more in my glass and reached for a cracker.

"She seems really nice."

"That's good." Matt had called the print shops we worked with to see which one could work us in the soonest. There would be a huge overtime charge on this project, which we'd pass along to Westwood. Ed wasn't going to be happy. But then he wasn't happy right now either.

"You should hear her talk."

"Who?" Laura's words didn't register

right away. I quickly re-ran the conversation. "Mom? She started talking today?"

"No. Her roommate." A wrinkle of irritation pulled at Laura's eyebrows.

I needed to pay attention. One thing at a time. I was home now. I popped a piece of cheese in my mouth. "This is good."

Laura smiled. "Glad you like it."

"I do."

Laura leaned toward me and brushed a light kiss on my lips. "I'm glad you're home." She stayed close.

I kissed her back. "I'm glad I'm home, too." If I could just get the office out of my thoughts.

She threaded one hand over my shoulder and across my neck. Her hand curved around my head, cupping the smooth spot under my ear. Oh, her skin against mine felt good. Soft. Warm. Her fingers lightly caressed the side of my neck as she kissed my cheek, the corner of my mouth, my lips. Mmmm . . . I could taste the wine, warm on her lips. Or was the alluring flavor from mine? Didn't matter. Her kisses were a formula for seduction. A familiar dance we'd perfected over the past 23 years.

I pushed back into the cushion, drawing Laura with me. It was as if a thousand tiny kisses were massaging me from the inside out. Every muscle in my body felt liquid.

Laura eased the wine glass from my hand and set it on the coffee table next to hers. "Relax," she said softly.

I leaned back onto the couch. I couldn't lift my eyelids if I tried. But I didn't want to. Her touch was bliss. Validation.

I opened my eyes the smallest bit. I was on the couch, a quilt covering me. The fireplace had been turned off. The wine, cheese and crackers were gone. Laura was standing, staring into the darkened fire pit.

"What time is it?" My voice was a rasp.

Laura looked at me over her shoulder. "Too late." Soft seduction was gone. I recognized the tone of a thousand similar nights. An edge. "I'm going to bed."

"I'll be up in a minute." All I wanted was more sleep. A minute might turn into a few hours if I was lucky.

"I've locked up." The soft shuffle of her slippers faded from the side of the couch, stopped at the foot of the stairs. "I turned down the heat."

I pulled at the quilt, turned into the couch. I punched at the cushion, trying to slip back into dreamland. The cuffs of my shirtsleeves had ridden up, pulled tight against my wrists. I turned on my back and pulled them down, a vague unease tugging at my mind. The fire. Wine. Food. Laura's kisses. Her intention clear.

My hand fingered the buttons of my shirt. All closed except the top two. I'd undone the top one while Matt and I plotted the Westwood account earlier. Laura had undone button number two an hour ago. My belt was buckled, my shirt rumpled but still half tucked into my slacks. The results of my survey weren't looking good.

Ice. Definite ice. That's what I'd detected in Laura's tone. A chill that had nothing to do with the temperature in the room. Everything to do with the fact that I'd fallen asleep on her sultry seduction.

I wasn't in hot water; I was in the deep freeze.

STASHA

"What time is it anyway?" I pushed back from the conference table and looked at my wristwatch. I had to blink three times before I could focus on the numbers on the dial. "Almost midnight?" I half stood. No one else was making a move. I sat back down.

"Does Cinderella have to get home?" Ben. Sarcastic. Of course.

"No, I don't have to get home." Just because Ben was single he seemed to think no one else had a life. If I'd known the meeting was going to run this late, I would have called Josh again three hours ago. Now, it was too late, unless he was waiting up. But if Josh was worried, he knew he could call me here. Where else was I these days?

But then, his schedule wasn't set in stone either. Back when I worked at the coffee shop, he'd left me sitting at home plenty of nights while he chaperoned a busload of junior high kids on a band trip or coached

341

them at an out-of-town ball game.

So . . . you're keeping score? You're alone one night; it's only fair for Josh to sit by himself another?

No, it wasn't like that.

Then why the defensive attitude?

I wasn't being defensive. Only fair.

Marriage isn't 50-50. Sometimes it's 90-10. You give 90, he gives 10.

I'm not giving 90! That's not right.

Not defensive?

I shifted in my chair. I'd read articles on how the first year was the hardest. So far, marriage didn't seem all that difficult. So what if Josh left the cap off the toothpaste? I bought my own tube to use. If he wanted crusty toothpaste in the morning, he could have it. What was hard was trying to find time to be together. Now that we were married we saw less of each other than when we were dating.

I pushed my fingers through my limp hair. The mousse I'd used at seven this morning was long gone. I didn't want to chance a glance in a mirror. My makeup couldn't look much better. If I looked like I felt, Josh should consider himself lucky if he was asleep when I got home. I covered my mouth to hide a yawn.

"We've got to get this tagline nailed

tonight." Justine twisted a pen between her fingers. "We told the Westwood people we'd have something by tomorrow."

It almost is *tomorrow.* I didn't mind staying up this late; I did mind having to actually think this late at night. What I really wanted was to be at home, snuggled in bed beside Josh.

And that was the problem. As much as I loved Josh, I was starting to love this job too. The paycheck was nice, but even that didn't beat brainstorming with other creative people. It was even more exciting to see one of my ideas come to life. Like the bank commercial. Ben had put in a good word for me on that one. My work on that commercial was probably the reason Matt tapped me to sit in on this account.

I looked around the table. Ben, Justine, Elle, and me. We were all about the same age. Eager to make a mark in this business. There was a stress-induced, deadline mentality that came along with each project. Baptism by brainstorming bonded us. I'd sit here as long as it took to come up with a winning idea. After I went to the bathroom.

"I need a pit stop." I slid my chair away from the table and headed for the ladies' room. At least Ben had nothing against a potty break. Too much Diet Coke was a good excuse to get up and walk around. Refocus my thoughts.

With my shoulder to the door, I rolled into the bathroom. Lack of sleep topped off with caffeine was making me punchy. When I did get home, I probably wouldn't be able to sleep. I pushed my way into a stall, sat down, closed my eyes. Ah, my eyelids felt so good against open-too-long scratchiness. I'd just sit here a minute.

My head bobbed and popped up as if I'd been pinched. I couldn't have fallen asleep that fast. I glanced at my watch. Mere seconds had passed. I looked again, just to make sure. And then, I saw it — the entire Westwood campaign right on my wrist. As fast as possible I did my bathroom thing, swished my hands under the faucet, and ran down the hall to the conference room. "I've got it!"

Three sleepy-eyed faces stared at me.

"Look." I was wide awake now. I tapped at the wristwatch on my arm. "Remember when I asked, 'What time is it, anyway?' It's right here." I held my arm out so everyone could visualize my plan along with me.

"Uh-huh," Ben said. He rolled his eyes at Elle and Justine. "Sit down, MacKay."

"No, really. This is brilliant. Well, maybe not genius, but it's great. Listen up." I turned the top off my Diet Coke and took a quick sip. My explanation to this sleep-deprived crew might take a while. "Here's what I came up with." I slipped my watch off my wrist and held it out for the others to see. "Look."

Ben raised one eyebrow at me. "What exactly were you doing in the bathroom?"

"Shhh!" Elle shot Ben a look. "Have you come up with anything tonight?"

"Yeah," Justine chimed in. I had no doubt she'd been on the receiving end of Ben's cynical comments one too many times.

I pointed to my watch. "There are 12 numbers on the face."

"Oh, duh-hh." Guess who?

I ignored the cretin. "Figure it out." I laid my watch on the table and held up both hands, fingers spread. As I spoke I wiggled a different finger with each letter. "W-E-S-T-W-O-O-D." I took a quick breath. "M-A-L-L. That's twelve."

As if a light bulb was hanging over her head, Elle grinned. Justine was next. "I get it." Ben lowered his chin and stared at me.

"See," I said, picking up the watch again. "We make a big clock and instead of numbers, we spell out Westwood Mall around the face. We can use smaller watches for some of the other ads, always substituting letters for the numbers. For the TV ad we can have people looking at the time on their wrists, on the wall, on the big clock at the mall. It will all spell out Westwood Mall. Shoppers can ask for the time and we'll have someone look at their watch and say, "It's time to shop at Westwood."

I stopped for breath. Ben was staring at me. I was explained out. If Ben didn't get it, I was sunk. He was the lead on this team; if he wasn't onboard, this train was going nowhere. Justine. Elle. We all looked to Ben, who was closed-mouthed and narrow-eyed. He'd been talking in run-on sentences all night. Now he'd closed up like a clam. Justine had worked with him the longest. She waved her hand in front of his face. "Speak."

Ben licked his lips, still staring at me. "You know what this means, don't you?"

"What does it mean?" I asked.

"It means," Ben threaded his hands together behind his head and broke into a grin "we have time to go out for a drink before the bars close." He rose from his chair, reached across the table and high-fived me. "Way to think, MacKay. Way to think."

"I love it." Elle pulled me into a one-armed hug.

"Ditto." Justine squeezed my arm.

"This calls for a beer." Ben already had

one arm in his coat. "I'll buy the first round."

Ten minutes ago I'd been asleep in the bathroom; now I felt like I could run a marathon. I ran to my cubicle and grabbed my coat. There was a natural high that came along with a good idea. Reason to celebrate. Besides, there was no way I could lay down and sleep now.

An icy wind whipped my black jeans against my legs as the four of us ran down the sidewalk from the agency to the bar and grill at the end of the block. Sometime during the course of our brainstorming, thick snow had begun to fall. It blanketed the sidewalk, creating a white carpet leading to our impromptu celebration.

Four pairs of feet stomped into the bar portion of the café. We took a high-stooled table captive. From out of nowhere four mugs of beer appeared.

"Here's to Stasha!" Justine raised her glass to the middle of the table. Elle and Ben clinked their thick mugs against hers. I raised mine and took a cold swallow. Beer was not my favorite beverage, but I wasn't planning to complain when we were celebrating and Ben was buying.

"What time is it anyway?" Ben's boisterous voice boomed over the loud music.

Justine, Elle, and I knew the answer. "Time to shop at Westwood Mall!" We clinked glasses again and took another drink. There weren't many people left in the bar this late on a weeknight. Those who were there turned our way with do-you-have-to-be-so-loud looks. Their night might be winding down, but the four of us were in our prime.

In what seemed like a minute, and before I could say "no thanks," there was another drink sitting in front of me. When I did get home, I'd sleep like a rock.

"I suppose," I reached in my purse and pulled out my lip gloss. The spices from the buffalo wings we'd shared felt like they were eating the flesh off my lips. I ran the thick gloss over my lip, dropped it back in my bag, and took out my car keys. "I've gotta get some sleep."

Elle stifled a yawn. "Me too."

Ben wrapped his hands around his beer mug. "Be ready to hit it hard tomorrow. We're going to have to crank this campaign out in the next couple of days."

Already I was regretting the hour I'd spent at the bar. Two drinks and a platter of chicken wings amounted to 60 minutes of sleep I'd bypassed. I couldn't wait to get home and crawl into bed. It was going to feel so good to cuddle up next to Josh and drift off to sleep. I hoped I wouldn't dream about the Westwood campaign. I was going to be breathing Westwood for the rest of my waking hours this week.

There weren't many cars on the streets of Carlton at one in the morning, but there was a heavy layer of snow. I drove carefully, conscious of the fact that two beers combined with the late hour and snowfall — and a drastic drop in the adrenaline rush I'd had earlier — were a recipe for an accident.

Made it. Josh had parked his pickup on the street. I pulled my car through a layer of snow into the driveway, parking in front of the garage where Mr. Miller kept the car he rarely drove. As long as we kept the driveway shoveled, Leon was a happy camper. I could see Josh had shoveled sometime earlier in the evening, but another inch or so had covered the driveway since he'd come home.

I turned off the car and the headlights. I knew the night was cold. I hadn't realized how dark it was with no moon or streetlight to illuminate the snowy, icy path I needed to march through to get to the back door.

I got out of the car, standing still for a moment to let my eyes adjust to the dim light. Small snowdrifts along the side of the driveway only made the edge of the driveway darker. The back door wasn't far, but I could barely see it from where I stood. The porch light was off. Not a good sign. We'd finally convinced Mr. Miller that we needed the back light left on in the evening. Electricity was cheaper than a broken leg. The last one in at night flicked it off. Josh must have come home late, assumed I was home, and turned it off before he headed upstairs.

Good grief. Didn't he see my car wasn't here? I dropped my hands and took a tentative step forward. Once I was on the sidewalk, it was a straight walk to the steps. The house cast a dark shadow. I knew there was a small rise where the shoveled driveway met a snow-packed footpath. A perfect place to fall in fashionably high, narrow-heeled boots. I lifted one foot high, stepping carefully into the snow, then the other. I hoped no one was watching. I must look like a majorette without a band. I slid one foot forward and found the lip of the sidewalk with the tip of my shoe. Whoops! There was a slick of frosty snow under my foot. I waved my arms and dropped my purse but stayed upright.

Instant anger kept me warm as I bent and picked up my bag. What kind of inconsiderate guy was Josh to not notice my car wasn't here? When he walked in the apartment and found me not at home, he could have turned the light back on. Didn't he stop to think what it would be like for me to walk this path in the dark?

Apparently not.

All he thinks about is himself. Earlier, I'd wanted nothing more than to climb into bed beside my husband, but now I felt like decking him, if I ever made it inside.

I took another step. The snow underfoot was hard and uneven. The leather soles of my boots might as well have been hockey pucks for the way they shimmied on the icy surface. Why didn't Josh shovel this part? At least I'd be able to walk, even if it was dark. My boots were going to be ruined, if I didn't break something first.

And now you're thinking only of yourself.

Well, I was the one about to break her neck. How would he feel then?

By the time I reached the first step of the porch my new brown boots were white with snow. As I took the first step, my foot slid out to the side. "Ouch!" A muscle in my upper leg screamed silently. I limped up the remaining steps and let myself in. My feet were freezing, my boots wet with snow. I was already planning the speech I'd give him. If my boots were ruined, he'd better not dare say a word about the money I'd have to spend to replace them.

I'll bet Josh will think twice about not shoveling next time. Righteous anger helped me up the back staircase to our apartment. This was all Josh's fault. He was my husband, after all. He was supposed to look out for me.

As I let myself into our apartment, I was tempted to wake Josh up and give him a piece of my mind. I was the one who'd worked 16 hours straight today. The least he could do was make sure I had a clear path to get home.

Common sense prevailed. If I woke Josh up now I'd be awake another hour and start a needless fight. I was home, safe and sound. I needed sleep if I was going to be productive through another long day tomorrow. Best to let sleeping husbands lie.

I peeked into the bedroom. Josh was sleeping on his side, his back to the door. The clock on the bedside table read 1:30. Josh didn't need to know what time I'd finally come home. I didn't need him to smell the smoky residue left on my clothes from our hour-long victory party at the bar.

As much as I'd been ready to vent my anger, now all I wanted was to have this long day over with.

I stood outside the bedroom door and took off my damp boots and socks, and then slipped out of my jeans and sweater. It was chilly without the extra layers. In my underwear I tiptoed across the bedroom; the old T-shirt I wore to sleep was under my pillow. I squeezed along the narrow space between the bed and the wall, eased my hand under the pillow, and pulled my nightwear from underneath. A reverse-order tooth fairy. I had to be careful, because now that I'd circled the room, Josh was facing my way.

I reached around my back and unhooked my bra, slipping out of it and into the T-shirt in one smooth move. As if the bed were made of eggshells, I carefully sat down. There was a deep breath from Josh. I froze until he exhaled. A slow lift of my legs, and they were under the covers. I eased myself back onto my pillow.

Every muscle in my body seemed to sink into the softness of the sheets. I sighed deeply and closed my eyes. Man, did my bed feel good.

"Where were you?" Josh's not-at-all-sleepy voice popped my eyes wide. If I'd thought it was icy outside, Josh's voice was colder.

"I-I thought you were asleep," I whispered. Muscles that had been limp moments before now began to tense.

"No." Just that. No more.

I swallowed hard. Spoke soft. "We were working on the Westwood project. I told you. Remember?"

Josh turned onto his back. "I thought the agency was 'no smoking.' " His voice held a sharp edge.

"It is." Two words that were a feeble attempt at evasion.

Silence. It wasn't hard to know what was coming next.

"Then why do you smell like an ashtray?"

An ice cube of defensiveness set my jaw tight. I hadn't done anything wrong. "We worked until midnight, then went out for a beer. Okay?" It wasn't as if Josh hadn't ever stayed out late with his friends.

Nothing from the other side of the bed.

I cleared my throat. "We needed to unwind."

"Unwind?" His voice was tight. "Ever think about doing that at home? With me?"

I stared at the ceiling. "Like you've never stayed out late."

"Not this late."

Even though he couldn't see me, I rolled my eyes. "We were having trouble coming

354

up with an idea for the Westwood account. I thought of one, and then Ben offered to buy a beer to celebrate."

"Ben?"

"I work with Ben. You know that."

"Working with and partying with are two different things."

"We weren't *partying.*"

"A married woman sitting in a bar, having a drink with a single guy isn't work."

If I hadn't known better, I would swear Josh had stepped out of a 1950s TV show. What was with the retro attitude? "Justine and Elle were with us."

"So, it was a party."

Good grief. "Sure. Whatever."

Heavy silence hung between us. I grabbed the covers and turned on my side, huffing my frustration into the air. Let Josh think what he wanted. One of us planned to get some sleep tonight.

I lay in the dark, sleep nowhere near. How could Josh be such an idiot? All I did was work hard and then —

"Are they married too?"

I knew perfectly well who he meant, but if he was going to act like some jealous soap-opera husband, I wasn't going to make this easy. "Who?"

"Justine and Elle."

"No."

I could hear him pull a long breath in through his nose. "So, you were sitting in a bar, drinking with three single people until almost" — there was a rustle as he angled his head toward the clock — "1:30 in the morning and —"

I sat up in bed. "When did you become my dad?"

Silence. Then, "When did *you* become him? All you care about is work." Josh threw back the covers and sat up. "And just so you know, I'm not your dad; I'm your husband." His voice held an eerie calm. "In case you don't remember."

I could feel my jaw drop. Backhanded sarcasm was my line of attack, not Josh's. "Remember?" I crossed my legs on the bed. "I don't understand what the big deal is. It's not as if you've never gone out with the guys."

Even in the dark I could see a wry grimace creep onto Josh's face. "My point exactly."

"What point?"

"I go out with guys."

"It was a guy and two girls. Women. Whatever."

"How would you feel if I went out for a drink after midnight with three of the single teachers on staff?"

"I wouldn't care." But I knew I would. Especially if I was sitting home alone waiting for Josh. And one of them was cute and flirty.

"Fine, then maybe I will." As if he was going to make good on his dare, Josh got out of bed and walked to the doorway.

"Where are you going?" He wouldn't leave, not at this hour.

"Why should you care?"

Why should I? I grabbed the edge of the covers and pulled them to my chin, lying down on the bed as if I could sleep.

Josh left the bedroom. I could hear him wander into the kitchen. Open a cupboard. Run the water in the kitchen sink. Every fiber of my being wanted to follow him out to the kitchen, wrap my arms around him, and tell him I was sorry. All I'd wanted the whole time I'd been working late was to be home with Josh. Now I was, and we were fighting.

I flipped my pillow and put my check against the cool side. This was so stupid. There was no reason for Josh to be jealous, and yet there was something about his jealousy that made me love him all the more. Maybe I should get up and apologize.

For what?

Exactly. I'd done nothing wrong. He

should be the one to apologize for starting this stupid argument. I flipped onto my back and stared into the shadows. I hated that he was mad at me. My after-work get-together was nothing but letting off steam after working too many hours. If only I hadn't gotten defensive. If I'd just calmed down and explained, he would have understood. Instead, I turned my late night outing into an argument that was costing us both a good night's sleep.

But still . . . A stubborn lump thumped where my heart used to be. It was ridiculous for Josh to get so bent out of shape over this. We might be married, but we weren't joined at the hip.

A man shall leave his mother and father and be united with his wife, and they will become one flesh. A verse the pastor had read at our wedding ceremony burned through my thoughts. I remembered how romantic that Bible verse had sounded the day of my wedding. Josh and I would be *one.*

A clump of tears pushed its way into my throat. I swallowed them down. I was not going to cry. I wasn't going to turn into some cliché of a wife, softening my husband with tears.

What about softening your own heart?

I didn't need softening. I was right, and

Josh was wrong. If anyone should apologize, it should be Josh. I punched at my pillow and turned onto my stomach. Enough of this. If Josh wanted to pout in the living room, let him. I was going to sleep.

I stretched, pushing my feet into the wrinkle of sheets, my arms over my head. After tossing and turning most of the night, I was surprised to see morning light creeping through my eyelids. I turned my head to Josh's side of the bed.

He wasn't there. Had he never come back to bed?

"Josh?" Loud enough for him to hear me anywhere in our small apartment.

No answer from any corner. I pushed back the covers and looked at the clock. Yikes! I'd overslept big time. I jumped out of bed and hurried to the bathroom. If Josh had eventually come to bed, I hadn't heard him. I also hadn't heard him get ready for work and leave. How could he let me sleep this late? He knew I had to get to work too.

I thought you weren't joined at the hip.

Obviously, we weren't, and now I wasn't going to have time for a shower. I scrubbed at my face with a washcloth, slapped on a minimum of makeup, and called it good, all the while doing a slow simmer. Didn't he care about me anymore? The tears I swallowed last night were back.

I grabbed my purse and hurried down the back staircase, reaching for the doorknob before my foot was on the last step.

"Morning, missy." Leon had a knack for catching me as I was leaving for work.

How long had he sat at his kitchen table this morning, eating his toast, drinking his coffee, waiting for me? Any other day I'd stop for a minute, today I didn't have time.

"Morning, Leon," I called. "Bye," I said in the same breath.

"Kind of late today, aren't you?"

I already had the door partially open, the doorknob in my hand. "Yeah, I'm late."

"Won't keep you then. Just wondering if everything was okay up there."

Just like that the tears in my throat filled my eyes. Blinking at them did no good. I doubted Leon heard the exact words Josh and I shot back and forth last night, but he had to know a loud late-night conversation couldn't be good. Either way, I had no words to answer him. I'd thought marrying Josh would be the answer to all of life's problems; instead, in some unfathomable way, our marriage had created more.

LAURA

Across the crowded art gallery I spotted Donnie. I didn't have to see his face to know what he was thinking. *How much longer do I have to stay?* I'd let him decide. The husband of the best friend of the gallery owner didn't have quite the obligation I did at this grand opening. Donnie might be able to duck out early; I'd be staying until the last crumb had been swept off the floor.

I bent to pick up a cocktail napkin someone had dropped, then glanced over to the buffet table Karen and I had set up late this afternoon. I had replenished the silver platters more times than I cared to count.

Once again my eyes found Donnie. He had found someone to chat up. At least now I could count on him staying a while. Every new contact was a potential client. If he thought he was doing business at this event, it would be worth his time to stay and pretend to understand the assortment of art on the walls. Karen didn't need to know that Donnie would rather be just about anywhere but here.

Our formal invitation to the opening of Karen's gallery had sat on the kitchen counter for almost a week. I had known it was coming for a month, about as long as I'd helped Karen plan the finger food and champagne menu. Making miniature cream puffs wasn't my favorite thing to do, but my sometime specialty was one of Karen's favorites. Last night I had been turning them out at top speed . . .

With a teaspoon I had scooped a small ball of the butter-yellow batter onto a cookie sheet. I had smiled to myself. I wouldn't tell anyone that the tiny puffs reminded me of little faceless doll heads lined up on a platter. Who would want to eat them with that image in mind?

"What are you doing?" Donnie had come into the kitchen from the garage and put his briefcase on the kitchen counter. As usual, he had missed supper. Since Stasha had moved out for good, I'd hardly cooked a meal. He probably was surprised to find me in the kitchen in the middle of a long evening.

"Hi to you too." Ever since he'd fallen fast asleep the night I had hoped we would reconnect in the love department, conversation was an art form in avoiding anything meaningful. I narrowed my eyes at his briefcase. Too often I'd seen his leather bag of work on the floor at his office, on the seat of the car, sitting on the sidewalk while he talked with an acquaintance. Who knew what might be growing on the bottom of the black leather? Whatever it was, I didn't want it on my kitchen counter.

Without saying a word, Donnie picked up his briefcase and put it on the floor. "Long day," he said.

I continued my measured scooping. Had there ever been a time when Donnie's day had been short? If I needed him somewhere at a certain time and place, I made sure he wrote it in his planner. This is what we'd come to. Me, a glorified secretary keeping track of Donnie's life outside the office. I put the filled cookie sheet in the oven, setting the timer for ten minutes.

While I waited for the timer to tick away the minutes, I busied myself sorting the already done miniature puffs into rows of a dozen. Why was Donnie just standing there staring into space? Certainly he had an hour's worth of work in that loaded-down briefcase of his. The oven-warmed air hung heavy between us. There was a time — years ago — when conversation would have come easy. Now I was racking my brain trying to think of something to say to this man who seemed more acquaintance than husband. It wouldn't hurt me to pretend the other night hadn't happened.

"I suppose I need to show up at this thing." Donnie tapped a finger on the edge of the invitation propped on the counter.

In an instant I knew exactly what Donnie meant. He didn't want to go to the gallery opening. I picked up the thick potholder and squeezed it between my fingers. I'd been friends with Karen so long I couldn't even remember how we met. Her husband and Donnie went back just as far. Donnie was a big boy. He should know the responsibilities of friendship by now. As if I was clamping my teeth on a bullet, I bit back the first words that came to mind and instead said, "I'm sure Karen and Todd would like to see you there."

He picked up the invite and studied it as if he'd never seen an invitation before. "The timing isn't great." Donnie set the invitation back on its edge and wrinkled his nose. "I don't have to wear a suit, do I?"

Oh, good grief. I couldn't help it. I threw the potholder on the counter and turned toward Donnie. "You know, this is supposed to be fun, not some obligation. If you don't want to go, don't. I volunteered to help Karen with the food, so I'll be there regardless. You make up your own mind."

And so he had come with me after all.

Chatter from the gallery infiltrated my memory. Now Donnie was still talking across the room. I hoped he'd stay long enough to make Karen think her opening was a success. She knew how easily Donnie got bored with anything that smacked of regular.

I turned to the couple standing beside me. "Can I get you anything? Refresh your champagne? More hors d'oeuvres?" It had been a long time since I'd played waitress.

"No, thanks." A woman I didn't know handed me her empty champagne glass as if I was hired help. "Everything is exquisite." She held out a crumpled napkin as well.

I took the glass and napkin from her diamond-studded hand, wondering if she'd made note of the fact that her beverage container really was glass and not some cheap plastic. Karen had insisted on only the best for this much-delayed opening. "If you need anything, just ask." I threaded my way through the crowded gallery, collecting three more empty glasses along the way to the makeshift kitchen in the back.

I was almost to the back room when Karen grabbed my arm, just about knocking two of the rented glasses from my hand. "Did you see? The mayor just walked in." Her eyes were too wide, glazed in an everything-has-to-be-perfect varnish. "Do you think I should go tell the *Register* reporter that the mayor is here?"

"If that reporter is on the ball, she's already seen him."

"But what if she hasn't?" Karen pulled a lipstick from the folds of the loose chocolate-colored tunic she was wearing and applied it to her lips. No wonder Karen kept lipstick handy; she'd kissed practically everyone who walked through the door.

I lifted my chin in the direction of the mayor. "There you go, problem solved." The frumpy reporter with a camera wasn't hard to spot standing next to the polished official.

"Do you think I should go over there?"

"Perfect photo op," I said, nudging Karen with my shoulder. "Don't forget to mention the grand-opening week discount."

"Oh yeah, thanks." Karen already had her back to me. She reminded me of a pinball, bouncing around her gallery, trying to rack up points by rubbing elbows with invited guests. We were all hoping every encounter would ring a bell of some sort — either a purchase tonight, or sometime in the near future.

I slipped into the tiny work area in the back, making sure the door closed behind me. The gallery patrons out front didn't need to see the messy version of their fancy party. I put the used glasses in a plastic bin, rinsed my hands in another bin filled with almost cool water, then simply stood and took a deep breath. The air back here was refreshingly clear, unlike the stuffy, polite-conversation-filled air on the other side of the door. Maybe Donnie wasn't so wrong in wishing he was home.

But it would do no good to hibernate with my wandering thoughts in this small room. I picked up a bottle of champagne and stepped back into the crowded gallery. And then, as if a magnet had pulled my gaze to the front door of the gallery, I stared as John, Cecelia's son from the nursing home, stepped into the party. What was he doing here?

I spun around on my heel and slipped back into the tiny storeroom, leaning my back against the door as if I'd just escaped capture after a wild chase. Who did I think I was running from? Cupid?

This was stupid.

Why should it matter if John sees you here?

What if he talks to Donnie?

What if?

He doesn't know I'm married to him. To anyone for that matter.

Maybe it's time he found out.

It wasn't as if I'd tried to hide my marriage. After all, I wore my wedding ring. I couldn't help the fact that it didn't look like a traditional wedding set. Donnie had picked out the unusual setting himself. If John assumed it was simply a ring, well . . .

You haven't exactly advertised the fact you're married.

I hadn't denied it. I stared down at my wedding ring, fingered the back of it with my thumb. If I was going to be honest with myself, I had to admit I had looked forward to seeing John at the nursing home just a little too much these past weeks. It was remarkably easy to banter with someone who didn't seem to have more important things to do. It wasn't hard to talk about everything but my husband with a personable, attractive man.

You're sure you haven't tried to give John the impression you aren't attached?

Oh, good grief. There was a casual picture of Donnie and me on Eleanor's bedside table. I could have easily tucked it in a drawer. Eleanor was in no position to complain if it went missing.

I recalled the day the old photo had been taken. Stasha snapped it years ago at a Fourth of July party in Matt's backyard. Even now I could feel a smile working at my lips. The raucous summer day was etched with volleyball, hamburgers and hot dogs, fireworks at dusk, and watermelon before we went home. I bit back the smile. That was back when Donnie and I actually did things together.

I didn't know if John had seen the photo. Even if he had, he probably wouldn't recognize us. The photo was ancient. Taken back when we were happy.

I blinked at the sudden stinging in my eyes. If John mistook us for brother and sister, let him. For all intents and purposes, that's all Donnie and I were. After all, the times Donnie had been to the home to visit his mother were so few and far between, anyone keeping track might easily imagine Donnie was a relative who lived across country, not merely across town.

I had to admit there was a part of me that enjoyed the jovial attention John gave me during his visits with his mom. What had been long, boring days by Eleanor's bedside had lately become the highlight of my week.

And nights? A flush crept up my neck. Even in my thoughts it was embarrassing to admit how much time I'd spent thinking about my newest friend.

There's a fine line between friendship and flirting, and you're walking it.

I picked up the bottle of champagne again. This was silly. I was acting like a teenager with a celebrity crush. Nothing would ever come of my feelings. Nothing could come from them.

What if things don't work out between you and Do—

No! I refused to act like a black widow spider, weaving a web to catch me just in case. Although I had to admit, John's strong arms would be a soft place to fall.

Stop it!

I set the bottle of champagne back down. I couldn't go out to the party feeling this conflicted, this flustered. Donnie wouldn't notice, but Karen might. What would I say?

I leaned my hands against the ledge where the party supplies were stored and balanced my weight against the ridge as if weighing my options. The party wasn't that big; I was bound to cross paths with John. Seeing him at the nursing home was one thing; bumping into him here was something else altogether. Then again, it might do Donnie some good to know he had little competition.

John is not competition.

Maybe not, but the idea of going out there and making small talk with John, knowing Donnie was hovering nearby, was simply too . . .

Behind me I heard the door open. A quick cloud of voices from the gallery filled the small back room, then sounded muffled as the door closed. I didn't have to turn around to know who had entered. It had to be one of four people — Karen, her husband, Todd, Carla, or Judy. We were the only recruits in Karen's small army tonight. It wouldn't pay to have any of them catch me taking a daydream break; they were getting paid as much as I was to play waitress, which was zilch.

I brushed my hands together as if I'd just finished something important. "What do we need out there?" I began to turn around to see who I was talking to just as I felt the too close warmth of another person at my back. Considering my thoughts just moments ago, it only took a second for my heart to leap to a conclusion. *What if this was John?*

In an instant, languid, liquid warmth seemed to fill my arms, my limbs. It had been a long time since I'd felt a sensation I could only describe as desire. Just as quickly, I realized John didn't even know I was here. The likelihood of my fantasy man being him was zero. The back room was small, but not that tiny. The only person who would stand this close to me was Donnie, and I knew better.

"What — ?" I looked over my shoulder to see who was invading my space.

"Hey, Laura." Judy's husband, make that almost ex-husband, was right behind me, a too-much-champagne grin on his face. "How's it going?"

How's it going? He could have asked the question two hours ago when he arrived. As it was, he and Judy had been doing a two-step that kept each other on opposite sides of the gallery all night. A small shiver of creepiness ran across my shoulders as Bill took one step forward. A step that now officially invaded my personal space. I took a step to the side, as far away as I was going to get in this minuscule, makeshift kitchen. I turned my back to him and started sorting appetizers as if I was trying to beat a speed record.

"Everything's fine," I said. What I really wanted to say was, "What in the heck are you doing?" My instincts told me it was best to keep my mouth shut and look busy.

I could feel Bill breathing down my back. "Did you shee Judy out there?"

Slurred words was not a good sign. What was it Judy had said about Bill's drinking? It seemed best to pretend I was too busy to talk.

"I don't shee why she can't come near me. We spent, what? Twenty years together, and now all of a shudden she's too good for me?"

I felt a breeze near the side of my face as Bill moved closer. Had Judy said Bill ever got physical when he was drinking?

"You know, Laura, I've always liked you." I felt his creepy hands on my waist. It didn't take but a second to realize my wild fantasizing of moments ago were about to become a reality — with the wrong man.

They're both the wrong man. You have a husband.

My hands froze over the platter of cream puffs. My body stiff, I gritted my teeth and pushed words past. "Move your hands." There could be no mistaking what I meant.

Bill ran his hands up my sides, down again. "Like this?"

"I said, move."

Now he slid in, wrapping his arms around my waist from behind, forcing me into a stiff-legged sway. "I'm moving."

373

I didn't feel threatened. There were too many people just outside the door to keep me from panicking. But I did feel violated. Who did Bill think he was putting his junior-high moves on me in the back room of the gallery? What gave him permission to press his body next to mine as if we had some sort of relationship?

Weren't you just, moments ago, imagining this same sort of rendezvous with someone else?

That was different.

Neither of them were your husband.

Anger and conviction finally moved my frozen limbs. I grabbed Bill's white-shirted arms and forced them away from my body. "Don't." I ducked away from his rude embrace. He was lucky I didn't turn and knee him in the groin. The creep.

As if she'd timed her entrance, Judy opened the door. Her eyes darted from me to her husband. I wasn't sure if she'd been looking for Bill or me.

I had nothing to feel guilty about, and yet I could feel a flush rise to my face. "Judy," I said, sidestepping Bill, "it's not —"

She rolled her eyes as if this was nothing new. "You can have him."

"I don't want him." As if.

"Well, neither do I."

"Hey." Bill looked between Judy and me as if he was waiting for one of us to claim him. I didn't feel one bit sorry for the two-timing leech.

Judy stepped around Bill and picked up the platter I'd been filling. "Here." She thrust the plate into Bill's hands. "Do something besides stalk me."

"I haven't been —"

"Just get." Judy pushed Bill out the door and closed it behind him.

"Really, Judy," I wasn't sure how to begin explaining the scene she'd walked in on. "I didn't — I wouldn't —"

Judy closed her eyes and sighed. "I know," she said looking directly at me, forgiving with her look even though there was nothing to forgive.

I lifted both arms, inviting Judy into a hug. Maybe it wasn't forgiveness I was seeing in her eyes. Resignation might better describe her gaze.

"You're so lucky." Judy's voice was muffled against my shoulder. "Donnie would never do something like this to you."

No, but you were considering doing it to him.

As if I could squeeze away my prior thoughts, I pulled Judy close, then released her. Her eyes were moist; her mouth twitched as she fought tears. "I never knew divorce would be this hard."

How could it be hard leaving a guy like Bill? I busied myself getting another platter of appetizers organized. "What do you mean?"

Judy brushed some crumbs from the ledge into her hand. "I just thought . . ." She stood at my side with her hand cupped around the small flecks of pastry and stared down at them. "I thought I'd feel good about finally being away from Bill. I wouldn't have to be on edge, worrying if he was going to come home blasted and be mean to me. I mean . . . I know I'm making the right decision, but —" she made an odd sound deep in her throat as she turned and threw the crumbs into the garbage can — "I miss him sometimes."

"You —"

Judy held up a hand, stopping my words. "And then he does something stupid like hit on my best friend." She gave me a knowing look. "And I can't wait for the papers to be final." She pressed her lips into a grim line. "Most of the time I feel like a hockey puck. First, I'm heading one way, then I get smacked in the other direction. I don't know from second to second what I'm feeling."

Judy lifted the bottle of champagne I'd

planned to serve. "To marriage. Yours, anyway." Just like that she turned and left the small room.

I grabbed a dishcloth from the plastic bin of water, wrung it out, and began wiping off the desktop we were using to store the cream puffs and lettuce wraps. Anything to avoid the thoughts skating through my head. Some of the ice we'd used for keeping things cool had melted into a puddle. I mopped up the water with the cloth, then noticed another puddle quickly forming. One of the containers must have a small leak.

Like your marriage?

What would a leaky, plastic bin have to do with my marriage? I lifted the tub, peering underneath. Maybe the excess water was just condensation. It didn't take a huge hole to empty a tub of water, only a tiny crack invisible to the naked eye, but a hole all the same. A drop here, a drop there, and if a person wasn't careful, you'd be left with what looked like a perfectly good container that held nothing. I might have to dump the whole container and throw it out.

Just what you're thinking about doing to your marriage. Throwing it all away.

Frankly, it didn't seem like there was much left to toss.

Donnie has been faithful to you. You have a wonderful life. You might be throwing out the very relationship I had planned for you.

If this empty shell of a relationship was part of God's plan, well, I wasn't so sure I trusted His —

Don't destroy what I have built. Whatever measure you use to give — large or small — will be used to measure what is given back to you.

I hadn't been to church or read my Bible in ages, yet from somewhere deep the reminder came to me. I certainly hadn't given much to my marriage these past years. I pressed my hands to my temples. I didn't *feel* like that hockey puck Judy had talked about, I *was* the puck. Smacked this way and that by changing emotions. I wished someone would just give me a good whack and send me into the goalie's glove. At least then I'd be safe.

DONNIE

"Hey, Donnie, good to see you." Ed Parcell, the marketing manager of Westwood Mall, hurried around the back of his desk. "The new ad campaign is going great." He shook my hand, then lifted his chin toward the door of his office in a tucked-away corner of the mall. "Let's walk out into the mall. You can see for yourself what you did."

If a guy was going to be technical, I hadn't done much of anything on this Christmas campaign. It had been my daughter who'd come up with the brilliant idea that had captured the imaginations — and pocketbooks — of the Christmas shoppers in Carlton. *Time to shop at Westwood Mall* had become something of a local catch-phrase. I had a hunch Stasha might be nominated for an ad award for this one.

Like father, like daughter. I would allow myself the proud cliché. Too bad I didn't have bragging rights. As far as most people knew, Stasha MacKay was a mere employee at the Dunn Agency, nothing more. I knew better. I already had my eye on her for a promotion. She deserved a step up for this one.

Faint strains of holiday music greeted Ed and me as we stepped from the long corridor into the main walkway of the mall. Everywhere I looked large clocks dangled from the high ceiling at varying heights. In place of numbers, each clock face spelled out the name of the mall. Dotted among the clocks, cutout letters spelled the tagline: *Time to shop at . . .*

Down on the floor, another of Stasha's ideas had come alive, bigger than life. Oversized stacks of fantastically wrapped presents balanced on top of the large display cases each and every shopper couldn't help but walk by. The packages were positioned so that it looked as if each stack might tumble at any second. On the bottom edge of the pile, right about knee high, was Stasha's second brilliant tagline: "Be careful what you wish for!" Only someone who couldn't read would miss the connection that shopping at Westwood was the answer.

I didn't only have Stasha to thank for this one; it had taken the manpower of our whole agency to bring her concept to reality in such short order.

"Looks great," I said to Ed.

He pushed his hands into his pockets and glanced at the floor. "Sorry if I got a little bent out of shape over this. Earlier, you know." "No problem." In this business, constant deadlines and pressure to reinvent the wheel with every project made "bent out of shape" standard operating procedure. "I'm glad it worked out."

"Sure did," Ed responded. "By the way, I put your name in to the chamber for Businessperson of the Year. We were really pleased with this campaign."

Now it was my turn to look at the floor. This business was a bungee-jump every day. Ed had been ready to dump us, and now he'd nominated me for an award. Go figure. I savored the thought, because by tomorrow he might change his mind. The competitor in me was already wondering who else had been nominated and if a win translated into more business. Either way, the publicity from the chamber contest had to be good.

"Thanks." I gave Ed a quick nod.

He pointed a finger at me. "Now don't forget, the mall is going to be doing some remodeling after the first of the year. We're going to want to roll out a new ad campaign to go along with our new look."

I should have known better than to hope for a year-end break. I covered my private thought with a smile at Ed. "I'll get a team right on it. Someone will call you." The ring of my cell phone interrupted me. Ed and I were almost done with our impromptu meeting anyway. I pulled my phone from my pocket and glanced at caller ID. *Matt.* I held out the phone. "Mind if I get this?"

"Go ahead; I've gotta get back to my office."

"Talk to you soon." I started walking as I flipped the phone open with my thumb. "Donnie here."

Matt didn't waste time. "I thought it was supposed to be Christmas. Goodwill to men. Peace on earth. Sheesh."

I didn't have to know the problem to imagine that in a few seconds Matt would start clicking his tongue through the phone. There, right on cue. I started toward the mall entrance where I'd parked my car. From the tone of Matt's voice I knew I'd be heading back to the office pronto. I pushed through the mall doors into the icy December air. The sidewalk beneath my feet held a thin layer of frost. Careful stepping was in order. Good thing I was used to multitasking. "What's going on?"

"You're not going to believe this."

"Try me."

"Ken Jenner called."

A phone call from the vice president of the largest hospital in Carlton wasn't uncommon. Our agency handled virtually all of the medical facility's marketing. Ken was the liaison. Even though the hospital was our largest account, I rarely lost sleep over it. Fifteen years ago the Dunn Agency had helped the new startup hospital in Carlton grab a major portion of the medical marketshare of the area. If Ken was calling, it was more than likely something minor. A misprint in the annual shareholder report. Print errors were a dime a half dozen lately. It wouldn't be the first time we'd redo a corporate brochure. We'd reprint the offending page and be done with it. If Ken wanted a major redo, we'd have to talk. The holidays were crunch time in any business.

"What did he want?" I opened the door of my BMW and climbed in. With any luck I'd be able to solve this one before I hit the traffic light.

"You know MedFirst got a new CEO."

"Yeah. Few months ago. I haven't had a chance to meet him."

"I'm not sure you want to." Matt had a deadpan way of letting me know there was more coming.

One-handed, I backed out of the parking spot, tapped at my brake, shifted into gear, and didn't say a word. I waited.

"The guy doesn't like the tone of the new ad campaign."

"He doesn't like the tone?"

"Ba-dum-bum." Matt's idea of a verbal rim-shot. The cue was funny on Letterman, not a bit humorous here.

"What does he mean by tone?"

"Your guess is as good as mine."

"Did you talk to him?"

"No, Ken said he was just the messenger."

"And we're not supposed to kill him, right?"

"You got it." Matt sighed. "I could tell Ken felt bad delivering the news." There was a pause. Too long. As if there was another ax hanging in the air.

"Well, it won't be the first time we've gone back to the drawing board on a campaign. I just wish it wasn't the holidays. Everyone wants to use up their vacation time. The freelancers are busy or don't want to accept more work until the new year. Timing's lousy." The stoplight turned amber, then red. I left a healthy space between my bumper and the car in front of me. It looked as if this problem wouldn't get solved by the time I made it back to the agency after all. I tapped at the steering wheel with my fingers, possibilities tumbling around my brain. "Can we push it off until after the first of the year?"

"There's more."

So, there was another ax. Inexplicably nervous, I jutted my chin in the air — might as well make it easy for the executioner. "What?"

"The new CEO wants to put their marketing business out for bids."

"Tell me you're kidding."

"No joke."

The light turned green, and I hit the horn. *Get going.* In my rearview mirror the mall receded. *Businessperson of the Year* suddenly seemed like a bad pun. Like the mall account, MedFirst was the agency's bread and butter. The ongoing income from our two longtime clients paid the bills each month. It was because of those accounts that we had the freedom to stick our necks out on more risky ventures.

"Five minutes. I'm on my way." I snapped my phone shut, tossing the hot potato onto the passenger seat. I pressed on the gas, then jammed on the brake. Morons. No one else might have to be anywhere important, but I needed to be at my office. Now.

I threaded from lane to lane, always ending up behind some driver who didn't seem to care when he arrived at his destination. There had to be a conspiracy. Every driver seemed to be trying to keep me from getting back to the agency.

We couldn't lose the hospital account. Even as I tried not to imagine the possibility, my mind grabbed onto the upshot. Yesterday we'd interviewed two possible new employees. If we lost this account, we'd have to lay off people instead.

A pit formed in my stomach as a new realization hit. As the newest hire, Stasha would be the logical one to go. She'd proved herself to be invaluable in the weeks since she'd jumped on board. I'd be foolish to send her packing. But what would the rest of the staff think if I laid off someone else instead?

Don't panic. Maybe we'd talk the hospital into reconsidering.

You've never backed away from a challenge. So what if the hospital put the account out for bids? The Dunn Agency was the best in the state. We'd simply win the contract back.

If only it was that simple. I'd been in business long enough to know that sometimes there was no reason for a client to pack up and leave; sometimes they just wanted something new. This new CEO was probably trying to see how much weight he carried in his new position. If that was the case, it would make the challenge all the harder. He'd take the hospital account for a walk just to prove a point.

There was a tightening across my chest. A muscle in the base of my neck throbbed. I didn't need this. Not when we'd been having a banner year. Our best to date. I took one hand off the wheel and tugged at the tight spot between my shoulder and neck. A heart attack might be a relief. Take me away long enough to get some perspective.

Wishing for a heart attack? You just might get an eternal *perspective.*

God knew I wasn't ready for that.

Yes, I do know. You're not ready for that.

A light sweat broke out along my upper lip. A clump of something pushed into my throat. For a second it felt as if I couldn't breathe. I opened my mouth, sucking air. No. Okay. I pulled a long breath into my chest, filling my lungs. Really, I was fine. Tense, but fine.

Get a grip.

I was trying. My hands tightened around the steering wheel. White-knuckle driving, as if I was on thin ice.

You are.

Minutes ago, back at the mall, I'd thought I had the good life in my grasp. All it had taken was one phone call to make me understand I had no control over anything.

I'm in control. Have you thought about praying?

Laura was the one who prayed in our family. Not me.

Maybe you should start.

If I knew how, I might.

You could ask Laura to pray for you.

Ha! How could I ask Laura to pray for my business when all she did was complain about how much time I spent there?

Maybe she's got a point.

Laura didn't have any idea how much work it took to keep an agency operating.

About as much work as a marriage?

More.

Are you sure? Have you looked at yours? If your business went belly up, what would you have left?

My business is not going belly up.

What if? What would you have left? There's more to life than your job.

A person can't live without working.

I'm not asking that.

What then?

If your business failed, what would you have left?

388

The band across my chest tightened. I pushed my lungs against the pressure. As long as I could breathe, I'd be okay. A vision of the agency building filled my mind. All it took was a tilt of the chin to see our floor of offices on the fourth story. It didn't take much to imagine the rest of my nightmare. There were enough downtown buildings with "For Sale or Rent" signs in the window. That wouldn't happen to the Dunn Agency.

At the price of your marriage?

Suddenly the constriction across my chest loosened. My marriage was one thing I didn't need to include in my agonizing thoughts. I may not ever win "Husband of the Year," but Laura would stick by me. She was the one constant I could count on.

I pressed my balled-up fist against my breastbone.

"Are you okay?" Matt looked up from the notes he'd been making.

"Heartburn." At least that's what I hoped it was. "Must have eaten something that didn't agree with me."

"So what's our plan?" Matt tapped his pen against the notepad on his knee.

I picked up my pen and scribbled while I talked. "Plan A. We set up a meeting with

Ken and this new guy. We go in and pitch like we've never pitched before."

"They already know our pitch."

"We convince them our ideas are already the cat's meow." Bad cliché. I was desperate.

"And if they don't bite?"

I wrote Plan B on the paper in front of me. "We shoot 'em."

"Ha, ha. Okay, you've had your moment of insanity. Now tell me, what's our backup plan?" Matt's tongue ticked against the roof of his mouth.

I tossed my pen onto the desk and stretched my arms out in front of me. "What it always is."

"And that is?"

"Come up with a genius idea they can't turn down."

"You make it sound so easy."

Now it was my turn. "Ha, ha."

Juggling my briefcase, I shoved one arm into my leather coat as I walked, then the other. "Ready?" I peered into Matt's office.

My business partner gave me a right-handed thumbs-up.

"I'd lift both of them if I were you."

He lifted his left thumb. "We need more than thumb luck, you know."

I rolled my eyes. "Keep thinking like that, and we'll have this account in the bag. The garbage bag."

Matt chuckled. "I crack me up sometimes."

"We've got a bigger nut to crack than you. Ken's expecting us. Let's rumble." I turned to lead the way out of his office just as Elle poked her head around the door.

She caught my eye. "You've got a phone call. It's your wife. I told her you were on your way to a meeting, but she said this was important."

"Mind if I use your phone?" I didn't wait for Matt's permission. I reached for the receiver and put it to my ear.

"I'll wait out here." Matt picked up his briefcase and walked out with Elle, winding his hand in a hurry-it-up motion.

I know, I mouthed as I punched at line three. "Donnie here."

"It's me. Laura." As if she didn't know if I'd recognize her voice. I took a finger and ran it around the edge of my collar.

For her sake, I took a quick breath trying to tamp down my impatience. A one-minute phone call wasn't going to impact the meeting I was heading to, one way or another. "What's up?"

"It's your mom. I'm at the nursing home."

"What about Mom?"

"She's just really restless today, and she keeps looking at me and saying something. You know how hard it is to understand her."

I'd have to take Laura's assessment on that. Inside my leather coat I shrugged my shoulders uncomfortably. I hadn't been to see my mom as often as I should have.

"So, what do you think she's saying?" I couldn't imagine what Mom could be trying to say that would make Laura feel that she had to report it to me.

"Donnie."

"Yeah, I'm here."

"No. I mean I think she's trying to say your name. Donnie."

A hot flush rose from the depths of my coat into my neck. What did Laura expect? That I would run out the door, speed to the nursing home, and help figure out if my mom was mumbling my name?

"I think you should come."

Apparently, that's exactly what she expected. I pulled a long breath into my nose, let it out slowly. "Laura." I cleared my throat. This wouldn't go over well if she thought I was verbally patting her hand. "Elle might have told you I'm on my way to a meeting. This might be one of the most important meetings I'll ever have. It might mean —"

"She's saying *Donnie.*"

"You told me you weren't sure what she was saying."

"She wants you. You're her son."

Who knew something as abstract as guilt could weigh so much? If I could pick up and go, I would. But our most important client was waiting. "I'll see what I can do."

"Before your meeting or after?"

Laura had no idea what this meeting held. "After."

I pulled the receiver — and the silence on the other end — away from my ear.

"Hey, Ken, how's it going?" I stuck out my hand and shook his as if we hadn't seen each other at the gallery opening. Funny how that night I'd been thinking what a shoestring operation Karen's gallery would be. There was a reason most famous paintings were housed in museums. Most people didn't have the spare change to indulge a money-losing hobby. I wasn't so sure Karen had figured that out yet, but she would soon.

Any good businessperson had to think as if they were on the verge of going broke on any given day. I only wished Laura had an understanding of that fact. I reached to straighten my tie. It would do no good to let Laura's phone call intrude on this meeting. I pushed the thought aside as I tugged my tie into perfect alignment.

"Thanks for agreeing to see us on such short notice. Things must be going well. The parking lot was filled." I might as well just kneel down and polish Ken's shoes.

Ken motioned Matt and me into chairs as he took a seat behind his desk. "The winter months are a busy time in this business." After another minute or so of casual chatting, Ken said, "I hope you don't mind waiting a few minutes. John was in a meeting when you called. He should be out —" In a swift motion Ken looked over my shoulder and pushed himself out of his chair. "Speak of the devil . . ."

I glanced at Matt. I wanted it on record that I wasn't the person who called the new hospital CEO the devil. Matt and I stood and turned to face our nemesis.

"John Barnes." The guy Matt and I had Googled a half hour ago was striding our way, hand out. "Pleased to meet you. Your agency has done some great work for the hospital." He shook my hand. "I hear you go by Donnie."

"Right." So, he'd done his homework, too.

"Let's move over to the conference room. We'll be more comfortable there." John

Barnes led us on a short walk down the carpeted corridor, all the while keeping up a jovial banter. "Sit here, Donnie." He patted the top of a high-backed, cushioned chair. "That's my favorite spot. You have a great view of the hospital complex from there." He took the seat to my left, around the corner of the long table.

If this guy was the devil, he had a great disguise. Charisma in spades. For the first time ever, I felt as if I was staring down my match.

An hour later, John Barnes stood, signaling the end of our discussion.

"Thanks so much for coming to meet with me. Us." John's glance took in Ken, even though the man had barely said a word. It was clear who was the alpha male in this pack. Barnes held out his hand. "I appreciate your time."

"Likewise," Matt and I repeated in unison.

Our handshake was a contest with no clear winner.

Less than five minutes later, Matt broke the silence as we got in my car.

"So, what did you think?"

"I think the guy is going to do whatever he wants," I said. There was something

395

about that attitude I was forced to admire. In Barnes's shoes, I'd do the same thing. There was nothing we could do now but wait for his decision.

"You hungry?" As he spoke, Matt took out his cell phone and dialed for messages with his thumb.

It took me a second to realize the pit in my stomach may not be due to the meeting we'd just had. Somehow in the course of this day I had missed lunch completely. "Yeah, I am. Let me call the office and let Elle know we're going to grab a bite." I pulled my cell phone from my pocket.

Before I could flip open the phone Matt paused and touched my arm. "Wait a sec." He listened a moment, pushed a button, handed his phone to me.

"Matt, it's Elle." Her voice was all business, and I pressed the phone tight against my ear as the wail of a siren howled toward the hospital. "I left a message on Donnie's phone, too. Whenever you get this tell him his mother was taken to the hospital by ambulance. MedFirst."

Right where we were.

STASHA

"Josh? Be there. Please." I tapped my foot, breathing a silent prayer that I'd hear Josh's voice in my ear. All I heard was the empty whirring of an answering machine recording the silence. "Josh?" I said again, as if just maybe he had suddenly appeared in our apartment at the other end of the line. I needed to hear his voice. "Call me."

I hung up the phone in my cubicle, uncertain what to do next. I'd tried reaching him all afternoon. The school secretary said he'd taken his junior high class on a field trip, in a tone that intimated I should have known. Even so, he should have been back by now. School had let out an hour ago. If he wasn't at school, he should be at our apartment.

If you had been home before Josh got to sleep last night, you might know what his plans were.

I grabbed my Diet Coke and took a swallow. I couldn't help it that the radio spots for the Carlton Symphony Orchestra's New Year's bash had somehow disappeared on the way to the radio station. The delivery service swore they didn't have a record of picking them up, but I knew better. At least I thought I did. No one in their right mind could keep track of the minutiae I was dealing with lately. Maybe Josh did tell me he had a field trip this morning when we were juggling turns in the bathroom getting ready for work. Who could blame me for not hearing? My time at work started in my head, long before I left the house.

I took another swallow. I'd spent hours last night trying to track down the symphony radio spots. They had vanished into the ozone. I only hoped the studio had a backup. If not, my boss — namely, Dad — was not going to be pleased to find out we'd need to rerecord them ASAP. An extra expense we'd have to eat.

The only good news about today was that my dad wasn't around, which made the bad news I'd gotten earlier all the worse. Dad was at the hospital with my grandma. A heart attack, the doctors were saying, at least according to the latest update from Mom.

Even her almost hourly assurance of "nothing's changed" hadn't stopped me from driving to the hospital when I could get away for a so-called lunch break. Somehow peering at my grandma through the ICU window glass didn't make me feel one bit better. *Please God, help her.*

I clicked my mouse, flipping from the report I'd been trying to write to my e-mail inbox. It was about to explode. Last night, in my frantic search for the lost recordings, I'd left a bunch of messages unread. I was paying for my procrastination today. I clicked on a message from Ben. I scanned his words reminding me I was supposed to have a trend report for the creative team meeting tomorrow. Argh! I couldn't concentrate. All I wanted to do was go to the hospital and find out how Grandma was doing.

Are you sure you don't just want to run away from work?

No. What I really wanted was to tell Josh what had happened. As soon as I shared the news about Grandma with him, I knew I'd be able to focus, at least for a little while.

I knew I'd proved myself enough around the agency in the past few months that now no one would question that my dad had hired me for my abilities, not our relationship. But running off to the hospital in the middle of a work crisis still felt like it smacked of nepotism. For a long time I'd been letting Mom hold down the fort at the hospital, and I'd been trying to pull my weight here.

Which was why I needed to talk to Josh; he would understand all the weird emotional balls I was juggling. Trying to make my dad proud. Worried about my grandma. Wondering when it would be okay to ditch work and go to the hospital. I just need to talk to someone who would understand.

I would.

I closed my eyes and let the tears I'd been fighting win the battle. I didn't even have time for God anymore. I didn't have time to read a Bible or pray, considering I worked from before sunup to after sundown. Who had time to go to church when Sunday was the only day left to get in an extra hour of sleep and run errands?

Maybe you're too busy.

Try telling that to my boss. Dad set the pace around here, and most of the time he made the rest of us look as if we were slackers.

Maybe your dad is too busy, too.

I'd thought that a lot growing up. It was only after I started working here that I understood why his time at home was limited. It wasn't always because he wanted

400

to be at the office after hours; it was because that was the very nature of his line of work. And now it was mine. For better or worse.

The sharp ring of my phone snapped me to attention. I snatched it up. "Josh?"

"I'm trying to reach Anastasia MacKay."

I cleared my throat and stared at the photo of Josh and me in Italy. *Focus.* Not that many people had the number to my direct line. My mind scrambled trying to connect the voice to someone I was supposed to know.

"This is Andrea." She paused. "Collins."

"Oh, Andrea. Hi!" I didn't have a clue who I was talking to.

"I wasn't sure you'd remember me."

My mind was already on overload, I'd just have to 'fess up. "Actually, if you could remind me . . . ?"

"We met at the women's networking seminar a couple months ago."

That had to be right about the time I'd come to work for the agency. A time that in advertising time was eons ago.

"We exchanged business cards," Andrea coached. "We talked about your trip to Italy. Your job at the Dunn Agency."

Yeah, she and two dozen other ambitious women climbing the same ladder. I held the phone in one hand and riffled through the small box of business cards I kept in my drawer with the other. I had no filing system unless you counted tossing a system. If I met Andrea months ago, her card would be near the bottom of the pile. Ta-da! Andrea Collins. Restaurateur.

"Andrea." I was going to have to wing it. "Let me see if I remember right." I looked at the card in my hand. "You own Andie's. The deli sandwich shop."

"Good memory."

Let her think better of me than I deserved. "What can I do for you?"

"I don't have a big budget," she started. "But I was hoping we could work something out. I'm planning on keeping the café open for dinner after the new year, and I was hoping to design some new menus. Maybe some table tents. A wine list." She cleared her throat. "I don't have a big budget. I think I told you that."

"No problem." I was making notes, mentally tallying the per-hour rate her job would entail. If Andrea had any talent with a computer and her imagination, she could save herself a bundle of money. But it wasn't my job to point that out. My job was to sell her on the Dunn Agency. I asked a few questions as I jotted notes. It was surprising how quickly it felt as if I'd been doing this kind of work all my life.

In a way you have . . . you've watched your dad.

One part of me listened to Andrea tell me her vision for her business, another part remembered the many times I'd been resentful that my dad had promised to be somewhere, take me someplace, and then had to cancel. It was only now, as I caught Andrea's vision for her business, that I understood how torn my dad must have felt. His job was to help make other people's dreams come true, not just mine.

I paused with my pen in mid air. If only I had understood my dad's work earlier. What more could I have learned? A strange kind of pride burbled in my chest. "Let me do some figuring, Andrea, and I'll get back to you." Despite all the balls I was keeping in the air today, my voice held a confidence I hadn't ever felt until just now. I'd walked in my dad's shoes, and they fit just fine.

As I stepped into the small ICU waiting area, it was as though my mom intuitively knew I was going to walk through the door. There was a magazine on her lap, but it was me she was looking at.

"How's Grandma? Is she . . . ?" Now that I was here, the tears I'd been fighting on the drive to the hospital gathered and fell.

"Oh, Stasha." Mom stood and wrapped her arms around me. "I'm glad you're here." She squeezed me tight and then released her hold. "It's been a long day."

Amen to that. "Where's Dad?" In this small room, it wasn't hard to tell who was missing.

"He's in with Grandma. They only allow one visitor at a time and only for a very short time every hour. You can go in next. I'll wait."

"I don't know if I can stay very long. I should get back to work. It's nuts today." The words were out before I could stop them, but the second I heard them . . . I didn't need to decipher the quick flash of something in my mother's glance. Lucky for me there was a rustling at the doorway, interrupting anything she might say. Her eyes flicked to the sound, and mine followed. "Dad!"

His face was pale in a way that had nothing to do with the awful lighting in the room. His eyes were red as if he might cry. Or had been crying. I noticed a grim-faced doctor a step behind him. I felt a thudding in my chest as all three of us turned to face the man in the white coat.

The doctor took one step into the room,

then stopped and rubbed the side of his face with his fingertips. Either he was one hip doctor, or he hadn't had time to shave. The doctor didn't bother with introductions. "I'm not liking the looks of things."

At his words, I felt as if all the blood that had been in my head a second ago suddenly decided to flow somewhere else. My head felt light; my hands were cold as popsicles. I wished Josh was here to hold me.

The doctor slightly shook his head as he spoke. "Your mother's vital signs are poor. There's a ventricular tachycardia that's worrying me. Her heart rate is elevated, over 200. An arrhythmia like that may cause the heart to supply blood insufficiently to her body."

I glanced from the doctor to my dad, then my mom. I hoped they understood what the doctor was saying. All I knew was it wasn't good. There was a swirling in my head, as if a strong wind was blowing hard, deep inside my brain. If this was how I felt when my grandma was sick, how would I react if she died?

Sheltered. Spoiled. I couldn't help the accusation that screamed inside my head. I'd never had anyone close to me die before. What if I fell apart?

This isn't about you.

I looked at my dad. His lips were pressed into a grim line. What must he be feeling? This was his mother. I looked at my mom. What would I be feeling if she was the one the doctor was talking about?

I blinked away the tears in my eyes and tried to concentrate on what the doctor was saying. What did it mean for my grandma? For my dad?

The doctor reached out and shook my dad's hand. "I'll let you know if anything changes."

My mom lifted her hand and rubbed a small circle between my dad's shoulder blades. He just stood there staring at the spot where the doctor had been.

"Can I help?" I sounded like a squeaky mouse. I cleared my throat and tried again. "What can I do?"

Dad straightened his shoulders. "I need to call the office."

"Dad." I put a hand on his arm. "I'm right here. I can tell you anything you need to know."

For the first time today, there was the smallest hint of relief on his face — and that made me feel incredibly good.

Unless something drastic happened to my grandma overnight, I knew my dad would be at the agency first thing in the morning. Which was why, instead of heading home, I turned my car back to the office. My cubicle full of work wouldn't make one iota of difference to what was waiting for my dad tomorrow morning, but tonight, it felt like the only way I could help.

My eyelids were heavy as I maneuvered through the practically empty late-night streets of Carlton. A set of red taillights glowed in front of me. A reminder of the hot coal of anger burning in my chest at Josh. He never had called.

Somewhere along the way to my apartment, I zoned out. Braking and blinking, driving and turning, without conscious thought. Too tired to be safe. The earlier set of taillights had been replaced by another. It seemed I wasn't the only person who had to work late tonight. I had the blinker on to turn into my driveway before I realized that the truck in front of me was doing the same thing. Josh.

As much as I'd wanted to see him earlier, now I found myself wishing he was already in our bed. Asleep — or anywhere but right in front of me. I was too tired to deal with whatever his reasons were for coming home so late. Or to defend myself.

I pulled my car into the driveway, parking close to the tailgate so I could keep the back of my car off the sidewalk. I shifted into park and took a deep breath. Come to think of it, I wasn't too sleepy to deal with Josh tonight.

"Hi." Josh stepped out of his pickup and gave me a sheepish wave, a slow back-and-forth of his hand and a goofy grin that said, *I've been out with the guys.*

A thousand words fought for first place in my throat. None of them good.

"Hi." I turned my back to him and pulled my purse out of the car. Maybe if I said as little as possible we wouldn't have to get into it tonight. It seemed lately, all we'd been doing was arguing, each of us justifying our side, neither one of us willing to concede the other might have a point.

I knew I'd been justified in worrying about my grandma, in working late to help out my dad. I also knew Josh couldn't possibly have a good reason for grinning like a Cheshire cat on catnip on a work night.

I threw my scarf around my neck as I tried to walk past Josh without touching him or stepping into the solid bank of snow lining the driveway.

"Hey, Stash." He one-armed me around the waist and pulled me into a sideways

408

hug. I tried to wiggle out of his embrace. Couldn't he tell that forcing his affection on me wasn't going to help matters? "Did you have a good day?"

I looked up at him. "Actually, no."

His arm stiffened as he caught my drift. "Oh." He scratched at the back of his neck. "The field trip went really well."

Oh, the bait-and-switch tactic. Don't ask me about my bad day; tell me about your great one. Yeah, that'll make me feel better. Just like the smell of beer and cigarette smoke. You'd think he would have figured out that trick didn't work. I pulled my coat around myself and stepped around Josh. "I'm going in. It's late, and I'm cold."

"Now what did I do?"

I looked at him over my shoulder. His hands were out, pleading, as if he really didn't have a clue.

I turned to him, keeping my voice slow and deliberate. "I've been working hard all day and most of the night. Grandma was rushed to the hospital, and she might not live. I've been trying to get hold of you since early afternoon, and you tell me your field trip went well." I plastered a fake grin on my face. "Some of us didn't have as good a day as you." I turned on my heel and took a step toward the house.

"Come on, Stasha, how was I supposed to know all that? Give me a break."

I stopped and turned. "Give you a break? Oh, that's a good one. Did it ever occur to you while you were on your great field trip that I might need you?"

He put his head back and looked up into the cloudless night, then tilted steely eyes to me. "Since when am I expected to check in with you while I'm at work?"

He had me there. I puffed a breath into the cold night. "You could have called me after school."

"Oh, sure, and get your standard brush-off." His voice rose in a dead-on imitation of me. *"I can't talk now, Josh. I'm busy. I have a meeting. I'm on the other line."*

"I don't say that to you."

"Yes." He stared at me. "You do."

I shifted my purse to my other shoulder. "If you'd carry your cell phone instead of leaving it on the kitchen counter all the time, at least I could leave you a message."

"Stash, the reason I don't carry my cell phone is because I can't have it on in school. I can't answer it while I have ball practice. And I hate cell phones." His voice grew louder. "And I don't see any reason why I should have to be available every stinkin' second of the day. You're not my

410

mother!"

"Thank goodness," I screamed back as a light went on inside the house. That's all we needed, Mr. Miller poking his nose into this. I lowered my voice. "You are my husband, and I don't think it's out of line to want to know where you are."

"And you're my wife, who I never see."

"It's not like you care. When I'm here, you're not."

"And you expect me to sit around waiting for you to have a spare minute to spend with me? You're married to me, not that stupid job of yours."

I put both hands on my hips and spoke slow. "Look who's talking! You're the one who started out this marriage being gone all the time." It was my turn to imitate him. *"I've got papers to grade. I've got junior high football practice. I've got basketball practice."*

"I'm not listening to this anymore." Josh stepped around me.

"Where do you think you're going?" Josh was right; I did sound like his mother.

"To bed."

"Oh, like that'll solve anything," I said.

"Like this will?"

He turned and stalked toward the back porch. My insides felt as if they were boiling. Earlier I'd been freezing; now I might as well be standing at the equator. Who did he think he was, stomping off in the middle of an argument? He wasn't going to leave me standing in the snow by myself. I'd see to it that he turned around.

I yelled as if I was hurling a hard-packed snowball at the back of Josh's head. "Sometimes I hate being married."

Josh stopped. My overheated words hung in the icy silence. He didn't turn around. I could see his breath forming a cloud near his mouth. Then he spoke softly.

"Me more."

LAURA

"Hark, the herald angels sing, 'Glory to the newborn King.' " The voices of another set of carolers echoed down the halls of the hospital, bringing sympathetic joy during this long week before Christmas. I glanced at Eleanor to see if she had any response to the familiar music. Nothing.

"With angelic host proclaim, Christ is born in Bethlehem."

I'd never noticed how many of the familiar carols referred so directly to the birth of Jesus. Maybe it was because I was holding what felt like a death watch.

There was a labored breath from Eleanor. I half stood from my padded seat, as if I could somehow help her breathe. There was nothing I could do as she fought to drag air into her lungs. I watched until she seemed to quiet again, then I sat back down.

I picked up my partially sewn quilt and pulled it onto my lap. It got dark early this

413

time of year in North Dakota, and the light in Eleanor's room was poor at best. Even though I was near the window, the late afternoon dusk did nothing to illuminate my work. The stitching I was doing to pass the time was moving at a snail's pace. But then, my mother-in-law had so much more to complain about. If she ever spoke.

The carolers paused outside the open door to Eleanor's room. I smiled awkwardly at a young woman near the door. *Thank you, I think.* The singers were offering comfort, but their songs only underscored how untraditional our holiday would be this year.

Eleanor had been in the hospital well over a week, never once coming fully conscious. The doctor had told us there wasn't much hope of recovery, but it didn't seem Eleanor was ready to let go yet. Each day she struggled through each breath. There was nothing to do but wait.

As the carolers began to move on, I raised a hand in silent thanks. Their songs were the only Christmas I was getting these days. Feeling restless, I pushed my quilting aside, rose, and stood by the window that looked out on one of the parking areas outside the hospital. Eleanor wasn't the only worry I had. In the brief visits I'd had with Stasha these past days, I'd sensed that something was not right in her voice. Her job? Her relationship with Josh? She was so much like her dad. I could only hope she wasn't too much like him. For her sake — and for Josh's.

My eyes scanned the parking lot. Donnie had promised he'd stop by to see his mother after work. I knew the chance that I'd see him striding across the lot was slim. Still, looking for him gave me something to do while I prayed for my daughter.

It was cold by the window, evidence of the December wind blowing hard outside. I wrapped my arms around myself, realizing how chilled I was. Eleanor was resting quietly. I would take this opportunity to stretch my legs and go get a cup of coffee. I was hoping when Donnie arrived we could grab a quick dinner together in the hospital cafeteria. The food wasn't nearly as unappealing as the old jokes made it sound.

I straightened Eleanor's covers and made sure the oxygen was flowing through a tube strapped near her nose. What I could do for my mother-in-law was limited.

You can pray.

I could. I had been. Praying was the only area of my life in which I didn't feel helpless.

That's because you're not.

As I left the room I smiled to myself. There was comfort in the little conversations I was having with God this week. Even in suffering there was a measure of assurance.

The elevator doors slid open on the lobby floor, which was vastly different from the mood of somber silence on Eleanor's floor. I could see yet another group of carolers assembling near the door. Good thing the hospital had several wings, or they'd be tripping over each other in their effort to bring cheer. A craft sale was being dismantled in another corner of the area. A floral delivery person stepped past me and into the elevator, a poinsettia held high. I felt as if I'd somehow landed in a different world. Maybe I'd been at the hospital just a little too much. No, I shouldn't begrudge Eleanor the time I spent here. Sitting beside her was my choice. Eleanor was certainly in no position to be demanding.

No, but if her son stopped by more often you might be able to get your Christmas shopping done. I wasn't going to take up that old argument now. Yesterday I'd extracted a promise from Donnie to visit his mother tonight. I wasn't proud of my tactics, but extreme times demanded extreme measures.

I think I had intimidated Donnie's assistant, Elle. I had firmly said, "I need to see Donnie."

My face and voice must have told her this wasn't a casual visit. She reached for the phone. "Let me see if he's available."

It didn't take but a second for her to say, "You can go in."

Matt was pushing himself out of a chair as I walked into the office. "Hey, long time, no see."

I dropped my purse in a chair and gave him a quick hug. The last time I'd seen him had been at Stasha's wedding, and there had been no time for a visit then, just as there wasn't one now. I was in no mood to issue a hollow invitation to stop by the house. "Things have been . . ." There was no explaining the way things had been.

"I'm sorry about Eleanor." Matt looked over to Donnie. "I always liked your mother. She was a feisty one."

Was. That was the word of the hour.

An awkward pause. Matt picked up a folder off the desk. "I'll let you two talk." He closed the office door behind him.

I didn't plan to waste my time. Or Donnie's.

"You need to come see your mother."

Donnie closed his eyes for a long second. "Laura, don't start —"

"Don't start what?" My tone wasn't good, but that didn't stop me. "She's your mother!"

"She's comatose." He stopped. Even he knew how bad that sounded. He tried again. "We've got a major situation going on right now."

I wasn't having any of it. "I'd say *we* have a major situation going on right now too. At least your mother does, and you don't seem to think it involves you."

"Laura, you don't understand. The bottom could fall out of the agency if I don't stay on top of things. You think I like sitting here till all hours of the night?"

"Do you think I like living at the hospital?"

"It's the hospital account that's giving me fits." Donnie tossed down his pen and pushed back his chair. "They're threatening to pull their account."

I really didn't know much about the agency's specific accounts, and right now I didn't care. "Donnie, your mom may be leaving this world."

There was an eerie quiet as Donnie and I stared each other down.

"Laura, I —"

"If you don't —"

We spoke over each other and stopped at the same time.

I picked up my side of the argument first. "If you don't come see your mother tonight, I'll —" I held my breath, hoping words would gather to fill the void. I had no idea what I'd do if Donnie wouldn't agree to come.

Donnie pulled his chair back to his desk, picked up his pen, and looked up at me, his expression inscrutable. "I'll come."

"Well, then." I wouldn't have to finish my sentence — my empty threat — after all. "Thank you." I lifted the hair from the back of my neck, which was suddenly too warm. "She'll like that." I thought about trying to muster a bit of a smile, but Donnie and I were long past that pretense. I bent down and picked up the purse I'd dropped in a chair. I turned to go.

"Tomorrow."

I quickly turned back. "What?"

Donnie flicked his eyes from me to the papers on his desk. He kept his gaze down as he replied. "I'll see her tomorrow."

He'd said he'd be here tomorrow; well, it was tomorrow now. Last night I had waited at the hospital past the hour I normally left for home, certain that guilt would compel Donnie to be at his mother's side. Eleanor may have never noticed that her son was missing, but I did. If he didn't show tonight,

419

I would know he was no longer the man I married.

An announcement over the hospital loud-speaker pulled me from my thoughts. Coffee. I had come here for coffee. Even though I'd practically worn a path to the cafeteria in recent days, it took me a moment to get my bearings. Left or right?

"Laura?"

I turned at the sound of my name. The voice belonged to Cecelia's son.

"John?" I could feel a warm flush rise into my neck at the sight of his familiar, handsome face. I hoped he had zero abilities when it came to intuition, or he would know the time I'd spent at my mother-in-law's bedside had included an unhealthy amount of time missing his easy banter.

Should I shake his hand or hug him? One greeting seemed too formal, the other too familiar. The problem solved itself as he took a step toward me and a visitor hurried between us. "Oops," the young woman said, dancing between us.

John and I each took a quick step back, smiling at each other across the expanse.

I filled the space with a question. "What are you doing here?" It only took a moment for me to answer my own question. "Don't tell me your mom is in the hospital too."

"No." John stepped near. "But I did hear that Eleanor was in the hospital. If you're here, it must be this hospital, huh?"

"Quite the detective." For the first time in a week I found myself grinning.

"How's she doing?"

My smile didn't last long. "Not good at all. Her doctor said it's only a matter of time. We have a do-not-resuscitate order in place."

Unlike Donnie, John looked straight into my eyes whenever I spoke about Eleanor's condition. "I'm sorry to hear that. It must be hard."

I was surprised to feel tears filling my eyes. For the first time since Eleanor had entered the hospital, I felt as though someone understood what I was going through.

"Yeah, it is." I blinked back the tears. "But it's like you said the day Cecelia moved in. Heaven isn't such a bad place to spend the rest of your life."

What was I doing quoting him? I cleared my throat, hoping John wouldn't realize how much time I'd spent combing through every conversation we'd had. I glanced away. "It's the getting to heaven that's the hard part." Again, tears stung my eyes.

He reached out and touched my arm. "You okay?"

Everything going on around us seemed to fade into the periphery as I stared at his hand on my sleeve. How could five fingers create such white-hot heat through the sleeve of my sweater? I didn't dare look up at him.

In the smallest of motions, he rubbed a tiny circle on my arm. "I missed you."

I couldn't help it; my eyes flew to his face. *Had he read my mind after all?*

"At the home," he added, as if he hadn't paused at all. "Mom's room seems really empty without Eleanor — and you."

"Oh," I cleared my throat, not trusting myself to speak. I moved my arm at the same time he tucked his hand in his pocket and began jiggling the change inside. The room seemed to come back to life. The automatic doors slid open, and a wave of visitors, stomping snow off their boots, entered the lobby. A sudden drop of my heart. *Was Donnie part of the group?* As much as I'd been conjuring him up, suddenly I half hoped he'd be detained. My eyes quickly scanned the new faces. No, no Donnie.

"You never did tell me, John — what are you doing at the hospital?"

He cast a glance around the vast entry area before settling on me. "I work here."

"You? You're not . . . ?"

"A doctor?" John filled in the blank for me. "No, nothing so illustrious. I work upstairs." He pointed in a vague way overhead. "I'm the CEO here."

"Oh my. Well, I guess I know who to complain to about the bill then."

He smiled. "I'm hoping you won't have any reason to complain. That's my job."

I smiled back. "So far, so good."

He gave the loose change in his pocket a final noisy shuffle. "I was just on my way to grab some coffee, then it's back to work. End-of-the-year reports drive me crazy."

I felt like a college freshman when I said, "I was on my way to get some coffee too." Fancy that. At least it was the truth.

"Then let's walk together. It'll be my treat."

As the elevator doors slid shut, I gave John a tiny wave and then blew across the top of my coffee cup. Amazing how bumping into John had changed my outlook. Eleanor might be okay. Stasha too. Donnie would show up and spend some quality time with his mother.

I stepped out of the elevator and sipped my coffee before starting my walk down the long hallway. The quiet here was ghostly compared to the scene down below and only served to remind me that life truly was for the living.

I rounded the corner into Eleanor's room. Possibly Donnie had come during my coffee quest. No such luck.

As I entered the room there was a sound from Eleanor. A gurgle. A gasp. Noises that were unfamiliar. I should know; I'd been beside her most of the time she'd been here. Quickly I set my coffee on the bedside tray and leaned near, calling her name as if I expected her to answer. "Eleanor? Eleanor!"

Her eyes opened, seemed to plead with me for something. Then, they fluttered, stayed open as if surprised at how quickly the end had come. The smallest of sighs. Before I could even think of calling for help, Eleanor was gone. The room held a quiet I could only describe as deathly. I was alone in a way I'd never been before.

I felt frozen in place; the only part of me that moved was the beat of my heart. In death, Eleanor's face held a profound peace. She'd been released from the body that in the end held her captive. And yet, all I could feel was sorrow.

All of a sudden it occurred to me that there were so many things I should have thanked her for. Frosted sugar cookies and homemade pickles. Things I never had the patience, or talent, to make. The valentines she'd send through the mail just so Stasha could open an envelope, even though we only lived minutes away. I should have forced Eleanor to write down her recipe for banana cream pie. I'd never found another to compare with it. And her caramel rolls. Why had I thought my mother-in-law would always be around to satisfy that craving? What had I been thinking?

My eyes landed on the quilt I'd been working on for much too long now. Small scraps of fabric, remnants of a life lived that was now gone. That red piece with tiny cornflowers was probably popular in the 1950s, yet not once had I thought to ask Eleanor where she had worn that skirt. Had she gone to a fancy party? There was no one left who knew. Scraps of Donnie's little-boy shirts contained memories only Eleanor held — now gone in a breath.

Why? Why hadn't I thought to ask?

Grit scraped the back of my eyelids as I closed my eyes against regret. If this was the way I felt, and I'd spent so much time right beside my mother-in-law, how would Donnie feel? He hadn't been here when she was alive; how would he feel when he realized there was no time left to make up?

I wasn't sure if the hollowness I felt was sorrow for what Donnie missed, or simply that what I once felt for my husband had disappeared along with Eleanor.

Emptiness. Vast barrenness. Sorrow.

For Eleanor. For Donnie. For me.

There was a rustle at the door. Had Donnie finally arrived?

I turned to the sound.

A nurse. Another disappointment. There was nothing left for her to do.

She walked into the room. "I came to check —"

I lifted my hand and motioned to Eleanor's body.

"Oh." There was no pulse to check. No heartbeat to count. "Let me get someone."

As she left the room, I turned back to the bed. I couldn't stand here forever, and yet I didn't know what to do. Call Donnie? Keep calling Donnie?

Another sound at the door. A soft knock. The nurse hadn't wasted any time. I didn't turn around. I'd let her tell me what came next.

"Laura?" Not the nurse. I turned. It was John. Not Donnie. John.

"I got to thinking maybe you'd like to join me later for supper."

My face must have told the story of what

had just happened in this room. He looked to the bed, then me. "Oh, Laura," he said coming near, drawing me into his arms. "I'm so sorry."

He didn't say anything more, just held me.

The thick, dry wall that had been holding back my grief imploded. I didn't wrap my arms around him. I simply turned my head into his chest and wept. Tears — wet, hot, filled with sorrow for the end of so many things — fell onto his shirt.

A sob shook my shoulders. John didn't let go. He held me closer, rubbing his hand in a comforting line up and down my back.

"Excuse us." The nurse and an aide tip-toed into the room. "We really should . . ." Her eyes flicked to the bed.

I stepped away from John and reached for several tissues from the box on the tray table. I dabbed at my eyes and blew my nose. "Thanks." I hoped my red eyes con-veyed how grateful I was for his comfort.

"Let's go stand out in the hallway." He pressed his hand into the small of my back and led me from Eleanor's room. He seemed to know I didn't need to see what happened next. Instead of the medicinal smell that had permeated my days at the hospital, John's cologne now wrapped me in an assuring blanket.

The next hour passed in a blur. The quiet tending of Eleanor's body. A call to Donnie's office only to be told he wasn't in. The funeral director who removed Eleanor to his care. Through it all, John stood by my side.

The sun had set by the time an aide motioned me into what had been Eleanor's room. "Here are her things." She handed me a plastic bag I had no use for.

"Thanks." The bed was empty. Remade. Waiting for another patient. I folded my quilt pieces and put them in the tote bag I had brought. How quickly life moved on.

"Do you need a ride anywhere?" John was looking out the darkened window.

"No. Thanks. I have my car."

"I can help you pack up Eleanor's things at the nursing home."

I hadn't thought that far ahead. There was that too.

John held out his business card. "Call me."

I reached out, the small linen card forming a bridge between our hands.

The sound of a throat clearing.

Donnie. He had come after all.

Donnie

"I've rescheduled your meeting with Andrew Martin." I could hear Elle clicking through my agenda. "The Brody people had no problem moving the meeting to next week. Don't worry about anything else; everyone is pitching in."

Most days I hardly had time to hit the bathroom; now it seemed I wasn't needed at all. Vague disappointment tapped against all the other emotions floating around today.

We'd buried my mother this morning. I shook my head. It was better not to imagine my mother in the frozen ground.

She's not there.

I was convinced of that fact. One look at my mother in her casket at the funeral home, and I realized her body was only the shell where she'd lived. I'd never been much for church stuff, but in the days following my mother's death I'd come to rely on the faith of my childhood for comfort.

Faith isn't only for children.

I was discovering that, too. But still, there was business to tend to.

"Is Matt there?" I asked.

"I'll check." I could hear Elle sigh. She sounded a lot like Laura did when I said I needed to call the office.

"Donnie," Laura had barely tilted her head, yet I knew what that look meant. *We have a living room full of relatives.*

"Ten minutes," I said. "They won't even know I'm gone."

"Hey, Donnie." Matt's tone was subdued. He'd been at the funeral this morning and offered his condolences at the cemetery. He told me not to worry about coming into work, to take as long as I needed. I told him I'd be back at my desk in the morning.

"Just a quick check, Matt. I was wondering if you've heard anything from the hospital people. Did Barnes make up his mind? Are they walking or staying?"

"Donnie. You've had a tough day. Don't worry; everything's under control." Matt might as well have patted my back and told me to go sit with my relatives.

"Did they call?"

"Let's talk about this tomorrow. Okay?"

Something in his tone wasn't right. "They're leaving, aren't they?"

430

"I didn't say that."

"You didn't have to."

There was a pause on Matt's end. Too long.

"So they pulled out."

"Donnie, let's leave this until the morning."

"Do you think I'm going to sleep tonight? I might as well have something to think about when I'm lying awake."

"I think you already have enough to think about."

True. But Matt didn't know I needed a diversion from what was really eating at me. Laura had been unusually quiet in the days leading up to the funeral. I could only imagine what it was like standing there as my mother took her last breath. I was silently glad I hadn't been there to witness Mom's last moments. I'd heard the theory that often people waited to die when their loved ones weren't there. Maybe my mother had sensed me on my way to the hospital. Maybe she had spared me that painful parting. What she hadn't spared me from was seeing the exchange between Laura and John Barnes. Sure, he was the hospital CEO, but I doubted he attended quite *that* personally to every death on his watch.

If you'd been to visit your mother more, you

would have known his mother was her room-mate at the home before the night she died.

Yeah, but would I have known what was going on between my wife and my mother's roommate's son?

There's nothing going on. I had repeated that a thousand times since I'd walked in on their exchange. But repetition did nothing to shake the odd feeling I carried with me.

"Donnie." Laura sounded surprised to see me, even though I promised her I'd visit when I could leave the office.

"Laura," I said, stepping into the room, noticing that the bed behind her was empty. "Where's Mom?"

She looked to the floor, then at me. Her wet eyes were red. She pressed her lips into a quivering line and shook her head.

"She — She . . . didn't . . ."

Laura nodded. "About an hour ago."

"Why didn't you call?"

"There wasn't time. I'd gone for a cup of coffee and when I got back, well, there wasn't time."

You should have been here sooner.

There was a burning sensation in my chest. I looked at Barnes. What did he have to do with any of this?

Laura followed my gaze. "Donnie, this is

John. His mother roomed with your mom at the home. He just hap—" Her voice caught. She cleared her throat, started where she'd left off. "He happened to be here when . . . when your mother . . ." She stopped completely and turned to Barnes. "John, this is my husband, Donnie Dunn."

"We've met," I said, taking the hand Barnes held out to me.

"Yes, we have," John said slowly. "But I didn't know you were Lau—" He stopped abruptly and verbally pivoted. "Eleanor's son."

A look I couldn't read passed between him and my wife. It didn't take a calculator to figure out he must have visited his mom a whole lot more than I visited mine. There was no sense beating myself up over a non-existent competition that was now over.

But now all that was in the past, and I had to know about the hospital account. "Matt, just say it. I can take it. If the hospital is going to pull their business, I'll find out about it."

Matt's tongue was clicking like a wood-pecker. "Actually, Barnes called yesterday."

"Yesterday! And you didn't tell me?"

He puffed air through the phone. "You didn't need that on your plate too."

I might have done the same thing under

the circumstances, but Matt knew me better than to withhold that kind of information. It was my mother who died, not me. I still had a life to live.

"Tell me what he said."

"There's a reason I didn't tell you Barnes called yesterday." Matt paused. Exhaled heavily. "I had the distinct impression he somehow knew about your mother passing away. He said they'd hold off on their decision until after the first of the year."

"I don't need the sympathy vote."

"That's what I thought, which is why I didn't tell you. There was nothing to tell."

"And?"

"And what?"

"Tell me the rest."

"I just told you what Barnes said."

"I heard what he said. I want to know what you think about what he said."

"You're starting to sound like my ex-wife."

"I might be your ex-partner if you don't hurry up."

Another pause. Another puff into the phone. "I think they'll walk."

At least I knew what the new year would hold.

Stasha and Josh spent Christmas Eve with us, but it was as if none of us was sure how we should act given the circumstances. A quick burst of laughter would be replaced by restrained conversation. The sound of wrapping paper being too carefully torn accented the awkwardness. When the kids said they thought it was time to head home for the night, it was as if we all breathed a sigh of relief. None of us had to go through the motions any longer. "Joy to the world" was going to have to happen someplace other than our house this year.

Laura was especially quiet as we picked up boxes and stray bits of wrapping paper. "I'll vacuum in the morning" was all she said.

I looked around the living room. The fireplace was as dark as the night. The Christmas tree lights were almost bright in the dim room. Why did I feel like I was walking on eggshells? "How about if I vacuum?" I asked. I wasn't even sure where Laura kept the vacuum these days, but I'd do anything to get rid of the tension in the air.

"No." Nothing more.

"Well then." I couldn't think of anything else that needed doing. Our opened gifts were under the tree, where I knew they'd stay until Laura had time to find drawer and shelf space for my new clothes and books, as well as the cashmere sweater and perfume I'd given her. Make that what Stasha picked out for Laura. I deserved nothing more than the polite "Thank you" and well-mannered smile I'd received from Laura. I cleared my throat. "Are you going to come up to bed soon?"

Laura gave me a long look. "Probably not. I want to finish up down here."

I'd help if I knew what to do. "Any plans for tomorrow?" Stasha and Josh were going to his folks' house for the day. Laura and I would be alone.

"No," Laura said. "None."

"It's official." I stood in the doorway of Matt's office.

He looked up from his desk. "Barnes called?"

"Yup. They're putting the account out for bids."

"Happy New Year, huh?"

The understatement of the day. We were only one week into the new year, and we'd just lost one of our biggest accounts. Normally, news like that would send my adrenaline pumping; there was no way we'd lose the hospital's business. But today, if I had any adrenaline, it had been siphoned away.

Matt pushed himself away from his desk,

walked around it, and stood toe-to-toe with me. He put one hand on my shoulder. "Maybe you should take some time off. Your mom just died; you've got her things to settle. You have a lot on your mind right now. I'll handle this. It'll be okay."

Donnie Dunn asked to step aside? No way. Yet, as I shook my head an unfamiliar tightness gripped the back of my throat. As if I'd break down here. I shrugged off Matt's hand. "Let's get a meeting set up this afternoon."

Through his closed lips his tongue worked its way across his teeth. After all these years, Matt knew when to stop. "If that's what you want."

"I want." I turned and walked back to my office. In reality I didn't know what I wanted. A cottage on the Riviera sounded good.

It's okay to grieve.

Once again tightness clamped my throat. Why now? I hadn't yet cried for my mom. The quality of her life these past months had been poor at best. I believed there was something better waiting for her. There was no reason for tears.

"No calls," I told Elle as I entered my office and closed the door. My day-to-day life had seldom included more than a passing thought about my mom. I knew she was just a short drive or a phone call away. But not now. I stood by my window and stared out at the cold January day. What I hadn't anticipated was the empty place her passing left inside me. Or how Matt's offer to head up this project without me would be a kindness I couldn't face.

I rapped a knuckle sharply against the window pane and then turned to my paper-loaded desk. Work had sustained me in the past. It would do the same now.

"What?" My head jerked up from the pile of paperwork lying in my lap. If you could call *dozing* working. I blinked at Laura, trying to remember where I was, what I'd been doing. Oh yeah, the recliner in my family room. Going over the new creative brief for the hospital pitch. "Did you say something?"

Laura poked a needle in and out of the fabric she was holding. She looked at her handwork as she spoke. "I've started sorting through your mother's things."

A large cavern opened inside me, and my heart dropped in. I'd been trying to avoid thinking about what to do with my childhood home, but the thought of going through my mother's belongings somehow felt worse. Those were her things.

Once when I was about six, I was caught snooping through her drawers. I was only looking for loose change to buy a comic book, but my mom hadn't waited for an explanation.

"Donald Peter Dunn."

The use of my full name instantly froze my hand in her jewelry drawer.

"Just *what* do you think you're doing?"

"Nothing." My excuse was only a whisper.

"Those are my private things. In this house we don't snoop. If you want something, you ask for it. Do you understand?"

"Yes." Another whisper as my fiery-hot hand slithered into my pocket.

"I don't want to *ever* have to remind you again. Outside." She pointed. I went.

I hadn't looked in my mother's things in the remaining 40-some years, and I didn't have any inclination to do it now. I turned my eyes to the paperwork in my lap. "It needs to be done, I guess."

"What do you want me to do with her things?"

"Do with them?" What did anyone do with their parents' former lives?

Laura put her sewing down and looked somewhere off to the side of my face, not quite into my eyes. "I can take the clothes to Goodwill. Stasha can use a couple of pieces of the furniture, but we're going to have to organize a sale or something."

"A sale? Give the stuff away." There, that should make it easy.

"Don't you want any of her things?"

No. Memories were enough. Laura was more sentimental. "Keep what you want. Let Stasha take what she wants. Do whatever with the rest."

She looked at me now. "I was hoping for a little help."

My eyes flicked to the papers in my lap. "I don't have time to organize a yard sale."

Her jaw flexed as she clenched her teeth. She took a slow, deep breath as she looked down at the quilt in her lap. "It might do you good to look through your mom's things."

Old clothes that smelled of stale perfume? No thanks. I'd rather remember my mom in other ways. *Like all the times she asked you to stop by and you didn't? How about the times Laura told you your mother called your name at the nursing home, when she could still speak? "No time," you said.*

I shifted in my chair. A couple of loose papers slid off my lap and floated to the floor. I lowered the footrest and bent over to retrieve what I'd dropped, a move that sent the rest of my papers sliding to the carpet. I swore under my breath.

"Talking like that's not going to help any-thing."

"Stop nagging at me!" Instantly I regret-ted the sharp words. All Laura had done was ask for help organizing my mother's belongings. She didn't understand that I couldn't. And I couldn't explain why.

Instead of apologizing, I scooped the papers into my hands and tried to straighten them. It was as if they were half-cooked spaghetti. Some of the papers bent, others were stiff, and none of them were doing what I was trying to get them to do. Angry words wrestled for position inside my mouth, along with a jumble of emotions I didn't dare examine. Retreat was my only option. "I'm going to the office."

I lifted my shoulders, waiting for the words I knew were coming. The room was so quiet I could hear Laura pulling a single strand of thread through a piece of red fabric.

A heavy wash of fatigue suddenly tugged at me. I really didn't want to go to my of-fice. All I wanted was to climb the stairs, slide into bed, feel Laura's arms around me, and slip into a deep sleep. I wanted refuge, not work. If only Laura would say some-thing. Just one word, and I'd sit back and let her win this one.

Nothing. A silent stalemate.

I shoved the papers into my briefcase, pulled my car keys from my pocket, and yanked my coat out of the closet. Stubborn silence propelled me into the garage, into my car, down the driveway, into the street.

I was halfway to the agency when I realized what was really bothering me.

Laura's silence was worse than anything she might have said out loud.

"Well, MacKay, I guess it's just you and me." Ben set his laptop across from me on the conference table and popped the top. "Any bright ideas?"

I gave him a long look, not sure if he was backhanding me with sarcasm or if he really wanted to talk shop.

"Hey," he said, giving me his "I'm completely innocent" look, "I can't help it if Justine had a hot date and bugged out on us."

"Lucky for her," I said, knowing he'd catch my drift. I wasn't thrilled to be working late on a Thursday night, especially alone with Ben. Not that I had anything to worry about with him. Only that I might get pockmarked with smart remarks instead of getting any actual work done. Then again, the idea of going home and facing the stony silence that had developed between Josh and me made a night at the office with Ben a picnic. Even my grandma's funeral hadn't done anything to soften the stiff politeness between us. Since our argument in the driveway, Josh and I had spoken to each other as if we were on a perpetual first date that wasn't going so great. Not much motivation to get home to that.

I lifted the top of my laptop. I arranged the notes about the hospital account on either side of my computer. There didn't seem to be a single fact Dad or Matt could have possibly overlooked. The briefing packet they'd handed out made a master's thesis look like a kindergarten reader. I had no idea when my dad had time to digest the information it contained, and yet during the team meeting he recited the facts as if he'd memorized them.

When they were looking for volunteers to brainstorm ideas, I raised my hand. Ben's had gone up just as fast. There were other people on the account, and we each had our niches. Since Ben, Justine, and I had developed a reputation for thinking outside the box, we'd been the go-to guys for some quick ideas. The three of us had spent all day racking our brains, rejecting ideas as fast as we thought of them. Nothing had struck a chord yet. The day had been long and unproductive. Justine didn't try to hide the fact she was happy to have an excuse to bow out of our evening session. For better or worse, it was Ben and me tonight. I only hoped our two heads would be enough.

We agreed that a short break for supper — alone — was a good idea. There probably wasn't a nutritionist on the planet who would call pizza "brain food," but I was hoping the few slices I wolfed down had done the trick. That and my "brain beverage." I twisted the top off a second cold bottle of Diet Coke and took a long swallow. "You start," I said, getting the jump on Ben.

"I thought you could be the brains behind this one."

I flashed a fake smile at him. "Very funny."

"I wasn't trying to be funny."

"I know better. Now give me something to work with."

The next hour reminded me of watching one of Josh's teams at an important practice. Ben and I batted ideas back and forth as if our lives depended on it. Sometimes he pitched. Other times I tossed. Nothing was falling into our mitts. I sat back and sighed. "This is hopeless."

Ben scratched at his head. "All I can think of is what we talked about all afternoon — how do we get past the idea that you have to be sick to be in the hospital? No one is going to pay for that kind of advertising."

"So what's the flip side of being sick?"

"Feeling good?"

"Keep talking." I did some quick clicking on my computer while Ben stumbled around trying to find footing for an idea. Waiting for a photo to download, I held up a finger. "Got it."

"Got what?"

"Give me a second." I checked another photo and then clicked back to the first. "How about instead of focusing on a hospital being a place to go when you get sick" — I turned my laptop computer screen so Ben could see the stock photo of a person lying in a hospital bed — "we turn the idea around and emphasize that the hospital is the place you go to get well. We could say something like —" I held both hands out, giving up the only idea I had. "Med-First, the Feel-Good Place." With another tap of a finger I switched the photo to a person sitting on the edge of a hospital bed laughing with family members.

All I had left was a long, what-do-you-think stare for Ben.

In the quickest of seconds Ben's expression told me he got it. EMTs rushing to an accident couldn't move any faster than our ideas started flowing. We tweaked the idea, added and subtracted, and by the time we were done, the original idea — "Feel Good" — felt great.

A slow smile spread over Ben's face. "MacKay, will you marry me?"

Grinning, I stuck out my left hand and flashed my wedding ring. "Too late." I twisted my laptop screen so we both could see the picture. "You like it?"

Ben tossed his pen onto the table and stretched his arms over his head. "Yeah, I like it. I think you're a genius."

Even though Ben usually wore sarcasm like a tight T-shirt, tonight he sounded different. I could feel a warm flush heading into my cheeks. "Right."

"Seriously." He sat forward, his forearms on the table. "I don't know why I didn't figure it out earlier. This business is in your blood."

My blush turned to ice thanks to Ben's snide reference to the fact that my dad owned the company. "Gee, thanks." My tone smacked of cynicism. If Ben could dish it out, so could I. "I'm sure in the morning I'll have a promotion along with a new Corvette." I snapped the cover of my laptop shut.

Ben sat back. "What'd I say?"

"Nothing." I pulled my arm away and shoved the papers around my laptop into a messy pile. Enough of this. I'd worked too long today to think straight. If Ben already had it in his head that I was Daddy's Little Protégé, there was nothing I could do to change his mind. If I knew how to do a back flip, I'd do one if it would prove to my coworkers that I was one of them. Unfortunately, mental gymnastics was all I had to offer. "I'm going home. We can work on this campaign more tomorrow when everyone else is here."

"Hey." Ben reached out a hand across the table and rested it on my arm. "Why are you so bent out of shape? All I said was that you were a genius."

"And that my dad owns the company, and that's why I have this job."

"I didn't say that."

"You didn't have to."

"So now you read minds?"

I snorted a laugh. "Believe me, Ben, I have no desire to know what goes on in your mind."

Ben traced a finger in a slow circle on the table. "I like knowing what *you* think."

What had he just said? He liked knowing what I think? Ben?

I stopped trying to tamp my papers into a

448

straight stack and stared at him. A weird quiet hung in the air. I spoke slowly. "What's that supposed to mean?"

He shrugged. "Just that I like the way you think."

Oh. Ben was fixated on the inane movement of his finger against the table. For the first time since I'd known him it seemed he was at a loss for words.

Suddenly, I was too.

I shuffled my notes. Why didn't he say something? Make some smart-aleck comment that would get things back the way they were?

There was paper shuffling on his side of the table too. Ben never looked through his notes during a meeting. And he was never quiet this long. If he didn't speak soon, I'd have to peek and see if he had turned into a statue. Silence was not Ben's virtue.

Plop. A small wad of paper hit the middle of my forehead.

Startled, I jerked my head up, causing another wad to bounce off my nose. Ben was in the process of firing off another paper ball.

"We're supposed to be working." I couldn't help but laugh as he bent his middle finger into his thumb, positioned a small clump of paper on the tip, and pretended to take aim. I held my hand up. A five-fingered shield. My "stop it" didn't mean much when it came with a giggle.

He snapped the paper at me. "Another bull's eye." Ben dropped his voice to that of a low-budget sports announcer. "The paper-wad champ prepares another missile." He rolled a scrap of paper between his hands. "He takes aim . . . He fires . . ."

"Stop!" I peeked between my fingers.

"A direct hit!" A diabolical laugh as he rubbed his hands together, gloating.

"You want war?" I laughed as I quickly gathered Ben's ammunition. "You're gonna get it." I peppered him rapid-fire with his own ammo.

"Truce." Ben held his hands in the sign of a "T." Ben was being kind; only one of my bullets had hit its mark. The rest dotted the table between us.

I laughed across the table at Ben. He smiled back at me. Ben seemed to know a paper fight was just what we needed to clear the weird vibe. Why didn't Josh know what to do to clear things up at home?

Ben seemed to sense the shift in my mood. He gathered the little balls off the table and tossed them into a nearby trash can. "I think we have an idea we can run with in the morning. Want to call it a night?"

I nodded. "Yeah. That'd be good." Now what? Go home and not talk to Josh?

"You okay?" Ben dipped his head to look me in the eye.

A nod would be a lie. A shake of my head would tell too much. But I had to talk to someone. "I —"

Don't.

The unexpected thought closed my mouth. Had I imagined it? Things were so easy between Ben and me right now. What would be so wrong if I confided in him? Asked his opinion about the way Josh was acting?

"I —"

Don't.

I closed my mouth and my eyes.

"Stasha?" Ben's voice held a gentleness that made me want to cry.

I needed someone who could understand. Why not Ben? *Lord, help me.*

"Hey guys."

My eyes flew open as Justine sauntered into the conference room.

"Bad date?" Instantly Ben was back to being Ben.

Justine grinned slyly. "No, I just missed you, Ben."

Ben thumped a fist against his chest. "Justine, you're breaking my heart."

She licked her glossed lips, shrugged off her coat, and slid into a chair. "I felt guilty ditching you guys. You mind?" She held out her hand toward my Diet Coke. At my nod she took a sip. "So, what'd I miss?"

A quick look passed between Ben and me. Ben spoke. "Actually, MacKay came through with her usual brilliance." He lifted his chin in my direction. "Tell her."

As quietly as possible I tiptoed into the apartment, set my purse on a chair, and carefully laid my coat on top of it. It only took a glance for me to see that Josh was asleep in bed. Guilty relief washed over me. At least for one more night I wouldn't have to pretend we were getting along.

Not wanting to take a chance on waking Josh, I undressed in the living room, tiptoed across the bedroom, and slipped into the bathroom where my robe hung behind the door. As I waited for the water to turn hot, I couldn't help but smile at all that Ben, Justine, and I had accomplished tonight. There'd been plenty of laughs as we worked our way through to some solid ideas for the hospital campaign. It was almost midnight, and already I felt the anticipation of going into work tomorrow. The rest of the team was going to be jazzed to see what we had come up with.

You should be jazzed about climbing into bed with your husband.

But I wasn't. Feelings I couldn't begin to name washed over me. Disappointment? Guilt? Disillusionment? None of them applied — or maybe they all did.

I avoided my eyes in the mirror. I didn't want to see what might be looking back at me. I'd gone into marriage so in love with Josh that I couldn't imagine ever feeling any different. And now? We'd barely been married half a year, and all we did was fight. A lump pushed its way into my throat. With a damp washcloth I wiped away the tears that fell from my eyes. What now?

Don't even think it.

As I hung the damp washcloth over the metal bar next to the sink, I couldn't help but face the truth. I was getting along better with Ben than I was with my husband.

Emptiness crept between the covers with me. I lay on my back, pulled the covers to my chin, and stared at the ceiling. Josh shifted onto his back. Through the window blinds, winter moonlight cast a cold shadow across the ceiling. The stark reality of my marriage glared down on me. Was this it?

"You awake?" Josh's voice seemed to come from someone I didn't know.

453

At the sound of his voice, the tears I'd fought in the bathroom returned. "Yeah." I knew what was coming. He'd criticize me for working too much. For staying out too late. He'd accuse me of loving my work more than him. And what could I say?

I listened as he pulled in a deep breath. Slowly let it out. *Just say it.* I was too tired of it all to argue.

A heavy silence weighted the air between us. Josh cleared his throat. His words were a raspy whisper. "This isn't working, is it?"

I closed my eyes as hot tears ran down either side of my face. "No," I choked into the night, "it's not."

I stopped by Elle's desk. "Is he in?" I tilted my head to my dad's office.

"Yes." She leaned toward me and spoke in a whisper. "But he's not in a very good mood."

Neither was I. "That's okay. I'm not asking for a raise." I only had a simple question. Nothing to do with work.

Elle motioned toward the door. "Don't say I didn't warn you."

I knocked softly on the partially open office door. "Dad?"

He looked up from his work. One glance at his face, and I knew Elle was right. My dad had had much better days than this one.

I stepped across the office and sat on the edge of a chair opposite him at his desk. I had to give him credit; he did his best to act as if he was glad to see me. The worry lines between his brows softened as he half smiled at me. We didn't try to hide our relationship around the agency. Still, we were careful to keep our in-office exchanges on topic — all business. Today I needed to cross that boundary, but not by much.

"Stasha," he said, sitting back in his chair, "great job on the hospital campaign." The words were right, but his voice wasn't. Any other day I might ask if he felt okay, but today I couldn't handle anyone's problems but mine.

"Thanks." I looked at my hands laying in my lap. I'd had a hard enough time deciding to talk to someone about my marriage, and now that I'd gotten up my nerve, I couldn't reach her. I looked to my dad for an answer. "Do you know where Mom is? I've been trying to call her, and she doesn't answer."

For a moment, my dad turned in his swivel chair and faced the expanse of glass behind his desk, then he pushed himself out of the chair, walked across his office, and quietly closed the door. For a reason I couldn't understand, my heart took up a thick, dull beat as my dad walked back to his chair, sat down, and turned to face me.

"Where's Mom?" It was a simple question. Why was he acting so weird?

"Stasha —" Dad stopped, tried again. "I was hoping —"

"Dad? What's wrong?" My voice was high, tight . . . scared. A little-girl voice needing assurance from her father.

"Stasha." He searched for words. "You — I — She —" His voice cracked.

"Is something wrong with Mom?" Panic coated my five words.

"Stasha, your mother has . . ." He blew a whoosh of air from his mouth as he looked to the ceiling. Then he lowered his eyes to me. "She's left me."

"Yeah, right." If this was my dad's idea of a joke . . .

He swallowed hard and looked down at his desk. "Your mother is staying at your grandma's house right now."

"No. She's not."

His eyes stared straight into mine. "Yes, Stasha, she is. That's why she's not answering the phone at home. She moved to your grandmother's house."

"Mom?" I had the surreal sensation I was watching a movie of someone else's life.

"There's no way."

My mind reeled through the last conversation I'd had with my mom two days earlier. She'd said something about taking some time away, time I assumed she needed after the vigil she'd held by Grandma. Her voice had cracked, but we were all emotional these days. She'd never meant — She couldn't have — "No. No way."

Dad couldn't seem to say anything now. The quiet was deafening.

"What happened?" I finally broke the silence. "I don't understand. You guys have been married for —"

There was no way my mom would ever walk out on my dad. No way.

He was lying. This was all some horrible, stupid lie.

I opened my mouth to accuse him, but I took one look at his face, and I knew the truth.

Bricks. A baseball bat. Something incredibly leaden landed somewhere between my heart and my stomach. I was afraid I might throw up. There was a ringing in my ears. I didn't want to have to try to comprehend the unimaginable — to understand, with absolute certainty, that if my parents couldn't make their marriage work, there was no hope whatsoever for mine.

LAURA

I have heard your prayer and seen your tears; I will heal you.

2 KINGS 20:5

All I had these days was time. Too much of it. Which is why I was allowing myself a break from my new routine of sorting through Eleanor's things. Possibly a morning of shopping would distract me from my thoughts. Unfortunately, walking around Carlton's small downtown shopping area wasn't doing the trick. Maybe this store. I pulled open the door and stepped inside. Candles, lotions, racks of new clothes. Certainly there was something here I needed. I picked up a heavy candle and sniffed. Lavender. Eleanor's favorite scent. I'd smelled enough of that going through her closet. Ah, vanilla. Donnie's favorite. I quickly set the candle down and moved on to another part of the store.

The boutique saleswoman lightly touched my elbow. "Are you Laura Dunn?"

For a second her simple question left me mum. Was I? For now, anyway, I still was. Of course I was. I nodded. "Yes, I am."

She held out her hand. "We met briefly at the opening of Karen's gallery. There were a lot of people there that night. Maybe you don't remember."

She was right. I didn't. With a finger I pointed to the upper half of my head. "Middle-age-brain syndrome. I'm sorry." I wasn't about to tell her what else had been going on that night — how Judy's husband had tried to push himself on me in the makeshift kitchen, how for a moment I'd imagined he might be John, how guilty I felt knowing my husband wasn't the person at the top of my imagination. Here I was, letting my thoughts run away from me again. I put out my hand. "Remind me of your name."

"It's Pamela." She cast a quick glance around the people-empty but clothes-crammed boutique. "Actually, I own this store. I've seen you in here before."

"That must mean I'm in here way too much."

She laughed. "Oh, in a business like this we never say anyone's in here too much.

Not possible."

"That makes me feel better." I fingered the silk sleeve of a blouse on display.

"Are you looking for something special? Or just browsing?"

"Oh." I dropped the soft silk. "Just browsing."

"Then I'll let you. Take your time." Pamela headed toward the back of the store.

Soft strains of syncopated jazz played over the boutique sound system as I walked through the store. Time was all I had today. No meetings. No appointments. Karen didn't even need my help. The only thing on my agenda was going back to Eleanor's quiet house where I would continue sorting through her things. I only hoped folding and boxing up would somehow order my thoughts. My emotions were as jumbled as the items in Eleanor's closets.

I looked through a rack of dresses, not really focusing on any of them. What was Donnie doing right now? Working, of course. But was his heart as heavy as mine? Was he at all concerned that I'd left? It had been almost two weeks, 14 long days — and nights — since I'd packed a bag and moved out. I hadn't heard a word from him, but I wasn't about to call. I'd talked to Stasha on the phone only once, but the conversation was as tension-filled as a downed power line. I hadn't expected her to understand; after all, she was a newlywed. In time, I hoped she might realize the why of what I'd done.

I gave my head a small shake and peered down at fancy baubles sitting atop a glass case. I was supposed to be taking a break from thinking about Stasha, Donnie, and the future of my marriage.

What future?

The ever-present clump of tears in my throat squeezed tight. No. I swallowed. I refused to look like a bad actress overcome with emotion in her favorite boutique. I picked up a bracelet and slipped it on. There now. A woman wearing this would have a perfect life. She'd be invited to lively parties, hang out with interesting people. *All because of a bracelet.* I smiled as I slipped the sparkly bauble from my wrist and put it on the counter. It had done its work without me spending a cent. I knew I wasn't the first woman to use shopping as therapy.

My fingers threaded through satin, silk, and fabrics I couldn't name. So much like the array of feelings I'd been thumbing through these past months, and especially these past two weeks. I picked up a long, light-blue chiffon scarf and drew the soft fabric along the back of my hand. Without trying, memories of better times with Donnie wrestled in hand-to-heart combat with all the awful times of this past year.

I'd never forgotten the details of our first meeting . . . Donnie Dunn had literally run right into me with his fancy BMW and smooth patter. By the end of the day I had crutches and a date. Within the year a husband. In spite of everything that had happened since, I still had to smile at the memory. It might not have been love at first sight, not technically. After all, he'd broken my glasses. I could hardly see the guy I had ended up marrying. I smiled as I put the scarf down and continued to browse.

There had been lots of good times, of course. We'd started the agency. Had Stasha and high hopes for everything that lay ahead. Now, looking back, it had all happened in the blink of an eye. We had a lovely home. Nice cars. A wonderful daughter married to a great young man. A lucrative business. Our dreams had come true. All of them.

All except the dream you had for your marriage.

Except for that.

My hand rubbed against a scratchy ribbon of lace. How could something that looked so delicate hold such irritation? So much like Donnie's and my relationship. What started out as a gigantic leap of love would end with a million little baby steps, tiny irritations that eventually led us apart. I moved away from the abrasive lace, but my thoughts stayed the course. Donnie's workaholism had eaten away any time we might have spent working things out.

Can you really blame him for everything?

No, I couldn't. I had a part in all this too. I'd filled my days and nights with activities to keep me from loneliness. From having to confront Donnie about what was missing in our relationship. Art guild. Book club. Tennis lessons. Bible study. Even quilting, for heaven's sake. If there was a club meeting or a class in Carlton, you could count on me to be there.

You still have all those things in your life. Shouldn't they be enough?

Ah, the question of the hour. Of the day. Of every long night I'd spent tossing and turning trying to find the answer to an impossible question.

"Would you like me to start a dressing room for you?" Pamela was at my elbow.

Without realizing it, I had collected an armful of garments. Why not? I had nothing better to do. I followed her to a dressing

463

room tucked in a back alcove of the boutique. A perfect place for me to hide away with my thoughts. "Thanks," I said, drawing the curtain between us.

"Just yell if you need anything."

"I'll be fine." Who was I trying to assure? Pamela or myself?

I took off my shoes, slipped out of my clothes, and pulled a gauzy, flowery, pink dress over my head. One glance in the mirror revealed where my mind had been when I'd picked it up. Not only was the color wrong for me; I'd also need a different life if I was going to wear a dress like this. I reached to pull it off.

Isn't that exactly what you want? A different life? The thought stopped me with the dress halfway over my head. There was no denying I'd been trying on a different kind of life these past two weeks. I let the soft dress float back down around my shoulders, past my waist, and over my legs. The hem of the skirt skimmed my ankles. If only a new life were as easy to assess in front of silvered glass.

I stood in front of the mirror and studied my reflection. On second thought, maybe pink was a good color for me after all. The dress was beautiful, soft and light in a way my life wasn't. My face, however, was another story. Pulling the dress over my head had mussed my hair and pushed my bangs off my face. Every worry line on my forehead appeared etched with permanent marker. I hadn't been trying, but I could tell I'd lost weight. No wonder the dress fit so well. I hoped Pamela only saw the surface — the makeup I'd carefully applied to hide what was going on underneath.

These past weeks I had mastered the fine art of avoiding looking at myself in a mirror. Today all my training left me. As hard as I tried to focus on looking only at the lovely dress, I couldn't keep my eyes from boring straight back into myself.

Every time I thought about what I'd done, something inside me did a belly flop, landing on solid cement each and every time. Even though I'd relived that one night a thousand times already, I couldn't prevent the scene from playing out one more time . . .

I had slipped out of bed and tiptoed into the bathroom, closing the door quietly behind me. The nightlight I kept in the wall was there doing its thing. A soft shadow was all I needed. I stood in front of the sink and laid my forehead against the cool marble of the countertop for a moment. I needed to clear my head. I needed to put some semblance of order to these thoughts that had kept me awake, more often than just tonight.

Things between Donnie and me had been strained before now, but when Eleanor died and he wasn't there, well, his absence in all of this was a deal breaker. It was that simple. Whatever reserve of emotion I still carried for Donnie had died that night. If he couldn't be there for his mother, why should I expect him to ever be there for me?

I lifted my head and stared into the mirror. It didn't take more than the dim nightlight to see the disillusionment in my eyes — disappointment masked as middle-aged crow's feet.

There was a cough from the bed just outside the door. *Oh, please Donnie, stay asleep.* Was he just as tired of this farce of a marriage as I was? I looked into the sink and stared at the drain. Maybe I didn't need order to my thoughts. Maybe what I needed was a break. A long one. Perhaps a permanent one.

"I want a —" I stopped speaking and closed my eyes. The final word stuck in my throat. Until I spoke again the possibilities were endless. There was still time to end my sentence with just about any other word in the universe. *I want a hug. I want a bicycle. I want a trip to Italy.* Oh yes, the possibilities were still endless.

I opened my eyes and looked down at my wedding band, the large diamond skewed off to the right the way it had for the past 23 years. It had never sat perfectly centered on my hand no matter how many times I wiggled my fingers or touched under the band with my thumb, trying to make it just right. Kind of like my whole marriage. Off center.

Out of habit I lifted my little finger and stroked the thin band with my thumb, pushing the diamond to the top of my left hand. There. As if that would make things right. I blinked, studying the solitaire in its unique setting. Once upon a time it had sparkled.

How long ago had that been? Long before countless layers of baby lotion had been swiped across one tiny bottom. Before bread dough and hamburger fat had worked their way around the facets, slowly clouding the starry prisms in my ring. Once upon a time, when two people got married they lived happily ever after. Too bad we weren't living in that time anymore. Too, too bad.

I closed my eyes, took a deep breath, and lifted my chin. I opened my eyes, looked at myself square in the bathroom mirror, and whispered the words, "I want a divorce."

As I had that night, I stared at myself in

the boutique mirror now. I had to face the truth: my marriage was over.

That next morning after Donnie left for work, I pulled a suitcase from the attic and started packing. I wasn't sure where I was going or for how long, only that I needed to leave. I was doing the one thing I thought I'd never do . . . walk away from my wedding vows.

For better or worse.

This was the worse. There was absolutely no better about it.

Even in the numbed state I'd been in when I walked out, I knew all the years Donnie and I had spent together deserved something. A phone call was the chicken way out. Still, I waited until I was unpacked at his mother's before I called.

"Elle, I need to speak to Donnie," I'd said in a tone that must have signaled to Elle that she should put me through to Donnie, busy or not. And she did.

I hadn't wanted to start this conversation by clearing my throat, but my words seemed stopped up inside until I did. Even I was surprised at how unemotional they sounded considering what I had to say. "I'm at your mother's."

"Okay?" There was a question there. He expected something to follow.

I wouldn't fail at this. It was now or never.

"You know how things have been lately. We've . . . I'm . . ." Where were all the words I'd been practicing?

"Laura, I'm —"

"No, Donnie." I wasn't going to let him railroad me. Not this time. I'd start there. "This time I need to talk. I've loved you for a long time. I suppose I do still love you." Was that possible? Did I still love him? This was no time to question. "When your mother died and you weren't there —"

"I was on —"

If I stopped now I'd never get it all said. "Donnie, you weren't there for your mother. You weren't there for me. You haven't been there for a long time." My voice was failing me. I took a deep breath. "I'm at your mother's. I'm going to be staying here. I —"

Thankfully, he interrupted. I had no idea what I planned to say next.

"Laura, what do you . . ."

"Want?" I could still finish his sentences. I gulped at the tears in my throat. I blinked against the sting. "I don't know, Donnie. I don't know. I just know we can't — I can't —"

The memory of those words was interrupted as Pamela's voice startled me out of

469

my thoughts. "Can I can get anything for you?"

A new life?

"No. No, I'm fine." But I wasn't. Leaving Donnie had not made things fine. My life was as unfinished as the conversation with Donnie. I'd only added two more words before I hung up that day. "I'm sorry." And I was. And in some sad way, I suspected he was too.

The chime of the front door was a reminder that I wasn't the only person in the world. And certainly not the only person with troubles. But I was just possibly the only person trying to solve them by staring at herself in a dressing room mirror. I pulled the dress over my head, pulled my own clothes back on, and draped the spring dress over my arm. If it was possible to buy a new life, I was going to give it a try.

"Laura. Hi!" Janet, one of the art guild board members, waved at me over a rack of slacks.

Oh, great. "Hi." I waved back, making a beeline for the counter. If luck was with me, I could avoid a conversation. Chit-chat wasn't my idea of therapy.

"Shopping for tonight?" So much for luck.

The only polite thing to do was answer her question. If I could figure out what was going on tonight that I hadn't been invited to . . . or had completely forgotten. My mind scrambled. An art guild event? I'd been in such a mental fog that blocking out anything wouldn't surprise me. "Tonight?"

"The chamber banquet?" Janet raised her eyebrows and grinned at me.

"Uh . . . I'm sorry." I shifted my new dress to my other arm. "I guess I'm out of the loop. I'm on lots of committees, but the chamber isn't one of them. I didn't know about the banquet tonight."

By now Janet had moved near me. She reached out and swatted my arm. "You are a *good* actress." She laughed. "You must be proud of your husband. Carlton Businessperson of the Year. Wow."

She might as well have pulled a trap door open right under my feet. I felt as if I was suddenly falling down into a dark, endless tunnel. Donnie had been named Businessperson of the Year, and I had no idea.

This will be what it's like to live separate lives. Is this what you want?

Was it? I had no clue. No inkling how to respond to Janet. I simply stared at her.

She touched the fabric of the dress hanging over my arm. "You're really going all out, aren't you? Very pretty. If you need an extra copy of the article in today's paper, I

471

can cut it out for you."

"No. That's okay. Thanks." I hoped I didn't sound as oblivious as I felt. Of course the *Carlton Register* had been delivered to the doorstep of my house. Donnie's and my house. If I'd been living there I would have seen it. I would have known about the honor Donnie would be receiving tonight.

Either Pamela had cranked up the heat, or I was having a meltdown. All I wanted was to get out of this store as fast as possible. I rummaged in my purse and pulled out my credit card, handing it to Pamela with a lame excuse. "I just realized I'm very late for something. I have to go."

She swiped my card and hung my dress on a clear plastic hanger while she waited for the authorization. My fingernails drummed against the countertop, tapping as fast as the emotions banging against my heart. Did Donnie wish I was going with him tonight? Was I proud he was getting an award for being a savvy businessperson, the very thing that had caused this break between us?

Is this what Stasha hadn't said the one other time I tried to talk to her? "If you loved Dad you'd go —" I thought she was going to say "go home." Maybe she had meant to tell me about Donnie's award.

Why hadn't she? Had she given up on us too?

Before I could answer my questions Pamela handed me a sales slip to sign. *Laura Dunn*, I scrawled. As I pushed the slip of paper back her way it didn't escape my notice that I wouldn't be buying this expensive dress if Donnie didn't work so hard. Was I ready to give up that privilege?

You'll get half of everything. A fact I learned from Judy's divorce attorney.

I pulled my purse onto my shoulder, slipped my finger through the hanger loop, and hoped the dress wouldn't get caught in the door as I pushed my way out. Hot tears stung at my eyes as I blinked my way to my car. *Why hadn't Donnie called to ask me to be at the banquet with him?* With my thumb, I punched at the automatic unlock button on the car door too many times.

Would you have gone?

I yanked open the back door and tossed the dress inside, then climbed behind the steering wheel and sat there in my cold refuge of glass and steel. *Would I have gone?* I didn't know. What I did know was that it hurt not to be asked. Hurt to think that Donnie was apparently moving on with his life while I wallowed in a messy pit of uncertainty. What would I do if my marriage really was over?

You won't have to do anything. You'll get half of everything. I jammed the key in the ignition and turned it, too far and too long. The engine screeched what I was feeling. I spun the wheels away from the curb and stepped on the gas. The loud honk of a passing car horn sent my foot slamming on the brake. I was in no shape to drive to Eleanor's house, but there was no one but me to get me there.

Is this really what I wanted?

You'll get half of everything.

Carefully I pulled away from the curb, scorching tears streaming down my cheeks.

The trouble was, I didn't want half of anything. I wanted it all.

Not all the money.

All the man.

Hardly conscious of where I was going, I drove through the streets that would take me to Eleanor's, my temporary home. As much as it hurt knowing that Donnie would be attending the chamber banquet without me, I felt a bubble of pride knowing he was the man they'd picked for the honor.

Part of me wanted to be there. Part of me was stubbornly glad I hadn't had to make the choice. I was happy for him and mad at myself for caring so much.

I turned into Eleanor's driveway and stared at the house I knew was all too empty inside. The stark truth was, I still loved Donnie Dunn. But could I stay married to him?

DONNIE

I stood in front of the mirror and tugged at my tie. Was it straight? I had no knack for this sort of thing. Laura was always the one to make sure I was presentable.

"Here." She would reach out her hand and wiggle my tie a millimeter one direction, then the other. I'd swear she hadn't done a thing but move it back to where it had been, but one glance in the mirror and I'd know something was better.

I looked in the mirror again. Either I was standing crooked or my tie was hopelessly lopsided. I tugged at the knot, undoing it completely, and started over. Twist, around, under, over, loop it through. There. Maybe. In what I knew was a futile move, I looked over my shoulder, hoping . . . I could use Laura's expertise tonight.

No such luck.

One more time I yanked off my tie. If Laura were here, I'd be grumbling. *Why do*

I have to get dressed up for this banquet anyway? One night I could spend relaxing at home, and instead I've got to put on a suit and eat rubbery chicken just to get a fake-wood plaque.

Laura would chuckle as she brushed imaginary lint from my lapels. *This is supposed to be an honor, not a chore.* Her eyes would sparkle as she'd lay a hand along my cheek. *Smile. I'm proud of you. Here.* Then she'd reach out and straighten my tie.

She should be here.

I looked away from the mirror. Yeah, she should. I pulled at the tie, shoved at the knot. Then I finally loosened the slipknot enough so I could breathe. Whatever it looked like, it was just going to have to do.

I reached for the bottle of cologne Laura had given me for my birthday. Then again, what did I need cologne for? In a fluid move I pulled back my hand and reached for my suit coat hanging on the knob of the bathroom door. I slipped my arms into the smooth lining and pulled the jacket on over my white shirt. In turn, I tugged at each of the cuffs of my shirtsleeves. The cleaners used a different smelling laundry soap than Laura did. They starched my shirts more, too. It felt like I was wearing someone else's clothes.

"Ready?" The word was out before I realized I'd spoken. It was Laura I was talking to. Laura . . . the one person who should be beside me tonight . . . and wouldn't be.

Polite applause surrounded me as I made my way to the stage and climbed the four rickety metal stairs to receive my award. As I approached the podium, a slow standing ovation began. I could already hear what Matt would have to say about that. *The crowd draaaagged themselves to their feet when Donnie Dunn accepted his award.* Leave it to Matt to keep me humble.

But Laura would have said, *Did you see that? They gave you a standing ovation!*

On automatic pilot, I shook hands with the chamber president and posed while the *Carlton Register* reporter snapped the standard photo as I was handed my plaque. I stepped to the microphone to give my remarks. Why hadn't I prepared anything to say?

I nodded to the crowd, waiting for the applause to stop, for them to settle back into their seats. From our table near the stage, Matt gave me a thumbs-up. Long-time business acquaintances nodded congratulations as I caught their glances. Off to my left I caught a glimpse of John Barnes, the hospital CEO. Was he here to flaunt the fact I'd lost his business? Even Stasha had begged off, giving work as her excuse. How fitting. But I suspected her absence was part of the mini boycott Stasha had been staging by not talking to me beyond office essentials. I couldn't think about that now. People were looking at me, expecting me to say something intelligent, or funny, or well, anything but what I was saying, which was nothing.

I looked down at the plaque in my hands and out at the crowd. I opened my mouth, then closed it. There was the soft *ting* of a water glass nicking a plate as it was lifted for a sip. There was a scrape of a chair as it was turned for a better view.

My mind a blank, I scanned the crowd not seeing any one face, just a mass of faces and eyes staring back at me. There was only one person I needed to see. One person who would give me the presence of mind I needed to say the expected words. I knew she wasn't here, and still I looked.

Someone called out, "Speech!" Embarrassed laughter followed.

I had no words for these strangers. The only person I needed to thank was the one person who wasn't here.

The house was dark as I let myself in the

side door from the garage. It was Laura who always thought ahead to leave a light on for us. For me. No matter how late I came home.

I flicked at the light switch and then tossed my keys on the counter. *You're going to scratch the countertop if you keep doing that.* Laura didn't have to be here to remind me. I grabbed at the keys and put them in my pocket.

Unsure what to do next, I stood in the kitchen. What was I supposed to do with this imitation-walnut framed award that summed up my professional life? I stared down at my name etched in gold script:

DONNIE DUNN
CARLTON CHAMBER OF COMMERCE
BUSINESSPERSON OF THE YEAR

If Laura were here, she'd already have a hammer and nail and be heading toward my office. I set the plaque down on the kitchen table, shrugged out of my suit coat, and *finally* removed my tie.

My eyes landed on the wall calendar hanging nearby. Laura's handwriting filled many of the small squares. Nothing was written on today's date. No record of the fact that on this day I was Businessperson of the Year and Schmuck of the Century.

Maybe I should have taken Matt up on his offer to go out for a drink after the awards banquet. Shooting the breeze with him would have filled some time, and a drink might have taken the edge off of the restlessness I felt tonight.

My stomach made a low rumbling noise. It couldn't possibly be digestion sounds. The banquet food wouldn't win any awards, and I'd been too keyed up to taste it anyway. Maybe I was hungry. What had I eaten since Laura left? Nothing that I remembered.

If nothing else, a late night snack would help pass some time. I opened the fridge. Jars of mustard, ketchup, jelly, and mayonnaise filled the shelves. Three small cartons of Laura's favorite blueberry yogurt were tucked along the side of one shelf, as if they were waiting for her to come home. A partial jug of milk.

What the heck. I reached for the milk container. How long had it been since I'd had warm milk to put me to sleep?

Since your mom used to heat it up for you in your favorite red mug and let you drink it sitting in bed in your pajamas.

I should have gone out with Matt. Wallowing in sentiment wasn't my style. I swallowed against the tightness in my throat and poured the milk into a mug. As I tilted the jug upright, a whiff of sour milk wrinkled my nostrils. *Phew!* Anyone who'd been paying attention would know that milk couldn't sit in a fridge for a couple of weeks and not turn bad.

I reached for the mug and dumped the contents in the sink, washing the rancid smell away with cold water. What wasn't so easy to wash away was the convicting thought. If I'd paid more attention to my marriage . . .

Talk about crying over spilled milk.

Resorting to clichés now?

The thing was that the cliché was true. Laura had brought so much to our relationship. And me? All I had offered her was what was left at the end of every long day, which wasn't worth much more than the sour milk I'd just dumped.

I wandered into the darkened family room and flicked on the television, then slumped into my shabby old recliner — the chair Laura had wanted to replace for the last ten years. Lumps of old stuffing made my back uncomfortable. I lay back in the chair the way I had a thousand evenings before, with my feet in the air, my eyes closed, the TV on.

It didn't take but a minute to realize there

was no way sleep was heading my way anytime soon. I thumped the recliner forward and stood up just as the picture changed on the television. A sudden bright beam bounced across the carpet and onto the coffee table. The small wedding album Laura had made of Stasha's wedding photos was illuminated as if a spotlight had been placed on it. I picked it up and sat down on the couch, quickly realizing my middle-aged eyes were going to need some light if I planned to see any of the photos. I turned on the table lamp, put on my reading glasses, and opened the album.

Stasha in her wedding gown. A silhouette photo of my once-little girl standing on the brick steps of the church, looking out over the bright-green, manicured lawn. Looking toward her future. Away from me. I felt a hiccup in my chest as I turned the thick page.

Stasha with her bridesmaids. They were laughing so hard that Stasha was doubled over. It was as if the photographer had just that second called out her name. *Stasha!* She'd looked up and *snap.* Captured forever. My joyous daughter. The bride.

Josh and his groomsmen. Five young men with promising futures.

I turned another page and was caught

unprepared. Stasha. Laura. My mother. All smiling. All beautiful. Each in their own way gone from me.

I closed my eyes and pulled in a deep breath.

I quickly turned the page. More standard photos. The kind a person found in every album. The wedding party. Stasha standing between Laura and me. Stasha and Josh between the two of us. There was a photo of just Laura and me. More photos of the flower girl, the ring-bearer, the ushers . . . anyone who was anybody, and the bride. Relatives from both sides of the family. Stasha and Josh cutting the cake. The first dance. Stasha and I swaying to a song I couldn't recall.

And that was the trouble. I'd been there for almost every one of these photos. And yet I had only the faintest recollection of posing for any of them. Of watching them being taken. It was as though a clone had stood in for me that day. Where had I been?

You were thinking about work. About the Brody account. That was the day you were supposed to hear if the Dunn Agency won the business.

That I remembered. We'd won the account, but in essence I'd missed my daughter's wedding.

What else have you missed in your quest to be the best?

I didn't want to think about the answer to that question. I closed the album and removed my glasses. Laura often told me she felt she was dragging me through life. I never understood what she meant until tonight. I'd sat in the bleachers for Stasha's elementary school programs. Cringed through junior high band concerts. I'd gone along. Reluctantly. My body had been there, but my mind had been a million other places. Well, actually only *one* other place, at work. And what did I have to show for it?

I placed the wedding album back on the table, put my forearms on my knees, and hung my head as I answered my facetious question.

I had a plaque.

In the pecking order of business, tonight should have been the pinnacle of my career. Oh, I was no Donald Trump, but I was Donnie Dunn, Businessperson of the Year. Isn't this what I'd worked for? To achieve exactly this kind of recognition from my peers? This was what life was all about. I was on top. The best. I had a plaque to prove it.

I remembered standing on the stage earlier in the evening. Trying to find words. Trying to find the one person in the room that mattered.

"You weren't there for your mother. You weren't there for me. You haven't been for a long time." Laura's words of goodbye.

Instead of pride, all I'd felt standing on that empty dais was that something was missing. Someone.

So, this is what Laura meant. I hadn't understood until tonight. How could I, when every other time in our married life she'd been there for me? How could I know this emptiness when Laura had always filled it?

A familiar tightness pushed into my throat. I dropped my face into my hands.

My climb to the top. It hadn't been worth this.

STASHA

Halfway up the stairs to our apartment I could hear the TV blaring. The good news was, if Josh was involved in a television program that meant I wouldn't have to talk to him. The bad news? We wouldn't come any closer to bridging whatever you called the gigantic expanse of nothingness between us. If Josh heard me come into the apartment, he was ignoring me.

"Can you turn that down?" I asked with a forced smile.

Josh glanced away from the TV and punched at the remote. "What did you say?"

"Hi." My greeting was tentative. Did Josh care that I hadn't been home for supper?

He stared at some crime drama on TV. "Hi." That was all. No more.

A glance to my left, into the kitchen, didn't tell me a thing. I couldn't tell if Josh had already eaten supper or skipped a meal. At 8:50 in the evening I knew better than to think he'd waited for me.

I took off my coat, grabbed a Diet Coke from the fridge, and sat on an overstuffed chair next to the couch where Josh was. "What are you watching?"

"*CSI*. It's almost over."

My cue to shush. It didn't take long for my mind to wander back to work, to the two new accounts we'd be pitching next week. There was research to do. Campaign development. Always more to do than there was time for. And that didn't count listening to Elle gush about her new boyfriend. Did he like her as much as she liked him? Who had time to listen? The only time I was tempted to give her a piece of advice was when she said, "You're so lucky to be married."

I bit my tongue. There weren't enough hours in the day for all I could tell her about being married. Somewhere in all my daydreaming, *CSI* ended and a new show began. Josh seemed as engrossed in this program as the other one.

A flame of anger began to smolder in my chest. Couldn't he turn off the TV and talk to me? Couldn't he feel the unsaid things hanging in the air between us? How could he be so involved in a story that had nothing to do with him and not give a rip about the drama that was playing out in our living room?

The longer I watched him stare at the screen, the madder I got. Didn't he care what was happening to us? Did he think sitting around and not talking was going to solve our problems? Inside my head I screamed, *What's wrong with you? Is that stupid show more important than us?*

If he was going to be oblivious, so could I. I focused my eyes on the screen as if I'd never seen television before. How long would it take him to notice that watching this program wouldn't solve anything? I looked at my watch, then crossed my arms over my chest. Two hours later, by the time the weather report was over, I realized if this was a contest, Josh had won. We'd sat in silence in our small living room for two hours in front of a blathering box. If it weren't for the sound coming from the television, this room could double for the *CSI* morgue when no one's around.

I couldn't not talk any longer. Maybe if I quit being so stubborn, tonight would be the night we'd figure out what had gone wrong between us. I pushed words out between my clenched teeth. "Do you want to talk?"

Josh sighed as if I'd asked him to run to

the store for nail polish at 10:30 at night. "Can we wait until after sports?"

The smoldering ember inside me flared into a bonfire. There. A perfect example. I'd throw it at him as soon as the sports was over. I packed his insensitivity into my mental suitcase. I wouldn't forget.

Josh leaned forward to watch the sports highlights. Why didn't he crawl right into the TV and live there? Did he even remember I was in the same room?

Impatiently I tapped my foot, picked up my can of Diet Coke, and then realized I'd emptied it long ago. I shook the can as if the motion would somehow add one more sip. How could he sit there and act as if some hockey game was more important than the problems we had? After an eternity, the music signaling the end of the nightly news sounded. Now. Now Josh would turn off the TV, and we could talk.

I waited. Letterman started cracking jokes that weren't one bit funny. But Josh seemed to think they were. Maybe the jokes would get him in a good mood. After the monologue he'd be ready to discuss us.

I woke with a sudden jump. False laughter from a mindless comedy was a sorry soundtrack for the stark reality playing out in my living room. I'd fallen asleep in the chair. My empty Coke can was overturned by my feet. Josh was slumped, asleep on the couch, the remote dangling from his limp fingers. So, that was how much he cared. How much both of us cared. We'd rather sleep than solve our problems.

I pushed myself upright in the chair and simply stared at Josh. None of this mattered anymore, and I didn't care. That thought was more convicting than any argument. *I didn't care.* We were going through the motions of a marriage, and that was all. Working. Watching TV. Not talking. If this was marriage, I'd been duped.

I slumped back in my chair. I always thought people who got divorced fought all the time. That they picked at each other incessantly. I never imagined it might be silence that spoke louder than raised voices.

An image of my mom and dad came to mind. Dad in his recliner. Mom in her corner of the couch. How many nights had they sat in their living room, saying nothing? *If* my dad was home. The only thing different about Josh and me was where we sat. So, this . . . *this* was why my mom left. There was nothing left to fight about.

I pushed myself out of the chair and walked into the bedroom, got down on my hands and knees. I bent and rummaged under the bed for the duffel bag I knew was there, somewhere. Ah. There.

Maybe you should pray while you're on your knees?

No. There weren't any words left to say that could help. I'd tried talking to Josh, and he wouldn't listen.

I'll listen.

I pulled out the duffel bag, set it on my side of the bed, and turned to my dresser. I wouldn't take everything. Not tonight. Only enough to get me through a few days. I would come back another time when Josh wasn't here and get the rest.

There was a loud burst of laughter from the TV in the other room. *Please Josh, don't wake up.* I'd been hoping to talk to him all evening, and now I knew what he'd apparently known all along. There was nothing left to say.

I parked the car at the curb and looked toward my grandmother's old house. It was completely dark. Why had I expected there would be a light on for me?

Icy air from outside was working its way into the car. I couldn't sit here all night getting up my nerve. I'd freeze to death if I waited until I was ready. But I knew that once I knocked on the door there would be no turning back. A lift of my hand, and my marriage would be over.

A deep breath. Another. I reached across the seat and pulled my duffel bag with me. Out of the car. One step closer to the beginning of the end. I stood at the curb and looked down the long sidewalk; small ridges of snow on either side pointed to my goal.

As if I was walking a gangplank, I tentatively put one foot forward, then the other. I knew what waited behind the door.

My mom. Unconditional love. Arms and words that would soothe the deep ache inside. Only a few more steps toward the door of my grandma's house, and I'd be on the way to healing. Mom would understand.

Okay. I'd stood here long enough. My toes were getting numb. The tips of my ears were like ice. A puff of warm breath clouded the air in front of me as I lifted my hand to knock. It was after midnight. I tried to imagine which bedroom in my grandma's house my mother might sleep in. All of them were at the back of the house. Would she hear my insistent knocking?

There was always the doorbell, but that friendly chime couldn't match the satisfaction I got from thudding my gloved fist against the door. I wasn't about to creep around the house like a burglar and tap at a window. I wanted her to open the door and take me in her arms.

"Mom!" I held my lips near the place where the door met the frame. I didn't want her to think some stranger was trying to pound his way through the door. "Mo-om!" It seemed like forever until a light went on behind the door.

A cautious voice. "Who's there?"

"Mom, it's me."

"Stasha?"

I could hear the deadbolt turn, the doorknob unlock. The tears I'd been swallowing flooded my eyes. "Mo-om, hurry. I need you."

"Stasha. What's wrong?" The door swung open, and I fell into my mother's arms.

"Oh Mom." I was sobbing now. "Mom. I — I — can't . . ."

She put her hands on my shoulders, pushing me away to look into my eyes. There was panic in hers. "What's wrong? Did something happen to your dad?"

"No," I sobbed, shaking my head. I hadn't imagined what my mom might assume. "No, it's not Dad." Once again I fell into her embrace.

Through my coat I could feel soothing

warmth as she rubbed my back. "It'll be okay. It'll be okay. Calm down. Whatever it is, it'll be okay."

"It's not . . . okay." I gasped out the words. "It's not —"

My mom pulled back her head and tried to lift my chin. "Did something happen to Josh? You have to tell me, Stasha. I can't help until you tell me."

I shook my head against her robe. "He's okay. It's — It's —"

"Well, then." My mom loosed her hold on me. "We have to close this door or we'll both end up with pneumonia."

I swiped my gloves under each of my eyes. "Just a sec." My voice was a croak. "I have to get . . ." I stepped off the threshold of the doorstep and reached for my duffel bag sitting just outside the door.

My mom was tightening the cloth belt of her robe. "What's that?"

I looked from her to my duffel bag. Didn't she know? "My stuff."

"What stuff?"

A little hiccup of tears squeezed my voice higher. "My clothes. For work."

A weird expression crossed my mom's face. She put one hand on the door frame, one closed fist against her heart. I stood facing her, duffel bag in hand, waiting for her to step aside so I could come in where it was warm.

"You can't come in here." She stood smack in the middle of the open door.

"What? Mom? It's so cold, and you just said —"

"I said, 'You can't come in here.' "

"But —"

"No."

"No?" I could feel my eyebrows practically touching. "What's that supposed to mean?"

"It means you need to turn around and go back home."

"I can't go to Dad. He won't be any help."

There was a long silence. From a block away car tires slowly crunched over icy streets.

"Stasha." My mom wrapped both her arms around herself. "I didn't mean for you to go to your dad. I said you need to go home." She lifted her chin as if urging me away. "Your home is with Josh."

I lifted one gloved hand. Pointed at her. "But you — You're not —"

"I'm not going to say this again." Her voice was calm. Firm. "Your home is with Josh. You need to go to him."

Looking into my eyes, she took one step back. One more. Then she slowly closed the door between us.

I stood frozen as the deadbolt slid into place and the light went out. A hot wave of tears spilled down my cheeks. What was I supposed to do now?

Go home.

LAURA

Just as I'd seen actresses do in countless movies, I stepped aside and closed the door between my daughter and me, leaning my back against the door as if Stasha might force her way in. Even as I did it I knew better; I had pressed against the door simply to hold myself upright. I'd just turned my daughter away.

I pressed my hands against my face. They were trembling. I was starring in no movie. The only drama being played out was happening right in front of me. On this doorstep. In this house. Stasha, Josh, Donnie, and me. We had no script to follow. No lines to recite. We were stumbling through life with no direction.

"Help me," I whispered into Eleanor's dark house. I knew who I was talking to. *Help us. Please.* The only sound I heard was blood whooshing through my ears, thumping through my heart — the sound of a mother questioning what she'd done.

If Stasha left, I hadn't heard her. No steps of retreat. No car starting at the curb. But then, I hadn't been listening for that. I tiptoed to the living room window and peeked through the drapes. Thank goodness, her car was gone. I hoped with all my heart she'd taken my advice and gone home to Josh.

What about you?

Yes, that was the looming question. What about me?

I tried sitting on the couch to think things through, but agitation pushed me to my feet. I wandered through Eleanor's house, turning on a table lamp here, another one there. I didn't want the glare of an overhead light; my thoughts were searing enough.

As if retracing my steps from the day I'd arrived at Eleanor's, I started at the front door. There was a stack of mail on the sideboard. Junk mail and bills where Eleanor kept them and where I put them now.

This is her home. Not yours.

I pushed my slipper-covered toe against a pair of Eleanor's beige walking shoes. I'd packed up so many of her things and yet hadn't been able to put away these shoes. As if I somehow expected her to use them. As if this mixed-up life I'd been living would somehow return to normal, if I waited long enough.

Is that really what you want? Normal?

No, not if I was honest. Not the normal I'd walked away from. But the limbo I'd been living wasn't satisfying either.

What do you want?

I coughed against the sudden constricting in my throat. Against the quick, true answer that was so hard to say. I wanted what used to be. What Donnie and I had at the start and lost somewhere along the way. That's what I wanted . . . the impossible.

Nothing is impossible with Me.

But how — *How?*

Your home is with Donnie. Go home.

Once again my breath caught in my throat. The road home was so much longer than the few minutes it took to drive. It was paved with obstacles. Complications so large I didn't know if Donnie and I could maneuver around them.

As often as I'd tried to block out our horrible conversation before I left, the words were as fresh as the day they'd been said.

"We need to talk." Of course it was *me* forcing the issue. It always had been.

With a sigh Donnie looked up from the stack of papers in his lap. I wasn't about to let his impatience, or his reading, get in the way this time.

"I can't live like this anymore." There. Finally. Let him try and tell me different.

"Like what?" He took off his reading glasses and tiredly rubbed the bridge of his nose, staring down at the floor.

Did he really not have a clue? I could feel fury pressing against my breastbone. "Like this!" My voice was shrill. How was I supposed to explain the nothing I felt about our marriage?

"Laura."

"Don't Laura me." I stood up from the couch and paced. "I'm sick of this. Of us. Of living like siblings. You could just as well be my brother for all the attention I get from you. You don't even know me anymore. You treat me like I'm some sort of glorified secretary. 'Pay this bill. Make this phone call. Pick up my shirts from the cleaners.' You could hire someone to do your errands. I'll bet Elle would be happy to do those things for you." The second I said the words I knew I'd gone too far. I'd used my deep fears as ammunition and shot myself instead.

Heightened silence, like the aftermath from a powerful explosion, hung in the air. Donnie put his papers on the end table and stood to face me. "Don't bring Elle into

501

this. I've never given you a reason —"

"Okay," I conceded, "so you haven't been unfaithful. Not in the way you might think of it. But look! Look at those papers lying there." I stabbed a finger toward his pile of work. "You've buried yourself in that stupid agency and buried us in the process. I'm —"

"And what about you?" The muscle in Donnie's jaw pulsed. In all our years of marriage, Donnie had been the levelheaded one. The person who talked reason into much of my emotional arguing. Here was a tone I'd rarely heard — and one I least expected. He spoke deliberately.

"Laura, when was the last time you noticed something I did for us? When was the last time you said, 'Thank you for the nice life we have'? When did you last ask me about some new client we're trying to get? You seem to assume I love every minute of having my brain sucked dry from that agency. Do you think you're the only one in this marriage who could use some encouragement? You say you don't know me anymore. Well, what ever happened to the Laura Dunn who did know me? That Laura Dunn used to be my biggest cheerleader. Where is the Laura Dunn who encouraged me to start my own agency? I could have punched a time clock at some other job and come home every night by six, but the Laura Dunn I used to know told me, 'Donnie, you were meant for this.' " He stopped and glared at me, letting his arrows hit their mark. He picked up his bow and aimed again. "The Laura Dunn I thought I knew used to bring an angel food cake with whipped cream and strawberries to the agency every time we won a new account. When was the last time you did that?" He answered his own question. "It's been years. You don't even know when we land a new account anymore." He stopped for a breath, eyes still flashing.

I didn't want to look at him. I didn't want to hear any more of the truth he was speaking. I'd been hunkering behind my own wounds and ready defenses for so long. "Donnie, I —"

His look stopped me. He wasn't finished, but his voice had softened some. "And where is the Laura who used to celebrate my birthday? Who used to bake a chocolate cake and sing 'Happy Birthday'?"

He never seemed to care about his birthday, about the cake, the celebration.

He stared straight into my eyes. "You didn't even give me a gift this year."

I could have reminded him about his

preoccupation that disastrous night. About the other sort of gift I'd tried to give him. But that wasn't his point, and I knew it.

He stared at me now, resignation in his gaze. His voice had dropped to just above a whisper. "What happened to her?"

His words that night still seared. Not all of this was Donnie's fault. I'd contributed my share to the falling-out. Going back home might be harder than leaving had been.

Maybe if I went back to bed . . . I wandered into Eleanor's room and sat on the edge of her bed — my bed now. I lifted my eyes and found myself staring at my own wedding day. The photo had been on that wall for nearly a quarter of a century. Donnie and me. Posing. Smiling. Impulsively in love. Had we ever thought our love would end up like this? That it would fade and wear so thin that no patch could hold it together?

No, I couldn't sleep. Not here. Not now. I went into the bathroom. At least there were no memories in this small room . . . Except for the Thanksgiving Donnie followed me in here and pressed me against the back of the door. Kissing. Caressing. His mother eating pumpkin pie just down the hall.

I hurried away from the memory, stumbling into the one room I'd avoided the whole time I'd been here. Donnie's room, Eleanor had called it even though he hadn't slept in his bed in almost three decades. I flicked on the overhead light.

She had made changes over the years. A new floral bedspread. Matching drapes. When out-of-town friends came to visit, this was where they stayed. They couldn't help but notice the montage of school photos hanging on the wall. First grade through senior year; only eighth grade was missing.

"The school lost his photos that year. I'm still disgusted." Eleanor wrinkled her nose when she told me about the incident almost a dozen years after the fact. Donnie and I were already married, and I knew Donnie had ditched his school photos in a garbage can in an alley that year instead of bringing them home. *"I looked like a nerd,"* he'd told me one night when we lay in bed laughing, sharing childhood tales.

"You should tell your mom," I laughed back.

"Yeah, I'd be the first married man ever to be grounded."

I couldn't help but smile now as I touched a finger to the empty spot in the frame.

You're the keeper of his stories.

I was. And Donnie kept mine. He was the

only soul who knew I once dreamed of living in a log cabin in the mountains of Wyoming. Far, far away from anything to do with meetings and committees, appointments and schedules.

"All I want to do is paint," I told him.

"Do you want to be famous?" he asked.

"No," I answered, way back then. "I just want to paint."

"Well," he said, turning on his side to look me in the eye, "that part we might be able to arrange."

Somewhere in the tangle of years those secrets and dreams had disappeared.

I sat on the edge of the flowered bedspread. The evidence of the young boy — young man — Donnie had been was all around me. Team photos and trophies lined the bookcase. The montage of school photos and an 8 × 10 of Donnie as a senior. Eleanor had kept these memories of her son. Who would keep them now?

You will.

A knot of emotion twisted and turned inside me. I lay back on the bed, the overhead light as piercing as the kind they use in an interrogation room. What would I do?

Go home.

I knew that was what I should do. But what did I want to do?

Go home.

But was that what I wanted?

It's not about what you want, it's about what I know is best.

I threw an arm over my eyes, blocking out the convicting light from above. I couldn't live at Eleanor's forever, running away from the nothingness of my marriage. What options did I have?

What about John?

I turned onto my side and curled into myself. I hadn't spoken to John since Eleanor's funeral. I'd been standing by Donnie in the foyer of the church, talking to out-of-town relatives, when I saw John hesitate on his way out of the church. Eleanor hadn't been much of a roommate for his mother, and yet our foursome had formed a bond of sorts. It was kind of him to come.

I put a hand on Donnie's arm. "Excuse me," I whispered. Let him think what he would. If he had visited his mother more, he would be the one thanking John for coming.

The clean, familiar scent of the comforting cologne that had surrounded me at the hospital welcomed me. "Hi." Now that I was standing near John, I was tongue-tied.

"Hi yourself." He smiled down at me. "You doing okay?"

My tears had been shed. Why couldn't I speak? I nodded.

He put a hand on my upper arm. "Really?"

Well, no, not really. Not with the shambles of my marriage standing five feet behind me. But John didn't know about that, did he?

He gave my arm a light squeeze before he let go. "If you need to talk, you've got my card."

Tucked in the inside pocket of my purse. Once again, all I could do was nod.

"Take care."

Finally, something I could say. "You too."

Thoughts of John, his comfort at the hospital, that last conversation, played and replayed in my mind as I limped through the days that followed. More than once I'd pulled out the business card he handed me, tempted to call.

Sorting through Eleanor's closets had been a mind-numbing task. Thinking about John was an easy distraction. Imagining what might be if I dialed his number. Certainly better than thinking about the muck my marriage had become. And yet each time I thought about calling John, I knew it would be wrong.

One long night I sat staring at the phone for an hour, John's card in my hand. His easy friendship was a temptation. Less tempting were the complications that first phone call would cause. It felt a bit as if I was ripping my heart in two when I finally tore his card down the middle, but I knew now was not the time to be talking to another man.

It's Donnie you need to talk to.

I knew *his* number. Why was it so hard to talk to the man I'd been married to for 23 — make that 24 — years?

Our twenty-fourth anniversary had come and gone in the weeks since Eleanor had died. Had Donnie remembered the date? I'd done my best to keep busy that day, pretending I wasn't harboring a quiet hope Donnie would call, would show up with flowers and an apology for all that had gone wrong. As if roses would solve anything now.

Wait until next year . . .

A peculiar chill ran down my arms. What *next* year? There would be no next year if we kept on like this.

Go home.

I pushed myself up from Donnie's old bed. I didn't understand this strange, silent conversation. Going home wasn't as simple as just going there.

Yes. It is.

No. It wasn't. I'd been waiting for some

sign. Some *thing* that would show me what I was supposed to do. Not this waffling.

There was a tightness in my throat as tears stung my eyes. Donnie and I were supposed to argue and fight. We were supposed to make threats and accusations. Then. Then I'd be justified in ending my marriage. Then I'd know what I was supposed to do. But how would we put our marriage back together if I simply packed up my things and went home?

If you are faithful in little things, I will give you much. Next year . . .

I didn't understand this inaudible exchange. Next year?

It's a promise.

A promise?

Trust Me. Go home. Your place is with your husband.

Warm tears filled my eyes as the words I'd said to Stasha convicted me. Nothing would be solved as long as I stayed at Eleanor's.

In my mind I traveled the short distance between Eleanor's house and mine. It was only a few miles on a map, but in terms of my heart it would take all I had to return. There was no guarantee anything would change once I walked through the door. Was I willing to face that possibility?

Nothing will change if you don't try. Are you

willing to just walk away from 24 years of marriage?

At one point I thought I was, but when I saw Stasha on the doorstep tonight, I knew sending her back to Josh was the only right thing to do. Maybe I needed to listen to my own advice.

And Mine. Go home.

With resigned reluctance I pushed myself off the bed, put one foot in front of the other, and debated my options as I walked back to Eleanor's — and my — bedroom. What should I do?

Feelings follow actions. Do you trust Me?

So, here it was at last. A gauntlet. Would I put my trust in Him? Or my fragile heart? I knew I had no power to change anything in my marriage. If I had, I would have done so long ago. Was there any other choice but to give His way a try? I swiped at my eyes with the cuff of my bathrobe. *Will You go with me?*

I never left.

Tears spilled onto my cheeks. He'd never left, but I had. I could change that. I would take His promise with me. I would do what I could to save my marriage. I would go home. I'd have to trust God to do the rest.

I pulled my suitcase from the corner of the bedroom where I had stashed it. I never

511

had put it away. Maybe there was a part of me that always hoped this night would come.

I opened the suitcase, then looked down at what I was wearing. *I was going home.* If so, I wasn't going to drive across town in my nightgown and Eleanor's old robe. *Really officer, I'm not an escapee from the psych ward.* I smiled as I slipped off the robe and threw it across the rumpled bed. I lifted my nightgown, wrapped it in a messy ball, and put it in the suitcase. Quickly I got dressed, making sure I wore my blue sweater. Donnie always liked me in blue. Maybe my sweater would be a subtle reminder of what we'd had . . . of what might be again.

What if he's not there?

Not home? Of course he'd be — Then I remembered the thing I'd purposely not thought about all night. Donnie's award. The banquet they held for him earlier this evening. What if he was still out celebrating? What if he'd been flirting with someone in real life the way I'd been toying with John in my thoughts? Maybe I shouldn't —

Trust Me. Go.

Before I could talk myself out of leaving, I reached for my diamond pendant on Eleanor's night stand. Donnie had given it to me on our fifteenth anniversary, and I'd worn it almost every day since. As I fumbled with the tiny clasp, another finger of doubt scratched at my thoughts. What if Donnie didn't want me back? What if these weeks of indecision had led him to a decision of his own? One that didn't include me? I hesitated with the clasp. Should I crawl back into bed and let a night of sleep guide me?

Go.

I closed my eyes. What would Donnie think if I crept back into the house in the middle of a dark night? As if I had to sneak back into his life. Maybe work was all he needed to be fulfilled.

I undid the clasp and laid the necklace back down. Leaning into my hands against the dresser, I stared into the mirror. I didn't look at my eyes; I peered deeper, past what I could easily see, to a dim place not visible except with my heart.

Scared. That's what I was. Petrified.

What if Donnie didn't want me anymore? *Oh, Lord. What if he —*

Like the beat of a terrified heart, a muffled thumping bled into my tumbled prayer. *Thump. Thump. Thump.* What was that noise?

I straightened and turned toward the sound.

My heart felt as if it tumbled into my

stomach. I knew what the sound was. *No, Lord.*

Stasha was back.

DONNIE

Like a lion trapped in a cage, I paced into
the kitchen, through the family room, a
detour into my home office, back through
the living room. Upstairs was no better. The
guest room was dead space. Stasha's
room . . . now her former room. Our bedroom. Laura's side of the bed, flat and bare.

I went back down the steps, retracing my
path. There was the book Laura had been
reading when she left, opened at the spine
as if she'd only left to get a drink of water.
On the wall was the landscape she'd painted
as a wedding gift to me. If I looked closely I
could see the tiny log cabin nestled in the
forest of Laura's imagination. On the floor,
near the corner of the couch where she
always sat, were scraps of fabric, a half-sewn
something spilling out of the basket. I bent
over and picked up the patchwork pieces.
There had to be several hundred of them,
sewn together in a jumbled sort of order.

515

Where had I been while Laura had done all this?

There was something familiar about the red fabric in my hand.

Mom's dress. My mind might be playing tricks on me, but I could swear this small red scrap had been part of the dress my mother had worn to my high school graduation. After receiving my diploma, I'd stopped center stage and grinned at the crowd. It hadn't been hard to spot my mom in the sea of faces. She'd been wearing a big smile and a red dress. Who could forget that?

And this. I touched my finger to another scrap. Brown plaid. My cowboy shirt? The shirt I'd insisted on wearing three weeks in a row? Mom had indulged my little-boy stubbornness, only if I agreed to let her wash the shirt while I slept.

What was Laura doing with all these snippets of my past? The years had gone by in a stupefying blur. I'd gone from a little boy roping invisible wild horses to a man who was still chasing something invisible.

And at what cost?

I knew the answer to that.

Maybe it's time to appreciate what you already have . . . not what you imagine will bring you happiness.

I folded the piece of fabric into an uneven

roll and put it into the basket. Laura would smile at my clumsy attempt to help.

If she ever comes back.

A bulldozer suddenly plowed through my insides, carving out a hole the size of a stadium. The chamber banquet should have served as a satisfying affirmation of my career. Instead, it had done nothing but remind me of what I had destroyed. There would be no sleep for me tonight. No warm milk. No comfort. What did any of it mean without Laura?

Go.

The restless urge I'd felt all night propelled me through my house again. *Go.*

Go where?

To her.

With sudden clarity, I knew what I'd been searching for all night. It didn't matter that it was well past midnight. What I needed to do couldn't wait one more night. One more second. It was Laura I was looking for. Longing for. Only her. Her affirmation was the only approval that mattered.

I hurried into the kitchen and pushed my arms into the wool coat I'd never hung up. In two giant steps I took the four steps down into the garage. For once there would be no search for my car keys; they were still in my pocket.

Practically in the same motion, I climbed into the car and started it, put the car into reverse, and tapped impatiently at the steering wheel as the garage door took its own sweet time lifting.

It was only as I backed into the street that I realized I didn't want to stand in front of Laura empty-handed. As if I had nothing to offer but what had been.

I'd been in a rush. Now I slowed the car, pondering as I drove the dark, empty street. Flowers were too easy. A dime a dozen.

Donnie? A cliché? You can do better than flowers.

A small smile lifted a corner of my mouth, a corner that hadn't turned up by itself in weeks. I made my living from good ideas. It was time I applied my logic to the rest of my life. I could do better. Much better. But at this time of night, where would I find the one thing that would prove to Laura I wanted to make things different?

In Carlton there weren't many shopping options after midnight, but I had to try. The clerk at the first convenience store wouldn't budge from his stool behind the counter to even take a look. "No," he said, giving me a look as if I'd lost my mind. Maybe I had.

The second store clerk seemed to have answered stranger requests. "That's a new one." He scratched his head. "Have you tried the grocery store?"

No, but I would.

What I found wasn't quite what I'd been imagining. Puny and a bit pathetic, but it would have to do.

"That'll be $2.48."

The price of my wife's heart.

I hoped.

I parked at the curb of my mother's house. It was lit up as if Laura had been waiting for me.

Maybe she's not alone. Like a seasoned detective my eyes cased the street. Laura's car was in the driveway. My mother's old car still occupied the garage. Other than what looked to be vehicles that belonged to neighbors, the street was orderly and calm. Nothing like the tumult inside my chest.

Maybe she'd fallen asleep with the lights on. Maybe not.

For the first time since I'd left my house, doubts began to surface. What if she wasn't glad to see me? What if the years I'd spent building a career had ruined any chance of restoring our relationship?

I took a deep breath. Another. I'd taken business risks all my life. I was used to rejection. One thing I'd learned was this: the bigger the risk, the sweeter the reward. And what lay at the end of this sidewalk was the biggest risk of all.

I got out of the car, my pitiful token in hand. Maybe this was a dumb idea.

It's not.

One more breath for courage. I walked the sidewalk, the path that would determine the next steps I would take. I stood on the doorstep. No tinny doorbell would do for this mission. I needed to let Laura know how I felt. I curled my gloved fingers into a fist and knocked. "Laura." The dark night caused me to whisper at first. The intent of my heart quickly overcame that. "Laura!"

The door swung open, and there she stood. Dressed in blue.

"Laura."

"Donnie?" She looked surprised. "I thought you were Stasha." She put a hand to her chest. "It's *you.*"

"Yeah." Why did I suddenly feel as if I was in eighth grade? "I . . . uh —" For the second time tonight I was caught wordless.

"I was just —"

I glanced down at the step. No, I needed to look into her eyes when I said what I'd come to say. "Laura, I'm sorry. For everything. So sorry."

Tears filled her eyes. "Donnie."

Saying my name could mean anything. *Donnie, I can't. Donnie, you have to go.* My heart started a horrible thumping.

She took a step back. Was she pulling away?

A simple motion of her hand gave me hope. "You have to come in," she said. "It's too cold."

I stepped into the foyer of my mother's house, a place I'd stood a million times in my life, but never, ever, had I felt this nervous in what had once been my home.

"This is a surprise," she said, a shy smile beginning on her face.

"Yeah. Well . . . I mean, I —" Another deep breath. "It's kind of a surprise to me, too. It's . . . late."

"It is. But not too late . . . ?"

The question hung in the air between us. Too late? Was it?

I had a way to find out. I pulled off my gloves and reached into the pocket of my coat, pulled out the crumpled brown paper bag. Some wrapping. I held the unlikely gift in one hand. "Here."

She dipped her chin. Looked at me sideways. "What's this?"

Long, skinny, flat. Under any other circumstance, and not twisted in a grocery store brown bag, she might think it was an expensive bracelet from the best jeweler in town. If it was diamonds she wanted, if that's what it took, she'd have them. Tomorrow. Tonight, my humble gift would have to be enough.

Lord, let it be enough.

I lifted my package to her. The brown paper crinkled as she tugged at the twisted top. I hadn't consciously turned it into some complicated coil.

"I can't imagine . . ." she said, finally freeing the opening. She reached her hand inside the bag. I couldn't watch her face. If my good intention was as ridiculous as it suddenly seemed, well, I'd know soon enough. I didn't want the image of her disappointment etched in my brain. I stared at a spot on the floor. Listened as her hand drew my cheap treasure from the paper.

Then laughter. Not the bad kind. Not the "what were you thinking?" kind. This laugh expressed pure joy. "Oh, Donnie."

I looked at her then. At the cheap box of preschool watercolors she held in her hand as if the box was made of pure gold. Laura opened the plastic lid and ran her fine fingers over the basic colors. Blue . . . green . . . she twirled the child's paintbrush under her finger. "I love it." Her eyes were wet.

Once again I couldn't look at her. There was too much to say. Too much I hadn't said for far too long. I had to start somewhere. "I was hoping you would."

"I do."

Now I couldn't take my eyes off her. "I love you, you know. I always have."

With her eyes she gestured to the paint box. "I know."

I took her in my arms and held her close. As if only one heart beat between the two of us. I breathed her in. Savored what I'd missed, not only these long strained weeks, but the years before them.

My throat was thick when I tried to speak. "I came to ask you to come home." I pulled my head back and looked into her eyes. "Will you?"

There was the slightest hesitation. I rushed to fill her pause. "I know there's a lot we have to talk through. I have to change some things." I cleared my throat. "A lot of things."

"I do too." Her voice was soft.

I loosened my grip on her. "I can't think of one thing you need to change, and I can find a thousand things to put on my list."

She eased back, wiggled the cheap paint box between us. "I need to paint."

Oh, yes. *Paint.* I grinned at her. She

needed to paint. Of course she did. "Something we agree on then."

I reached down and slid the small box from her hand. Then I wrapped my arms around her once more. "Painting. I'd say that's a good start. A really good start."

We stood with our arms wrapped around each other as if we were trying to make up for all the time we had let pass. I knew recapturing lost time would be impossible, but I was willing to give it a shot. I squeezed Laura close. From somewhere deep within, I felt a lightness I hadn't felt in years.

Her voice was muffled against my chest. Okay, so maybe I had to loosen my grip just a tad. "What did you say?"

She lifted her chin. "I said, 'I missed you.' "

I cupped my hand against the sweet curve at the back of her neck and pressed her cheek against my heart. Could she feel it beat? Could she hear what my heart was saying?

No more assuming that Laura knew how I felt. If things were going to be different, I was going to have to be different. I had learned the hard way and almost lost it all. Some things were much too precious to waste.

Time.

Words.

Love.

From now on I'd make sure Laura knew how I felt. Every day. Every night. Starting now.

I nuzzled my lips into the top of her head. "Let me tell you how much I missed you. After . . ." With the back of my fingers I nudged her head back and looked into her eyes.

I'd tell her how much I missed her . . . the way her eyes twinkled when she laughed. The smell of her perfume. The way she could walk into a room and bring sunshine along with her. I'd tell her all that and so much more . . . after I kissed her.

I smiled down at Laura. No more waiting. Now.

STASHA

"Your home is with Josh." It was so easy for my mom to say. She didn't have to live with him. She didn't know what we were going through. If she had acted like a mother and listened to me, instead of closing the door in my face, she would know how bad it was.

One thing was for sure. I couldn't drive around all night. The stupid heater on my car had suddenly decided to blow cold air, my gas tank was on empty, and I was too cold to think about standing outside and filling the tank.

What was I supposed to do?

Your home is with Josh.

I'd been hearing those five words for the last two hours.

Listen to them.

Checking into a motel wasn't an option. It was the end of the month, and we weren't exactly rolling in money, what with Josh's student loan payments and now a car that would have to go to the shop. Besides, why should I pay for a motel room when the night was practically over? And I'd never be able to sleep in a strange bed anyway.

Fueled by anger, I turned my car toward home. Toward my home. Not hers or my grandma's. Besides, it was just as much my apartment as Josh's. Why should I have to leave?

As I pulled up in front of the apartment, I sighed. Good. The lights were out — as if Josh would be awake at this late hour anyway. I grabbed my duffel bag out of the backseat and slammed the car door. I didn't care if the whole neighborhood woke up. A sleepless night would serve everyone right.

I stomped up the back stairs. Mr. Miller never slept with his hearing aids in, but so what if he did? Tonight I didn't care.

I whipped open the door of the apartment and, as if I was the lead person on a SWAT team, I threw my duffel bag in ahead of me. Look out!

Josh jumped from his spot on the couch as if I'd tossed in a grenade. "What in the —" He shook sleep from his head, looking from me to the now-broken zipper on my duffel.

With my boot I shoved the bag aside and stomped to the chair I'd spent several hours stewing in earlier in the night. I should have just stayed there for all the good my little trip had done.

I plopped myself down. "I'm so mad at my mother. If she wasn't my mother, I'd strangle her." I crossed my arms over my chest for punctuation.

Josh rubbed the stubble of his beard. "Either this is a really weird dream, or I missed something."

"My mother is so dense!"

Josh stepped over my broken duffel bag and sat heavily on the arm of my chair. "I have no idea what you're talking about."

"My mom. Tonight!" I couldn't even complete a sentence.

Josh reached out a hand and stroked my hair. I jerked my head away. "Don't."

"I was just trying to help."

"You can help by going and yelling at my mom for me."

"I would if I knew what I was supposed to be mad at her about."

"For not letting me move in with her." The second the words were out of my mouth I realized the irony. I was asking Josh to get on my mom's case for not letting me leave him. A tiny bubble of laughter brushed against the balloon of my tirade.

"You left me?" Josh had one eyebrow raised.

"Um-hmm." I had to bite the insides of my cheeks to keep from laughing. I wasn't quite done being mad yet.

"And I slept through it?"

I swatted at him with the back of my hand. "Yes."

The corners of his mouth were twitching too. "Am I a bad husband?"

A bit of a giggle pushed out my reluctant words. "About as bad as I am as a wife."

Josh lifted his right hand and swatted at his left one. "Bad husband. Bad, bad husband."

I didn't want to let go of my anger, but I couldn't help it. I laughed out loud. "You sound like a dog trainer — or a rapper."

With the middle two fingers of both hands turned down and his index and little fingers in the air, Josh improvised. "He's bad. He's bad. He's really, really bad. Bad husband. Bad husband."

A belly laugh pushed its way from deep in my stomach. "You're terrible."

"He's bad. And ter-ble. He's really bad and ter-ble."

"Stop. Stop it." I wasn't sure if I should hold my ears or my stomach. I hadn't laughed this hard since . . . since . . . too,

too long.

Josh dropped his new persona and started laughing along with me. It wasn't long before we were both struggling to breathe.

"That was soooo baaa-aad." I couldn't catch my breath. How could I go from being so angry to a laughing fit so quickly?

Josh tried to resume his rap. "Hee-ee's baaa—" Laughter stopped him as he slid off the arm of the chair, crosswise into my lap. Our eyes met as we alternated between trying to compose ourselves and falling back into our twin fits of hilarity. Finally, I gasped for air at the same time Josh did. His weight was heavy against me, and I tried to shift so I could breathe better.

"Here." Josh lifted himself while I threaded my legs over his. Now I was in his lap. Our smiles faded as we realized we were eye-to-eye, nose-to-nose . . . a position we hadn't been in for months.

Josh tipped his head and brushed his nose against mine. It was the tiniest touch, but it sent tingles through me. I leaned my face close to his and fluttered my eyelashes against his cheek. A butterfly kiss.

"That tickles." Josh's voice was husky.

I leaned near his ear and murmured. "It's supposed to."

He squirmed against my whispered words,

then turned and spoke softly into my ear. "You're so beautiful."

How could he possibly think I was beautiful after what I'd done tonight . . . or *almost* done? What must I look like after sobbing for so long? Or my angry tirade? Beautiful was not a word I'd used to describe myself, inside or out. I lowered my eyes so I wouldn't have to see his gaze. "No, I'm not."

His finger touched my chin and tried to lift it against my resistance. "Look at me."

I shook my head.

"Look at me."

Reluctantly, I lifted my eyes to his.

"I'm sorry if I've been a rotten husband. I —"

I stopped his words with a finger to his lips. "I'm the one who should be apologizing. I —"

His finger touched against my words. "Shhh . . ."

"But, I —"

"Shhh . . ." His lips brushed against mine. Pressed close.

I closed my eyes as the slights and resentments of the past months fell away. Josh's lips were so soft, tender against mine. What had I been thinking just an hour ago? What had I almost thrown away in my selfish anger?

My mom had been so right.

Tears pushed into my eyes and spilled onto my cheeks.

Josh pulled away. "What?"

A kitten-like sound worked through my tears. "I'm so — so . . . sorry. I just never thought —" I had to gasp for a breath — "marriage would be so *hard.*"

Josh rested his forehead against mine. "I didn't either." He wrapped his arms around me and let me cry.

After a while, I wiped my face with my hands and tentatively smiled at Josh. He met my smile with a soft kiss and a question. "So, now what?"

"I have no idea, but we have to do something." I laid my head against his chest. "Something different."

"How about right now we go to bed?"

Was he suggesting what I thought he was? It had been a long time since sex had been anything more than another obligation between us. After all my theatrics, how could he possibly want to make love to someone like me?

"Are you sure you want to?" Did he see the question in my eyes?

A silly grin was his answer, right before he stifled a yawn. "I meant to sleep, but I like

532

your suggestion better."

It felt so good to laugh with Josh instead of argue.

"Love you," I said, suddenly relaxed and sleepy.

"Me more."

For the first time in ages, we spoke together. "Same."

Stasha

Many waters cannot quench love; rivers cannot wash it away.

Song of Solomon 8:7

"First of all, I want to commend both of you for having the courage to do something about your difficulties this early in your marriage." The marriage therapist, Rhonda, reminded me a little bit of my mom. Not the way she looked, but the way her confident smile said, "Trust me. I'll help you."

After I got over being mad at my mom, we had a long talk about what happened that night on her doorstep. I knew now how hard it had been for her to close the door on me and how that had been the best thing she could have done. Mom had asked around and found Rhonda for Josh and me.

Now that we had the paperwork filled out, Rhonda folded her hands over the open folder on her desk. "Most couples wait to get help until their habits are so ingrained, and resentments so built up, that by the time they come to counseling it's almost too late." She looked at the two of us. "You're already a step ahead of most couples. That tells me you're committed to making your marriage work." She gave us an encouraging smile.

Josh and I exchanged a look. It was strangely reassuring to know we weren't the only couple to ever have problems. Josh reached out and covered my hand with his. For a guy who hadn't been thrilled with the idea of seeing a marriage counselor, his message was clear: We're in this together.

"Now then." Rhonda picked up a pen and pulled a yellow legal pad in front of her. "Why don't we start by having each of you tell me a little bit about yourselves. Where you grew up. How you met. What kind of work you do. Who'd like to start?"

Josh raised a finger. "I can."

The fact that he was willing to go first spoke volumes. We weren't going to fail for lack of trying.

I listened as Josh recapped his childhood. I thought I knew the basics, but I found myself tearing up as he described how his dad, as a child, had been ill with rheumatic fever and was left with a heart condition that didn't allow him to engage in much activity with his son. It had been Josh's athletic fifth-grade teacher who had kindled his passion for sports and planted the seed that would grow into his desire to become a teacher.

I let go of Josh's hand and rubbed his arm. "I didn't know that."

"Yup." Josh blinked a little too fast. "Mr. Schmidt."

What else didn't I know?

Rhonda made some quick notes before commenting. "Role models can be extremely powerful. I'm sure you're passing the same sort of enthusiasm on to your students."

Josh shuffled his shoes. "I try."

A swell of emotion pushed from inside my chest. This great guy was my husband. When was the last time I'd asked him about his day? Or given him a compliment for all his hard work? Already I'd learned something from this appointment. Instead of complaining about his job, I'd ask him about it.

My turn was next. It didn't seem I had much to tell. "Being an only child, I was the center of my parents' universe. Except when my dad was at work," I added. "And he worked a lot."

Rhonda made a note. "How did you feel about that?"

I'd never really thought about it. "I don't know, I guess I didn't know any different. That was just my dad."

"And what about your mother?"

What was there to tell? "My mom didn't work, but she kept busy with lots of meetings and stuff."

Once more, Rhonda wrote something on the pad of paper. "We may revisit that topic a bit later, but for now, tell me what a typical day is like for each of you. Josh, let's start with you."

He scratched the side of his head. "Well, I pretty much get up at 6:00, I'm at school before 7:30. Some of the kids like to come early to lift weights so I make sure the gym is open for them. Then I'm at school until 4:00, unless I have practice or a game, which is most of the time. If there's a game, I'm usually there until 9:00. Unless it's out of town, then I don't get home until the bus gets back and all the kids' parents have picked them up. That's probably around —" He looked to me.

"Late," I said, turning my eyes to Rhonda. This was the part I wanted her to hear. Josh was never home.

Neither are you.

As if the spotlight had suddenly shifted to me, Rhonda said, "And Stasha, what kind of schedule do you have?"

I licked my lips, thinking where to begin. I'd start where Josh had, from first thing in the morning. "I get to sleep in a little later than Josh does. He's usually leaving about the time I get up. Then I go to the agency and, well, most days are nuts. I always think I'm going to get home for supper, but then there'll be some" — I made two quote marks in the air — "emergency, and I end up grabbing pizza and working right through."

"So, you get home around . . . ?"

This time Josh spoke the word. "Late."

Before Rhonda could tell me what I already knew, I chimed in. "Basically, we never see each other."

Rhonda pressed her lips together as she looked at the two of us. The soft tick of a clock on the wall underscored time as it passed. Time together that Josh and I had already missed in our busy schedules.

"We talked about role models a bit ago," Rhonda said. "Do you see any similarities between the schedules the two of you keep and what you, Stasha, mentioned earlier about your mom and dad?"

I thought for a moment, then said, "I'm

just like my dad?" What started out as a question became clear as I spoke. "And mom." My mind was doing slow cartwheels trying to spin these random thoughts into a whole. I spoke slowly as I put my thoughts together. "In our family it was important to keep busy."

"Do you think it's possible that the role models you had growing up are affecting the way you relate in your marriage now?"

I stared at the floor and nodded. Josh and I were basically imitating what I'd seen growing up. Dad worked. Mom was off to club meetings and volunteer work. All good stuff, but look what their busy schedules had led to.

A small cough from Rhonda brought my eyes back to her. "What may have worked for your parents may not work in your relationship with Josh."

"But it didn't work for my parents," I blurted. The painful weeks of their separation were still hard for me to comprehend.

Rhonda glanced down at her notes. "Are your parents divorced? You didn't mention that."

"No," I hurried to add. "They're not. They've been married 24 years, but recently they . . ." The tumble of thoughts and ideas that had been sifting through my mind settled with sudden clarity. Why did the solution suddenly seem so clear? How could Josh and I expect to have a relationship when we didn't spend any time together?

Since I'd started working at the agency I hadn't had time for my friend Jen either. No time equaled no relationships. *Duh.*

All it had taken was — I glanced at my watch — less than an hour, and without Rhonda saying more than a few words, asking a few pointed questions, we had a diagnosis for our troubles. Time . . . or lack of it.

It was going to take some work, some major juggling of schedules, but now that we knew where to start —

A question from Rhonda broke into my musing. "I think we've covered a lot of ground in one session, and our time is almost up. Why don't we end our session today with something lighter? Most couples have good memories of how they met. Would you share that story with me?" She set down her pen and sat back in her chair.

With a glance Josh told me to start.

"We were in —"

"College," Josh stepped in.

"Yeah." I smiled at him. "We were both . . ."

"Juniors."

"And I was sitting on the grass outside the student union and Josh —"

"— wasn't about to let someone as cute as Stasha sit alone."

"We both missed our next —"

"Class."

"I got such a bad —"

"— sunburn."

By the time we were done, Rhonda was chuckling along with Josh and me. She closed the folder on her desk. "Do you realize neither one of you has finished your own sentence? In your case, that's a good thing. I have a hunch, with a little bit of work, you two are going to be just fine."

I purposely waited until Elle was away from her desk before approaching my dad's office. What I had to talk over with my dad was private. I tapped softly on his office door. "Dad? Can I talk to you?" My palms were about as sweaty as they were the first time I had asked him if I could go out on a date.

"Stasha." A big smile welcomed me in. Whatever he was working on he pushed aside. "My favorite employee."

I couldn't help but laugh. "Shhh . . . not so loud." I closed the door behind me, crossed the office, and sat across from him.

"I'm just being honest," he defended himself. "You are."

So, there would be no beating around the bush. No small talk. Being an employee was exactly what I'd come to talk to him about. I stared down at my hands. My fingers were clenched so tight the tips were turning white. How to start? I forced my hands open and shut. How did other people talk to their bosses? It was hard to know where the line was between worker and daughter. The daughter in me wanted to burst into tears. The employee part of me knew that even if he was my father, I needed to be mature about this. I took a deep breath and looked somewhere over his shoulder.

"Dad, I love my job, but I just can't do it anymore." I didn't want to look at him and see the disappointment in his eyes. But I couldn't look away from him forever either. I forced my eyes to meet his level gaze.

He stared at me for a long moment, then picked up a paper clip and began slowly rotating it between his fingers. What was he thinking? I couldn't begin to interpret the look that crossed his face now. I gripped my hands together. Say something.

"It's not worth it, is it?"

"What?" My eyebrows just possibly met in the middle of my forehead. That was the last response I expected to hear from my dad.

"It's not worth it, is it? All this." He tossed the paper clip into the air and watched it nosedive onto the desk.

I'm not sure what I expected, but it certainly was not empathy. My chin trembled as I shook my head. "It's not."

He swiveled his chair so that he faced the window . . . the whole world that existed beyond the walls of the agency. The four walls that up till now had made up his world — and mine.

Beyond the door of his office, I could hear the muffled sound of phones ringing, Elle back at her desk answering, transferring. The daily world of an advertising agency never stopped. This private time between my dad and me wouldn't last long; there was work to do, and I knew my dad felt the pressure. His inbox was filling as he stared out the window. Mine was too. And yet, as if he had nothing more important to do, he sat and gazed out the window.

Finally he spoke. "It took you less than a year to figure out what took me 24 years." He turned his chair to face me. "I'd say you're way ahead of the learning curve."

He was surprising me with every sentence. "I am?"

"You are." There was no doubt in his voice. He put his elbows on the desk, rested his chin on his hands, and closed his eyes. "Stasha, if you want to walk away from this crazy business, I'll give you my blessing." Was this my dad? Before I could answer that question, he opened his eyes and raised a finger. "But before you do, I want to ask a favor of you." He paused as he picked up the paper clip again. "Would you hang in with me just a little while longer?"

I wasn't sure if he was expecting an answer. I needed more information before I could agree to anything, so I waited.

"I want to make some changes." He stopped, reworded. "I need to make some changes. Not just around here, but at home, too. I'm hoping I can work things out so this job won't be so consuming for any of us. The way I've been working is not healthy." He shifted the paper clip to one hand, and with his other he held his thumb and forefinger a quarter inch apart. "Do you think you can give me just a little bit of time?"

Was this my work-is-my-life father? If nothing else, I had to stick around to see how his plan played out.

"A little bit," I said, holding my fingers in the same position my dad had. I had come here to make some changes of my own. Sweet talk from my dad was one thing; working on my marriage was a whole different category. I'd tell him about tomorrow now and deal with other changes in another conversation. First things first. "I'm going to need to leave early tomorrow."

My former dad would have reminded me of campaigns waiting to be developed, of pitches to be made, of clients who needed something. There was always a fire that needed tending. Here was a test. I waited to hear his response.

Dad dipped his head in a short nod. "Fair enough. I know that whatever the reason, it must be important."

"It is." I put on my game face. The old me would have foamed at the mouth, trying to justify why the thing I had planned wouldn't interfere with my work. But I had my bases covered. If my dad wanted me to stay on, well, I had some new rules of my own, and my marriage came first.

"Thanks," I said, standing up. If this were just any-old boss, I might stick out my hand and shake his; instead I went around the desk and gave him a hug.

He squeezed me back, then let go. "Better get to work." I knew he meant both of us. Old habits were hard to break.

I crossed the office and was reaching for the doorknob when he spoke once more. "By the way, how are things with you and Josh?"

A smile covered my face before I turned around. "Great, Dad. Things are really great."

And I planned to keep them that way.

"Hey! You kids settle down back there." Josh shouted over his shoulder, then turned in the school-bus seat so his players couldn't see him chuckle. "I sound like a dad," he said to me.

"Or a good coach." I put my hand on Josh's leg and gave it a squeeze.

"Thanks," he murmured. "I'm trying to teach them how to act when they leave town. Sometimes junior high boys are like . . . like —"

"Junior high boys?"

Josh grinned. "Yeah, like that." He put his arm across the back of the seat, then dropped it onto my shoulder. As if to prove his point, from behind us there was a loud, sappy sigh, followed by smooching sounds.

Following the cue, Josh and I turned and gave each other a quick kiss. Noisy gagging came from the rear.

"They're just jealous," Josh said, giving

my nose a brush with his finger. He turned and called out, "She's my wife, guys. Give it a rest."

The rhythm of the school bus was oddly relaxing as it bumped down the highway, toward a town and a basketball game 50 miles away. Josh and I would have almost an hour to sit beside each other.

Now that — with Rhonda's help — we'd mapped out some strategies, it was hard to understand how we thought we could have a marriage without ever seeing each other. I'd made a commitment to attend as many of Josh's games as possible. Josh had agreed that on nights when I had to work late, he'd pick up to-go food and join me at the office for supper. After all, we both had to eat; we might as well do it together.

Together. That was the key word. We were in this marriage, this life, together. Thick or thin. For better or worse. My dad might cringe at all the clichés, but I didn't care. Josh was my first priority now.

Somewhere on the way to the ball game, I dozed off. I woke as Josh eased my head off his shoulder. "We're here now," he whispered. Then he sharply clapped his hands and turned to his students. "Let's rock and roll, guys."

Shouts and hoots were followed by the

clamor of junior-high-sized feet as they piled off the bus.

I planned to be close behind them. I'd take my place on the bleachers right behind the team and cheer them on. The junior high basketball team — and my husband.

DONNIE

It was a late afternoon meeting in Matt's office. Just him and me, catching up on the events of the day. A typical meeting like we had almost every day.

Matt threw his pen onto the desk and leaned back in his chair, folding his hands behind his head. "So, the hospital pitch goes down tomorrow."

I knew what Matt meant, but I wasn't going to let him off the hook so easy. "I'm not so sure I like your phrasing. 'Down' isn't the direction I'm hoping for." Then after a moment I said, "So, what do you think our chances are?"

"Well, we made the final cut," Matt said. "They must have liked our pitch the first time out. I'd say 50-50."

"Some gambler. There's only one other firm in on this second round."

"Then we've got as good a shot as the other guy."

"That's one way of looking at it." I turned to look out the window. The morning was crisp and clear. I turned back to Matt and said, "Well, I guess we'll find out our fate tomorrow."

"Or the day after that." He made a twisting motion with his hand. "Or the one after that. This whole deal has strung out longer than I thought it would."

"You don't have to tell me," I said.

Matt sat forward in his chair, resting his forearms on his desk. "So, what gives, Donnie?"

"What?" Was I that transparent? I did my best to look oblivious.

"Something's wrong." Matt nodded his head to the chair across from his desk. "Sit down."

Matt had known me too long. I should have known he'd catch on to me. I sat back down as if I was a kid in the principal's office. The thing was, something *was* wrong; I just wasn't sure how to put it into words.

"So, what gives?" Matt wasn't about to let me off the hook. "You've been subdued lately."

Oh, great. He made me sound like a moody female, but he'd hit the mark. Subdued was the perfect word. "Male menopause?"

Matt picked up his phone and pushed a button. "Elle, hold my calls." He hung up the receiver and didn't say another word. He simply stared me down.

I pulled at the tight muscles in my neck. "Matt, my heart's not in it anymore."

"Your heart?"

"Okay, my brain. My guts. All of me. What we do is superficial. We convince people to buy stuff. And what does it matter?" I was on a roll; I might as well say it all. "While I was so busy being Mr. Advertising, I almost lost my wife." There, I'd said the one thing I'd been trying to keep from Matt. "Laura left me for a while."

"Laura left you?"

"Yeah," I said, challenging his incredulous gaze. "She's back, and we're working on it. But if I'm not working for my family, what's the point? So, I've got a big fancy house to go home to at night. What good is it if Laura's not there?" My eyes drilled into him, daring him to counter me. I waited for Matt to tell me how great our business was. How fulfilling.

Matt clicked his tongue against the roof of his mouth. His eyes darted away from mine. When he spoke, his tone held an odd mix of emotion. "You're preaching to the choir, buddy. In case you forgot, Kathy divorced me. If I remember right, her exact words were 'You don't need a wife. You're married to your agency.' "

Even though their divorce had happened years ago, there was a remnant of pain in his eyes. I had an inkling of what that kind of pain felt like, and I didn't ever want to know his kind of sorrow. The fight was gone from my voice when I finally spoke. "I need to do something different, Matt. I don't want to lose Laura."

"I don't want you to either."

For a brief second his eyes met mine. Quickly we both looked away. This conversation would be a lot easier if we were shooting buckets. Right about now I'd pivot and dribble to the half-court line. A long shot. That's what was coming next.

I'd already spilled my guts. As long as I was disemboweled, what did I have to lose by saying the rest? I pushed myself out of my chair and walked back to the window of Matt's office. His view wasn't much different from mine. I'd soon see if we had the same vision when it came to this business. I turned to face him, put my hands on the window ledge behind me, and leaned back as if I needed the support.

"I haven't been running this business for a long time."

"What do you mean? You put in just as much time as I do."

A shake of my head stopped him from continuing. "This business has been running me. It's running all of us." I paused. "Think about our staff, Matt. How many of them are married? Or used to be married?"

He didn't need to answer my question. We both knew the statistics. The mindset of this business. Hire them young before they have commitments. While they still have the fire to burn both ends at the same time. If they flame out, so be it; there would always be someone else to step in with fresh ideas. An agency wasn't built by encouraging quality family time; it was built on long hours and cutting-edge concepts.

I wanted to change that, if it was possible.

I returned to my chair. My ideas were half formed. Maybe half baked. Then again, brainstorming built our business; maybe inspiration could save it. Or at least change it enough to let all of us have viable relationships outside of these walls.

Just as I opened my mouth to speak, there was a quick tap at the door. Elle stuck her head in. "Excuse me. Donnie, you asked me not to let you forget you have an appointment at four o'clock. It's 3:45 now."

I looked at my watch. Elle was right.

Where had the day gone? Every day would be like this one if I let it, time passing in a blur until I missed supper at home and most of an evening I could spend with my wife. Laura and I had spent the past weekend sorting through the pieces of our relationship. What worked. More importantly, what didn't. One thing we agreed on — we didn't want to lose each other. And for that to happen there were some things that had to change.

I lifted a hand to Elle. "Thanks." I turned to Matt. "I've got to make this quick." I didn't have my plan in any sort of order. What I had were random ideas. Concepts that sounded good in my brain might not translate into the real world. But I was willing to give them an airing if it meant keeping Laura.

I laid my forearms on his desk and opened my hands. Might as well lay it all out and see if my musings held up to daylight. "Here's what I'm thinking. One of the reasons we lost the hospital account is that we were so busy pitching new business, we didn't have time to effectively service the clients we already have."

Matt sat forward in his chair. What I said had apparently hit a bull's eye of some sort. Maybe it was good I didn't have a lot of time to lay this out. As long as I knew I had his attention, I'd go for broke. I planned to talk fast, giving Matt no time for discussion.

"Obviously, I hope we get the hospital account back. If we don't, we'll need to fill in that gap. I'm wondering if we can do it by growing the clients we already have. Why reinvent the wheel when we've got a steady client base? I think we need to service them better so they don't even think about leaving. We can expand what we do for them. Print. Media. Brochures. Signage. We're good at concepts; let's get better at the nuts and bolts."

Matt was nodding. So far, so good. This next part was tricky. I was out on a road most agencies didn't travel. "Matt, I'd also like to do some work for nonprofits."

Before I could raise a hand, Matt jumped in. "Why do you think they're called 'non' profit?"

I'd been doing too much negative thinking during the days Laura was gone. Now that she was back, I'd had a burst of creative energy, a generosity of emotion I wanted to share with the world. I had a ready remark for Matt. "This town has given us enough. More than enough."

My eyes took in his plush office, the bank

of windows overlooking downtown. I knew it wasn't only this town. Someone else had a hand in this too. "I think it's time we give something back to Carlton. And one more thing." I stood up. I really did have to run. I'd drop my little bomb on Matt and head for cover. "I want to give up on the idea of moving into the Minneapolis market. We have enough clients to keep us busy right here. Instead of constantly vying for more business, let's service what we have."

I could see Matt was ready to counter, but I was quicker. I knew that what I was going to say was sappy, but I didn't care. "Matt, the truth is, I have a new client, and her name is Laura."

Only ten minutes late. Laura would forgive me. She knew that for me, ten minutes late was early. I shrugged out of my coat and tossed it over the back of the kitchen chair. I loosened my tie and headed for the stairs. "You ready?" I called up the steps.

"Yeah." I could hear quiet excitement in Laura's voice. How long had she been planning this?

Too long.

"It'll only take me a second to get out of these clothes." I was unbuttoning my shirt as I walked down the hall. Several boxes lined the walkway, and I danced around them. There was a pile of folded bedding on the floor outside Stasha's old room. I stopped in the doorway and looked in. Laura was standing near the picture window that faced our backyard, looking out. I crossed the room and wrapped my arms around her from the back, nuzzling my lips into the soft crease of her neck. "What are you thinking?"

"That the light is perfect."

I chuckled as she turned in my arms and wrapped hers around me. "And here I thought you were going to say you couldn't wait for me to get home."

She smiled up at me. "Yeah, that too."

I gave her a quick squeeze, then let her go. There was work to do. On our marriage. In this room. I was hoping that by working together, the two of us could kill two birds with one . . . okay, I'd say it . . . stone.

As soon as I changed out of my work clothes, into jeans and a denim shirt, we'd get started. I wasn't a handyman, and Laura knew it. The easy way would have been to hire someone to come in and do the work. But the easy way wasn't the way to Laura's heart. Working side by side with her was.

If my silent prayers were answered, by the time Laura and I hauled Stasha's old bed out of the room, by the time we painted the walls, ripped out the carpeting, and laid down the do-it-yourself hardwood floor, Laura would have her art studio and her husband. The husband she married all those years ago. The one who promised "for better or for worse, in sickness and in health, till death do us part."

We had survived the "worse." Now I planned to show her the "better" part of my promise. If it took the rest of my life, so be it. I had until the end of time to show Laura how much I loved her.

Starting now.

■ ■ ■ ■

ONE YEAR
LATER . . .

■ ■ ■ ■

LAURA

Karen raised her hand. "I nominate Laura Dunn to a second term as art guild president."

Before anyone had a chance to second the motion, I held both palms out to the eclectic membership sitting in front of me. "It's been a great year for our guild." I motioned to Karen. "One of our members realized her dream of opening an art gallery here in Carlton." There was a smattering of applause. Karen was selective about the artists she featured in her gallery, and not everyone in this room had made the cut. The ones who had were the ones who clapped the loudest. Including me.

My technique was rusty, and my style had changed in the years since I'd spent time in front of a canvas. And yet, one of my acrylics had met with Karen's approval.

"That one," she said a few months ago when I gave Karen a tour of my own private gallery: three paintings, still on their easels in my recently revamped studio. Of the three paintings, Karen pointed at my favorite. I hadn't realized how much of a favorite it was until I was faced with handing it over for sale.

"You're sure?" My plump, joyful peasant woman stared back at me. I'd concocted her story in the weeks I worked on her. She was grinning at something. *Someone* approaching her. *Who was it?* I wondered as I applied the layers of color. Of course, I should have known that it was her fisherman husband. He'd been gone for oh so long, and now he was back. Her arms were open wide, waiting to embrace him. Her feet seemed to dance on the wooden steps where she stood. *He was home!*

And so was I. Stasha had a mini fit over the fact that we'd turned her old room into my art studio.

"Why didn't you use the guest room?" she asked, hands on hips.

"Because," Donnie said, exchanging an amused glance with me, "the light is better in your room. Your *old* room."

Josh had put his arm around Stasha as if he sided with her, too. Good. They could be miffed at us together.

I smiled to myself as the art guild applause

faded. "I want to thank you for the opportunity to preside over this unique group of artists, but I'm afraid I'm going to have to turn down the privilege of serving another term. I have some projects I plan to pursue this coming year, and I won't be able to give this group my full attention." No need to add that rebuilding my marriage was at the top of my list of projects.

On automatic pilot, I took note of a nomination for a new president. Her election was swift and sure. I easily surrendered my spot behind the podium as our new leader took my place. I waited impatiently until the meeting was adjourned.

"Talk to you tomorrow," I mouthed to Karen as I slipped into my coat. My mind was already out the door, heading home. I didn't envy her the extra hour she'd spend after the meeting, surrounded by members seeking her advice on gaining a spot on her gallery wall. I knew the *exact* size of the spot she needed to fill.

Earlier, when I'd arrived at the meeting Karen had fairly burst with the news: "Your peasant woman sold!" Up until now, I knew where my woman was — hanging in Karen's gallery. I'd harbored a secret hope she'd stay put until I got used to her being away from my watchful eye. Now, I'd have to let her go to someone else's imagining.

"Is she going to a good home?" was all I could muster.

Suddenly Karen sounded guarded. "Of course she is." She turned her back on me. Apparently, the gallery owner wasn't going to pat the artist's hand and console her over her first sale.

Remember when I told you to trust Me?

I did. I'd clung to that promise more than once these past months. Days and nights when Donnie and I tried to talk about what went wrong . . . and what might make things right again. Old habits were hard to break, but we were committed to recreating this thing called marriage. Donnie and I agreed to be intentional about doing whatever it took to jump-start our relationship. We'd taken each other for granted for so long, that we'd almost lost our love in the every-dayness of life. Donnie was making it a point to be home for dinner. I agreed to cut down on several of my evening commitments, which was why turning down a second term as president had been surprisingly easy.

Trust Me.

I took a deep breath. I'd learned that trusting was something I could do. Well then. Give myself a mental pat on my back.

My first sale. I hadn't imagined my dream of painting would involve painful partings with my work. But then, I hadn't imagined much of what had happened in the months just past.

As I had so often when I was tempted to hang on to old resentments, I repeated my new mantra, a Bible verse I'd stumbled on late one sleepless night. *I am bringing all my energies to bear on this one thing: Forgetting the past and looking forward to what lies ahead.*

Forget the past. Look ahead. I planned to do that right now. Shouldering my purse, I tiptoed out of the post-meeting chatter. I didn't want idle talk to delay what I had planned for the rest of the evening.

I hurried to my car and slipped behind the wheel. After meeting for a quick dinner earlier tonight, Donnie had gone to the office, and I'd run off to my meeting. We were getting better at coordinating our schedules, but tonight I was hoping to get home before he did. I needed to work on finishing my latest project — a secret project that had nothing to do with painting and everything to do with my marriage.

I stood in the doorway of the family room. Donnie had his head bent over a copy of

Advertising Age as CNN droned in the background. Why did I suddenly feel so nervous? The worst that could happen was that Donnie would say something like, "Oh. Thank you, I guess." I wasn't hoping for much. Only that Donnie would be as pleased with the finished product as I was glad to have it done.

I hadn't even realized I'd cleared my throat until Donnie looked up from his magazine. He raised his eyebrows. *Did you want something?*

Now or never. "Close your eyes," I said, a nervous twitch tugging at the corners of my mouth. Donnie played along. He laid the magazine across his lap, closed his eyes, and rested his head against the back of the recliner. His lips were slightly pursed as if this were some new kind of kissing game.

Well, if that's what he wanted . . . I picked up the bundle I had hidden beside the doorway and crossed to his chair. Leaning down, I planted a kiss smack-dab on his lips, then I placed the completed project in his lap. "You can open your eyes."

"I liked what happened when they were closed," he said, eyes still shut.

I bent and gave him another quick peck. "Now look."

Slowly Donnie opened his eyes, gazing

566

first at me, then down to the crazy patches of my quilt. *His* quilt. He ran a hand over the small pieces of patchwork. His eyes were shining as he looked back up at me.

I blinked back sudden tears. "I made it for you. It's — it's — from your mother's —" My throat was tight, my voice thick with emotion.

"I know," he said softly, once more running his palm across the cotton cloth.

"You know?"

He nodded. "I saw it in your basket when you were —"

He didn't have to say it. We both knew those tiny stitches held together so much more than scraps of fabric. I'd taken Eleanor's jumbled box of clothes with only the thought of taking them off her hands. It turned out there was a grander plan for the castoffs.

Donnie fingered one of the red scraps. "My mom wore this dress to my high school graduation. And this . . ." He touched the brown plaid. "This was my favorite cowboy shirt."

Now it was my turn to say softly, "I know."

His moist eyes met mine. He tried to say something. Then he simply dropped his head and cried. I sat on the arm of the chair, leaned in close, and cried with him.

Not knowing what I was doing, I'd cut and sewn and prayed by Eleanor's bedside, not realizing I was piecing together a final gift from her to her son. Yet here it was, a crazy quilt of memories, some good, some not so great . . . a perfect picture of our imperfect marriage.

As Donnie drew in a shaky breath, I stroked his hair, thankful for all the bits and pieces that made us . . . *us.* What would a marriage be like if it was all good times? Would we value moments like this at all? I had a hunch Someone knew what He was doing a lot better than we did. And that was perfectly all right with me.

Donnie swiped at his face with the back of one hand. "Thank you," he finally managed.

"You're welcome," I said, sliding from the arm of the chair to squeeze next to him in the oversized recliner.

He put his magazine on the floor, unfolded the quilt, and swished it over us. The cool rush of air caused me to snuggle in closer. Donnie pulled the blanket up to our chins, tucking us in together. He put an arm around my shoulder and held me close. "This is nice."

"I thought I'd never get all those pieces sewn together," I said, nestling into his chest. "And then the backing, and the binding . . . who knew?" I smiled up at him.

He kissed my forehead. "You'd better stick to painting."

I threaded my arm out from under the quilt and smoothed my hand along the comforting surface. "My first . . . and *last* quilt," I announced. "Appreciate it."

Donnie rested his chin atop my head. "I do. Believe me, I do."

I lifted one heavy foot, then the other. I raised my eyes from the dirt path and looked up. How many steps were there on this terraced hillside, anyway? I pulled in a lung full of air, puffed it out. "Whose stupid idea was this?"

From close behind me Donnie piped up. "Yours." I felt a soft poke as his walking stick nudged my backside. *"Sorridere."* The Italian word for "smile." In Donnie's fractured accent, the word sounded more like "sorry derriere" — Donnie's view of me these past three days.

I wasn't going to give him the satisfaction of seeing me grin. Besides, I was too tired to turn around. We'd spent the last three days hiking the Amalfi coast with our small tour group and Italian guide. We had three more days to go. Four days in Rome would cap off our trip. If I lived that long.

"Almost at zee top." Giovanni, our guide, was unfailingly encouraging. "Eess all down heel from there. Zen back to zee 'otel. Warm bath. Deener."

As the path widened, Donnie fell into step beside me. "Ah, zee magic word . . . deener."

In spite of my exhaustion, I laughed out loud.

Members of our tour group stood at the high point of the small mountain we had spent most of the day climbing. Donnie and I waited until they had their fill of the view, then we stepped to the summit, gazing out together at the incredible blue of the Mediterranean Sea. I mentally riffled through my paints, already imagining the broad, colorful strokes of this picture. I wanted to paint it all.

I turned and looked back over the steep, dusty path we'd hiked to get here. I didn't want to leave anything out. The dusky green olive trees, the brighter verdant leaves of citrus groves. The polka dots of lemons hanging from the branches. It had taken Donnie and me 25 years to reach this spot. Twenty-five years of hills and valleys and mostly long, flat stretches of in-betweens.

So, here it was. Laid out in front of my eyes. The secret. The hard-won knowledge that there was, after all, no secret to a good marriage. It was hard work. Dusty paths. Ups . . . like lemon trees and deep blue seas. And downs . . . like illness, death, and disagreements. And mostly, it was the everydays. Meals to make. "How was your day?" conversations. Laundry.

Colors didn't exist to paint what I suddenly saw spread out beneath me. It was all up to me . . . and Donnie to add color to the days ahead.

It seemed, finally, we were up for the challenge.

Donnie put his arm around me and looked into my eyes. "Happy?"

I blinked against the stinging. "I am."

"Good," he said, drawing me close. "So am I."

We looked out over the vast sea together. At all that lay ahead. Dreams for our marriage that shimmered like diamonds in the brilliant Mediterranean sun.

A NOTE FROM ROXY:

Thank you for reading this book about marriage. My husband and I celebrated our 32nd anniversary while I was writing *The Secret of Us.* It seemed that after all those years I might have something to say about the topic of marriage. And I did. Too much, actually. As I began writing this story, I quickly realized there was no way I would begin to scratch the surface of all that a marriage encompasses.

There is so much to say about marriage, but if I had one piece of advice to give to a newlywed, I'd tell her (or him), "Marriage is work. Hard work." I remember when I was a starry-eyed bride. I thought a good marriage was something that simply happened. We'd live on love. *Yeah, right.* Then I got married. And I realized that marriage is about love and so much more. It's about sharing a bed *and* a bathroom, a checkbook *and* the remote control. (Well, okay, let's face it, *he* gets the remote.) But that's my point: Marriage is all about compromise, communicating, standing firm, and giving in. And, oh yes, it's about love.

Whether you're currently in love or out of love, I hope this book has given you some new things to think about regarding this God-given gift called marriage.

CONVERSATION QUESTIONS

Talk about how even "good things" (committee meetings, Bible study, work) can pull a marriage apart.

Feelings follow actions. Do they? Can you think of an example when this was true for you?

Marriage can involve long dry periods. Discuss how these times can make it seem as if a marriage is in trouble. Talk about ways to overcome the idea that something is "wrong."

Lack of communication, or miscommunication, is a major factor contributing to most marriage problems. Why is it often so hard to communicate what we need to say? Why do we expect our partner to read our mind?

Speaking of clichés: "It takes two to tango."

Can one person make a marriage last? Are there ever acceptable reasons to end a marriage? If so, what are they? If not, what can be done to revive a faded love?

Talk about the little irritations in a marriage. It's easy to spot them in a partner, less easy to notice your own. What are some ways to minimize the impact of the little things that interfere with wedded bliss?

We all carry role expectations into a relationship. Talk about the expectations you have. What sorts of duties do you consider to be "women's work"? What belongs to the men? Are these expectations realistic?

Talk about young love. What happens when the flush of the honeymoon period wears off? Is wedded bliss realistic? If not, how can we do a better job of letting newlyweds know that real life involves some very ordinary days?

Discuss the pitfalls, and the comforts, of a long-term marriage.

Any thoughts on how to keep love alive?

ABOUT THE AUTHOR

Roxanne Sayler Henke lives in rural North Dakota with her husband, Lorren, and their dog, Gunner. They have two, very cool, adult daughters, Rachael and Tegan, and an equally cool son-in-law, Dave. As a family they enjoy spending time at their lake cabin in Northern Minnesota. Roxanne has a degree in Behavioral and Social Science from the University of Mary and for many years was a newspaper humor columnist. She has also written and recorded radio commercials; written for, and performed in, a comedy duo; and cowritten school lyceums. She is the author of five previous novels: *After Anne, Finding Ruth, Becoming Olivia, Always Jan,* and *With Love, Libby.*

You can reach Roxy through her Web site at:
www.roxannehenke.com

577

MGR
EGra